WASHOE COUNTY LIBRARY

D0773039

APR 1 5 2002
DATE DUE FEB 2 5 2001

MAR 3 0 19--

NOV 0 1 2001

LAST
BUCKAROO

LAST BUCKAROO

MACKEY HEDGES

SALT LAKE CITY

WASHOE COUNTY LIBRARY
RENO, NEVADA

Sierra View Library
Old Town Mall
4001 S. Virginia
Reno, NV 89502

This is a Peregrine Smith Book, published by
Gibbs Smith, Publisher
P.O. Box 667
Layton, Utah 84041

Copyright © 1995
by Mackey Hedges

All rights reserved. No part of this book may be reproduced
by any means whatsoever, either electronically or mechanically,
without written permission from the publisher, except for
brief excerpts quoted for the purpose of review.

All the characters in this work are fictional. Any resemblance to
persons living or dead is purely coincidental.

Cover design by Scott Van Kampen

Edited by Gail Yngve

Cover illustrations by William Matthews
William Matthews Gallery
1617 Wazee Street
Denver, Colorado 80202
(303) 534-1300
front cover painting is "Cold Grounds" (private collection)
back cover painting is "Bow Legs" (private collection)

Printed and Bound in the United States of America

99 98 97 96 95 5 4 3 2 1

First Edition

Library of Congress Cataloging-in-
Publication Data

Hedges, Mackey, 1942—
Last Buckaroo: a novel by Mackey Hedges
p. cm.
ISBN 0-87905-661-4 (hb)
I. Title
PS3558.E3164S55 1995
813' .54—dc20
94-37227 CIP

To buckaroos—

the handful of men who
know the only future that life holds
for them is a dirty bedroll and a
worn-out saddle.

They have been around
for many decades in one form or
another, and they live on today;
but this is especially
for the buckaroos who cowboyed
after Will James and before the
environmental movement—a
vanishing breed.

CHAPTER *1*

I t's been almost thirteen years now since I first met Dean McCuen, but I can 'member it like it was yesterday. I'd spent the last four months in a cow camp down in southern Arizona for the Two Bar outfit. Ol' Charley Duncan was the cow boss. He was a good man. I reckon he's dead by now though. He was gettin' pretty long in the tooth even then. I think he must be about ten years older than me. My God! that'd make him over ninety now.

Charley had loaned me one of the company pickups to go in to town for a haircut and a few new clothes before the spring work started. He'd said, "Tap, you can take the truck on the condition that you pick up some supplies for the ranch cook."

The little town of Demar was old and tired, but it had about all a man needed to get along. There was a post office, a fillin' station, a general mercantile store, a restaurant, and three bars. The man who ran the fillin' station, I can't recollect his name right now, would cut your hair if he wasn't too busy greasin' somebody's car.

I don't 'member there being a tree in the whole area, and I know there wasn't a yard with grass. The only paved street was the one that ran down through the middle of town. It wouldn't have been paved either 'cept it happened to be the state highway that went to Yuma.

In the summer, that blacktopped road got so damned hot that the kids who didn't have shoes couldn't play with the ones who lived on the other side unless they could get somebody to carry 'em across. The other six streets that fell inside the city limits were all dirt. In most cases, it was hard to tell where someone's yard ended and a street began.

All the businesses were owned by "gringos" 'cept for one bar that Degarmo Lara owned. Most of the folks who lived around town were either Mexican, Indian, or a mixture of both.

There was one stoplight in the middle of town. The city fathers chipped in to buy it. They thought that the stoplight made the town seem more substantial. They also hoped it'd slow down some of the through traffic so that a few of those people would stop and do a little business. I don't think the idea worked very well. In truth, if it weren't for the few outlyin' ranches and the monthly welfare checks, the whole economy of Demar would have fallen on its can.

At the moment that I met Dean, I's out on the edge of town. I was sittin' 'side the highway, tryin' without much success to get in the shade of the speed–limit sign. My head felt as big as a fall pumpkin. My mouth tasted like I'd eaten supper with a buzzard, and my stomach was on the brink of losin' whatever it was that I'd put in it the night before. I figured I'd probably live 'cause I knew I's too sick to die. I'm telling you, to call what I had a hang-over would be like describin' smallpox as a rash.

As I laid there propped against my bedroll, the sky spinnin' above me, my mind drifted back over the events of the past few days. Try as I might, I couldn't make a lot of sense out of the few pieces of clear thought that I could recollect.

I didn't have no trouble at all 'memberin' the first few hours that I'd been in town and the things that took place. I could remember my haircut and even the greasy, dirty hands of the barber. I figured I wouldn't need no hair oil for a week after that stop. I could remember lunch at the diner and the cute little gal who waited on me. I wondered if she realized I was old enough to be her father. I hoped not.

After that, things started to get a little hazy. I'd had two beers with my lunch. When I stepped out into the hot sunlight, I got to thinkin' how cool and refreshin' they'd tasted. With that in mind, I'd decided to stop off at the Shade Tree Bar next door for one more beer before startin' in on my shoppin'.

I's kinda disappointed to see that there wasn't anyone in the bar I knew. I hate to drink alone, and I was feelin' pretty sociable about then. I'd spent the past four months with no one to talk to but a couple of horses and a mirror. I's lookin' forward to a little friendly conversation and a couple of sociable drinks. The only other person in the bar 'sides me and the barkeep was an old gal slumped over a table in the back. When I walked in, she raised up and looked at me 'fore droppin' her head back on the table. Now, it's always dark in the Shade Tree, but it wasn't so dark that I didn't notice this woman wasn't much to look at.

The bar was cool inside, and one beer had led to two. Somewhere around the fourth or fifth drink, I switched over to whiskey.

As the afternoon turned into early evenin', a few more people drifted in. It wasn't long 'fore the place started gettin' noisier and friendlier. Pretty soon there was quite a little crowd. People were slappin' each other on the back, jokin', and buyin' one another drinks. It was one of those nights in a little country bar where everyone seems to be just one big happy family. There were Indians and cowboys, miners and town people—all just as friendly as God meant for folks to be. I felt like these were sure some good citizens, and I was right there in the middle, backslappin' and buyin' drinks with the best of 'em.

It was at about the height of the evenin's festivities that I happened to glance over at the table in the corner where earlier the ol' drunk gal had been slumped over. I'm not sure where that toothless old cow had gone off to, but sittin' there all alone in the same chair at the same table and wearin' pretty near the same clothes was the cutest little dark-haired gal I'd ever seen.

Well, she glanced up from her empty glass about the same time that I'd looked over at her. It was just like in one of them Hollywood movies. Our eyes met, she smiled shyly at me, I blushed and looked down at my boot toes. It was true love.

I separated myself from the crowd at the bar and made my way across the room to her table. It was my first attempt to go any distance since I'd entered the bar. I didn't think I's drunk, but I's surprised at how much difficulty I's havin' walkin' straight.

Being a true gentleman, I offered to buy this young lady a drink. She musta been out on the desert for some time 'cause she came damn near to swallowin' the glass when the drink was poured.

Sittin' there buyin' drinks for that little lady was the last thing that I can remember about the evenin'. In fact, it's about the last thing I can remember until I woke up a day or so later.

My awakenin' come real sudden-like. Someone had aholt of my neck and was hollerin' somethin' about killin' me. Someone else had aholt of my arm and was screamin' to leave me alone, that she and I's lovers.

The man tryin' to strangle me kinda unnerved me, but when I heard the woman's voice say somethin' about us gettin' married, it sobered me up and got me to lookin' around.

Well, in a lot less time than it takes to tell it, I took in the room and the feller with a death grip on my Adam's apple. The man was Charley Duncan, the boss who'd lent me the company truck a couple of days earlier.

The room was a dirty little ten-by-twelve frame job with a woodstove across from the bed we were in. There was a rough board table and bench against one wall. To the left of the bed was the place where the door used to be. All that was there now was the frame of a screen door, only there was no screen on most of it. All of the corners were full of cobwebs and there was no glass in the window. The bed had been a big fancy brass thing, but that had been a long time ago. The brass had turned green and the mattress sloped off to one side. The blankets that were on it were so ratty and dirty that a coyote woulda been ashamed to den up in 'em. And stink! Good God Almighty, but they did smell! Kinda reminded me of a night I spent in the YMCA locker room down in Houston.

And then there was the woman. I had a slight recollection of goin' home with that cute little thing I'd been buyin' drinks for, but somewhere along the line I musta gotten mixed up. Merciful Lord, was this thing next to me ever a mess. She had a face a little like a gummer cow, only if I's the cow it woulda hurt my feelin's to be compared to her. I think this thing musta been the same old gal that was passed out in the bar when I first went in. I could tell then she wasn't much to look at, only now, close up, she wasn't only ugly but was downright scary. She didn't have no teeth 'cept for a couple of rotted fangs at the corners. She had a good start at growin' a mustache, and a half a dozen long black hairs were comin' outta the side of her nose. There was a wart on her right cheek, and an ugly scar started up in the hairline and ran down across her eye. The scar gave that eye a droopy look.

I couldn't see much of her figure 'cause she had on some sorta nightgown that looked like it was made outta tater sacks. I can tell you this much though, she sure musta done some hard work somewheres along the line 'cause from the grip she had on my arm, I could tell she sure had muscles. I figured her for an ex-ditchdigger or maybe a hay bucker or somethin' like that.

By and by, Charley got tired of tryin' to separate my head from my shoulders and let me go. As he turned to leave, I heard him say somethin' about leavin' my saddle and bed outside and that he'd used my wages to pay for some of the damages I'd done. He also said a lot of things about the marital status of my parents and where he hoped I'd rot after I died.

After he'd gone, I just sat there for a minute or so tryin' to catch my breath. My moment of rest was cut short by the voice of my "True Love" tellin' me how happy we were gonna be.

Bein' alone with that woman scared the hell out of me. I don't mind tellin' you, I didn't waste any time gettin' my hat on and jumpin' into my pants. As I swung my feet over the side of the bed to slip my boots on, I stepped right smack into the old crock pot that was sittin' there. From the warm, soft ooze that squished around my foot, I could tell someone had used it the night before. I didn't even bother to wipe my foot off. I just shoved it into my boot and hit the floor a-runnin'.

As I went out the door, I turned to look back for one last glimpse of the old woman. When I did, I tripped over my bedroll that Charley'd left outside, and I went sprawlin' headfirst into the dirt.

I was scramblin' to my feet when I looked up and saw a beat-up 1939 Chevy pickup comin' down the dirt street. Behind the wheel was Tommy Bass, an Indian I'd worked with once before. I gave out a yell, and 'fore Tommy even had the truck stopped, I'd thrown in my saddle, bed, and tack and was hollerin' for him to get the hell outta there.

As we drove off, I saw we were in the worst section of "Poor Town." Poor Town was about a block square on the very edge of Demar. Mosta the people who lived there were either old, alcoholic, or illegal.

Tommy liked to talk, and he started in as soon as I's inside. Seems he's just leavin' his girlfriend's place a few houses away. He started in tellin' me stories about what all had took place in town durin' the last couple of days. I's sure he was tryin' to kid me. But then we drove into the main part of town.

There, still smolderin', were the ashes and charred ruins of the Shade Tree Bar. The restaurant next door was only burned along one side. Degarmo Lara's place had a big For Sale sign where the front window used to be. What was left of the company pickup that I'd borrowed from the ranch was wrapped around the pole that had held the city fathers' prize stoplight. Tommy said that no one had moved it 'cause they were waitin' for the Highway Patrol to come and fill out some sorta report first.

Well, when I saw all that, I began to think there might be a splinter of truth in some of what Tommy was sayin'. He hauled me out to the edge of town and dropped me off. I crawled to the side of the road and laid down to die. About six hours and twenty cars later, I staggered to my feet and started gettin' serious about tryin' to thumb a ride. About an hour passed 'fore a big black 1956 Mercury come slidin' to a stop and this friendly voice told me to throw my stuff in the back and jump in.

My saddle and bag of tack made it in okay, but my bedroll wouldn't fit through the door. That old canvas bed tarp had fifteen or twenty blankets and all of my clothes inside it. On top of that, it didn't appear Charley'd made no real effort to roll it up very tight. The whole thing was about the size of a rolled-up mattress off a double bed.

I half carried, half dragged the big bundle around to the trunk and waited for the kid to open it. As I's wrestlin' it into the trunk, I couldn't help but see some of the other stuff that was back there. Over to one side was a couple of cases of canned food and some pots and pans. Farther to the back was a suitcase and some other boxes of different sizes.

Right in the middle, though, was the thing that caught my eye: it was the prettiest little A-fork saddle I ever laid eyes on. One glance told me it was old, but damn, it was in good shape. Round skirts, full flower-stamped, six-inch cantle, three-inch dalley horn, outside stirrup leathers that looped through the seat, and twenty-eight-inch taps. Oh, what a beauty!

We scooted stuff around till we made a hole big enough to get my bed in, then the two of us jumped up and down on the trunk lid till we managed to get it closed.

When I's settled down in the front seat, I sat back and took stock of this feller who had picked me up. He was about twenty and stood somewheres around five-ten. He only weighed around 150 pounds, and he's dressed in the most God-awful dude getup I ever saw.

Startin' at the top, he had on a flat-crowned, wide-brimmed, brown hat with some sorta beaded hatband. Next, around his neck he wore a red handkerchief, not a scarf, but a farmer-style snot rag. He had on a black shirt made outta some sorta shiny material with white snaps. His Levi's were new and just barely broke in. He was shod in a pair of cheap rough-out boots with square toes and walkin' heels. This young guy spelled Dude from top to bottom. The only thing that didn't fit was the old saddle in the trunk.

That right there was my first glimpse of Dean Michael McCuen. I seen a thousand more who looked like him but never met another who could compare to him.

9

CHAPTER 2

As the miles rolled along, Dean and I got to talkin', with him doin' most of it. Seems he's fresh outta the army and was figurin' on makin' his fortune as a cowboy. I can't recall where he called home, but it was one of them foreign states back East someplace. He'd got discharged from a base over in New Mexico and had been hittin' mosta the ranches along the way, lookin' for work. So far he hadn't had much luck. I could see why.

Now, right here I'm gonna tell you somethin' I did that I'm not too proud of. You see, I wasn't real sure just where I wanted to go. All I knew for certain was that I wanted to put a lotta miles 'tween me and southern Arizona. And I wanted to do it fast. This kid looked like he could be my ticket so I told him kind of a lie. Actually, it wasn't "kind of a lie." It was an out-and-out lie. I told him I was headed north to go to work for an outfit on the east side of the California Sierras. And then I just sorta dropped a hint that there might be a job there for him, too.

Well, young Mister Dean grabbed the bait and swallowed the hook in one bite. He pulled the car over, whipped out his map of the western U.S., saw what road we needed to be on, and headed the big black car north. His plan was to take 95 up to Las Vegas and then cut off across Death Valley and come out over on 395.

It all sounded good to me, and the more I thought about it, the more I liked the idea of spendin' the summer in some nice cool cow camp up in the Sierras. I wasn't exactly sure just how I was gonna get rid of this kid or who to see about a job, but I figured I'd come up with somethin' when the time was right.

The miles went rollin' by, and 'cept for an occasional stop for gas, we just kept headin' north. Gradually my headache went away, and I got used to the nasty taste in my mouth. Along towards evenin', though, my stomach began to think my throat'd been cut. I wasn't sure when my last real meal had been, what with bein' drunk for two or three days. Now I was sober and I needed food.

Finally, just 'fore sunset Dean pulled into one of them rest areas. It was too early in the season for the *touristos* to be out in force, and we were the only car in the place. It was sure a peaceful little spot with big ol' cottonwood trees and a little creek runnin' through it. There's about a million frogs tryin' to out-croak each other down along the banks and not many 'skeeters or gnats out yet.

Dean found a place to park down by the creek with a good grassy space where we could sleep. By the time he'd opened the trunk and we'd unloaded the beds, pots, pans, and boxes of canned food, the first stars had started to show over in the east. I went to rustlin' up wood from under the old trees to get a fire goin' while there was still light.

It was that very first night that I figured out why that kid was so damn skinny. When he started diggin' out the food I didn't think he planned on sharin' any with me. To my way of thinkin', he didn't open enough cans to feed a four-month-old baby. I was wrong though. He divided the little can of stew right down the middle, same as he did the little can of peaches. My share of both didn't come to more than half a dozen spoonfuls. As I think back on it, I'm not sure he didn't give me the biggest part.

I'd heard about them army guys goin' on them survival hikes where they see how long they can go on little or no food. I figured this kid had been on so many of them that he'd been completely weaned. I also heard that on them hikes those army fellers take to eatin' bugs and snakes and such. Well, I wasn't far from that point myself.

When we were done eatin' I told the kid I'd wash up the pot and plates while he got his bed laid out. As soon as I had everything down by the creek and out of sight, I proceeded to lick every bit of grease I could off of 'em. When I's done, it didn't take a hell of a lot of water to finish cleanin' up. Then I started in schemin' on how I's gonna get that little stew can outta the fire. I figured there had to be one or two good licks on the inside of it.

When I got back up to the camp Dean had his bed, if you want to call it that, all rolled out. It was some sort of a little bag so small that a man couldn't even turn over in it. The thing looked like it was made out of the same stuff as women's stockings. Dean said it was what the army used, and it was called a mummy bag. Said it was supposed to keep you warm even when it was ten below.

As I drug my big ol' canvas-covered bed over to the grassy spot, I told him I had my doubts about how many soldiers ever slept in one of those things when it was much below freezin' and come out warm. I untied the rope that kept my bed rolled up, unsnapped the hooks that held the sides together, and took out a couple of blankets. I offered the kid the blankets but he said he didn't need 'em. Just the same, I laid 'em between us just in case he changed his mind. Then I crawled down inside my own nest.

As I burrowed in, I remembered back to one fall in the thirties when I was workin' for the Rail Road Ranch up in Montana, gatherin' beef. The snows had come early that year, and it was miserable. It was so cold at night that we'd taken to doublin' up in our beds. There was ten of us in the crew, not countin' the cook and the cow boss. We'd put one man's bed on the bottom and the other's on top and sleep two of us together. I's just a kid then, and even though I was cold and miserable, it still seemed kinda like a big adventure. It'd kill me now to lay out there on that cold frozen ground all night and ride all day in damp clothes.

I wondered how many of them ol' punchers woulda wanted to double up with that kid and his army mummy bag.

As I started to drift off, a light breeze came up, and I caught the faint scent of pines. The smell of pines always reminded me of home in southern Idaho. I don't remember smellin' the pines much as a kid, but after I left home, every time I caught their scent I remembered home, even though I hadn't been there in years.

CHAPTER 3

The next mornin' I woke up to the smell of fried bacon and coffee. Even 'fore I's completely conscious, my mouth started to water and my stomach began to grumble. It didn't take me long to quit the blankets and get dressed.

Dean was hunkered over the fire, workin' on whatever it was that he's cookin'. Beside him was a can with a picture of a big heapin' platter of bacon. The writin' on the can was in some foreign language, but I could figure out what it probably meant just by the picture.

I staggered down to the creek and threw a couple of handfuls of cold water in my face and went back to the fire. When I got back, my worst fears had come true. It was a repeat of supper. That whole can of foreign pig meat had shrunk down to next to nothin'. Even though Dean had divided it right down the middle, my share still only came to a couple of bites. Layin' on my plate next to the little pile of bacon was the smallest egg I ever saw. I didn't even know that chickens could lay eggs that little. I woulda washed it all down with a half gallon of coffee except that the kid's little coffeepot only held three cups, and he's drinkin' one of 'em.

Dean was sittin' crosslegged, leanin' back against one of them big cottonwoods, munchin' away on one of his little pieces of bacon. As he ate he chattered away about how we should be gettin' into some real cow country by noon. He wanted to know about what the name of the ranch was that we were headed for and what town it was near, but his mind was workin' so fast that I didn't have time to say anythin' 'fore he asked another question.

To be on the safe side, though, and keep from havin' to answer too many of his questions, I swallowed my food and went over and started rollin' my bed. I noticed that the two blankets I'd laid out were wrapped around the kid's sleepin' bag. I gathered 'em up and stuck 'em back inside the canvas tarp.

I had my bed about halfway rolled when Dean come over and started rollin' his little bag. He asked me how I carried that thing when I's horseback. Before I could answer, he told me how his bag could be rolled up long ways and tied right behind you on your saddle.

I started in to tell him that you don't carry your bed behind you, that you use a pack horse or a pickup, but 'fore I got started he's off talkin' about somethin' else. That was one good thing about the boy—if you didn't want to answer him, all you had to do was wait a minute or two and he'd be off talkin' about somethin' else. I found out later that he only talked like that when he's nervous. Nowadays he's kinda quiet and don't talk much at all.

We carried our beds over to the car, me with my

fifty-pound monster and Dean with his little grocery-sack-size mummy bag. Then we went back over and started cleanin' up the camp. That boy left a campsite cleaner than a hotel maid.

When the fire was out, we hopped into the car and drove back to the highway. With the windows rolled down and the radio tuned into one of them country-western stations, it was hard to carry on a conversation. The breeze was cool so I laid back and let the big black car eat up the miles. Even though I was still a little hungry, life didn't seem so bad.

I slept through most of the southern part of Nevada and all of Death Valley. When I woke up, it was the middle of the afternoon, and we were over on 395.

I's hungrier now and that made me feel grumpy. I decided that it was about time for me to get shed of this young lad 'fore I starved to death. I'd found a $10 bill in my pants pocket the night before so I's feelin' pretty independent.

I told Dean to pull over at the next town and I'd buy us somethin' to eat. My plan was to get each of us a good meal and then tell the kid "adios." I figured I could find some kinda work that would keep the wolf away from the door, even if it was washin' dishes. A lot of cattle are run along the edge of the mountains, and I didn't figure it would be too long 'fore I'd be able to land a ranch job someplace.

A few more miles down the road, we come to a little town. We pulled off and parked in front of one of them places that can't decide whether it's a bar or a restaurant.

When we got inside, Dean headed straight for the rest room and I headed straight for the bar. There's a little group of locals down at the end celebratin' somethin' when I walked up. I ordered a beer, but 'fore I could pay for it, a big man pushed himself free from the crowd and said for me to put my money away. He said his wife had just had a baby and that he's buyin' all the drinks for the rest of the day.

I thanked the new father and congratulated him. While I was talkin' I noticed that he and most of the group with him were dressed in western work clothes. I thought that maybe someone in the crowd might be able to tell me what the chances of landin' a job in this area might be. I also figured if I's kinda friendly and sociable I might enjoy a few more of them free drinks.

I'd just finished sippin' the foam off my beer and was gettin' down to the real stuff when out of the rest room walked Dean. It was also about this time that the happy new father laid back his head and let out with a screechin' rebel yell and hollers, "Yes, sir! That old mare of mine sure went and had herself one fine stud colt!!"

Mr. McCuen didn't want to be left out of the festivities, and not knowin' that the man was talkin' about his wife and new son, Dean walked up to the bar, looked over at the feller, and said real casual-like, "What color is the little guy?"

That was when the party ended. The group froze. It got so quiet that I could hear a fly buzzin' in the front window twenty feet away. The proud father looked at Dean like he couldn't believe what he'd just heard. Before the new daddy had a chance to say anything, Dean added, "What did it cost you to get her bred?" Then he said, "If she's normal, she'll come into heat in twenty-four hours after she gave birth, and you can breed her again."

17

I looked over at the father. He was changin' colors like a chameleon. First he was sort of pale; then he started gettin' red splotches on his cheeks. The veins in his neck started poppin' out, and he started swellin' up. Then I heard the first noise that anyone'd made since Dean started talkin'. It sounded like a cross 'tween a growl and a moan, and it was comin' from the stranger, even though his mouth was clamped shut.

Suddenly the father let out a screech that made the hair on the back of my neck stand up, and he rushed at Dean with his head down. I figured the boy would be caught off guard, but he sidestepped the man so smoothly that the enraged father went crashin' into the bar.

Dean turned to me and said, "What the hell's the matter with him?" Before I could answer, the stranger was after the boy again. This time he threw a roundhouse punch at Dean's head, but Dean stepped aside again, grabbin' the arm as it went whistlin' by his face. He twisted the arm up behind the man's back with his right hand and wrapped his left forearm around the man's neck. It was then that I noticed how big the stranger was. He stood at least two inches taller and weighed fifty pounds more than the kid.

Dean shoved the big man up to the wall and said, "What's your problem?" But the fight wasn't out of the man yet. Before the boy knew it was comin', the stranger swung his left elbow backwards, catching Dean on the side of the rib cage. The blow was hard enough that it knocked the wind out of the kid and sent him flyin'. He landed on the floor, gaspin' for breath. The stranger closed the distance in two steps and let fly a kick that woulda broken some ribs if it'd connected, but Dean had rolled outta the way.

The boy staggered to his feet, still gaspin' for air. He grabbed a table and pulled it 'tween 'em in an effort to stall for a few more seconds while he caught his breath. They danced back and forth on opposite sides 'fore the new father finally grabbed the table and flung it aside. By then, though, Dean had got his wind back.

Now, I ain't much of a scrapper at best, and there's nothin' I hate worse than to get into a fight when I'm sober. It seems like the bruises hurt so much worse. But I just couldn't stand there and let this dumb kid get beat to death. I sorta stepped forward and said, "Hey, pard, the boy's had enough. He didn't mean no insult. Just let him apologize, and I'll buy the next round."

The big man stopped and looked over at me. In fact, everyone in the place was lookin' at me. Then the stranger said, "When I get done with him, Pop, there ain't gonna be enough left to apologize." With that, he turned his attention back to Dean.

When he looked in the boy's direction, so did the rest of us. That kid was over there goin' through the damnedest bunch of gyrations you ever seen. He stretched his arms down straight, then turned both palms up and raised 'em up slowly toward his chest, takin' a deep breath at the same time. Then he snapped his hands over, palms down, and pushed down, lettin' his breath out in a long loud flow. He did this two or three times. All of a sudden he snapped his left leg forward and landed in a half-crouching position. In a flowin' motion, he placed his hands and arms in one of those old-style boxing stances with the left arm way out in front and the right hand back next to his face. He held his hands in a kinda claw-like manner, sorta like you'd hold 'em if you was to be catchin' a ball without a glove on. Then he began to wave 'em around in a circle, still keepin' 'em close to their original position.

I haven't been around a whole lot, but I've watched enough TV to know that this was some sorta oriental fightin' stance. The big man recognized it, too, but wasn't impressed. He said somethin' like, "Gonna try some of that Kung Fu crap on me now, are ya? Well, come on and give it your best!" But instead of lettin' Dean throw the first punch, he shot a left jab at the boy's face.

Dean brought his right arm forward, blockin' the punch and knocking the other man's arm to the outside. At the same time, he shot his right foot forward and kicked the man in the chest. As his right leg returned to its original position, he pivoted on his left foot, faked a low kick with his right foot as he came around in a full circle, let out a deep guttural squall, and hit the big man with the back of his right fist square alongside of the head.

I was so impressed with all of the boy's jumpin' around and kickin' that I didn't notice one of the locals sneakin' up on him. The newcomer jumped out of the crowd and grabbed the boy in a bear hug, pinnin' his arms to his side. Dean shot a kick backwards, hittin' the new man in the shin, causin' him to let go, but by then the big man was back on his feet and in the fight again.

At that point I don't know what got into me. One minute I was standin' there watchin' and the next I was out there tusslin' with the second man.

I guess when I jumped in, though, all them locals took it as an invitation to join in, too. From then on it got kinda confusin'. Fists and hands and bottles and boots came at me from everywhere. The air seemed to be filled with jabs and uppercuts, all landin' somewhere on my body.

Every once in a while, through all of the commotion, I got a glimpse of Dean out there in the middle of the room. He was surrounded by the new father and three or four of his friends. The boy was jumpin' around, spinnin' and screamin' and kickin' in every direction. It was hard to tell if he was doin' any real damage, but he sure made a lot of noise and seemed to be a real tiger.

I was gettin' tired fast, and I knew that the kid couldn't keep up all that leapin' around too much longer either. But just like in the movies, when the cowboys are surrounded by ten thousand Indians, the cavalry comes chargin' to the rescue. Only this time it wasn't the cavalry, and there was no bugle soundin' the charge. It was the local sheriff and his deputy. They arrived with sirens blarin' and red lights flashin'.

I could hear 'em comin' a couple blocks away. By the time they came crashin' through the door, there was only me, Dean, the new father, and one other feller left in the place. Everyone else had lit out. Even the bartender and the waitress were standin' outside, watchin' through the window.

The sheriff was a big man a little past middle age. He stepped up and smacked the bar with his nightstick so hard that it sounded like a gunshot. Everyone froze in their tracks. He looked over at the new father and said, "What in the name of holy hell is goin' on here, Floyd!?"

Floyd pointed at Dean and said, "He insulted Emmy, Bill."

About that time the bartender sneaked back inside and

said, "Yep, that's right. Floyd's tellin' the truth, Bill. I heard it."

I thought to myself, "Floyd? Emmy? Bill?? These guys are all on a first-name basis. This ain't gonna be good for us."

Sheriff Bill turned back to the new father and his partner and said, "Floyd, you two go on home. Me and Brad can handle things from here. And don't worry, son. No one's gonna make light of my niece in public and get off easy."

When the two were gone, the sheriff turned back to me and Dean and said, "Boy," looking at Dean, "I'd get a lot of pleasure out of hurtin' you, so don't give me no trouble. Just keep your mouth shut and walk out and get in the back of that patrol car. Brad here'll drive your car, if you got one."

They didn't search us, but before we left, they had us empty our pockets out on the bar. They took Dean's car keys and my pocketknife and let us keep everythin' else.

When we got to the little station, they had us sit down in front of a desk while Deputy Brad filled out the usual papers and reports on the incident. That done, they led us back to one of the two cells and locked us up.

We both plopped down on the bunks and stared at the opposite wall. Finally, Dean said, "Will you please tell me what's going on?"

I started at the first part where the guy told me about his wife havin' a new baby and went from there. Before I got halfway, Dean was smilin'. By the time I finished, he was laughin' his fool head off. Listenin' to him carry on got me to laughin', too. Pretty soon we were both holdin' our sides and rollin' around.

Suddenly, Sheriff Bill came crashin' back there and smacked the cell door with his nightstick. He told us to knock it off or he's gonna start bustin' heads. Guess he didn't hear the story or maybe he just didn't have a sense of humor. Anyway, we'd sit there for a few minutes, then one of us'd start to giggle and the other one'd follow. I reckon we sounded like a couple of little schoolgirls.

After a while, I asked Dean where he learned that foreign fightin'. He told me that he'd gone to a private school back East and had taken up boxing there. When he got in the army, he went down to the base gym one evenin' to do a little sparrin' and found that they had karate classes a couple of nights a week. He said he'd only been studyin' it for about eighteen months and that he really wasn't that good.

We were sittin' there talkin' when the deputy came in and told us that the justice of the peace had arrived and wanted us up front.

Our hearing was as simple and short as you could imagine. We were charged with disturbin' the peace. We could plead guilty and each pay a $150 fine or spend two weeks in jail. If we wanted to plead innocent, a trial date would be set, and we could post bond and go free till then. It was that simple.

They gave us a chance to talk it over alone. Dean was all for pleadin' innocent, but I reminded him that the girl he was supposed to have insulted was related to half the people that'd be on the jury.

In the end, Dean and I decided to plead guilty. Dean paid his fine and offered to loan me the money to pay mine, but I said no. This looked like a good chance for me to get away from him without hurtin' his feelin's. And 'sides, none of us likes to get caught in our own lies. I'm no exception. I really didn't want to tell him that I'd lied about havin' a job just to get him to give me a ride.

Life in the jail wasn't all that bad. They brought in three good meals a day from a restaurant down the street. I got clean sheets twice while I was there, and they sent my dirty clothes out to be cleaned. The only work I had to do besides keeping my own cell clean was to sweep the office every mornin' and empty the trash cans.

After three days, they quit lockin' my cell door except at night. I'd sit up front and watch TV durin' the day. Later, when no one was there, I'd answer the phone and take messages for the sheriff.

One evenin' while me and Deputy Brad were playin' checkers, he asked what'd started the ruckus that had got me locked up. By the time I finished tellin' the story, he's laughin' 'bout as hard as Dean and I had that first day. Then he told me all the gossip about everyone else who was involved.

Seems Floyd was a big ol' farm kid whose only claim to fame was that he'd been the local football hero when he was in high school. He'd married the daughter of Sheriff Bill's brother, who still lived on the family ranch a few miles outta town where Floyd worked for him.

I guess Brad musta thought my story about the fight was worth retellin', 'cause a day or so later I noticed a change in the way the sheriff acted towards me.

One evenin' instead of bringin' me my supper, he asked if I'd like to go down to the restaurant with him and eat there. We sat in the cafe and talked and told lies till the place was ready to close.

The day after that, the proud father, Floyd, brought his wife, Emmy, and his new son down to the jail. His wife brought a cake for all of us to eat. They'd already heard the story of what happened at the bar, and Floyd apologized. I did, too, but I wasn't really sure just what for.

Floyd asked if there's anythin' that he could do to help or make me more comfortable. I told him I'd be needin' a job when I got out and asked if he knew of anyone wantin' a man to take care of cattle up in the mountains for the summer. He and his wife said they'd check around and let me know.

Their outfit didn't have any summer range on the forest. They kept their cattle down in the valley on permanent pasture. They said if I wanted to take a job irrigatin', they could probably help me out.

A day or so 'fore I's to get out, Sheriff Bill came in and gave me a piece of paper with the names and phone numbers of every rancher in the area that had a cow camp in the mountains. He told me to use his phone to try and line up a job. Guess he figured it was cheaper to pay the phone bill than to have to arrest me for vagrancy and have to feed me some more.

None of the numbers turned up a job. Most everyone had already hired their summer help, but one man did give me a suggestion. He told me that if I knew how to shoe and pack, I could probably get on at one of the pack stations that operated in the area.

I got out a phone directory that listed all of the numbers from Bridgeport to Olancha. I's surprised to see that there were at least fifteen or twenty pack stations. I started at the top of the list and began to work my way down. Some weren't open yet and others already had their help lined up. Finally, I got lucky.

Along toward the middle of the column, I came to a listing for a Lost Lake Pack Outfit. It had a Bishop, California, number that turned out to be an answerin' service. The lady on the other end told me that there was no regular phone at the pack station, just a mobile unit in one of the pickups. She said that she took their calls and made the reservations for 'em.

When I told her that I's lookin' for work, she said she'd talked with the manager just that mornin' and she knew for a fact that he needed another packer. I gave her my name and the number of the jail and asked if she'd have the manager return my call when he came in.

The next day I's sittin' at the sheriff's desk playin' solitaire when the phone rang. It was a feller named Lonney Blain, the manager of the Lost Lake Pack Station. He wanted to know if I's still lookin' for work. Then he wanted to know if I could pack and shoe horses.

It didn't take us long to make a deal; I needed a job and he needed a packer.

Lonney arrived that evenin' to pick me up. My official release date wasn't till eight o'clock the next mornin', but Sheriff Bill said, "What the hell, just stay outta trouble until after eight."

As we loaded my gear in the back of the company pickup, Lonney and I were sizin' each other up out of the corners of our eyes. After I got in and we were headin' back up into the mountains, Lonney said, "I wasn't expectin' someone as old as you."

I told him that I wasn't expecting someone as young as him for a boss either. He didn't appear to be much older than the kid that had picked me up in Arizona.

Somewheres along the drive to the pack station, he asked me why I wanted to quit a job workin' for the sheriff's department and go packin' in the mountains.

The question really threw me for a second or two. Then I remembered that I'd answered the phone when he called. Lonney'd just assumed that I's workin' there and not one of the prisoners. I's kind of afraid to tell him the truth but decided to anyway. When I's done, he just laughed.

By the time we got to the pack station, it was way past dark. There was no electricity, and the other help was already asleep. I found an empty cot as quietly as I could and threw my bedroll out.

I'd been restin' pretty regular down at the jail, and I woke up early the next mornin'. It was just barely gettin' light when I first opened my eyes and started lookin' around. I didn't get up or anything. I just laid there without movin' and took in what was around me.

It was dark in the room, but I could make out the doorway and a window on each side of the room. Another door led into a back room, and from the snorin' I could tell there was at least one other person in it. The whole room was only about ten by ten.

I was in a bed just inside the door and up against the front wall. The door was at my feet. Next to my bed was a small table and across from it was another cot.

I laid there lookin' past the little table at the man in the next bed. There was somethin' wrong, but I couldn't put my finger on it at first. Suddenly it came to me. I jerked up straight into a sittin' position, rubbed the sleep from my eyes, and looked again. I was starin' straight into the sleepin' face of the kid, Dean McCuen!

CHAPTER 4

I musta laid there for a full ten minutes, just starin' at that boy and thinkin' what a strange sense of humor fate has. Then I decided to get up and take a look around. I crawled outta bed as quietly as I could, slipped on my clothes, and stepped out the door. It was just barely gettin' light, and there was a bite to the early mornin' breeze.

The first thing I noticed was that the bunkhouse was facin' north. It seemed to sit right in the middle of the woods. Huge red fir and giant tamaracks were everywhere. It looked as though only enough trees'd been cut to make room for the buildings and the corrals. Off to the right was a low log buildin' with a tin roof. This turned out to be the cookshack and the place where Lonney slept.

About thirty yards off to the left was another log buildin'. This one was a little bigger than the cookshack. It was where the tack and pack equipment was kept. In front of it was a pole hitchin' rail. Another thirty yards west of the tack buildin' were the corrals. They consisted of three pens, each about two-hundred-foot square. A manger ran the full length of their west side. To the north of the pens was the haystack. It looked like it held about twenty tons of hay.

I walked up to the corrals for a look at the stock. In the upper pen, there were about fifteen head of geldings. The middle pen held twelve mules, and the lower pen held another fifteen head of mares. It was early in the season and none of the stock had been used much. They were all fat and slick.

When I turned around and headed back, I noticed the old two-seater outhouse. It sat back behind some willows and scrub tamaracks. Only the little shake roof showed above the undergrowth. I probably wouldn't have seen it if it weren't for the worn path leadin' from the side of the bunkhouse back into the willows.

I was headin' for the outhouse when Lonney stepped out of the cookshack and started bangin' an ol' disk blade that was hung from a tree limb. I decided to go get a cup of coffee first.

Because I was up and dressed, I was the first one down to the cookshack 'cept for Lonney. I ducked my head and went inside the log building. It would have been dark inside, as there was only one window along the south wall, but there was a Coleman lamp burnin' over by the cookstove. Lonney was just finishin' up fryin' eggs. The coffee and bacon were already done. I walked over to the stove and poured myself a cup of coffee while Lonney and I exchanged small talk about how we slept.

Right here, I think I'd best fill you in on a few things I found out about the Lost Lake Pack Station. It took me two seasons to learn these things, but after I tell you, it'll

29

make it easier to understand how the outfit operated.

First off, the Lost Lake operation was one of the oldest pack stations in the mountains. It had started way back in the early 1900s. The present owner was a lawyer who had gotten the place in exchange for payment on a bad debt. The "Legal Beagle" lived down in the Bay area, someplace around San Francisco. He had put the place up for sale as soon as he got it. When it didn't sell, he hired Lonney to run it. I'm not sure just what the details of their agreement were, but I do know that Lonney got a percentage of the profit in addition to a regular wage. That was probably the reason that Lonney ran the place the way he did.

He knew any money that got spent on improvements was gonna be charged off as part of the operatin' expenses and would cut into his share of the profits. For that reason, almost no money was spent on fixin' the place up. The buildings were patched with whatever materials were available. This gave the place a sorta rustic, western look when in reality it was just plain run-down. The saddles and pack equipment were all old and worn; they'd all been torn and patched someplace.

Now, let me tell you about the stock. Most pack stations and dude outfits operate on the idea that old gentle animals make for a smooth, safe operation. This wasn't Lonney's way. He'd put together a string of about fifteen head of the nicest dude horses that I was ever around. For the most part, the twelve head of mules weren't too bad either, though some would kick, and all of 'em were hard to shoe. But Lonney had also managed to collect fifteen head of the dirtiest, crankiest bunch of chicken-feed rejects I could ever imagine.

This was Lonney's third year of runnin' the place for the lawyer, and Lost Lake had already made quite a reputation among the other outfits operatin' in that part of the mountains. It was said that if you wanted a "High Mountain Adventure," the Lost Lake Pack Station would give it to you. If you wanted a nice relaxin' horseback trip in the mountains with lots of time to fish and take pictures, you'd best use one of the other outfits.

There was a big sign on the side of the barn that said, "NOT RESPONSIBLE FOR PERSONAL INJURY OR DAMAGED EQUIPMENT." People shoulda read between the lines. There were always a couple of lawsuits goin' on from people who had been kicked, bitten, or bucked off. This doesn't even bring into account the complaints about broken fishin' and campin' equipment. We didn't have a lot of repeat business, but no one ever left there without some sorta story to tell.

Only one thing came outta all this. It was said IF you could pack for Lost Lake, you could pack for anybody in the mountains.

The first feller to come through the cookhouse door was a giant of a kid. He's about twenty-five and stood close to six foot six. He musta weighed 250 pounds. I found out later that his real name was Malcolm Kister, but Lonney just called him Slick.

This Slick didn't talk a lot. Lonney said he's studyin' to be a vet. He's only workin' there for the summer and would be goin' back to school in the fall. He'd worked for Lonney the summer before and was sort of a leadman, takin' over when Lonney was gone.

Slick was always tradin' stuff. He'd trade horses, cars, guns—just about anything. He got his name 'cause some of his deals leaned a little toward the direction of larceny.

A story I once heard was that one summer Slick was keepin' a little sorrel horse down at his folks' place in the valley. When he got ready to leave for college, his mom asked if he'd sell her the horse. Slick, of course, said he would and 'cause she was his mom, he'd give her a real good deal on the pony. He sold her the horse for $400 and went to leave again. As he's pullin' outta the driveway, his younger brother came up and asked if Slick would sell him the little horse. Slick asked his brother how much money he had. When the kid said $175, Slick agreed to the deal. He grabbed his brother's money and left for school.

It wasn't till the animal got cut in some wire a couple of months later that Slick's mom and brother figured out what had happened. Up to then each one had thought that the other was just jokin' when they called the horse his or hers.

About five minutes after I's introduced to Slick, Dean came in. Even though it was now pretty well light outside, it was still kinda dark in the cabin 'cause Lonney had turned off the Coleman lamp. Dean walked over and filled his plate from the pans on the stove and sat down next to me. When we were introduced, Dean looked up from his plate and stuck out his hand. At first I didn't think he was gonna recognize me. Then all of a sudden it dawned on him who I was. He went to carryin' on like we were lost kin.

After Dean settled down and we all got to eatin', Lonney lined us out on the day's work. Dean had been hired a week or so earlier. His job was to feed the stock, haul off the manure from around the hitch rail, and help saddle the horses. He's also to drive any animals that we weren't usin' or shoein' up to a meadow a mile or so from the corral. In the evenin' he had to go out and gather these loose horses and bring 'em back to the corral.

Lonney kept the books and scheduled the trips. He also did most of the shoein' and packin' when there was more business than Slick and I could handle. He always cooked breakfast 'cause he was the first one up. The other meals were just sorta up to whoever was around and who was hungry. My job was to help Slick and Lonney with the shoein' and packin'.

As I said before, it was still early in the season, and a lot of the backcountry was snowed in. On this particular day, there was only one party goin' out so Slick would be takin' them. They'd be gone three days.

The campers, four fishermen, hadn't arrived, but we went ahead and caught the stock that they'd need. We caught four saddle horses for them plus one for Slick. Then we caught three pack mules. We tied all of 'em but Slick's horse to the hitch rail. While Dean was puttin' grain morrals on 'em, the rest of us went to saddlin'.

None of the dude horses or mules seemed to pay any attention to anything except their grain. But Slick's horse, a big black-and-white pinto called Patches, reared over backwards as soon as Slick tightened the cinch.

When he came up, the nose bag had slipped down over one eye, and he started buckin' blindly into the other horses that were tied. This caused a couple of the mules to pull back, tearin' the hitch rail from the posts that it was fastened to. They ran backwards till they came to one of the big fir trees. They were all still tied to the rail and half of 'em ended up on one side of the tree and half on the other.

Even Dean didn't seem to get too excited about the whole thing, so I got to figurin' this must be an everyday occurrence, which is what it turned out to be.

While we were untanglin' the mules and dude horses, Slick led Patches down to a little round corral hid in the bushes by the outhouse. I couldn't see the corral unless I was right up on it. Lonney had built it down there outta sight to keep from scarin' the customers.

Slick put the pinto in the round pen and chased him around for ten or fifteen minutes to loosen him up. By the time he came back, we'd gotten the other animals straightened out and were puttin' the rail back on the posts where it'd come from.

While we were waitin' for the fishermen to arrive, we started in catchin' some of the horses that needed shoes. We tied these animals to the inside of the corral fence so that when Dean took the other horses up on the hill to graze, these wouldn't be able to get away and go with 'em.

The fishermen still hadn't arrived when we were done catchin' horses so Lonney had Dean get saddled and ready to take the loose stock up the hill.

The horse that Lonney picked out for the boy to ride was a big, stout, buckskin gelding with a forty-five brand on his hip. He was easy to catch, but I didn't like the look in his eye. When Dean threw his saddle on, the horse humped up and I coulda stuck my hat under the cantle.

The dumb kid never even noticed. In fact, the boy didn't bother to untrack the big animal. He just cinched up and climbed aboard his fancy old centerfire saddle.

As soon as his butt hit the seat, the old horse fired. In two jumps the kid was on the ground and the buckskin took off, runnin' and buckin' around the corral.

Dean gathered himself up and caught the horse. He led the buckskin back and climbed on again. I think if the kid had watched the horse and known how to get on, he coulda talked the pony out of another fight. But the boy didn't know nothin'. He never even took the slack out of his reins.

This time the horse let him get both feet in the stirrups before he went at it. Dean lasted one more jump this trip than he did the first go-around. But that was only 'cause the horse bucked back under him and Dean happened to land in the saddle instead of on the ground.

The three of us were all cheerin' him on, but the advice we gave couldn't help much. Things like "Keep a leg on each side" and "Stay a long time" don't tell you a whole lot.

When Dean got up, I could tell he's mad. He stomped over and snatched up the reins. He led the horse away from the manger where he was eatin'. Lonney held the buckskin by the head till the kid was set.

For a minute it looked like they were gonna be okay but Dean shifted his weight and turned around to look back at Lonney. When he did, the buckskin let out a fart and fired again. Dean only lasted a couple of jumps, but he left claw marks all over that old saddle and the horse's neck. He landed on his back with a big wad of mane and two saddle strings in his hands. The horse kept on buckin' after the kid was off, just to show that he's mad too.

The taps on the ol' A fork were sure flyin' and flappin'. Then the horse took off down through the willows, past the outhouse and the little round corral.

Slick's pinto musta seen the buckskin go by and tried to jump the gate, 'cause the next thing we heard was a loud crash and both horses come flyin' up the outhouse trail toward the corral.

The horses tied to the hitch rail saw 'em comin', too. They spooked and pulled back again, tearin' out the hitch rail that we'd just finished repairin'.

While Lonney and I went to untanglin' the dude horses and pack mules, Slick and Dean set about tryin' to capture their saddle horses. The buckskin and the pinto were now involved in a horse race, goin' round and round the outside of the three pens while the loose horses were runnin' around the inside.

The horses to be shod were tied to the big stout tamarack poles that made up the corral, and every time the loose horses would go by, they'd all pull back, tryin' to get loose, too.

By and by, the two free saddle horses were caught, the dude horses were untangled, and the hitch rail was put back together, but the fishermen still hadn't arrived.

Lonney decided that Dean probably wasn't gonna get the buckskin rode, so he had the boy tie up the old horse, and he picked out a little sorrel mare called Lady Jane. Dean switched his saddle to the other horse and got ready again to take the unused horses up to the pasture. When Dean was all set, Lonney, Slick, and I went over and opened the gates.

Then we started hazin' the loose horses outta the pens.

Everything went okay till one of the mules saw his partner tied to the hitch rail. The big brown mule trotted out of the bunch. As he went by he sniffed the face of one of the other horses that was tied. That horse squealed and stomped his front foot. The mule nipped the horse to show his annoyance, and the whole damn bunch pulled back again.

All the noise and commotion scared the guilty mule, so he trotted over to the main bunch, and they all lined out and headed up the hill as though nothin' happened.

The three of us went to untanglin' horse and mules and repairin' the hitch rail for the third time that mornin'. Before we were done, the fishermen arrived. They'd got in late and spent the night in one of the public campgrounds not far from the station. From the looks on their faces and the way they acted, they musta decided to have a couple of drinks to relax before goin' to bed. They were all still about half-lit.

It didn't take the three of us long to get their gear packed and them mounted. We necked the three pack mules together, Slick climbed on his pinto, Lonney handed him the lead rope, and they were off.

Suddenly, from up on the hill came the thunder of hooves. Then the whole herd of loose horses that Dean had been trailin' to the pasture came flyin' into sight. They saw the animals the fishermen were on and headed straight for 'em. The mounted horses saw the loose bunch comin' off the hill at a dead run and figured they were bein' attacked. The startled fishermen dropped their reins and grabbed their saddle horns. The whole bunch, loose horses and fishermen together, shot past Slick and the pack string, doin' ninety. The pinto tried to join the stampede, and when Slick pulled him up, the horse bogged his head and went to buckin'.

By the time Slick got the pinto under control, he'd lost his pack mules and they'd joined the runaway, too. There wasn't a damn thing Lonney and I could do but stand there and watch as the whole cavvy went thunderin' outta sight with fishermen screamin' and pack equipment flyin'. Then we heard a noise that sounded sorta like one of those ol'-time air-raid sirens, and from out of nowhere came Lady Jane and Dean. The boy's face was ash white and his eyes were bugged out of their sockets like a stomped-on frog. The sorrel mare was stretched out like a race horse headed for the wire. Dean was screeching "whooooa" in a voice so shrill it woulda shattered a crystal glass. He was tryin' his damnedest to stop Lady Jane, but the reins had slipped through his fingers and his hands were now pulled clear back to his ears.

The two of 'em tore past Slick and flew down the trail, followin' the fishermen, the loose horses, and the pack mules. In less than a minute every animal on the place that wasn't still in a pen was outta sight.

We found out later from the fishermen that Lady Jane passed the pack mules like a bullet fired from a high-powered rifle. Where the trail turned back to the left, she went straight, jumped a six-foot switchback, and ended up out in the lead of the whole parade.

Dean got her stopped at a narrow spot in the trail, and, of course, all the other animals had to stop, too. This made Dean a hero to the fishermen, who were now dead sober.

Slick had Dean ride on ahead till they came to a wide spot in the trail. The two of 'em got the fishermen off their horses and tied those animals and the three pack mules to trees. Then Slick helped Dean trail the loose stock back to the pack station where Lonney and I helped drive 'em to the little pasture on the hill.

It was close to noon now so Lonney and I spent the rest of the day shoein' horses while Dean repaired the gate on the round corral and tried to reinforce the hitch rail.

I'd like to say this was an unusual day, and in some ways I guess it was. But the truth is, there's some sorta rodeo or wreck around the Lost Lake Pack Station nearly every mornin'. A lot of 'em coulda been avoided but Lonney and Slick were both wild. They had no fear of personal injury and couldn't see why anyone else should. Dean was just dumb. So that's the way we went through the summer: terrorizin' customers and givin' people stories to tell their friends.

Later that afternoon while we were shoein', Lonney told me about Dean's first day on the job. He and Slick had helped the kid start the horses up the trail toward the pasture on the hill. After they got him lined out, they went back to shoein' and gettin' ready for the next day. When Dean got back, Lonney asked him if he got to the pasture okay. Dean said he thought so, but when Lonney asked how many horses he'd put through the gate, the kid had to admit that he didn't know. Lonney sent him back with instructions to count all of the horses inside the fence. An hour later, the boy came back and said that there were twenty-eight. Lonney told him that there's supposed to be thirty-two and sent him out to look for the four missin' horses.

I guess Dean was gone most of the mornin'. When he did wander in, Lonney asked if he'd found the missin' horses. The kid told him, "No, but they can't be far."

Lonney asked, "If you didn't find 'em, how do you know they're not far?"

Dean said, "I rode far and they weren't there, so they must be near."

That kinda shows you how Dean's mind worked back in them days.

That night after supper I walked up to the barn. I was sittin' there, leanin' against the buildin', when Dean wandered up. I could tell somethin' was the matter from the way he was actin'.

He plopped down beside me without sayin' a word. He picked up a little pine stick and began scratchin' in the dust. We sat there like that for five minutes or so 'fore he finally said, "Tap, Lonney says if I don't get to where I can handle these horses pretty quick, he's gonna have to let me go. He said as soon as business picks up he won't be able to let me keep on ridin' the gentle ones. What can I do?"

I sat there for a minute or so, thinkin'. Then I said, "Let's go see Lonney. I might have an idea."

When we got down to the cookshack, Lonney was layin' on his bed, readin'.

"You got any objections to me tryin' to teach the kid here to ride?" I asked.

"Depends on how you plan on doin' it," was Lonney's answer.

I explained to him how I figured we could do it usin' a couple of the pack mules. Lonney said he didn't have a problem with the plan as long as we didn't cripple any of the animals.

With the boss's okay, I told Dean to get his saddle and meet me up at the corral. By the time he got there, I'd caught one of the long ears and was waitin' for him.

We slipped his saddle on and cinched it down tight. Then I took an ol' catch rope apart and flipped it around the mule's flank. After I picked up the free end, I ran it back through the honda.

I had Dean climb on and take a deep seat. When he said he was ready, I sat back on the loose end of the rope. As soon as the rope went tight around the mule's flank, he fired. Dean made about two jumps before he loosened up. When I saw that, I slacked off on the rope and the mule quit buckin'. When Dean had his seat back, I tightened up on the rope again and the mule started all over. We did this for the next fifteen or twenty minutes, lettin' the mule rest every time Dean needed to get reset.

Every evenin' I wasn't in the backcountry, we'd go out to the mule pen and flank out one or two. Before June was out, Dean had gotten to where he could ride most any horse in the cavvy, except for the buckskin and an ol' palomino named Gold Dust.

It wasn't long 'fore mule ridin' got to be quite a game, with Lonney, Slick, and Dean all playin' at it. This horsin' around didn't do a lot to make any of them mules gentle, but it was kinda fun and gave us somethin' to do after work.

One evenin' we were all out there playin'. Lonney was

up, and Slick was on the rope. The mule that Lonney was to ride was a great big black animal called Ike. Must've weighed close to thirteen hundred pounds. Lonney got set and Slick gave a heave on the flank rope. The mule jumped and kicked backwards with both hind feet, catchin Slick square in the chest. Slick flew across the corral, lookin' like he was rollin' on his spur rowels. When he came crashin' to the ground, he was clutchin' his ribs and gaspin' for air. From the noises he made, we all figured he was dyin'. Lonney jerked the tall man's shirt open to see if Slick had any broken ribs stickin' out. Then he began to laugh. Dean and I went rushin' across the corral to see what was so funny about a dyin' man. There on Slick's chest were two of the prettiest mule tracks you ever seen. The three of us thought it was hysterical, but it was a half hour before Slick got enough air so he could laugh, too.

As the days got warmer and the passes opened in the backcountry, we got a lot busier. This meant that there were times when Dean got drafted into helpin' with the packin'. He started out just leadin' a string when we had a big group. Later he got to load and balance the panniers. By the end of the summer he'd gotten to where he could throw a respectable-lookin' box hitch, and Lonney let him take a few of the spot trips by himself.

The boy was a natural. He did his own job, and he took an interest in anything that the rest of us were doin'. Whenever an animal got sick or hurt, he's right there while Slick was doctorin'. When we were shoein', he was right in the middle, handin' us our tools or helpin' throw the ones that wouldn't stand. When Lonney had to patch a pack outfit after a wreck, Dean was there again. In addition to all this, there wasn't a job that he thought he was too good for. He shoveled manure, swept the bunkhouse, washed the dishes, and chopped wood.

Little by little, the way he dressed was changin', too. The first thing he did was recrease that flat-crowned hat to where it looked more like the one Lonney wore. I gave him a silk scarf to replace the snot rag he wore around his neck, and Lonney traded him a couple of half-worn work shirts for one or two of those fancy western dress shirts. It didn't take long for the new jeans to get broken in. One night we all sat down and helped him make out an order for a pair of custom boots.

By September, when Slick had to leave for school, Dean looked 'bout like the rest of us. He knew his way around most of the backcountry and could pack fairly well. He was a long way from bein' a horseshoer, but he could level a foot and tack steel under a gentle animal. He'd gotten to where he didn't talk so much, and when he asked a question, he'd wait till you'd answered him 'fore he asked another. Most everyone, the customers and us, liked him. He always seemed to be interested in everybody and the things that everybody had done. He hardly ever talked about himself, and when he did, it was usually to make a joke outta somethin' he'd done wrong. All in all, he was becoming a pleasure to be around.

CHAPTER 5

After Slick left for school, everything seemed to change. The weather started turnin' cool, and a breeze was always blowin'. All summer there had been scattered thundershowers, but snow was mixed in 'em now. The business slacked off at the pack station, and we had a lot more spare time.

In the summer, most of our business was movin' pack trips with families or makin' spot drops for scout or church groups. Now they were mainly fishermen who were content to stay at one lake as long as the fish were bitin'.

It got daylight later, so we slept in longer. A lot of our work switched from packin' to repairin'. We went to spendin' lots of time just patchin' up the equipment and buildings. There were still horses to shoe and a few scattered trips to take, but for the most part, we were just markin' time, waitin' for deer huntin' season to start.

Only two things that happened that fall are worth retellin'. The first one took place about a week before deer season. I had packed a family of five way back to one of the farthest lakes that we traveled to and dropped 'em off. A day or so later we got about a foot of good wet snow. Some backpacker came by the pack station the next afternoon and told Lonney that the family was back there freezin' and wanted to come out early.

The next mornin' at daylight Dean and I saddled up five head of ridin' horses and two pack mules along with our own horses and headed out. The sky was overcast, and it snowed off and on all the way. It was about eighteen to twenty miles back to the lake where the family was stayin', and we had one low pass and one high one to cross 'fore we got there. We made pretty good time by trottin' on the flats. Of course, we had to walk the horses in the steeper country. Even so, we still made it to their camp by three in the afternoon.

When we got there, I don't think I've ever seen a sadder group of people. Most all the wood in the area was wet, but they'd managed to find a couple of pine knots and had gotten them burnin'. All they had to wear in the way of extra clothes were some light jackets and sweaters. The five of 'em were huddled around the little fire, stompin' their feet and wavin' their arms, tryin' to keep warm. They hadn't knocked the snow off the tent and it was saggin' in the middle. They were all cold, wet, and scared.

Dean and I set right to work gettin' 'em mounted and headed back toward the pack station. We figured they'd travel slower than us so we wanted 'em to get goin' as soon as possible. After we got 'em on the horses we wrapped their sleepin' bags around 'em for warmth. Then we took their plastic ground cloth and cut it into three pieces and punched a hole in the middle of each to make ponchos for the kids. As soon as that was done, we pointed 'em towards home and went to tearin' down the camp.

In less than an hour, we had the whole thing packed and lashed on the mules. We shoulda been faster but all of the groceries were out and had to be repacked before loadin'.

We caught up to the family not much more than a mile from their camp. They were creepin' along at a snail's pace and didn't seem to be in a hurry. It was snowin' pretty hard right about then so I tried to explain to the father that if we didn't hustle it up a little, there's a good chance we'd get stuck on this side of one of the passes. That would mean that we'd have to spend the night. Dean and I had on warm coats, slickers, chaps, and gloves but I still wasn't in a hurry to spend the night out there if I could help it. The whole family seemed to understand, and for the next ten minutes or so we moved right along. But gradually the pace started slowin' down again. By this time, I had an idea. I stopped the parade and tied each of their horses to the one in front. Then I gave the lead horse to Dean. Now they were all strung out like a pack string.

The light was fadin' fast so we struck out at a pretty good clip. We weren't trottin', but we were sure movin' right along. The mommy of that outfit wasn't real happy about the pace we set, but we never slacked off.

Shortly after eight, the storm blew away and the stars came out. With the stars came the cold. By midnight we'd crossed both passes and were at a fork in the trail. The right track went along a ridge high above the south side of Lost Lake while the left-hand fork went down to the north shore of the lake itself. We usually traveled on the right fork as it was a more direct route to the pack station. That night we decided to take the left branch for safety reasons.

At the northwest end of Lost Lake was a pay phone where backpackers could call a boat taxi from the resort to come pick 'em up. By doin' that they saved about three or four miles of hikin'. Dean and I decided to take the family down to the phone and let them ride the boat. They'd get back an hour or so ahead of us, but they could stay at the lodge and be warm.

By one o'clock we were on the trail just above the boat dock and phone booth. We dropped the family off there an' told 'em we'd meet at the lodge. We watched 'em start down the hill toward the phone booth, and then we took off.

It was well below freezin' now and darker than the inside of a mine shaft. We were movin' as fast as we could without shakin' the packs apart, and in an hour we were at the lodge. When we got there it was snowin' again and there was no one around. We figured the family had gotten someone to take 'em to the pack station and were waitin' for us there.

It was close to three when we got back to the corrals, but no one was there either. I went in, woke Lonney, and told him what had happened. He jumped in the company pickup and headed for the lodge. Dean and I set about unpackin' and grainin' the horses.

Somewhere around four, maybe four-thirty that mornin', Lonney got back with the family. He had all five of 'em ridin' in the front of the pickup with him. They were dead tired and about half-froze.

Seems that when they got to the phone, they found out

they didn't have any change to call, and we were long gone. They'd taken turns standin' in the booth, tryin' to keep warm and waitin' to be rescued again.

Lonney offered to let 'em spend what was left of the night in the cookshack, as it was the only buildin' we had with a stove.

The father said, "NO!" Then he threw the campin' equipment in the back of their station wagon, slammed the door, and said he was headin' home. He stomped on the gas and shot outta the little dirt parking area like a jet. They were still scatterin' pine cones, dust, and gravel as their taillights faded into the darkness.

Dean and I turned around and headed for the bunkhouse. We were kinda expectin' a pretty good tip for our efforts. We'd been in the saddle for almost twenty-four straight hours. As it turned out, we didn't even get a Thank You. Guess they figured it was our fault it snowed. In any case, I bet the family will remember that trip for a long time.

CHAPTER 6

The other event that happened at the pack station took place in the middle of deer season. Dean and I'd taken a party of ten hunters back to a spike camp we'd set up at Lake Linda. Nine of the men had hunted there before and knew the area better than Dean or I did. The tenth man was on his first huntin' trip.

By the end of the third day, the group had filled about half of their tags just huntin' around camp. Dean and I knew of a rocky ridge farther west where we'd seen a couple of good bucks earlier in the season, so we suggested this place. The only hunter we were able to talk into goin' was the new man.

The next mornin' we got up way before daylight, saddled our horses, and woke the hunter. We rode in the dark till we got to the ridge. There, we dismounted and led him on foot to a rocky point that offered a good view of three draws that were natural deer trails. I figured any big bucks that'd gone down to the valley to feed that night would have to come back on one of those trails.

On the ridge where we were, it got light a good forty minutes before it did down in the valley and it wasn't long 'fore we were occasionally able to make out the forms of an animal workin' its way up the draws. In the half-light, it was impossible to tell their size or even if they were bucks or does.

Just as it was gettin' light, Dean tapped me on the shoulder and motioned for me to look at the head of the left draw. I looked and then I looked again. There, about seventy-five yards out, standin' in a clump of big granite boulders, was some kind of animal, but I couldn't tell what the hell it was. The outline looked a little like a deer, but it was too dark to tell for sure.

I thought it might be a doe standin' in front of a dead snag. Then for a second I thought we were lookin' at an elk. There was somethin' about the head that wasn't right, though. I've seen enough deer over the years to recognize certain patterns in the way they move and carry themselves. This animal put its feet down real deliberately and even seemed to stumble at times. I couldn't be sure just what was wrong or even what I's lookin' at, but I knew this was no normal deer.

We watched the strange animal for fifteen minutes before our trance was broken by a movement less than thirty yards to the right. Comin' outta the mornin' shadows was a beautiful four-point. I nudged the hunter and motioned for him to take the new animal, but as he was aimin', Dean signaled for him not to shoot. The nice buck was now less than twenty yards from us and would be out of sight in a few more feet. Again I motioned for the hunter to fire, but Dean put his hand on top of the rifle.

Now the hunter couldn't shoot and the deer walked through a notch in the rocks and was gone.

Dean motioned for the hunter to shoot the farthest animal. I's kinda ticked off at the kid and thought to myself, "Go ahead, smart guy, have him shoot the S.O.B. Let's see just what the hell it is." By now I's almost certain it wasn't a deer.

The hunter moved his rifle back across the rocks, took aim at the unknown creature, and fired. I have no idea where that bullet went but it didn't even scare the animal. His next shot struck to the left, and the beast jumped to the right just as the third round hit in front of it. Then the animal froze and started pawin' the ground like a buck sheep. The hunter's next shot smacked a boulder, sprayin' the animal's rump with splinters.

The animal shot forward, runnin' straight toward us. The closer he got, the less I could believe what I was seein'. It was a deer, all right, but it had the damnedest set of horns I'd ever seen. By now the buck was less than forty yards away and closing fast.

The hunter jumped from our rock hiding place, stepped into plain view, and fired again. It was a clean miss. The deer didn't slow down; in fact, he sped up. Now he's less than twenty yards away and it was evident he planned on goin' right over us. I started to grab the rifle and shoot the deer myself. I had never seen a rack like this, and I didn't want it to get away.

Before I could climb over the rock and grab the gun, the hunter fired his last shot. The animal fell dead less than twenty feet from us. We all jumped up and rushed over to see what it was. The buck was big and old. His muzzle was gray and his teeth were just little snags. He had cataracts in both his eyes.

We decided later that the bad eyes were the reason he walked so strange. It probably also accounted for the deer not changin' direction when the hunter stepped out.

He had a twenty-eight-inch spread, which isn't too fantastic, but he had nineteen points on one side and twenty-nine on the other. That's far from being a Boone and Crocket Club record for a non-typical rack, but it was the biggest set of horns I'd ever seen.

Dean and I set about cleanin' the big animal and gettin' him loaded on my horse. All the while, the hunter kept rattlin' on about the deer and how he thought it was goin' to attack him. He talked constantly, and we finally got to where we weren't really payin' too much attention.

When we got to camp, everyone was gone, so we hung the deer in the tree next to the other five bucks. As the other hunters came in, our man would grab each one and tell him about shootin' this monster. The more he told the story, the wilder it got.

The final account went somethin' like this: he'd spotted the buck just as the sun was comin' up and wanted to shoot it then, but I'd stopped him. Finally he had insisted. When he fired and missed, the animal charged us. He stepped from his rock cover and shot the deer just as it was closin' in for the kill. Dean and I'd stayed crouched behind the rock while he alone faced the attacking beast.

My first impulse was to jump up and tell everyone what I thought really happened. Before I could, though, Dean started in, backin' up everything this bastard said. The kid told 'em how brave our hunter was and how he'd stood his ground and faced the charging killer deer alone, with no sign of fear. I couldn't believe what I was hearin'. That night when we were alone, I asked the boy why he'd said those things.

His reply was, "What difference does it make? We couldn't change his mind. Besides, the story makes him feel good and it doesn't hurt us any. He's a hero. Let him enjoy it."

I thought it over, and even though I didn't like it, I had to admit that the boy was probably right. As it turned out, Dean was a whole lot more right than I figured. Nine of the hunters each coughed up $10 apiece for a tip for us. But the brave deer slayer gave Dean and me each $50.

CHAPTER 7

I don't know when it was that Dean and I decided to travel together. It was one of those things that just sorta happened.

We knew that after the last hunter left, there wouldn't be anything for us to do but pull the shoes and truck the horses down to the valley. Lonney planned to stick around for awhile to drain the water lines and close up the camp for the winter. Then he'd be outta work, too.

Our last night together, Lonney went down to the valley with us for a couple of drinks and a final good-bye. We'd all made pretty good money and had a lot of fun, and none of us knew where we were headed next.

When we quit sayin' good-bye, it was four days later. We were almost 150 miles to the north in Carson City, and we were all about outta money. Lonney and Dean looked to have lost at least one fight, and the car had been in a wreck. I was sick with the dry heaves and pukin' blood, Lonney was seein' snakes, and Dean was so sore he could barely move.

We pooled our resources and came up with enough to get Lonney a bus ticket back to Bishop. From there he figured on hitchin' a ride to where he'd left his truck. He wanted to get back as soon as possible 'cause he was afraid that the water pipes at the cabin mighta froze and busted while he was gone.

Dean and I drove to a highway rest area on the edge of town where we used the rest room to wash up, shave, and change clothes. Then we set about lookin' for a job. I'd never been in this part of the world, so we found a pay phone and called every ranch listed in the directory.

A funny thing about that area. They got legalized prostitution there, and they call all the cathouses "ranches." We sure got some strange answers when we'd call one of those places by mistake. One of 'em told me they didn't go in for that kinky stuff and for me to go back to San Francisco where I belonged. Another asked Dean what his speciality was. He said, "I can ride a little if they don't buck too hard."

The black lady's voice on the other end said, "Honey, you'll have to do better'n that to work here."

We finally drove down to the unemployment office where Dean got a job at a car wash, and I got a job doin' dishes at one of the casinos. Dean picked me up after work, and we drove around till we found a cheap motel that would let us pay when we were ready to leave.

The closest I'd ever worked to this part of the country was way up near Gerlach, about 175 miles farther north. I's only in my early twenties, then, and more than forty years had gone by since then.

Back in them days, the ranch was owned by what I

thought was an old man named Ben Bird. He wasn't as old as I was at the time we were in Carson, but he sure seemed old to me as a kid. It was Ben Bird who had given me the nickname Tap. I'd drifted into his place one winter and asked if he had any horses he wanted "tapped off." I thought that term "tap off" sounded pretty western, and I wanted to impress him with just how much I'd been around.

Back in them days, I considered myself pretty "forked." So Ben hired me to start a string of what he called colts. They were stout, full-mouthed animals. Some of 'em might even have been smooth.

I got bucked off a lot that winter, and it seemed like every time I did, ol' Ben was right there, cussin' me for spoilin' his horses. He also got to callin' me Tap, and pretty soon, everyone else on the place was, too. After that, the name just stuck.

On the chance that some member of the family might still be runnin' the outfit, I wrote and asked about a job for me and Dean. I also wrote a dozen or more other letters to different ranches all the way from California to Utah.

It was gettin' on towards the middle of autumn and a lot of the bigger outfits go to layin' men off as soon as the fall gatherin' is over. Gettin' a job at that time of year can sometimes be a little slow.

Dean and I musta scrubbed pots and washed cars for about ten days 'fore I got a letter postmarked Gerlach, Nevada. The card was short and blunt. *Got a camp job for two men. The cabin is cold and the horses are green. If you are interested, call me 6:30 P.M. October 25 at the following number.* It was signed, *Ben Bird.*

I figured the card musta been written by one of the grandkids. The old Ben who I knew woulda been way up in his eighties by then, and his two sons were named Ed and Ted. There'd been another boy named Ned, but he and his mom had died back 'fore I ever worked there.

The evenin' of the twenty-fifth I went down to the motel office and asked if I could use their phone. As soon as the voice on the other end answered, a bolt of fear went through me.

I remembered how that sound used to strike terror into my heart as a kid. I knew right off this was no grandchild. Nobody could sound as mean as Ben Bird, nobody but the old man himself. With the sound of that voice, a thousand memories went shootin' through my mind, pictures of the past that I hadn't thought about for many, many years.

Forty years ago Ben Bird was big, gray-haired, old, and mean. In an area where rustlin' was common, no one touched his cattle. The people who weren't afraid of him at least respected him. I don't think he feared any creature that God ever put on the face of the earth. He woulda fought a bear as fast as he would a man. Ben had a tongue that could cut like a knife, and he said just exactly what he felt, not caring if it hurt somebody's feelin's or not. If the person didn't like it and wanted to fight, that was fine, too.

I grabbed my wits and told him who I was and that I's answerin' his card. His reply was, "So?"

I said, "So what?"

"So, do you want the job or not?"

"That depends," I said, "on what the job is."

"It's the winter camp job down at the Parker place. Same job it was when you were here before."

I couldn't believe it. I hadn't said anything in my letter to him about havin' worked there before, and here he was talkin' to me like I'd just left.

I asked if he knew who I was. "Sure," he said, "ain't you that round-assed kid outta southern Idaho I called Tap?" He said this almost as a statement, not as a question.

I hadn't thought of myself as a kid for a long time. The part about havin' a round ass embarrassed me and reminded me again of all the times I'd gotten bucked off. I admitted he's right. Then I told him that the kid I had with me was pretty green.

Ben said, "I don't need no gunsal kid runnin' around the place, but I do need you. If I have to hire him to get you, then I guess that's what I'll have to do."

Ben musta been mellowin' in his old age. There's a time when he woulda told me to get shed of the boy or stay in town, and that would have ended it.

He said he'd pay me $400 a month and give Dean $200. I told him just to give each of us $300 and not say anything to the kid.

His reply to this was, "Have it your way. I don't give a damn. Just get your ass out here as soon as you can."

CHAPTER 8

I went back to the room and told Dean to start packin', that we had a job. The next mornin' we went in and picked up our checks. Then we went back to the motel, paid our bill, and packed the car. There wasn't a lot of money left now, but it would get us to the ranch.

By noon we'd reached Gerlach. It hadn't changed a lot in the time I'd been gone. Back then the railroad used to change crews there, and the town got a lot of business from the railroaders. It didn't look like the trains even stopped anymore. I guess the miners from over at Empire were keepin' the town alive now.

We gassed the car and got somethin' to eat before headin' out. We left town, goin' past the hot springs, and then turned off on the road that ran along the edge of the Black Rock. It's shorter and smoother to drive on the ancient lake bed, but it'd rained recently, and it didn't look like that would be a very good idea right then.

It's only sixty miles from town to the ranch, but the road is so rough and winding that it takes a good two to three hours to get there. I's surprised at how much of the country I's able to remember after bein' gone for so long.

As we drove I pointed out different sights to Dean and told him a little about Ben Bird's place and what we'd be doin' that winter. I couldn't remember whether the ranch ran two or three thousand head of mother cows, but I did remember it ran lots of horses. The flats and hills used to be full of mustangs, and we'd had a ball runnin' 'em. Ben had juniper traps scattered all over. Some were big, fancy keyhole affairs, while others were just little round pens with a wing comin' off of 'em.

Back in them days, chicken feed was two cents a pound while a fat two-year-old steer only brought a nickel. Horses used to be a big part of a Black Rock rancher's yearly income.

The Parker camp, where Dean and I were to winter, had been an old homestead back 'fore Ben got it. The place sat right in the middle of his winter range. He still hayed the meadows and kept up the buildin's and corrals.

After we finished helpin' with the fall gatherin', our job would be to move down there and watch the cattle on the winter range. When we found any that were gettin' skinny or weak, we'd bring 'em in and feed 'em till they were stout enough to go back out. Most winters there was some ice to chop and there was a little fence to keep up. Come spring, we'd start gatherin' the cattle into the meadows, brand the calves, and start driftin' everything north toward the summer range in the mountains.

When we pulled into the ranch headquarters, it was as if time had stood still. The old poplar trees and stone buildings were exactly as I remembered 'em. The only change was the addition of a new machine shed that held some fairly modern hay equipment. Before, what little hay we used to put up had been put up loose with teams.

As I stepped outta the car in front of Ben's house, I could hear the steady chugging sound of a diesel power plant, and that, too, would have been a new addition since I was here.

All the buildings, with the exception of the new machine shed, were made of rock and sat in a straight line, with Ben's place bein' first, followed by the cook-shack, bunkhouse, and barn.

This was a real rawhide outfit and nothin' was spent on anythin' that didn't make money. There wasn't any of them white board fences on this place. In fact, there wasn't anything on this place that got any paint.

No one answered when I knocked at the main house, so I started over to the cookhouse. Before I got there, an elderly Indian woman stepped out, wipin' her hands on the front of her dress.

I asked if Ben was around, and she told me that he and the rest of the crew were up in the foothills movin' cattle. Then I asked if Ed or Ted was around. She looked confused at that question and then told me that they were both dead. Ed had been killed in the Second World War and Ted had been killed in a truck wreck. They were buried out back next to their mom and brother. She asked if we were the two new men that Ben had hired. When I told her that we were, she said she'd been told to have us take our gear over and put it in the bunkhouse.

The bunkhouse was a large rock buildin' with a long covered porch that ran across the front of it. When I walked in,

I came into a big room with a potbelly stove in the middle. Down the left side were six eight-by-ten cubicles with a bunk and a dresser in each. They were open on the front so they faced the stove. This didn't do much for privacy, but it did make 'em warmer in the winter. Opposite the front door was another door. It used to go to the trail that led down to the outhouse. Now it opened into a bathroom that had been added on.

Dean and I threw our bedrolls out on the only two open bunks and went outside. We walked around, lookin' at the barns, corrals, and shops. The gates and doors all swung, but for the most part, everything was old and pretty well used.

While we were wanderin' around, a stock truck came rollin' in. It had five horses in the back and three men up front. Old Ben was drivin'. The truck backed up to a dirt loadin' ramp, and the men got out and walked around to the back. When they opened the tailgate, two more men stepped out. That was like Ben not to waste gas on a second vehicle when he could still fit part of the crew in back with the horses.

Except for the fact that his hair was now snow white instead of gray and he didn't move as fast, I couldn't see no difference in Ben. His eyes were sharp and his voice was firm. Like his stone buildin's, he didn't seem to age.

The riders led their horses out of the truck and toward the barn where Dean and I were standin'. As they came up, I thought I saw a trace of a smile on Ben's face when he saw me. It only lasted for a second 'fore it was gone, replaced by his normal scowl.

I shook hands and introduced Dean. Before anything

more could be said, Ben growled, "Where's your saddles?" I told him they were still over in the car. "Well, go get 'em unloaded and in the barn. Tomorrow I don't want to have to wait around here all mornin' while you look for your chaps in the dark."

As we walked off, Dean asked, "Is he always like that?"

"No," I said, "sometimes he wakes up in a grumpy mood."

That night after supper all of us that slept in the bunkhouse sat up swappin' lies and tellin' Wild West stories. By the time I hit the blankets, I'd fairly well sized up the other four men. There were some details that I learned later, but for the most part, I'd formed a rough idea of what I thought of each man.

One kid about Dean's age, called Wade, bragged about bein' AWOL from the army and about how bad he was. When Dean asked him questions about where he'd been stationed and what outfit he was in, the kid stuttered and had a hard time comin' up with answers. I pegged him as a phony and probably a liar.

The youngest member of the crew was an Indian boy from the Owyhee reservation up on the Idaho-Nevada line. His name was Luther. He's out here on probation from the reform school east of Elko. Despite his age, he's still a hell of a hand. His aunt was the cook.

Pete Courtley was the third member of the crew. He was about thirty-five and stood six-foot-two. He probably weighed over two-fifty. From his beer belly and the large veins showin' in his nose and cheeks, I pegged him for a payday alcoholic. He'd worked on every ranch from Eagleville to Winnemucca. He turned out to be a fair hand but nothin' to get real excited about.

The fourth man, Deak Iverstine, was a small man around forty. He'd had a ranch of his own, somewhere between Gerlach and Susanville, but had lost it when his father-in-law turned him in for rustlin'. The father-in-law had ended up with the ranch, and Deak had gone to prison for five years. When he got outta the pen, his wife slapped him with divorce papers. Deak was good, by far the best hand on the crew, and he knew it. He's quiet and, in some ways, sullen. I always had the feelin' he looked on the rest of the world with contempt.

Nearly all buckaroos spend a lot of money and time on their gear, but Deak was a real "Shadow Rider." He carried a seventy-foot rawhide riata, wore silver spurs and ol'-style black Angora chaps, and packed a big six-gun with ivory grips. He musta had six or eight silver-mounted bits with fancy headstalls. He rode a saddle similar to Dean's, only newer. It had a silver horn cap, cantle plate, and conchos. He was pretty to look at and a pleasure to work with, but I had to be careful on sunny days 'cause you could go blind from the light reflectin' off all that horse jewelry.

CHAPTER 9

The next mornin' the cook clanged the ol' school bell out front of the cookshack at a quarter to six to let us know breakfast would be ready in a few minutes. At six she rang it again, and we all staggered in and took our seats. Breakfast on Ben's outfit was, and had always been, the same: fried eggs, biscuits, gravy, some form of beef, and coffee.

After we got done eatin', we went back to the bunkhouse and finished gettin' dressed for work. This time of year that meant gettin' enough warm clothes on to stand the morning chill and still not be so weighted down that you died of a heatstroke later on in the afternoon.

Ben met us at the barn and pointed out the string of horses that Dean and I'd be ridin' till we left for camp. While Dean and I set about shoein' 'em, the rest of the crew loaded up and trucked out to where they'd be gatherin'.

Dean and I each got four head of horses. Each string had three snaffle-bit horses and one broke bridle horse in it. None of my horses were hard to shoe, but we had to gang up and throw two of Dean's to get them shod.

Dean and I worked straight through the day, as Ben didn't believe in eatin' lunch and only furnished two meals a day. We were just finishin' up the last horse when the stock truck pulled in that evenin'.

The next day was a repeat till we got saddled and ready to load the horses in the truck. Dean's horse, a little bay called Piss Ant, was all humped up and walkin' on eggs. Dean tried to loosin' him up by walkin' him in circles, but the horse was on the peck and lookin' for a fight.

Ben came over and said, "Take him to the round corral and run him around a little before you load up."

I knew then that Ben must be mellowin' in his old age. When I's a kid, he damn sure never told me to take any of my cranky horses over and loosen 'em up. In fact, he use to cuss me for not steppin' on 'em and jumpin' 'em out.

We went over to the round pen, and Dean tied his Mecáte reins to the saddle horn. He popped the ol' horse on the tail with a pair of sack hobbles that were hangin' on the fence. That was all it took to tap the cranky S.O.B. off. He fired and went straight up in the air. When he come down, the long tapaderos popped together over his head, and he went to hoggin' it around the corral. Dean kept after him, makin' him move out till he quit buckin'. Before the horse could get his breath, the kid untied his Mecáte and stepped on. Mosta the buck was out of the horse by now, and all he did was make a few halfhearted crow hops before walkin' off.

Dean rode him over to the truck and we finished loadin' up. Ben, Deak, and I rode inside the cab while the other four found places on top and in the back. Ben drove us out to the edge of the foothills where we unloaded.

We had two big canyons to ride that day, so we started up the ridge that separated 'em. It was a steep climb, and we had to stop several times to let the horses rest 'fore we got to the top.

Near the summit there were little patches of snow left over from the last storm, and it was quite a bit colder than it was down in the valley. The wind was blowin' out of the north and it stung my face when I turned into it. It musta been close to eleven before we finally topped out.

The view from the summit was sure somethin'. I'll bet we could see for a hundred miles in any direction. About the only signs of man were a few dirt roads down on the valley floor and an occasional dirt water tank that reflected and sparkled in the sunlight. It was some view.

I've always thought them folks who talk about how desolate Nevada is are the ones who never take time to get off the paved roads. Dean gazed out over the country and turned to me and said, "I know folks back East that would pay a thousand dollars to be sitting up here lookin' at this."

Ol' Ben looked over at him and mumbled, "Them same friends that would give the thousand to be here are the ones that are wantin' to take the land away from us. They ain't happy with their jobs, so they can't stand the thought of us out here makin' a livin' and enjoyin' ours." With that, he turned his big roan and started off down the ridge.

When we got to a place where you could look down both canyons, Ben divided us up. He sent half of us down one and the rest down the other. The upper part of the country was pretty rough and had a lot of junipers. A little farther down it opened up. The grass got better, and there were springs and little groves of quakies all along the sides. There were lots of deer, and it was nothin' to chase thirty or forty head outta one of them quakie patches.

It was cool and the cattle hadn't gathered on water yet, so we had to do a lot of up-and-down ridin'. One good thing about it, though, was that the cattle were all native and had been summerin' in this country since they were born. About all you had to do was get 'em started and they'd trail right on down and out on the flat.

From the looks of the sun, it musta been sometime around three when we hit the flats at the bottom. Deak, Pete, Dean, and me got to the bottom first. We spent about forty-five minutes gatherin' up the cattle that we'd pushed out. By the time we had ours bunched and held up, the leaders from the canyon that Ben and his crew was comin' down started driftin' in with ours.

Once we had 'em all gathered, we started trailin' across the flat to a fenced holdin' field three or four miles away. We probably picked up another fifty head as we were crossin' the flat.

When we got to the fence, Ben counted the cattle through the gate and wrote down the total in his little tally book. There musta been close to 300 head, but I never bothered to ask. Without another word, Ben turned his horse, and we trotted the five or six miles back to the truck.

When we got in, it was close to dark. Pete wrangled the cavvy from the horse pasture while the rest of us unsaddled and put down hay for the horses we'd be ridin' the next day. After we'd caught a change of horses, we drifted on over to the bunkhouse and waited for the cook to ring the dinner bell.

That was the romantic life that we followed for the next week and a half—risin' before sunrise, rubbin' our butts on a saddle all day, and ridin' home after dark.

One evenin' Ben said he wanted me to come over to his house after supper. I'd only been in his place once or twice, and that had been a long time ago when his boys had asked me over. It seemed to me then that Ben considered his house a place where he could escape from the problems of the ranch. The hired help was just not welcomed there.

After we finished eatin' and everyone else had gone back to the bunkhouse, I walked over to Ben's place and knocked on the door. In his roughest voice, he told me to come in.

Ben had sealed off the rest of the house and was only livin' in the front room. He'd made the couch into a bed, and from the dirty dishes at his desk, I assumed that was where he ate. His clothes were stacked in one corner. The walls were covered with photographs of his wife and boys, along with 4-H ribbons and trophies that the kids had won.

He moved some newspapers from a chair and motioned for me to sit down. Then he started in with a little small talk about how we'd made a pretty good gather and were only out seventy-five or eighty head. He said that Deak and him would pick those cattle up later on, after the snow pushed 'em down from the high country.

Then he said he was goin' over to visit his younger sister in Susanville, and that he was gonna leave me in charge. He'd only be gone a couple of days, and while he was away he wanted me to gather the roundup field and cut out the oreana pairs that needed brandin'. He wanted us to get 'em marked and ready to ship.

He said that as soon as he got back, we'd cut out the steer pairs and ship them first. Then we'd cut out the drys that hadn't brought in a calf and ship 'em.

After that, he planned on me and Dean movin' down to the Parker place, where we'd be winterin'. We'd start goin' around the fences, patch any troughs that needed it, and check out the windmills. The rest of the crew would wean the heifer calves and trail the main herd down.

Ben kept his heifers in and fed 'em till spring. Then he picked out the biggest for replacements and sold the rest.

On a lot of outfits in the fall, they preg test and vaccinate the cows, but Ben was from the old school. He didn't vaccinate, dehorn, or preg test. He kept lots of replacement heifers and sold off everything that didn't bring home a calf.

The next mornin' when we were all down at the barn saddlin' up, Ben walked in and said, "I'm goin' into town for a couple of days. Tap, here, is in charge." Then he turned and walked out.

Everyone was lookin' at me.

I haven't had a lot of experience at playin' boss 'cause I usually don't stay long enough for anyone to trust me with that kinda responsibility, so this was sorta new to me. I didn't really know what to expect from the crew.

I cleared my throat and proceeded to tell 'em what we'd be doin' for the next couple days. When no one threatened to quit, I figured I's accepted as leadman.

Everything went pretty well that first mornin'. We gathered the roundup field and bunched the cattle at the southeast corner. Then we started in cuttin' out the ore-ana pairs to brand.

Along toward one, it warmed up and the cattle got lazy. In the mornin' it'd been easy to make pairs. The cows were all lookin' for their calves, and the calves were wantin' to suck. Now the cows wanted to lay down, and the calves had their bellies full and weren't interested in their mamas.

Wade was holdin' rodear on the right side of the herd and was only out twenty or thirty yards from the fence. The sun was warm, the cows were quiet, and I guess he and his horse both sorta dozed off. An old cow with a branded calf decided to take that opportunity to slip on out. Deak was sortin' at the time, and he saw what was happenin'.

He hollered over to wake the kid and to get him to turn the old cow back. Deak's voice startled Wade, and he woke with a sudden jerk. The kid's unexpected, quick movement spooked his horse and it jumped ahead. That threw the boy off balance and he tumbled backwards. As he fell, both legs flew up in the air and his right foot went through the coils of his rope.

The little yeller horse he was ridin' was already buzzed up by all of the jumpin' and jerkin' on his back. When he saw Wade hangin' off to one side, he took off at a dead run, kickin' with his hind feet at the helpless boy.

When the horse came to the fence corner and couldn't run no further, he turned to the left and and took off run-nin' down the fence. As the horse spun out of the corner, Wade was flung out to the side, and his head smacked into one of the railroad-tie corner posts so loud I could hear it clear across the herd.

I jerked my rope down and started shakin' out a loop as the horse came flyin' down the fence line.

Dean was closer to where the horse broke out of the cattle and he tried to cut him off. His idea was to turn the horse back into the herd, but the palomino ducked past him and continued runnin'.

Dean's attempt did manage to slow the horse down, and I closed some of the distance between me and the runaway. I made a long throw, and the rope settled around the horse's throat. By the time I got my slack pulled and took my dalleys, the horse was probably forty-five feet out on my rope. I'd hoped that when he was caught, the horse would stop, but he kept on runnin' in a big circle around me. He was kickin' hard at the boy 'bout every third jump.

Deak came sailin' out of the herd. He rode up alongside of the stampedin' horse and tried to get aholt of the reins, but his horse kept shyin' away from the body that was floppin' off to the side between the two horses. Suddenly, Deak whipped out his pistol and shot the palomino horse in the head.

The yellow pony dropped like he'd been hit with an ax. Even 'fore he finished fallin', Deak had leaped from his own horse and whipped out his big belt knife. He cut the leather thong that held the rope. He did that just in case the horse got back on its feet. It turned out it wasn't necessary; the little palomino was stone dead.

I rode up, jumped off my horse, and looked down at Wade. His eyes were wide open and a little trickle of blood ran out of his nose and ears. I reached down and touched his eyeball. When he didn't blink, I figured he's dead.

By now the rest of the crew was all standin' around watchin'. No one seemed to know what to do. It was Dean who took over. He bent down and listened to the boy's chest, then looked up and said, "He's still alive. Deak, go get the stock truck. Luther, go get a couple of the longest quakie poles you can find out of the fence line. All of you, give me your coats and jackets. Pete, get back over there and hold those cattle we cut out. Don't let 'em get mixed now."

When that was taken care of, he wrapped Wade in our coats, and we waited for the truck to get there. Dean took two of our coats and slid the long, skinny quakie poles in the armholes, makin' a crude stretcher. He had me jerk the saddles off my horse as well as his and Deak's. He laid the saddle blankets down on the bed of the stock truck. When that was done, he had all of us except for Pete slide our hands under Wade and lift him onto the homemade stretcher. He told us that by rights we shouldn't even be movin' the kid, but there was no other choice. When we had Wade on the stretcher, each of us took the end of a pole, and on Dean's command we lifted him as gently as we could into the back of the stock truck and laid him down on the saddle blankets.

Again Dean wrapped him in the coats. He told Luther to take our horses over to where Pete was holdin' the cut and to help him trail the horses and the oreana pairs back to the ranch. He had me climb in the back of the truck with him and told Deak to head for the ranch, sayin' that when we got there, we'd grab some more blankets. Deak tried to drive as fast as he could and still miss as many bumps as possible, but it was a slow, rough ride to the ranch.

At the ranch I ran and gassed up one of the company pickups while Dean and Deak grabbed a mattress off one of the beds. We moved Wade as gently as we could from one truck to the other and then wrapped him in a dozen blankets. The trip from the ranch into Gerlach went a lot faster than the one from the roundup field to the head-quarters, but it still took better than two-and-a-half hours. When we got there, I ran into Bruneau's Bar and told someone to call the hospital in Reno.

Quite a crowd had gathered around the truck, and everyone was givin' advice and makin' suggestions. In a few minutes a lady came outta the bar and said that an ambulance was on the way and that we were to take off and meet 'em on the road.

This time Dean took the wheel, and Deak and I stayed in the back with Wade. He shot outta Gerlach and was on the road past the Empire mine in less than five minutes. It was evenin' and starting to get cold now. Somewhere just north of Pyramid Lake we spotted the flashin' lights of the ambulance comin' toward us. We pulled off to the side, and I jumped out and started wavin' my arms. The ambulance came to a screeching stop, and in no time they had Wade transferred from one vehicle to the other. They wanted one of us to ride with 'em to fill out all of the necessary papers as they drove to the hospital. Dean and I didn't know anything about Wade 'cept for his name, so Deak was elected.

CHAPTER *10*

As Dean and I drove back toward Gerlach, we passed the place where I embarked upon my short career in crime. I debated on whether or not to tell Dean about it and, in the end, decided not to, but that didn't stop me from rememberin' it.

It was back in the early part of the fifties, and I was workin' for a horse trader named "Fat" Ron Griffen. There were quite a few horse traders then, and each had his own method of operatin'. Ron had a truck with an eighteen-foot rack on it, and he traveled around the country, goin' from ranch to ranch and auction to auction. He'd trade one broke horse for two unbroke ones, or he'd buy your horse for cash. Ron made it a point to always try to get a little money to boot on all of his trades. He'd take all of the ol' chicken-feed horses to the nearest auction and drop 'em off. The old wore-out ranch horses were taken to ridin' stables and to towns where they made good kids' pets. The horses that would buck consistently were sold to rodeo stock contractors.

As horse traders go, I guess Ron was fairly honest. He tried never to give a person a horse that he thought would hurt 'em, and he never drugged any of his horses. But that's where his honesty ended. He'd sure skin you any other way that he thought he could.

My job was to help with the drivin', take care of the stock, and try out all of the horses that we traded for. We'd come into Gerlach that day by way of Cedarville. Ron's last stop had been at a sheep outfit where he'd traded a couple of old, gentle ranch horses for three head of colts and a border collie bitch.

Ron didn't usually deal in dogs, but he couldn't squeeze no money outta the sheep man, so he took the dog in hopes he could sell it down around Fallon. The sheep man said that the dog was well broke but that she was in heat and that his herder couldn't get his other male dogs to work, with her shakin' her tail in their faces.

As we were chuggin' along down the road a few miles north of the reservation line, Fat Ron spotted nine head of ewes out in the brush. He pulled the truck over and said, "Let's see if this damn dog'll work." Ron opened his door and waddled out. (He wasn't called "Fat" Ron for nothin'.) He grabbed the little female and hoisted her up to where she could look over the sagebrush and see the sheep. Then he set her down and said to the dog, "Get around!"

The little pup shot off like a rocket, and in no time she had the sheep bunched and was herdin' 'em back to the truck.

Ron told me to get my rope and see if I could snag one of the woollies. Well, with that little pooch bunchin' the range maggots right there next to the truck, it weren't no trick at all to rope 'em, and in no time we had all nine caught and loaded in the back with the horses.

We drove on into Fallon and went directly to the auction yard where we unloaded the sheep and one old crippled horse that Ron hadn't been able to find a home for. The next day was sale day, and Ron wanted to go out to the auction to see if any horses were gonna be run through.

When we got there, I ran into a couple of ol' friends, and Ron and I got separated. I was sittin' in the coffee shop, swappin' lies with these fellers, when one of the men who worked out back came in and wanted to know if I knew anything about the sheep that Ron had brought in. He said the brand inspector would like to have a little talk with us.

I's already feelin' pretty guilty about my part in rustlin' them stinkin' things, and now I's sure that we'd been caught. I tried to find Ron to warn him, but he'd gone out to Swingle Bench to see a man named Bray about tradin' off the three colts we'd got from the sheep man. I knew I couldn't hang out there at the sale yard till Ron got back without runnin' into the brand inspector, so I walked out to the main road and hitched a ride back to the hotel.

The more I thought about it, the scareder I got. As I sat there in the room, I became convinced I was gonna end up in the pen. That thought in my mind, I gathered up my saddle and bedroll. I went down and bummed a ride as far as Ely with a miner who wanted some company. My plan was to hitchhike to Utah and stay with relatives till the heat wore off. I's surprised to see they didn't have roadblocks set up on the edge of town. Maybe that would come later.

I was standin' there on the corner when this feller in a pickup pulls up and says, "You lookin' for a ride or work?" I said it depended on what the job was and where it was. He told me he had a place over on the back side of the Shell Creek Range and was lookin' for someone to help with the fall gatherin' and brandin'. I didn't know where the Shell Creek Range was, but the feller said his place was pretty far out and that sounded good to me.

The man's name was George Stanton, and he and his wife were the only ones on the place now. They boarded the kids out in Ely so they could go to high school. It was a little outfit and only ran five or six hundred cows.

I told him a phony name and made up a social security number. After a couple of weeks, everything was goin' great. George and I got along fine. He was a hard worker and was damn sure a cowman. When it turned off cold, he and his wife had me move into one of their kids' rooms.

Then one day right after lunch, George walked up to me and handed me my check. He told me to go get my stuff packed and my bed rolled. He said, "Mister, I don't know who you are, but I do know who you aren't."

He'd gotten a letter from the social security office tellin' him that there was no such person with a number that come anywhere near the one that I'd given him. He told me he didn't know what kind of trouble I's in and didn't want to know, but he couldn't take chances, livin' that far out. Then he said the thing that hurt me the most. He said, "If you lied to me about your name, I don't know if I can trust you not to lie to me again." With that, he turned and walked off.

I got my stuff gathered up, and George hauled me into

town. He never said a word all the way in. I think he really liked me, and I know it hurt him to find out that I'd lied. Well, I made up my mind that I was gonna go back and face the music, no matter what it was.

I bought a bus ticket back to Fallon. I rented a room and started makin' phone calls. It wasn't long till I found out who ran sheep north of the Pyramid Reservation line.

The next day I found a high school kid who was skippin' school, and I told him I'd buy the gas and give him ten dollars to haul me out to the headquarters of the sheep outfit. When I got there, I went up to the house and told the owner who I was. Then I confessed my part in the rustlin' venture. I told him I was willin' to pay for the sheep or go to jail.

He looked at me for a minute and then started to laugh. He said they lost sheep all the time when they were trailin' em. He said most of the time if they didn't find 'em in a couple of days, the coyotes killed 'em. Then he added, "If it'll make you feel any better, I'll take two dollars a head, but I'd rather have you go to work for me. I'm gonna need another herder in a couple of weeks when we divide up the winter bands."

I was feelin' pretty guilty, but not that guilty. I gave him $20 instead. That night I slept better than I had for a long time.

CHAPTER *11*

I t was between nine and nine-thirty by the time Dean and I got back to Gerlach. We hadn't eaten since breakfast that mornin' and both of us were pretty hungry. Also, we still needed to find a phone to see if we could get aholt of Ben.

The only place in Gerlach that was open was Bruneau's. The same lady who had called the ambulance was tendin' bar when we walked in. After we told her that we hadn't eaten all day, she went back in the kitchen and came out a few minutes later with a couple of plates of steak and eggs. I was ready to wash mine down with a case of beer, but Dean asked if we could have some coffee.

The way I felt, I coulda gone on a good runnin' drunk that woulda lasted for days. The only thing that kept me from it was Dean. He kept remindin' me we had to talk to Ben that night. He also said it wouldn't be right to leave the old man two more men short.

After supper, we asked the lady bartender if she knew where Ben stayed in Susanville. She told us that he stayed with his sister and gave us her name. With that information it wasn't hard to get the number from the operator. I'll tell you right here, I sure wasn't lookin' forward to makin' that call to Ben. To be honest, I was wishin' I'd rode in the ambulance with Wade. I had a pretty good idea what Ben was gonna be like.

When the voice of an elderly lady answered the phone, I thought about tellin' her what'd happened and lettin' her pass the information on to Ben. In a moment of weakness, though, I decided I'd best tell him myself. Ben came on the phone with a gruff, "What do you want!?" I told him that Wade had been hurt and that we'd taken him to meet the ambulance on the way to Reno.

Then Ben said, "Well, what do you want me to do about it?"

I said I thought maybe someone oughta make arrangements to get Deak home. When I said that, Ben sorta settled down and wanted to know the whole story. He never said a word till I's finished. Then he did just what I figured he'd do. He went into a rage. "Damn that crazy, trigger-happy Jew! What the hell's the matter with him, anyway!? If he wanted to kill somethin', why didn't he go join Moshe Dayan and shoot rag heads?"

I tried to explain again how it had happened, but Ben wasn't hearin' nothin' except one of his horses had been killed. He wasn't interested in Wade's condition or even how we were gonna get Deak back from Reno. All that seemed to bother him was the fact that he'd lost a good horse.

Somewheres along the line, I did manage to scrape up the courage to say somethin' like, "You could at least check to see if Wade's alive. Maybe he needs somethin' from the ranch."

Ben's answer to that was, "All that little draft-dodgin' bastard probably wants is sympathy, and if he does, I can tell him right where to find it. All he has to do is look in the dictionary somewheres between *shit* and *syphilis*." And with that he slammed down the phone. Well, that was Ben. Emotions like pity, kindness, mercy, and sympathy didn't register with him. They were just words. He didn't expect any of the feelin's that them words implied to be shown toward him, and he didn't give 'em out either.

The Black Rock Desert was dry and hard when we crossed it comin' in from the ranch, so we decided to save a little time by takin' the shortcut across the big alkali bed. We turned right, just below the hot springs on the edge of town, and started out.

When we hit the desert, it was darker than the inside of a black cow, and it was hard to keep your bearings. There were no landmarks, and the desert floor was covered with car tracks goin' in every direction.

By midnight, though, the moon was up and it was so bright I coulda read a newspaper without any extra light. It was easy to see the hills along the edge then. We aimed directly for Douglas Peak. That's where the dry lake road meets the one that runs along the foothills.

It was close to two when we pulled up in front of the bunkhouse. The night was clear and cold, and I could only see a few of the brightest stars 'cause of the moon puttin' out so much light.

When we got inside the bunkhouse, it wasn't much warmer than it was outside. I can't speak for Dean, but I didn't waste a lot of time 'fore sneakin' down between my blankets. It's true I's tired, but the main reason I's in such a hurry was that it was the only warm place I could find.

It didn't seem like I no more than got warm when I heard the cook ringin' the big bell for breakfast. The four of us—Pete, Luther, Dean, and me—stumbled over to the cookhouse and took our seats. Six or eight cups of coffee later, I was finally able to think halfway clear again. I figured I's still in charge, so I told everyone we'd go back and finish the sortin' we'd started the day before.

No one seemed to object, so we went down to the barn and saddled our horses for the day. We loaded 'em in the back of the stock truck, and we all crowded into the front. Dean drove us out to the north end of the roundup field.

The cattle hadn't scattered too badly, so it wasn't much of a chore to gather the field again, even though we were two men short. Because it was still early in the day, we didn't have no trouble in makin' pairs out of the ones that had been so hard to get together the afternoon before. By noon, we were headin' home with the unbranded oreana pairs.

Pete went back an' got the truck while Dean, Luther, and I trailed the cattle. It only took us a couple of hours to get the cattle home, so there was still plenty of time 'fore supper. Pete had gotten there ahead of us and had wrangled the horses. Everyone changed mounts and turned out the ones we'd been ridin'. When Luther and Dean had fed them, we were through for the day.

It was too late to start any new projects, and 'sides, my tail was draggin' from bein' up for most of the night. I don't know what anyone else did, but I went over and passed out on my bed. I didn't hear the dinner bell, and no one woke me, so I slept right through supper. The next thing I heard was the bell callin' us to breakfast.

After we'd finished eatin', we went down and got our horses saddled and gathered up all of the brandin' equipment. On Ben's outfit, that didn't amount to a whole lot. We got three or four branding irons, a syringe, and a couple bottles of blackleg vaccine. Luther got a little diesel to start the fire. When that was done, we were ready to get the cattle in.

There was only 103 head to do, and most of 'em were pretty big. Because of their size, I decided we'd best head and heel all of 'em. Dean couldn't rope, and I figured I'd better work the ground to make sure that everything got done the way I wanted it. That left Pete and Luther to do all of the ropin', which didn't seem to hurt their feelin's.

Everything moved along slowly but smoothly after we figured out a system. Luther was a damn good roper, and Pete didn't have to be ashamed of what he could do either. Dean didn't have any idea in the world what was goin' on. In the end, all I had him do was give the blackleg shot and tail the calves down when they were only caught by one hind foot. That left me free to take the rope off the head and put it on the front feet. I also had to do the ear-markin', brandin', and casteratin'. With a good full crew, I've knocked out better than ninety calves in an hour and a half, but we were still goin' at it at three-thirty when Ben pulled up to the corral with Deak and a big Indian.

I don't know how the others felt about the new arrivals, but I's sure glad to see 'em. I'd been worn out for the last hour, and we still had fifteen or twenty calves to go. Ben took over the brandin', Deak started cuttin' the bulls, and the new man went to helpin' Dean knock the calves down. Then he'd take the rope off the head and put it on the front feet. All I had to do then was the earmarkin'. Luther and Pete kept on ropin'.

It seemed like no time at all 'fore we were done and Ben had Luther out wranglin' the horses for the next day. He had Dean and me help Pete trail the freshly branded pairs down to a field below the house, where we could keep an eye on 'em for the next day or so.

While we were catchin' our horses, Ben pointed out the ones that the new man was to have in his string. I could tell from the little bit Ben talked to the Indian that they knew each other. We found out later Ben had cut this new man a string of broncs that woulda made me miss breakfast if I thought I was gonna have to ride any of 'em. Some mornin's, just gettin' a saddle on took him the better part of an hour. Dean and I decided that watchin' him ride out in the mornin' was one thing we were gonna miss when we moved down to the Parker.

I guess right here is as good a place as any to tell about this new feller. As I said, he was a Shoshone Indian and a damn big one at that. He was clean shaven and looked to be somewhere in his late twenties or early thirties. He didn't have a scar on his face, but he was missin' two teeth on the left side of his mouth. Over six-foot-three-inches tall, he musta weighed around 225 pounds. He moved with the smoothness and grace of a cat. From the way he handled the big calves, I could tell he wasn't packin' much tallow.

When it came to workin', he could ride rougher horses than I ever thought about gettin' on, even when I was younger. He came closer than any of us to bein' as good a roper as Deak. A good cowman, he knew how to handle livestock. He was as strong as a bear and never got tired. All in all, he was just one hell of a hand, but he sure wasn't any pleasure to be around. Somethin' about how he looked at us and acted was kinda scary.

I could tell that Deak knew he was a better hand than the rest of us, but Hooper (that's what Ben called the Indian, Hooper John) seemed to look down on the whole world with disgust. If he smiled, it was a sneer; if he laughed, it was when someone messed up or got hurt.

I was raised around Indians and worked with 'em most of my life. A lot of the time they're quiet and keep to themselves till they get to know you. Hooper wasn't just quiet, he was sullen. He'd speak English as little as possible, and I never heard him say anything that wasn't sarcastic.

He'd talk to Luther and the cook, Luther's aunt, more often than he did the rest of us, but then it would be in Shoshone. Northern Paiute, Goshoute, Banock, Shoshone, and Comanche languages are fairly close. Most of 'em can understand each other if they have to. My Banock grandmother had made it a point to try to teach me to speak Banock when I's a kid, so I was able to catch a little of what Hooper said to Luther. Generally, it was directions or orders on how to do different things. A lot of the time, though, it was comments on what a bunch of dumb asses us *endosa wa* (white male sex organs) were.

Later on, Ben told me that Hooper was from up around McDermitt, and that he'd worked for Ben off and on since he was fifteen. Ben had bailed him outta jail several times when Hooper'd been locked up for assault.

He said Hooper tended to be a little headstrong and short-tempered at times, but if you handled him right, he was a good man.

A few days later, Luther told Dean his aunt had said that the first time Hooper came to work, he got into a fight with a Paiute cowboy from the Summit Lake Reservation. When Ben stepped in to break up the fight, Hooper came after him. Ben pushed him aside and picked up a switch made out of a broken pick handle. When Hooper charged in the second time, Ben smacked him up alongside the head and knocked out two teeth. Another time Hooper got mad about somethin' and pulled a knife. Ben broke Hooper's arm with a single tree that time. One day when we were ridin' together, Pete sorta summed up what I felt Hooper was like when he said, "Y'know, that Hooper's the kinda Injun that woulda built a fire on your chest if he caught ya a hundred years ago."

After supper that evenin', Pete and Dean started in askin' Deak about Wade and about his stay in town. Deak told us that Wade was still in the intensive care ward. He said Wade had a serious skull fracture and a lot of bad bruises, but the doctors figured he'd live.

About that time, Deak started laughin'. He said he'd gotten a room and left word at the hospital, tellin' 'em where he was stayin'. He bummed some money from one of Wade's doctors to eat on but not enough to go any-place. All he could do was lie around watchin' them soap operas on television.

Sure 'nough, he got word that Ben was comin' down to pick him up. When Ben arrived, he paid the hotel bill and left money at the hospital to pay the doctor back for what he'd lent to Deak.

When they got in the truck, Ben told Deak he wasn't gonna charge him for the horse that Deak had killed and he wasn't gonna dock him for the time he'd spent in town. But he sure as hell wasn't payin' for his room and meals while he was out cattin' around Reno. Ben said he was takin' the money for that outta Deak's next paycheck.

Then Deak laughed again and said, "You know, that ol' bastard is tighter than a duck's ass, and that, fellers, is waterproof."

CHAPTER *12*

ith Ben back, the work went a lot smoother and faster. He'd done this so many times that he made plans and decisions almost by habit rather than thought.

The next five days were spent cuttin' out the steer pairs and shippin' their calves. The sixth day, the last that Dean and I would spend workin' with the crew, was used up cuttin' out the drys.

There were a hundred little jobs that had to be taken care of 'fore Dean and I could leave for the Parker place. We had to pull the shoes on the horses we'd been ridin' and get the camp horses in. Harness for the feed team needed to be oiled and patched. We had to get groceries gathered. The truck that we were to use at camp had to be greased and have the oil changed.

Then there were the thousands of little items that had to be rounded up, packed, and loaded in the truck. We had to get the fence tools, lanterns, extra parts, oil for the windmills, and barrels of gas for the pickup. And lastly, we had our own personal stuff to get ready. It had takin' us an extra day to finish gettin' everything together. That made Ben so nervous that he almost fell apart.

While we were pullin' the shoes, Dean asked me why we were changin' horses. I told him that ever since Ben lost a lawsuit, he'd made a special point of sendin' only foolproof horses to camp. All the horses we'd been ridin' were young, and a couple of Dean's were still a little humpy. None of 'em were what I'd call bad, but they sure weren't kid ponies.

Dean wanted to know what kinda lawsuit would make a man have his men change horses. So I told him the story as I'd heard it years ago.

It seems that back in the days 'fore they had Workman's Compensation and Labor Relations Boards, Ben had a man stayin' out in camp. The man had a string of Ben's regular horses to ride, which meant they were probably only green broke. Back in those days, anytime a horse got gentle, Ben sold it.

One day this man was out ridin' and he got bucked off. He broke his leg, and his horse got away. It took him a couple of days, but he managed to crawl and drag himself to one of the neighbors's cow camps. There was plenty of food and wood, so he decided to hole up there till help showed up.

When Ben went down to the man's camp a few days later and found the horse standin' out front with the saddle on, he guessed what'd happened. He got the rest of the crew out and even hired one of the first planes they had in the country to come and look for the missin' man. There were no fences in those days, and no one had any idea where the man had been ridin'. After a week of searchin', they gave him up for dead.

Two months went by 'fore someone found the missin' cowboy. He'd put a splint on his leg and was able to hobble around. When they hauled him back to the ranch, Ben agreed to pay the man for the time he'd been laid up in the other ranch's cow camp. But then Ben told him he's gonna deduct the cost of the search plane and the groceries that the man had eaten. In the end, Ben wanted the man to work another six months for nothin'.

The cowboy went into town and hired himself a big high-powered attorney, and they had a trial. Ben ended up losin' the case. He had to pay the court costs, the man's wages for the time he was laid up, plus give him some extra money for endangerin' the cowboy's life by leavin' him out there with those half-broke broncs. Ever since then, Ben had made it policy never to put men in camp with a string of green horses.

The last night before Dean and I were to leave for the Parker place, everyone was layin' around the bunkhouse. Dean, Luther, and Pete were sittin' over by the stove. Dean was writin' a letter, Luther was lookin' at a western catalog, and Pete was starin' at the wall, probably dreamin' about some long-gone bottle. Hooper and I were in our little cubicles lyin' on our beds. I was readin', and I think Hooper was gettin' ready to go to sleep.

Deak's bed space was the one to the left of mine, and Hooper slept to the left of him. Deak was sittin' out front of his cubical, greasin' his riata. Everything seemed peaceful enough till Deak got up and started lookin' around. The first sign of trouble come when I heard Hooper say, "What the hell you lookin' at?"

Deak answered, "I'm just tryin' to find a piece of scrap leather to make a new burner for the honda in this rope." Deak musta found what he's lookin' for, 'cause he came back and sat down again.

I never heard Hooper get outta bed, and from where I's layin', I couldn't see him. The next time I heard his voice, though, I looked out and saw his shadow on the far wall. I could tell he'd gotten up and was standin' in front of Deak.

"I don't want you over there starin' at me when I'm tryin' to sleep. Understand?"

Deak's voice sounded quiet and calm when he said, "Back off, son. I'm not out here to play any of your silly kid games."

That musta been the wrong thing to say 'cause the next thing I heard from Hooper was, "Kid games!? I'll show you a kid's game." There was the sound of movement and Hooper's voice again. "Man, I'm gonna cut you long, deep, wide, and con-tin-u-ous-ly." When he said the word *continuously,* he pronounced it slowly, separatin' it at every syllable so that it sounded more like five separate words.

I still couldn't see Hooper, but his shadow on the far wall looked as big as King Kong. And the outline of the knife he had in his hand was as big as one of them Japanese swords.

I's pretty sure that if I couldn't see him, Hooper probably

couldn't see me. So quietly as I could, I eased around and slid my old hog leg out from under my pillow. I had no idea what I was gonna do next, so I just laid there, holdin' the big pistol and waitin'.

Slowly Deak leaned over and put his rope down on his bed. When he straightened up, the pearl-handled six-gun was in his hand. The hammer was back, and it was fully cocked.

He looked Hooper square in the eye and said, "Son, if you so much as move one inch in my direction, I'm gonna blow a hole in your chest so big, they'll be able to drive a truck through it." He paused a moment, then added, "Now, you can back up and cool off or come ahead and die. The choice is yours."

It seemed as if time had stopped. I looked over at Dean and Luther. They were both frozen solid, starin' at the two men. Pete had picked up a copy of the *Livestock Journal*. He acted like he was so absorbed in the cattle market reports and grain features that he didn't know anythin' was goin' on.

I looked back at Deak. He hadn't moved or blinked.

The silence was broken when Hooper said, "You gotta put that gun down someday. When you do, I'm gonna circumcise you a second time."

As Hooper backed toward his bed, I heard Deak say, "You do whatever you think you got to do, boy, but when you do it, you best do it right. Remember, you've got to sleep sometime, and when you do, I promise you'll never wake up."

I guess I don't need to tell you that I didn't get much rest that night. Everytime I heard a mouse run across the floor, I's wide awake. I's sure that come mornin' we were gonna find Deak dead in his bed or hear that cannon of his go off and find Hooper dead. I've often wondered if that big Indian ever realized how close he came to dyin' that night. I was afraid of Hooper, and even if he didn't show it, I'm sure Deak was, too. Frightened men are dangerous.

Come mornin', neither Deak nor Hooper acted like anything had happened the night before. They didn't actually ignore each other. They just acted normal, which was almost the same thing.

CHAPTER *13*

That night it snowed about two inches, but the mornin' broke clear and cold. The path to the cookhouse didn't have a track on it when we trudged over for breakfast. Ben wouldn't allow a thermometer on the ranch, so it was hard to tell just how cold it was. Ben claimed thermometers only made you feel colder. Still, it was so cold that the snow squeaked as we walked across it and our breaths made big misty clouds in the mornin' air.

After breakfast I took off for the Parker with the truck and our gear. The old pickup had a set of stock racks on the back, and they were loaded from the floor to the top rail.

Luther helped Dean with the horses. Once they were away from the headquarters and lined out, Luther went back. All Dean had to do then was keep 'em followin' my tracks for the next twenty-five miles. There were ten saddle horses, countin' the one Dean was ridin', plus the work team. All of 'em had been down the road to the camp many times, so they trailed right along.

Even with the fresh snow on the road, I's still able to get

to the Parker place two or three hours ahead of Dean. No one had stayed in the camp since the hay crew had left that summer. Pack rats musta moved in right after the hay hands pulled out. They'd built nests in the woodstove and in the flour bin. I opened all the doors and windows and started tryin' to make the place livable. By the time Dean got there with the horses, I had the house swept out and most of our personal gear inside.

The little house had never been real fancy, but it was easy to keep warm. It was made outta used railroad ties laid one on top of the another. Then they'd been covered with chicken wire and plastered. There were only three rooms: a kitchen, a living room that we used as a bedroom, and a smaller room off to the side that we used for a pantry and storage room. There's a wood cookstove in the kitchen and a wood heater where we slept. The only furniture in the place were two beds, a kitchen table, and four chairs. An outside door opened into the kitchen, and another one opened into our bedroom.

Someone had put up a net wire fence around the yard, but over the years cattle and horses had rubbed it down. I imagine there'd been a yard, too, but now sagebrush was growin' right up to the edge of the building itself. There were no trees, unless you count the big willow bush that grew out beside the well.

Out back and to the left of the kitchen door, about a hundred feet away, was the outhouse. To the right, about the same distance, was the corral where we kept the work team and the horses we'd be ridin' the next day. Straight out from the door was a well with a hand pump. It was set up so you could pump water into a pipe that carried it to the corral, or you could fill a bucket to carry to the house. To the west side of the house was a ten-by-ten shed that was stacked from the ground to the ceilin' with firewood. Out front of it was a choppin' block and a sawbuck.

The corral was made outta juniper posts set in the ground on end like a stockade. To the back was a three-sided shed that ran the full length of the corral. The roof was gone in places but it gave the horses some protection from the wind. A feed rack in the middle of the corral held enough hay for three or four days, and to the right of that was a large pole gate that opened into a round corral. The round corral was about forty feet across and was made of willows. It was probably close to eight feet high, and the walls were way over a foot thick. In the middle was a big, stout, juniper snubbin' post that wore the marks of a lot of use.

Back of the corral were two forty-acre hay fields. We'd be usin' one to hold the horses and the other to hold the weaker cattle that we'd be bringin' in to feed. In the fence line that divided the two fields was a large stack yard where the hay that'd been baled that summer was stored. The fence around the stack yard was made of six strands of barbed wire with juniper posts set every eight feet. Between the posts were willow stays standin' on end. They'd been placed so that they were about six to eight inches apart. There were two big wire gates at each end of the stack yard so that you could drive the team in one end and out the other and go into either of the hay fields. The gates were made almost as stoutly as the outside fence.

The Parker place was like the rest of Ben's holdings. There was nothin' fancy about it, but everything worked.

The wire in the fences was old and rusty but tight. The corral posts were all different sizes, and some weren't too straight, but none of 'em were rotten. Some of the wooden gates sagged a little, but they all swung. The house was small and smelled of pack rat urine, but it was warm and the roof didn't leak. The well sat 'tween the outhouse and the horse corral and probably woulda been condemned by a health inspector, but no one ever got sick from drinkin' the water. All in all, it was a pretty fair place to spend a winter.

When Dean got there, we turned all the horses but one into the east hay field, as it was closest to the round corral. We kept the one horse in the corral to wrangle on. Then we set about finishin' unpackin' the truck.

There was an ol' shed out front of the house that had probably been used as a garage back in the days of the Model T. Someone had built some saddle racks in it and put some pegs on the walls to hold harness, so we stored that part of the gear along with all the fence tools and spare parts for the windmills in there. On the side of the shed was a place where some dirt had been piled up to make it possible to load horses into a truck. The gas and the barrel pump were put over by it.

When all of that was done, we went to the house and started sortin' out the groceries and puttin' 'em on shelves. There was a propane Servel refrigerator in the room that we used as a pantry, but it was so cold in there that we didn't even bother to light the refrigerator. We just kept the door on that room shut, and it worked as well as a walk-in cooler.

By now it was gettin' on towards four, and there wasn't much daylight left. We laid in a supply of firewood, pumped up the Coleman lamps, rolled out our beds, and got ready to fix supper.

After we'd eaten, Dean washed the dishes while I went down and hauled up a load of hay for the wrangle horse. By the time I got back, it was dark. The stars were out and the air was cold and crisp. Dean had a fire goin' and the lamps lit. As I walked up from the corral, the little cabin sure looked cozy, with the soft glow of the lamps shinin' through the dirty windows.

Dean was sittin' at the kitchen table, writin' another letter, when I came in. I sat down and started readin' a mystery novel I'd found in the outhouse. It was so warm and peaceful sittin' there that I's only able to read for a half hour or so 'fore I started dozin' off. I went in and unrolled my bed, shed my clothes, and crawled in. I think I's asleep 'fore I finished stretchin' out.

Dean and I spent the next two days patchin' fence, cleanin' springs, and servicin' windmills. Four units were in the winter range allotment. We were only able to get around the fences and check out the water in the first unit 'fore the cattle were to get there. We would have to work on the other three units later on.

The plan was for Ben and his people to bring the first bunch of cows to us as soon as they quit bawlin' for their calves. It wouldn't have done no good to move 'em earlier 'cause they'd just gone back. Later the crew would wean the heifer calves. As soon as those cows had settled down, the men would trail 'em down to us, too.

The mornin' of the third day, Dean and I saddled up a

couple of our new horses and trotted back toward the ranch headquarters. About twelve miles from the winter range, we ran into the lead cattle. There would be a little over 900 head in this first herd, and they were strung out for two or three miles. There was only Ben and three men drivin' 'em, but the cattle knew where they were goin' and were lined out single file, movin' right along. As soon as we got there, Ben sent Deak back to the ranch to get the stock truck to haul their horses home when we were done.

By goin' cross-country we were able to save some time, but we still ended up movin' the cattle over eighteen miles. That's a pretty long push for one day, no matter how you look at it. By the time we reached the gate and Ben had counted the last animal through, it was almost dark.

Deak still wasn't back with the truck, so after cussin' and fumin' for a few minutes, Ben and the other two men started back to headquarters. Dean and I only had seven miles to go to our camp, so we struck an easy trot and were there in an hour and a half.

From the followin' day through the rest of the winter, our routine was pretty much the same. We'd get up, fix breakfast, harness the team, and feed the weaker cows. Then we'd turn out the team and saddle our ridin' horses. We'd load 'em in the pickup and make a circle of the water holes, choppin' ice and checkin' windmills.

If we found any cattle at the water holes that looked like they needed a little help, one of us'd unload his horse and start back with 'em. If we didn't find any poor cows on water, we'd check the country along the foothills.

At first we didn't have many skinny cattle to feed. That

gave us time to go around the fences and finish repairin' the windmills in the other three units. As winter wore on, though, and we brought in more cattle, the feedin' took up a little more of our time.

That was our normal routine, but that doesn't mean that every day went that way. There were two little items that Ben threw in that I haven't mentioned yet. Their names were Bill and Bob. They were a matched pair of big Belgian workhorses that made up the team we were to use for feeding.

Bill was a good-lookin', nervous gelding that would spook and run at the drop of a hat. Bob was a matchin' mare that was as quiet and docile as Bill was high-strung. Her hang-up was that she'd kick the hell outta anything that got near her hind end. That little trait made hookin' the tugs to the single tree an interesting challenge every mornin'.

The first day we went to hook 'em up, we didn't know about these little quirks. I took Bill 'cause he acted the most excitable, and Dean had ol' quiet Bob. We had the harness on, the lines snapped into their bridles, and the pole straps fastened into the neck yoke. I told Dean to go ahead and hook up his tugs first and then I'd get mine. As soon as he reached down to hook the inside trace chain to the single tree, that rotten old bay bitch let fly with both hind feet. She caught Dean along the right side and knocked him over the double tree. The noise spooked Bill, who jerked away from me, and the two of 'em took off. We had to go get a saddle horse and run 'em down. By the time I caught up, they were three or four miles away, headed for the home ranch.

Another mornin' we were down in the stack yard, loadin'

up. Dean was up on the stack, throwin' the bales down to me, and I was stackin' 'em on the wagon. For some unknown reason, Bill spooked and bolted. The sudden lurch knocked me off. Dean saw the team start, and he dove from the top of the stack and landed on the loaded wagon.

In three jumps the big lumberin' giants were goin' wide open. They shot through the wire gate at the end of the hay corral and tore it from the posts. The center of the gate caught on the point of the tongue, and the wire wrapped around the sides of the horses, addin' to their excitement.

Dean was layin' spread-eagle across the top of the stack with his fingers diggin' into the bales like a terrified tomcat. I think he'd intended to grab the lines that were tied to the front of the wagon and bring the horses to a stop, but it was all he could do to hang on as the team and wagon went flyin' around the field, bouncin' over the frozen cow pies.

The pair made a circle of the meadow and then saw our saddle horses in the other pasture. They ran through the fence that divided the two fields and started toward the saddle stock. When the cavvy saw the terrified giants comin' across the field at 'em and heard Dean screamin' "Whoa! Whoa!" over and over at the top of his lungs, they took off, too, with the team in hot pursuit.

Little by little, bale by bale, the load started to shake apart. Soon the whole mess was scattered across the field. Dean's perch was some of the last to get dumped. The saddle horses finally ran into the round corral to get away, and the team stopped just outside the big gate.

Those two horses caused a dozen other wrecks that winter, but those were the worst.

CHAPTER *14*

You'd have thought that livin' out like Dean and I were, we wouldn't have many visitors, but that wasn't the case. Rock hounds, arrowhead hunters, weekend miners, sightseers, and people who'd gotten lost were often showin' up at our place. Then once every week, Ben or Deak came down with a load of groceries and a barrel of gas.

Probably the most unusual character who'd stop in and visit was Basco Charlie. He's an old codger who'd been born there on the edge of the Black Rock. His mother was a Paiute from Summit Lake, and his dad had been a sheepherder and a coyote trapper. Both were long dead. Charlie'd never been to school a day in his life and had never been more than hundred miles from the place where he's born. His main camp was an abandoned miner's shack ten or fifteen miles from where Dean and I were stayin'.

When he was younger, Charlie used to work as a buckaroo, a mustanger, and a sheepherder. Durin' Prohibition, he ran a little still up in the hills. Now he's old, broke, and ugly. In the winter, he made his livin' trappin'. In the summer, he guided tourists and rock hunters. He also sold arrowheads that he made. Charlie passed them arrowheads off as genuine Indian artifacts.

As he traveled around the desert, Charlie was always lookin' for lost gold mines, buried treasure, and a stash of old Indian guns. He knew and gathered every edible plant that grew in that part of the country. For meat he ate mustangs, jackrabbit, snakes, and an occasional deer.

Charlie had an ol' blind horse that he packed and a black gelding that he rode. They were both mustangs he'd caught and broke himself. At night he never hobbled 'em, just turned 'em loose to graze. In the mornin' if they weren't around, he'd holler a couple of times, and they'd come trottin' in.

Ben had made sure that we understood Charlie was to be fed and his horses taken care of anytime he came by. Ben told us not to let Charlie know that it was his idea to furnish the grub. He said Charlie more than earned a few meals by keepin' the coyotes thinned down. But Ben didn't want Charlie gettin' the idea that he's an easy mark.

I don't know if you could call Charlie a hermit or not. It's true he lived alone, but he liked people and loved to talk. He told Indian stories that his mother had taught him. He told about the old days on the desert. And he told yarns about encounters with flyin' saucers, hidden caves with giant elephant skeletons, and mysterious army experiments that he'd witnessed. He'd lived alone for so long that I think he actually believed a lot of the tales he told.

Whenever he came by, it was always about supper time. He'd eat with us and then sit up and tell stories till we were too tired to keep awake. Then he'd go spread his bed outside. If it was real cold, he might sleep in the shed where we stored our saddles, but he'd never stay inside with us.

One night he got to talkin' about Wild Willie, the bronc stomper. Willie was kind of a legend in these parts when I was a kid, and he and Charlie had camped together a couple of winters. Dean made the mistake of askin' Charlie to tell him about Willie. That was all it took to get the old man started.

Charlie leaned back in his chair, spit a long stream of tobacco juice into the firebox of the kitchen stove, and started in.

"Willie was a first-class bronc stomper back when it took a real hand to make a livin' just bein' a buckaroo. He'd go around from ranch to ranch, breakin' horses for fifteen dollars a head.

"Willie had a few minor problems, though. He'd rode so many buckin' horses that his brains were a little scrambled. Sometimes he acted a little peculiar. There's some folks around here who'd went so far as to say that Willie was about half a bubble off center.

"I 'member one time when he's over at the hospital in Winnemucca havin' his head stitched up and an arm set. The nurse asked him for his religious preference. Willie reared back on his hind legs and roared, 'I'm an old he-wolf and a bronc-stompin' fool. I'm long, tall, lean and mean, quick, fast, bad, and deadly!' With that, he let out a bloodcurdlin' scream.

"That ol' nurse thought that beller was some sorta western cowboy yell. The truth is, it was brought on by the doctor stabbin' Willie in the rump with a shot for tetanus.

"Willie told me that when he's a kid, his dad had pleaded with him not to become a buckaroo or a bronc stomper. His dad told him, 'Mark my words, son, if you follow this cowboy trade, one of these days you'll find yourself old, stiff, and broke. You won't own nothin' but a dirty bedroll and a wore-out saddle.'

"That's just about the physical and financial shape ol' Willie found himself in that night he camped across the dry lake over by Antelope Springs. He'd finished his supper, hobbled his horses, and had just slid down between the dirty sogans in his ol' canvas tarp when he saw it.

"If Willie had a-knowed anything at all about that Greek mythology stuff, he'd a-knowed right off what he's a-lookin' at. As it was, though, all Willie recognized it to be was a damned albino mustang. Only, this broom-tail had wings and it drifted down out of the evenin' sky. The moon was full, so Willie said he got a good look at the pony as it fell in with a bunch of range horses that was trailin' in to drink at the spring.

"Over the years Willie'd claimed to have seen a lot of things fly that most folks just took for granted was earth-bound. Willie'd seen things like blue snakes and pink elephants fly. He'd seen most of 'em after spendin' the better part of his summer wages in the gyp joints and juice shops below the tracks in town.

"As Willie laid there watchin' the horse, he started sizin' it up and appraisin' his confirmation. He decided that if it weren't for that albino color and them wings, the animal would make a better-than-average ranch horse. Thinkin' along them same lines, it finally dawned on Willie that maybe them wings could be more of an asset than a flaw.

Why, think of all the time he could save when they were gatherin' cows. And wouldn't he be somethin' to run mustangs on, too! Well, these thoughts got his old brain to churnin', and he started schemin' on just how he's gonna get this flyin' cow chaser captured.

"Willie'd run a lot of mustangs in his day, and he knew most all the tricks, from water trappin' down to relayin' 'em. But as he went over these methods in his mind, he couldn't see how any of 'em could do much to put him in ropin' distance of the winged horse. Then, like most plans that come out of the minds of geniuses, the idea just popped into his head. He'd set a trail snare, front foot the ol' pony, and while he's down, hobble his wings. From then on he'd treat 'im just like any other bronc.

"Along toward mornin', right after the coldest part of the night and just 'fore the eastern sky started changin' color, the white horse quit the bunch he's grazin' with and drifted back to the spring for another drink. After fillin' up, he took off into the western sky.

"Willie spent most of that day workin' on his trap. He knew from watchin' that most all the horses used the same trail down to the spring. Even the white horse used it, landin' up on the higher ground and then walkin' down to the water. The way Willie saw it, his main problem was how to keep the other horses outta his snare till the white horse came in to water. He finally decided to use an old mustanger's trick. He burnt big piles of sagebrush and old junipers till he had enough ashes to make a line across the trail farther back from where the flyin' horse had landed. Willie knew that the range horses wouldn't cross the line 'less they were really thirsty. He was hopin' he'd have his prize caught and tied by the time that happened.

"The moon was a few minutes later comin' up that night than it had been the night before; but when it did, Willie was ready. He had his snare set and propped up across the trail. It was anchored to a buried juniper post that he's sure wouldn't pull out. Back a few yards from the snare, Willie had himself half-buried and covered with sagebrush. He'd already built a loop in his riata and had enough extra rope with him to hobble them wings. Now all he had to do was sit and wait.

"Along toward ten, when the moon was at its brightest, Willie saw the horse come into sight. Slowly it circled the spring, checkin' out the area. Two or three bands of range horses were grazin' back of the charcoal line, not bein' thirsty enough to chance crossin' it yet. Willie was scared the big horse would get suspicious when he saw the other horses millin' around back there. Evidently the white horse musta figured they'd already been in to water, 'cause after a single pass or two, he flew down and lit. The big pony only looked back once at the others before startin' down the trail toward the spring.

"As soon as the snare went tight on the albino's right front foot, he went plumb nuts. Even though the moon was full and you could see almost as clear as day, Willie said it was still hard to tell just what all that horse did 'cause he was movin' so fast. About all Willie could see for the first few minutes was white hooves, hair, and feathers goin' in every direction.

"When the horse started to slow down, Willie sprang from his brush hidin' place and flipped a hulahand shot with his riata. The ol' gut line shot out straight and true. When it settled, it was right around the white pony's throat latch.

"Willie ran around so that he was on the left side of the horse and bided his time for just the right moment. He threw all his weight into the rope, catchin' the animal with all four feet off the ground. This slammed the poor old pony down to earth so hard that it knocked a good deal of the wind out of him, and the horse paused for just a second in his fight for freedom. It was durin' that second that Willie dropped on the horse's neck, slipped a hackamore over the white nose, and jerked the horse's head up to his knee. In this position, Willie was able to hold the horse till he got both front feet hobbled. Then he stepped back and rested for a minute while the horse fought some more.

"Willie knew that with both front feet hobbled and one of 'em tied to the ground, 'bout all the horse could do was stand up and throw himself again.

"After a few minutes' rest, Willie went back to work. He was pretty sure he could never get the white horse to a set of corrals, so that meant he was gonna have to top him off right out there in the brush. He knew the first thing he had to do was get them wings hobbled, and no matter how he sized it up, it wasn't gonna be no small task. He figured he'd best start off by throwin' the horse down again. He done this the same way he did the first time. He stepped over to the left side, picked up his riata, and throwed the horse, only this time he had another rope, and as soon as he had the horse down, he tied one hind foot up to the horse's neck. Then Willie proceeded to tie the wings down to the pony's side. He thought for a while about clippin' them wings like you do a chicken's but decided against it.

"When he had them wings tied down good and tight, he rolled the old horse over and into his saddle. It took some doin' to get his saddle cinched up good and tight, what with them wings bein' right there where his latigo tied off, but he got her done to where he figured it was good 'nough.

"With the horse saddled and the hackamore on, all that was left was to climb aboard and stay a while. Willie stood up, hitched his chaps a notch tighter, checked the straps on his spurs, pulled his hat down over his ears, and spit out his chew. He took a deep breath and was ready for war. Sliding the blind on his hackamore down over the pony's eyes, he untied its hind foot. Then he slipped the hobbles and snare off its front feet and let the big horse stagger to its feet.

"As soon as the pony got his footing, Willie grabbed a handful of mane, hooked his elbow over his Mecáte, and pulled the horse's head into him. Then he swung into the saddle. Willie sat there for a few seconds, gettin' himself set and checkin' out the feel of his riggin'. As soon as he was sure there wasn't much else he could do, he reached over the top of the horse's head and slid the blinds on the hackamore up towards the animal's ears.

"For a second or two, the horse just stood there, blinkin'. He seemed to be tryin' to get his bearings and tryin' to figure out what'd happened since the lights were turned out.

"Willie was from the old school of twisters who figured

the best way to get the Injun sign on a bronc was to get your licks in first and not let up till the horse showed signs of wantin' to quit. With that in mind, he reached up with both spurs and hung 'em in the points of the pony's shoulders. Then he drug 'em back to his cinch, makin' the rowels sing and the hair fly. That was all it took, and the white horse came uncorked.

"Now, when it came to readin' and numbers, Willie mighta been a little on the slow side; and even though he had been unloaded off a few broncs, he was by no means a green hand. He'd stayed on a good many horses that'd bucked off some pretty fair men. But this horse was sure 'nough makin' him hunt a deep seat. Even with his wings tied down, the horse still went higher and came down harder than anything Willie'd ever ridden.

"After half a dozen of those high straightaway jumps, the horse sucked her hack to the right and went into a tight spin. Willie was gettin' dizzy, and a thin trickle of blood that had dripped from his nose was bein' spread sideways across his cheek. Suddenly the horse straightened out and went into a series of high sunfishin' jumps, first to the right and then to the left. Willie was tryin' to figure out the horse's pattern, but the horse kept changin' it.

"Finally, Willie thought he could tell the old horse was slowin' a little. After another series of spins to the left, he could really feel the mustang wearin' down. That's when he went after the pony for real. He said he hooked him in the shoulders and thumped with his quirt. And just to show the horse what a real twister could do, he jerked off his hat and proceeded to fan the albino's ears on every jump. His confidence back again, he took a deep breath and hollered for all the coyotes to hear, "I'm an ol' he-wolf, and it's my night to howl!" With that, he let out his best imitation of a timber wolf's cry.

"I've heard Willie give that wolf call before, and in reality it sounded more like a tomcat with its tail caught in the outhouse door. That war cry was probably poor Willie's downfall. It terrified the horse so bad that he went straight up in one of those skyrocket jumps of his again. By now, though, with all the leapin' and twistin', the hobbles on his wings had gotten loose, and that jump was all it took to slip 'em free.

"With his wings loose, the horse took new heart and started in to show poor Willie just what a real buckin' horse could do. He always swore he stuck on for several jumps that were two or three hundred feet high. He even claimed to have stayed on when the horse did a complete flip with a pause. But when that white mustang got within twenty or thirty feet of the ground, Willie decided to bail out 'fore things got worse.

"Well, Willie staggered into town a day or so later, ridin' bareback. He looked pretty rough and seemed to feel even worse. He tried to tell people about his ride on a flyin' white horse. He even showed some of the folks who would listen a half a dozen white feathers that he claimed to have picked up after he got back to the spring. No one paid him much mind. Most folks already figured Willie was packin' a few bricks short of a full load, and all his stories about a flyin' white horse just went to prove they were right.

"But ya know, I'm not so sure as most of them folks. Ya see, I found Willie's saddle the next spring. Found it along the banks of a little dry creek over on the other side of the big alkali flat across from Antelope Springs. I found it about a hundred feet up in the top of a big cottonwood tree. And you know, there was a couple of them funny little white feathers stuck in the broken cinch.

"Willie was still startin' colts when he was up in his sixties, but he's dead now. Died back about '52 or '53. Ol' Ben Bird and Roy Sam found him there in the stone corral across from the Red House field. They couldn't tell if his horse killed him or if he died of natural causes. Roy thought they oughta take him in so as to find out how he died. Ben said it didn't make no difference; he's dead, and knowin' what kilt him wouldn't change that.

"Willie didn't have no kin left, so Ben and Roy just dug a hole in the corral and planted him there. I reckon Willie would have approved of their choice of a place. Ben had a little sign made up and hung on the gate to the corral. I think it read, 'Wild Willie Bremhaugh, last of the old-time bronc peelers,' and then it had the date that they found his body.

"Some tourist showed up in Gerlach with the sign a few years later. The stone corral's about gone now, too. Leastwise, it's all fallen down. Ben gave me Willie's saddle. I'm still ridin' it. Roy Sam took the white feather outta Willie's hat and put it in his medicine bag for luck. Willie always swore it was the last of the ones he had left from his ride on the flyin' horse."

When he's done with his story, Basco Charlie finished off another cup of coffee and went out and turned in. When he's gone, Dean looked over at me and said, "If

Charlie knew how to write, he could make a fortune. Someday you should type up a few of those tales and see if you can't get 'em published." Then we both laughed and went to bed.

Dean and I heard a few years ago that Charlie'd been killed. Seems some social misfit by the name of Fox came up to the Black Rock country from Southern California. He set up a minin' claim on the edge of the dry lake. Charlie stopped in to visit, and the miner killed him for trespassin'.

CHAPTER 15

Ben came by the day before Christmas and brought us a turkey dinner that the cook had fixed. He's on his way to Susanville to spend the holidays with his sister. When he came back, he stopped and gave us each a pair of nice insulated gloves for a gift.

Deak brought us our supplies the week after New Year's. He told us that Ben had let Pete and the big Indian, Hooper, have a couple days off for the holidays. They were both in jail in Winnemucca for disturbin' the peace.

Deak and Hooper had been startin' a little bunch of three-year-old colts and halterbreakin' some yearlin's. Pete and Luther had been feedin' and lookin' after the heifer calves. Now Deak and Luther were havin' to do it all. Ben had decided to leave the other two in jail. He told Deak that he'd go in and bail 'em out when it was closer to spring and he needed 'em for brandin'.

Stayin' busy the way we were, it didn't seem like no time 'fore the days started gettin' longer. The next thing I knew, it was the end of February and there were little white-faced calves standin' around the water holes with their mamas.

With the longer days, we had more spare time in the evenings. Dean decided to use the extra daylight to learn to rope. After a week or so of practicin', he got to where he could catch the end of a bale of hay pretty regularly.

To teach him how to rope heels, I had him practice sittin' on his horse, makin' his loop stand up around the base of the snubbin' post. He found an old, rotted saddletree out in the dump and took the horn off it, making a hook that held the horn to his belt. When he wasn't horseback, he practiced taking his turns around the old horn. In the end, he got to where he could take his dallies as fast as any man I ever saw.

When he got to where he could catch more bales than he missed and could stand his loop up around the post more than half the time, I figured he's ready for the real thing. We cut ten or fifteen pair from the bunch that we were feedin' and put 'em in the round corral. Then Dean practiced heelin' the calves.

We roped calves every evenin' when the weather was decent. On the ones where it was snowin', Dean would set up a bucket under the ol' three-sided shed in the corral and practice ropin' it at different distances.

By April, Dean was as good a roper as Pete. He couldn't throw the fancy shots nor rope as far as Hooper and Deak, and he had to run his outside cattle a little farther than the rest of us, but he usually got 'em caught.

When May came and we started gatherin' and brandin', Dean got to spend as much time ropin' as the rest of us.

Ben taught him to cut the bull calves and do the ear-markin'. I showed him how to watch the smoke and look for the rusty color on the hide to tell if a brand had taken.

The biggest surprise that spring come when Hooper and Deak started teachin' Dean and Luther how to make the fancy shots that they threw. It took lots of practice on live cattle to learn to throw the classy catches. Many's the time them two top hands gave up their turns at ropin' to let the kids work on a new shot.

Ben didn't even seem to mind that it was takin' us longer to get done. In fact, he got to where he'd stand back and give advice right along with the rest of us.

By the end of the month, Dean had to order a new rope and rewrap the horn on his old slick fork saddle. His first rope was as limp as a dishrag, and the original horn wrappin' was burned in two.

Dean and Luther may not have been in the same class as Deak and Hooper John, but those two youngsters did-n't have to take a backseat to no one at brandin'. They weren't arena team ropers, but they were damn sure good at draggin' calves.

After we finished brandin' and 'fore we started trailin' the cattle to the mountains, Ben got us all together in the cook-house and asked us what our plans were for the summer. He said that after the cattle were on the summer range, every-one would go to irrigatin' and hayin', 'cept for Deak and Luther. They'd be stayin' in camp up on the mountain.

Dean and I talked it over and decided we'd stick around till the cattle were moved and settled, then we'd pull out. We told Ben our plans the next day. He said that Hooper had decided to leave, too, and asked if we'd take him with us as far as the reservation town of Nixon.

I wasn't particularly wild about bein' around Hooper John when he had money, 'cause that meant he'd probably be drinkin'. One of the last people I wanted to go partyin' with was him. Some people draw trouble like a magnet, and Hooper was one of 'em.

Before I had a chance to answer, though, Dean popped up and said, "Sure, we'd like to have him ride along. It'd give us a chance to talk over ol' times and to say good-bye."

I thought to myself, "Talk over ol' times? Hell, we've only known him for six or seven months, and the sullen bastard hasn't said ten words to either of us durin' that time."

Ben looked at Dean, then back at me, shook his head like he couldn't believe what he'd just heard, and walked off without sayin' another word. I could tell he's thinkin' about the same thing I was. Ben knew that havin' Hooper around civilization and whiskey was like smokin' in a powder magazine. He just wasn't the type of person you invited out for a few social drinks and light conversation. Oh well, it was Dean's car. I was just along for the ride, too.

Dean had been writin' back and forth to Lonney over the winter, and in his last letter Lonney had asked if we wanted to come back to the pack station for the summer. I could tell Dean wanted to go, so I said okay.

It took us another six days to finish trailin' the cattle to the summer range. It's always slow goin' that time of year. Cows with young calves don't travel very fast. Every afternoon when we stopped, we had to take a couple of hours to make sure everything was mothered up 'fore we could go home. If you don't do that, you end up makin' a lot of leppie calves. Even though the days were longer, we still never got in 'fore dark.

The day after we finished movin' the cattle, Hooper, Dean, and I pulled the shoes on our horses while Luther and Deak got their supplies ready to move to the summer camp. Pete was already out irrigatin'.

After we were done with the horses, Dean went over and tried to start the old black Mercury. The battery just growled a couple of times and died. He hadn't driven it for over six months and had only started it once or twice in that time. One tire was low, too, so we pulled it off and put on the spare. Dean took the battery over to the shop and put it on the charger. I rolled the tire over to the compressor and blew some air into it.

The next day after breakfast, the three of us shaved and put on our Sunday best. Our boots were polished, our hair was combed, and we were soaked in aftershave lotion. We looked like we were either goin' to a funeral or a weddin'. Dressed like that, we trooped over to Ben's house and knocked on the door. Ben never invited us in. He just stepped outside and handed each of us an envelope with our checks in it.

There was no sentimental good-byes or anything like that from Ben. He'd seen too many men come and go over the years to get emotional about someone leavin'. He didn't even say thanks or good luck. All he said was somethin' to the effect that one of us smelled like a French whorehouse, and that if we wanted our jobs back in the fall to let him know in time so he didn't go and hire someone else. Then he turned and walked inside. I have to admit, I was a little disappointed, but I hadn't really expected any more from him.

Dean got the battery in the car and gassed it up at the company pump. Ben had agreed to the free gas earlier in exchange for takin' Hooper in with us. By the time Dean pulled the car up in front of the bunkhouse, Hooper and I had all of our gear out front. We managed to get the three saddles and one bedroll in the trunk and the other two bedrolls, our tack, and clothes stuffed in the backseat. Then the three of us piled in the front and headed for town.

Ben had left Hooper in jail from January through March, but Dean and I hadn't been off the ranch since we got there in November. The way I had it figured, it was party time. Gerlach wasn't my idea of a town to throw a proper fling, since it only had two bars and the local women had burned down the cathouse, but it would do for a starter. I didn't even care if we did have Hooper with us.

I hadn't looked at my check, but I knew that even with the deductions for winter clothes and social security taken out, it still had to be way over a thousand dollars. I figured if I played it right, I could get a few new clothes, a real haircut, replace some worn tack, and still stay fairly drunk all the way from Gerlach to the pack station.

The first hitch in my plan came when we got into town. When I opened my pay envelope, I found a check for $2,200. There was a note that said, "Forget about what you owe me for the winter clothes. You and the kid did a good job. Ben."

Dean had a matching check and also a note. His note read, "I've paid you a full wage with no deductions for either your stamps, winter clothes, or the fact that you're a green kid. I did this because you were worth it. You work hard and learn fast. If you will divorce yourself from that wore-out old drifter, stop readin' Will James books, and realize that today a good cowman has to do a lot of things that aren't done from the back of a horse, you will stand a good chance of amounting to something. The old saying, 'A rolling stone gathers no moss,' still holds true. You have a job here anytime you want it. Ben."

When Hooper opened his envelope, there was no check. Just a note saying, "You still owe me $225 for the remainder of your fine and the damages you did to the bar in Winnemucca."

I was expectin' Hooper to throw a squallin' cat fit, but instead he just smiled and said, "Must be old Ben don't count so good anymore, or else he's gettin' soft. I think I owe him more."

The problem we had was that there was no place in Gerlach that could cash a check as large as ours. That meant that we'd have to go clear to Wadsworth or Fernley 'fore I could start my party.

When we got back in the car and headed for Nixon, it seemed like I's the only one in bad spirits. I'd had my heart all set on startin' a real history-makin' drunk, and now it was bein' delayed.

Dean was floatin' 'cause of the note Ben had written, and Hooper was happy 'cause Ben had dropped about half of the bill he owed. I sat in the car and pouted all the way to the reservation. Dean and Hooper chattered away. Actually, Dean did most of the talkin', but Hooper would answer him once in a while and was civil.

Nixon was a Paiute town, and Hooper was a western

Shoshone, but he claimed to have friends there. I doubted that. I figured he might have someone there that knew him, but I doubted if he had any friends anywhere. He gave us directions to a small house on a dirt side street. The house was little and looked just like the other houses scattered around, 'cept this one was neat and didn't have any ol' junked cars or pickups sittin' around it.

When we stopped, Hooper started unloadin' his things from the backseat while Dean went around and opened the trunk. Suddenly the door on the front of the house opened, and a little girl of about three came flyin' out. She started hollerin', "Daddy, Daddy!" and actually jumped or flew the last six feet into Hooper's arms.

There are no words to tell you how surprised I was at the sight of Hooper John holdin' a little child. The tiny girl started rattlin' away in Paiute so fast that I never caught a word. When I looked toward the house again, there was a small, almost frail-looking girl of eighteen or twenty comin' outta the door. She came slowly down to the car, tryin' not to look at either me or Dean. She walked up to Hooper and hugged him and the little girl at the same time.

Hooper turned around to us, holdin' the little girl out at arm's length, and said, "This is Amy, and this is Lydia." Amy buried her face in his chest and Lydia looked down.

Then Hooper pointed at us and said, "These are my friends Dean and Tap." Amy wouldn't take her face out of her father's chest, but Lydia did manage to stick out her arm and shake hands with us. The handshake was as soft and light as dandelion seed, but she never looked us in the eye.

We finished gettin' Hooper's things outta the car and were closin' the trunk when Hooper said, "Wait!" He unbuckled the rawhide riata from the fork of his saddle and handed it to Dean. "This is good rope. You use it."

Then he turned to me, pointed with his chin toward Dean, and said, "He is a good guy. You take care of him." With that he turned and started for the house, still carryin' the little girl in one arm and the saddle in the other. Lydia followed along behind, draggin' his bedroll.

CHAPTER *16*

When we got to the junction outside of Wadsworth, we had a choice of goin' east to Fernley and then over the hill to Highway 50 and on into Carson City, or we could go west into Reno. At either city we'd catch Highway 395 south to the pack station turnoff.

I's all for goin' into Reno and startin' my party there, but for some reason, Dean wanted to go east to Fernley. It was his car, so what could I say?

When we got to Fernley, no one would cash our checks either. Ben did most of his bankin' in Susanville, and that was across the state line in California. Everywhere we went the story was the same, "Sorry, we don't take out-of-state checks."

Here we were with over $4,000, and we couldn't even come up with someone who would sell us a hamburger. We still had over a half a tank of gas, so Dean decided to head for Silver Springs and Dayton.

I's sure that with all of the out-of-state gamblers in

Reno we coulda cashed our checks there, and I coulda been on my way to settin' the world's record for the most liquor consumed in a twenty-four-hour period. Now we were headin' the opposite direction.

I was really poutin' by then and wouldn't talk. What made the whole thing even worse was that Dean was so damn cheerful and happy. He didn't even seem too upset when we pulled outta Dayton with just barely enough gas to maybe (just maybe) make it to Carson City.

It's pretty well built up now, but there used to be a stretch 'tween Dayton and Carson City that didn't have a building of any kind on it. That was where we were when the old black Mercury started to heat up. Dean stopped and let it cool off. Then we checked it all over but couldn't find anything the matter. When the heat gauge showed that it had cooled down, we started out. In a couple of miles the temperature started to rise again. This time the engine started makin' a funny knockin' noise too. After we stopped and let it cool down the second time, it wouldn't start.

I don't know the first thing about mechanics, and Dean didn't know a whole lot more. We were standin' there bangin' on the starter and the distributor with a rock when two miners pulled up. They took about a two-minute look at the situation and said that either the water pump or the oil pump had given out and that we shouldn't have driven it. They said the engine was probably frozen now. With that good news to cheer me up, I's about ready to scream.

The two miners were on their way to visit one of the local cathouses on the outskirts of Carson, and they offered to tow us that far.

We pulled up in front of "The Happy Mink Ranch" just as the sun was settin'. One of the miners pushed a button at the gate; it opened, and we went inside. There was a bar across the back wall from the door and several tables in between. Four or five half-dressed girls were scattered around the tables, visitin' with other customers.

The two miners went over and started talkin' to a big black lady who musta weighed close to 300 pounds. I figured she was probably the madam 'cause I had a hard time imaginin' anyone payin' very much to go wrestlin' in the sheets with her.

The big woman hollered somethin' through the door into the next room, and another four or five girls came trampin' out and lined up. The miners each grabbed one and took off down the hall.

That left me and Dean standin' there, starin' at the girls. I sorta cleared my throat and motioned for the black lady to come over. I explained to her that we weren't really customers. We just wanted to find someplace that would cash our checks.

She waved to the girls, and they disappeared into the back room where they'd come from. Then the three of us went over to the bar, where I told her our whole story and showed her my paycheck just to prove I's tellin' the truth.

The old gal turned out to be an all right kinda person. She laughed a lot and gave us each a free drink. She let Dean use the private phone in the back where he made a collect call to Lonney.

As luck would have it, Lonney was on the line to the answerin' service in Bishop when Dean called. Dean was able to talk to him right then. Lonney told Dean to sit tight and that he'd get help to us some way. He said that if we left the Happy Mink, to tell Sadie (Lonney said that was the black lady's name) where we could be found.

We sat around there sippin' free drinks and talkin' with Sadie for the next couple of hours. Somewhere durin' the course of the conversation, Dean mentioned that we hadn't eaten since breakfast. Sadie invited us to come into the back where the employees ate. The place had its own cook for the women, but she was off by then. Sadie had one of the women show us where the refrigerator was and told us to help ourselves.

Well, the next thing I knew, Dean and this woman were a-chatterin' away about different recipes. Then he and this little lady started fixin' us up a proper supper. Pretty soon a couple more of them young things come over. By the time we were done eatin', Dean's on a first-name basis with all of 'em. They were tellin' him stories about different cowboys they'd met, and Dean was tellin' them about buckin' horses and ol' Ben Bird and his own home back East.

After we got done eatin', one of them gals asked Dean if he'd help her with some knittin'. Seems she's makin' some sorta sweater for her baby back in Los Angeles, and she wanted to get him to hold the yarn for her while she rolled it into a ball. I didn't know it then, but that yarn comes from the factory wrapped in a skein, which is sorta like a coil of rope, and it has to be rolled up into a ball 'fore you can go to knittin' with it.

When I walked out to go thank Sadie for the supper, I looked back and there sat Dean, both arms stretched out in front of him with this yarn wrapped around his hands.

In front and on both sides of him sat about six half-naked women, all of 'em just a-chatterin' away like they were at a church quiltin' bee.

Me and Sadie sat there swappin' stories and drinkin' till somewheres around two in the mornin'. She mighta been a big woman and not much to look at, but it's been a long time since I've sat down and visited with someone as interestin' and easy to talk with as ol' Sadie was.

She knew I couldn't cash my check, but she never held back on the drinks or said anything about me payin' for 'em later. I guess she enjoyed talkin' to an ol' wore-out saddle tramp as much as I enjoyed talkin' with her. When I couldn't keep my eyes open any longer and figured I wasn't holdin' up my part of the conversation, I excused myself and went out to the car, where I crawled into the backseat and went to sleep.

About four in the mornin', I woke up to someone bangin' on the car door. It was none other than Lonney. After Dean's call he'd driven all the way from the pack station to pick us up.

He stuck his head in the car window and said, "I've heard of people that were so damn ugly that they couldn't get a girl in a whorehouse, even if they had a fistful of twenty-dollar bills. Now that I've seen you, I know just how ugly that is."

I thanked him for the compliment and told him that I'd never thought he's all that good-lookin' before, but right now he looked pretty good to me.

He wanted to know where Dean was, so I told 'im that as far as I knew, he's still inside knittin'. Lonney looked at me and gave me that sly smile of his and said somethin' about me leadin' young Dean astray.

I told Lonney that Dean was a good man to stay in camp with, and that he always pulled his part of the load when it came to work, but he sure wasn't much of a party animal. Havin' him around on a fling was a lot like havin' a Baptist minister for a chaperone.

Lonney opened the car door for me, and I untangled myself from around our gear and crawled out. The first thing I noticed was that there were a lot more cars in the lot now than when we got there. There was even music comin' from inside.

When we got to the gate, Lonney pressed the buzzer, and we walked in. The lights were dim, and it was hard to see at first, after comin' from the well-lit parkin' lot. The music comin' outta the jukebox was so loud that we had to scream to be heard. There were people dancin' in the middle of the room and others sittin' around at the different tables.

As my eyes became accustomed to the dark, I looked around for Dean but didn't see him. I hollered in Lonney's ear that Dean was probably still in the other room, holdin' the yarn. We were workin' our way across the dance floor when Lonney tapped me on the shoulder and pointed toward the bar.

There behind the counter, wearin' nothin' but the skimpiest little pair of pink bikini underpants and a lace brassiere, was Dean.

He was mixin' drinks and dancin' around to the beat of the music. When he saw us, he leaped up on the bar, let out a bloodcurdlin' scream, and hollered, "Come on, everybody, let's twist!!" Then he went to shimmyin' down the top of the bar, doin' some sorta bump-and-grind dance.

Without goin' into a lot of sordid details, let me just say that was the start of one of the wildest five-day benders I've ever been on. We partied till all three of us were broke, and we had to sell the old black Mercury to a junk dealer to get enough money for gas so we could make the trip back to the pack station.

We pulled into the parkin' lot at Lost Lake, drivin' on one flat tire, so hungover and wrung out that none of us even noticed it was flat. After a day of restin' up, we started to work. Lonney'd already told us that Slick wouldn't be back this summer 'cause he wanted to take some special courses that were only offered durin' that part of the year. That meant more work for all of us.

Lonney hadn't brought up any of the horses yet, as there was still too much snow in the backcountry. All of the passes were closed, and the backpackers said a lot of the trails had big drifts across 'em.

We spent the next few days oilin' saddles, cuttin' firewood, and repairin' corrals. When most of the heavy work was done, Dean and Lonney took the stock truck down to the valley and started haulin' up hay, while I stayed at camp and did more work on the pens.

When Lonney figured everything was ready, he took Dean, and they started haulin' horses. Some of the pack stock were on pasture down by Bishop, and some were clear up near Fallon. After they got back with the first load, I started in shoein'. By the end of June, we were in full operation, except for the fact that there were still a couple of high country lakes that we couldn't get into.

One day in July, Lonney and Dean came back from a

three-day pack trip. After the animals were unsaddled and turned loose, Lonney took me aside and told me that Dean was either the bravest or craziest S.O.B. he'd ever seen ride a horse.

Seems they were on a trail that ran above one of the backcountry lakes when Dean's horse blew up and started buckin' down through the rocks toward the water. Lonney said it was almost fifty yards straight down. When Lonney heard the noise and turned around, Dean and his horse were already halfway to the lake. The ol' pony was really turnin' the crank, but every time the animal hit the ground he come near to fallin', it was so steep. Lonney said the thing that impressed him the most, though, was Dean. He said the kid had somehow jerked down his quirt and was over-and-underin' the horse every jump. I guess the dirty little beggar finally gave up when they hit the water. When I asked Dean about it that night, he kinda chuckled and said, "I figured I was gonna get killed, and I wanted to get a few good licks in before I went down."

A couple days after that, Lonney went in by himself to drop off some fishermen at Rainey Lake. That afternoon his pack string came home without him or his saddle horse. Dean and I were shoein' when the pack mules showed up. We didn't think too much about it. All of us turned our empty pack animals loose and drove 'em home rather than lead 'em. Sometimes we'd stop off and visit with other packers or hikers, and the loose stock would drift on home ahead of us. About three that afternoon, we started gettin' worried. We saddled up and took off at an easy trot.

Rainey Lake wasn't all that far, maybe eight or ten miles

is all. We crossed Trout Creek and followed the trail across the broken slide rock without findin' any sign of trouble. We were able to follow Lonney's tracks both comin' and goin' across the meadows.

When we got to the lake, we found the fishing camp and talked with the fishermen. They said Lonney'd left 'fore noon and should have been back long ago. We turned and started retracin' our tracks back toward the pack station. As we dropped down through the switchbacks from the rock slide to Trout Creek, I thought I heard a cry. The closer we got to the bottom, the clearer it got. We found Lonney lyin' there by the trail where it crosses the creek.

He was badly hurt, that was easy to see. Neither of his legs would work, his jaw sat at a funny angle, and he couldn't talk clearly. His right arm hung at his side, and even though he could move it, he couldn't hold it up. He was covered with dried blood and looked like he'd crawled on his belly across a slaughterhouse floor.

We got a fire goin' and wrapped him in our saddle blankets. He was conscious but couldn't talk. I knew he was in shock from the feel of his skin. A couple of hikers came by, and Dean threatened to kill 'em if they didn't give us their sleeping bags right then and there.

It was dark by then, and there was no way we could get Lonney out 'fore daylight. I took off, anyway, at a hard lope across the rocky trail. The shoes on my horse's hooves made sparks as I crossed the granite, and he musta fell a dozen times 'fore I reached the lodge at Lost Lake.

I got the owner up, and he called the Forest Service. Within minutes, they had a man on the line from an air rescue helicopter outfit down in the valley. The pilot musta had a map in front of him, 'cause when I told him that Lonney was located where the main trail crossed Trout Creek, he acted as if he knew the place. He told me that he couldn't get a helicopter down in the canyon at that point, but if we could get Lonney up on the ridge to the south, he could make a landin' there. I told him to be on the ridge at daylight, and we'd be there.

The owner of the lodge got a couple of the biggest, stoutest kids that he had workin' for him out of bed and told 'em what was goin' on. He gave me a thermos of coffee and a couple of heavy quilts that I tied on my saddle, and I started back.

After I left, they rounded up a portable stretcher, some signal flares, and more blankets. Then the owner and his crew started out on foot.

I got there a good hour ahead of the rescue party, even though they took the boat across the lake while I rode clear around. When I showed up, the two hikers were sittin' across from the fire, glarin' at Dean. Lonney was unconscious or asleep now. There was a big pile of firewood stacked near the fire, and Dean kept feedin' it into the flames at regular intervals.

I asked Dean how it was goin', and he just shrugged. Then the hikers started in. They wanted me to know that when they got out, they were gonna press charges against both of us. Seems they didn't like sharin' their sleepin' gear with someone all covered with blood, they didn't like havin' to haul firewood for a stranger, and they damn sure didn't like bein' threatened by some stupid cowboy.

I offered 'em the coffee and the quilts that the lodge

owner had sent, hopin' that would quiet 'em down, but once they were comfortable, they got even more difficult to listen to. Suddenly Dean jumped up and jerked a limb off the firewood pile and started for 'em. I grabbed him by the arm about the time he was gonna take a Babe Ruth swing at the closest one.

Well, they shut up right then and never said another word till the rescue party arrived. Then they started in all over again. The lodge owner took 'em aside, and I heard him tell 'em not to be too hard on Dean. He said the boy had been in a mental institution and that Lonney was his only friend in the whole world. He said that if anything happened to Lonney, Dean might become violent and hurt someone.

The rescue team and Dean talked it over, and everyone agreed that it would take about an hour to pack Lonney from the creek bottom to the south ridge. The helicopter couldn't get in till daylight, and that would be somewhere between four-thirty and five. We already had a supply of firewood, and there was no wood on the ridge, so it was decided we'd stay right where we were till three. Then we'd start out.

It was midnight or thereabouts, so we had three hours to rest. No one slept, though. We sat around and talked or wondered off along the creek bottom to gather more wood for the fire.

At three, we wrapped Lonney in the heavy quilts and strapped him to the stretcher. The climb out was steep but made a little easier by the series of switchbacks. I walked in front with a flashlight, shinin' it on the trail for the men who were carryin' Lonney. A man took each corner of the stretcher, and two brought up the rear. The two in the back would trade off with the ones on the stretcher every couple hundred yards. They also led our saddle horses.

We left the two hikers down by the fire, grumblin' about havin' to sleep in dirty sleepin' bags. It took us every bit of an hour and a half to reach the ridge. We got there just as the helicopter showed up. The doctor shot Lonney full of painkiller and loaded him onboard. The rest of us took off for home.

As luck would have it, we didn't have any trips scheduled for that day, so Dean and I were able to get some rest. That evenin' the lawyer who owned the pack station showed up. The owner of the lodge had called him. Dean and I'd met this guy once or twice, so we knew who he was even though we'd never talked with him very much.

He told us that Lonney was in serious condition with a broken jaw and collarbone. The most serious injury that Lonney had suffered was to his back. Right now the doctors weren't sure just how bad it was, but it looked like he might never walk again. The owner said he'd get someone up there to run the place just as quickly as he could, but he wanted to know if we could hold things together for a week or so till he could find someone.

We told him we'd try, but we weren't sure if two of us could do it. He told us to do the best we could and to cancel any trips that we couldn't make. He gave us instructions on how to use the mobile phone in the pickup and the number of the answering service in Bishop.

A week or so later, we got a letter from Lonney. In it he told us about the wreck. He was on his way out when the colt he was ridin' got scared. They were right in the middle of the narrowest part of the trail where it crossed a granite slick, high above Trout Creek. Suddenly the horse had turned in toward the bank to try to spin around. When the colt found that it was too narrow to turn completely around, it reared over backwards. They went over the edge and fell clear to the creek bottom, where they landed in the top of a big yellow pine. The two of 'em had landed upside down with Lonney still in the saddle on the bottom. They hit so hard that the impact broke the horse's neck. When Lonney came to, he found himself in the top of a tree with a dead horse on top of him. The horse's head and neck were lyin' across the top of Lonney's right shoulder, and he thought that was the reason he couldn't use that arm.

Somehow he managed to reach around and get the knife off his belt. He figured that if he cut the cinch or latigo that held the saddle, the horse would fall free, and he would be able to get down. But when he'd tried that, the dead horse didn't budge.

Lonney said he could see then that his only chance now was to cut the horse's head and neck off. That would change the point of balance, and he figured the animal would fall then.

He started in cuttin' away at the neck and didn't have much trouble till he got to the bone. That took him another hour to get through, but as soon as it was separated, the head fell to the ground, and he was able to work the rest of the body off him.

It was after the horse was off that Lonney realized how badly he might be hurt. His right arm wouldn't work and neither would his legs. With only his left arm still functioning, he tried to make his way down out of the top of the big tree. He ended up fallin' thirty or forty feet through the limbs, bouncin' from one to another. Durin' the fall, he probably broke his jaw.

He laid there on the ground till he saw Dean and me ride by on our way in. He tried to call to us, but we couldn't hear him over the sound of the creek. He knew that once we got to the fishin' camp, we'd turn around and start back to the pack station. His only chance of us findin' him that day lay in the possibility of bein' able to drag himself along the creek bottom to the trail. With nothin' but the upper part of his body and one arm, he pulled himself along for almost a quarter of a mile to the place where we found him.

In the letter, he asked if we would go back and get his saddle out of the tree and send it to his stepdad's place.

The next day we took an extra horse and two or three lash ropes. We rode back to the creek crossin'. Dean tied his horse down in the bottom and started workin' his way up the creek. The underbrush was heavy in the bottom, and it was slow goin' for him, even on foot. He figured it wouldn't be hard to find the right tree 'cause, after all, there'd be a dead horse layin' at the foot of it.

I was to go along the trail up above till I could see or hear Dean. The plan was for him to climb to the top of the tree where the saddle was and for me to lower a rope down to him. Then he'd tie the loose end of the rope to the saddle, and I'd haul it up to the trail, where I'd put it on the extra horse.

I missed Dean on my first trip across the granite slick, but on the way back I saw him. It took all three of the lash ropes plus my sixty-foot catch rope to reach from the trail to the top of the tree. That meant that Lonney had fallen somewhere close to 180 feet before he landed in the tree.

It took several tries to get the string of tied-together ropes out to where Dean could reach 'em from his perch in the treetop. We finally made it, though, and I hoisted the saddle back up to the trail.

We'd brought an extra latigo to replace the one Lonney'd cut, so I put it on the saddle and cinched the rig on the extra horse.

CHAPTER *17*

W hen Dean and I got in that afternoon, the owner and the new manager were there to meet us. The new
man's name was Dave Robison, and
he was as opposite of Lonney in
looks as he was in his ideas on how to run the pack outfit.
Even their backgrounds were completely different. Lonney
was about six feet tall and skinny. Dave was short and
squatty. Lonney came from a broken home and had left
high school in the eighth grade. Dave came from a fairly
well-to-do family and had graduated from college. Dave
was married, while Lonney didn't even have a steady girlfriend. Lonney was on the go all the time and worked
harder than any of us. Dave wasn't lazy, but he liked to
work with his brain and leave most of the manual labor to
others. Lonney was uncomfortable around strangers and
didn't say much till he got to know you. Dave was a born
talker and got along well with all of the customers.

The biggest contrast that Dean and I had to adjust to was
the difference in their views on how to operate the pack

station. Lonney's idea was to run it on a shoestring—spend as little money as possible on improvements, hire as few people as necessary, and get by with horses and mules no one else wanted. Lonney believed in givin' the customer a rustic high-mountain adventure. They might never come back, but they'd sure have some tales to tell.

Dave, on the other hand, wanted a smooth-operatin' place with no excitement or surprises. He wanted an outfit that looked western but was as neat and well kept as a city ridin' stable.

Two weeks after Dave took the job, it was hard to tell we were workin' for the same place. He and his wife Malisa (everyone called her Missie) moved into the cookhouse where Lonney'd lived. Missie cooked for us and gave ridin' lessons. The meals were a lot more varied than the fried meat and potatoes that we usually ate, and the customers seemed to enjoy the free ridin' class.

Dave got permission from the Forest Service to clear an area north of the parkin' lot and to build a ridin' arena there. He hired two college kids to start cleanin' and workin' on his building projects. They also put a new roof on the cookhouse and converted a back closet into an indoor bathroom for Missie.

Twelve of the crankiest horses and mules were cut out and traded for gentler, more dependable ones. The pack boxes were painted red with the company name on 'em in white. Little signs that said Office, Bunkhouse, and Barn were stuck up on the various buildings, and a list of rules and regulations was posted out front of the hitchin' rail.

Dave started advertisin' in a couple San Francisco and Los Angeles papers, along with some horsey magazines, and business tripled. With the increase in pack trips, Dean and I were seldom home for more than a day at a time.

By the first of September, when school started and business slowed down, Dave had his arena done. He told Dean and me that if we'd help him build a ropin' box and catch pen, he'd supply the steers, and we could team rope in the evenin's. That sounded like a fair 'nough deal, so we jumped in and had it done in a couple afternoons.

True to his word, Dave went down and picked up four head of Corriente steers from someplace in the valley. He also brought up two of his ropin' horses. The days were startin' to turn cooler. The two college kids left for school, and everything became more relaxed. Dave liked to rope, and with the slowdown in business we had a lot more time for it. There were days when we'd run those poor ol' steers through three times in the afternoon and three more times in the evenin'.

Dave staked Dean to one of his ropin' horses, and within two weeks Dean had become a respectable heeler and a pretty fair header. Dean and I even talked about someday entering a couple of them century ropin's, where the total age of the contestants has to add up to a hundred or more.

One evenin' in the middle of September, we were out there givin' the steers their exercise. Dave and I were each ridin' one of his rope horses, and Dean was ridin' one of the new horses that Dave got in trade. For some reason, Dean decided to try out the riata Hooper John had given him. He took the rubber wrappin' off his saddle horn and got ready to heel for Dave.

Missie turned the steer out, and the two ropers shot

down the arena after it. Dave threw and missed, and Dean came in and made a long throw that settled around the steer's neck. By now, though, they were at the far end of the arena. The steer ducked into the catch-pen area. But instead of stoppin' and waitin' for someone to pull the rope off, he came runnin' out, headed back for the other end of the arena.

Everyone, including Dean, had expected the animal to stay in the catch pen, so when he came lopin' out, it took us all by surprise. Dean was in the process of coilin' up his rawhide rope when the steer came out and ducked past him. The slack in his riata went under his stirrup and fender. That spooked his horse, and he jumped and straddled the rope. As soon as it went tight under his front legs, he spun around and went to crow hoppin' across the corral.

As hard as the horse was buckin', Dean coulda ridden him blindfolded with both hands over his head. But he wasn't thinkin', and he reached down and put his right hand on his saddle horn. What he didn't notice was that he'd reached through the coils of his rope. With the steer runnin' one way and the horse buckin' the other, it didn't take long before the rope went tight around Dean's hand.

I was clear back at the other end of the arena and couldn't do anything but watch. Dave didn't realize that Dean's hand was caught. About all Dean could do was sit there and ride it out till the last of the rope finished burnin' around his hand. When it was all over, the rope had cut off Dean's little finger at the first joint. The one next to it was broken.

We got him down to the hospital in Bishop as quickly as we could, but there wasn't much they could do but splint the broken finger and trim up the loose ends of the other one. That little wreck sorta took the fun out of the summer for Dean.

A few days later, we took a couple of men from Oregon on a four-day fishin' trip. One evenin' while we were sittin' around the campfire, one of 'em told us about a friend of his who owned a ranch up on the Snake River. He said his friend might be needin' someone to stay in his cow camp for the winter.

That was all it took to get Dean cranked up and thinkin' about pullin' out. He'd been kinda down in the dumps since Lonney's accident, and the loss of the end of his pinkie finger didn't do a whole lot to cheer him up. He didn't recognize the signs, but I did. He was wantin' a change of scenery and didn't know it.

Dean got the name and phone number of the ranch up on the Snake, and as soon as we got outta the backcountry, he told Dave he needed some time off. He had a doctor's appointment, anyway, and he wanted to buy a pickup.

We still had trips scheduled, so I didn't tag along. Dean hitched a ride down to the valley with some tourist and was gone for three days. When he got back, he had a new hat, new boots, all new clothes, and a brand-new Ford pickup. He also told me that he'd talked with the owner of the ranch and that the man was holdin' the job open till he talked with me. I got to talk with the man a lot sooner than any of us expected.

The next day after Dean got back, he and Dave took a troop of Boy Scouts to one of the lakes, about twelve miles from the pack station. It took fourteen head of pack stock to get all of the camp gear and food moved in, so each man led seven head. That's a pretty long string, even in flat country. Dean was a little upset that Dave hadn't had me come along to help, but Dave wanted me to stay back and shoe up some horses.

They had a few minor wrecks on the switchbacks 'cause of the length of the pack strings but nothin' too spectacular. When they got to the meadow that bordered the south end of the lake, Dean and Dave hobbled their saddle horses, and Dean started unpackin'. Dave got wrapped up tellin' Wild West stories to the scout leaders and a bunch of the boys. In the end Dean had to unpack all of the mules and horses without any help.

As Dean'd finish unpackin' an animal, he'd hang the empty pack bags or boxes back on the sawbuck saddle. Then he'd throw the lash rope and cinch over and hook it under the horse's belly. With that done, he'd take the rope and throw a couple of half hitches around the fork of the packsaddle and tuck the extra rope in the empty bags or boxes. Then he'd let the animal go off to graze. Dean's tyin' down the bags and boxes this way allowed the animals to be turned loose without any chance of the pack gear bouncin' off as they trotted home.

When Dean was all done, he walked over, unhobbled his horse, and climbed on. As soon as Dave saw Dean was ready, he finished his story to the scouts and stepped up on his horse. To make a dramatic exit, Dave pulled out his big Colt .45; hollered over to Dean, "Let's head 'em home!"; and fired two quick shots in the air.

Those pack animals musta figured he was shootin' at them, 'cause they took off across the meadow like a grizzly was after 'em. Of course Dean and Dave's horses were a-wantin' to be right in amongst 'em, too. Rather than fight 'em, the boys gave the horses their heads and they took off, too. Well, Dean's did, anyway. Dave's was a-hoppin' up and down, tryin' to catch up, only he couldn't 'cause Dave had forgot to unhobble him.

The little horse was doin' his best to run with his front feet tied together, only Dave didn't know it. He shoved his six-gun in the holster and jerked down his quirt. "Buck with me, will ya!!" he hollered, and he went to over-and-underin' the poor little horse. Dean thought it was so damn funny that he came near to bustin' a gut, laughin' so hard.

Finally, Dave realized what'd happened. He got a real silly look on his face and then got off and unhobbled the horse. Dean was still laughin' like some sorta crazy man and kept it up every few minutes all the way home.

Like a lot of little men, Dave couldn't take bein' made fun of. He took himself pretty serious. When they got back to the pack station, he told Dean that enough was enough and to knock off the nonsense.

Dean looked over at him with a real serious expression on his face and said, "Buck with me, will ya!!" Then he busted out laughin' all over again.

That was all it took. Dave told him to roll his bed and hit the road.

Dean said, "That suits me just fine." The kid was still laughin' when he come over to where I's shoein' one of the mules and told me what'd happened. Then he headed for the bunkhouse to get his gear together.

I was in the process of loadin' my shoein' outfit in a gunnysack when Dave showed up. He wanted to know what I was doin'. When I told him I was gettin' my stuff together, too, he wanted to know why. I told him that Dean was my ride out of there, and if he was leavin', I was too.

We were over by the bunkhouse gettin' the last of our gear loaded in the back of the new pickup when Dave came over. He had both our checks in his hand. Before he handed 'em to us, he said he was sorry and that if we were willin' to forget about what'd happened, so was he.

Dean said he was sorry, too, and that more'n likely it was his fault, but he'd kinda like to be movin' on, anyway.

Then Dave looked over at me and said, "What about you, Tap?" I said somethin' to the effect that someone had to follow the stupid kid around and straighten up things behind him, so I figured I'd best be goin', too. Dave handed us our checks, and we all shook hands 'fore we pulled out.

CHAPTER *18*

Dean and I drove down to Bishop, where we bought a case of beer, cashed our checks, and then drove over to the city park. We sat in the parkin' lot behind the Forest Service Visitor's Center, sippin' our brew and talkin' about where we ought to head next. I suggested we head south and see if we couldn't find somethin' down in the Imperial Valley. I'd never been there, but I'd heard they wintered lots of yearlin's in the area.

In the end, Dean talked me into givin' the Oregon ranch a call. We found a pay phone, and I dialed the number Dean had given me.

As soon as the owner, Mr. George Wilcox, got on the phone and told me where the ranch was located, I was ready to tell him that we weren't interested. The ranch headquarters were clear up in the northeast corner of Oregon, just south of the Washington line. The camp he wanted us to stay in was actually located in Idaho, right on the bank of the Snake River.

The job was simple enough, though. All he wanted us

to do was look after 500 head of cows on his winter range and pack protein block to 'em. There would be no hay to feed, no ice to chop, and good, gentle horses to ride. He'd pay us each $300 a month and furnish our groceries. It didn't sound all that bad, except it was so damn far away. Without lookin' at a map, I guessed it to be close to 800 miles as the crow flies from where we were to the Washington State line.

Our call ended with me tellin' Mr. Wilcox I had to talk it over with Dean, and that we'd let him know in a day or so. The truth is, I wasn't too wild about headin' that far north with winter comin' on, but Dean seemed to like the idea. He said that after the summer at the pack station, he was tired of crowds. Five or six months alone sounded pretty good to him.

We went back to the park and popped the top on a few more cans till it was dark. I kept arguin' for goin' to Southern California or even Mexico, while Dean kept pushin' for someplace without any people.

Finally Dean gave in, and we decided to head south. With that settled, we drove around till we found us a nice, quiet restaurant, where we filled up on steak and salad. After we'd eaten, we went to the cocktail lounge and had a couple of highballs.

I'm not sure if it was the liquor or the good food, but when we walked out, I was sure feelin' relaxed and ready for bed. I curled up in the passenger's side of the truck and was conked out 'fore we were outta town. When I woke, we were parked beside the road, and Dean was sleepin' behind the wheel.

It was just crackin' daylight, and the eastern sky was

streaked with orange clouds where the sun was comin' up. I looked around and tried to figure out where we were. The truck was parked off to the side of what appeared to be a blacktop country road. There was a big irrigation canal not more than fifteen feet from the truck, and alfalfa fields surrounded us.

I crawled out of the truck and stretched. When I got back in, Dean was wakin' up. I asked him where we were.

"Somewhere on the outskirts of Fallon, I think," he said.

"Fallon?!!" I shouted. "Hell, that's 150 miles *north* of where we started. I thought we decided to go south for the winter!!"

Dean shrugged and yawned.

He said that after I went to sleep, he decided to run on up and visit Lonney for a few days. After all, what difference did it make? We had plenty of money and nobody waitin' for us.

I thought about it for a minute and decided that he's probably right. I had over $1,500 in my pocket, and I knew Dean had at least $350 or so left, even after buyin' the clothes and the truck. If we didn't get too wild, we could spend a day or so with Lonney and still have plenty of money to make it down to Southern California.

We drove on into town and found a phone where Dean called the number that Lonney had given him in his last letter. Lonney was stayin' at his mom and stepdad's place, and his mom answered the phone. She gave Dean directions on how to get out to their home.

Dean had told me that Lonney'd said in his letters that he was stayin' with his folks and goin' to saddle-makin' classes. The state workman's compensation insurance was footin' the bill for him to learn a new trade and helpin' out with his livin' expenses.

After we ate breakfast, we drove east out of town till we found the little place where Lonney was stayin'. It sure wasn't very fancy to look at. The outfit consisted of about five acres. There was a little house, a small shop, and an even smaller house next to a tumbledown barn. Lonney's stepdad was a mechanic, and the place was covered with junk cars and trucks. He also gypo-traded cattle, and the two or three acres back of the barn held a dozen or so skinny cows, bad-eyed calves, and crippled bulls.

Lonney's mom had told him we were comin', and he was sittin' out front in his wheelchair when we pulled up. That was an uncomfortable greetin' for me. I didn't know how to act or what to say. Lonney'd always been so active, and to see him tied to that chair made me feel kinda mad. I'm not sure who or what I's mad at, but I sure felt like he'd gotten a raw deal from fate or God or somethin'.

We went inside and met his folks. Durin' the course of the conversation, it was decided that we'd take Lonney into the saddle shop and spend the day with him there. Then we were to bring him home and have supper with the family.

Lonney's instructor was the owner of the saddle shop. He'd learned the trade in prison. Lonney was just beginnin', and he spent most of his time either stampin' leather or watchin' the older man.

After lunch, I got to prowlin' around the shop. In the back, I found a pair of silver-mounted Garcia spurs and a fancy spade bit. The spurs were the old California drop-shank style. They had a real pretty pair of wide, flower-stamped straps on 'em with big silver conchos, buckles, and keepers. The silver-mounted bit was the Elko star pattern. The little brow-band headstall had silver conchos on the corners and a good set of braided rawhide reins.

I asked the shop owner what he had to have for the whole layout, and he said $500. That would be a steal today, but back in 1977, that was better than a month-and-a-half's wages. Still though, it was sure a pretty getup. For the rest of the day, I kept driftin' back there to look at the spurs. Pretty soon I got to daydreamin' about how they'd look on my ol' boots. I could see myself struttin' around the brandin' fire, with all those other fellers watchin' my feet and wishin' they had them hooks strapped on their heels.

Finally, toward the end of the day, I couldn't stand it any longer. I told the saddle maker that if he'd throw in a pair of shotgun chaps that were hangin' in the front window, I'd give him the $500 he wanted.

He hemmed and hawed a bit and finally said he'd do it.

I justified the deal in my own mind by sayin' that I might as well get myself somethin' nice, 'cause I'd probably just end up drinkin' the money away.

Lonney called his mom that afternoon and told her that we wouldn't be back for supper. At six they closed down the shop, and all of us went out and ate. We'd talked about havin' an ol'-time party, but somehow pushin' Lonney around in that wheelchair took the fun out of it for all of us. We ended up back at his folks' place a little 'fore midnight.

Dean and I spread our bedrolls out on the floor in Lonney's cabin and slept there. Even though we stayed up talkin' after we got home, the next mornin' I got up early and went outside. Lonney's mother was out pickin' beans in her garden. She and I got to visitin'. It ended up with her cryin' on my shoulder.

She said that after Lonney got outta the hospital, he'd tried to kill himself. It had only been since he'd started goin' down to the saddle shop that he'd quit drinkin'. She told me Lonney's stepdad was a good man, but Lonney and he had never gotten along, even when Lonney was younger. It was hard on both of 'em now, havin' to live this close together. The insurance paid all of the hospital bills and paid the shop owner to teach Lonney a trade, but there wasn't much money left over for groceries. That caused her husband to grumble and complain, and she was caught in the middle. The picture wasn't a real pleasant one.

Dean and Lonney came out about then, and Lonney's mom invited us over for breakfast. After we'd eaten, I went back and rolled my bed while Dean sat at the table with them and talked. I still don't know why I did it, but somethin' made me reach down in my pants pocket and take out the roll of bills I had left. There were nine hundred-dollar bills along with a couple of tens. I took the nine big bills and put 'em on the dresser in the room where Lonney slept. What the hell, I figured. I'd just blow the money on a big drunk. Besides, I knew Dean still had a couple hundred dollars and that would get us to Brawley, California. I's pretty sure we could get work there.

I carried my bed out and was puttin' it in the truck when Dean came outta the main house. He told me we were gonna take Lonney down to the shop and we'd leave from there. Lonney's mom would come in that afternoon and pick him up.

At the saddle shop, the conversation got around to what we planned on doin' for the winter. Dean told Lonney about the the camp job up on the Snake River for Wilcox. That got Lonney to tellin' about the winter he'd spent on the Snake at Pittsburgh Landing for the old Circle C Ranch. He said that Wilcox's winter range was only a few miles north of where he'd camped, but he'd never been to their place. He'd heard that the Wilcoxes had been runnin' cattle there on the river for a long time and had a reputation of bein' good cowmen and good people to work for.

Lonney rambled on and on about the area, the way a blind man does when he's talkin' about things he saw 'fore he lost his sight. I don't think Lonney was tellin' us about the country as much as he was relivin' a time and an experience that he'd never be able to enjoy again. He remembered that winter as bein' pretty mild and said a lot of deer and elk had come down durin' the colder months and stayed in the area. For the most part, the country was fairly steep, but there was lots of grass with big pines on the upper ridges. All in all, he felt there were a lot worse spots for a man to hole up for winter.

The picture Lonney painted almost had me wantin' to call up Mr. Wilcox and offer to pay him for the privilege of workin' up there. But I just couldn't convince myself that anyplace that far north could keep from bein' cold.

Finally, Dean said we'd best be gettin' on down the road, so we all shook hands and said our good-byes. Dean and I drove back into town and filled up with gas at the station across from where the road turns south to Hawthorne and down into Southern California. A block or so farther east is where the road takes off that goes on up toward Winnemucca and then into Oregon.

When the truck was full, Dean turned to me and said, "Well, which way do we head, north or south?"

Hell, I couldn't decide. "For once, let's make up our minds logically," I said.

"How do we do that?" Dean asked.

"The same way a good cowman makes any important decision. We list all of the good points on one side of a piece of paper and all of the bad points on the other side. Then we flip a coin and call it in the air," I told him.

"Sounds logical to me," was his answer, as he dug in his pants pocket for a coin. Five minutes later, we were on the road headed north.

CHAPTER *19*

Dean and I pulled out of Fallon on 95, headed north. Dean figured on callin' the Wilcoxes when we stopped for gas at Winnemucca. As we drove across the big alkali flats that lie between Fallon and Lovelock, I couldn't help but think about what it musta been like for the ol' pioneers that trudged through this area on their way to California.

Back in the late thirties, an older couple had hired me to take 'em on horseback across the Forty-Mile Desert. It lies just a few miles west of the highway we were on. They were doin' research for a book that the man was writin' on the history of the California Trail. It was in the fall that year, too, and the weather was fairly cool. We had one packhorse carryin' nothin' but five-gallon cans of water, another with our tent and groceries, and a third with our beds.

Even with all the stoppin' to take pictures and make notes, it only took us three days, but I could still imagine what it musta been like for those people with their slow-movin' wagons bein' pulled by wore-out oxen.

Back when I made the trip, the trail was fairly easy to follow. There was a steady string of ol' broken wagon parts, the iron hardware off harnesses, and rustin' pieces of discarded junk. The ol' man'd told me that this stretch of the trail was the most dreaded of the whole trip. By the time that the people got there, most of their teams were used up and the wagons were all but wore-out.

He said more people and animals died in this area than on the rest of the trail. He had copies of diaries and journals written by the people who had made the trip. In some of 'em, they claimed to have been able to step from one animal carcass to the next, and said that no place along the main trail was without fresh graves.

As we clipped along at sixty miles an hour with the radio blarin', it was hard to imagine the tragedies and the heartaches that had taken place all around us. We covered the distance 'tween Fallon and Lovelock in a little over an hour; it had taken the pioneers better than a week.

Early afternoon, Dean and I pulled up to the curb in front of the Star Casino in Winnemucca and went in to eat a late lunch. While we were eatin', Walt and Elaine Finch came in. I hadn't seen 'em in more'n fifteen years. Walt and I'd worked together up on the C S, and Elaine had cooked for the outfit. We sat around drinkin' coffee, swappin' lies, and catchin' up on where different people that we knew were workin'.

We were there for an hour or so when Elaine said she had to go do some grocery shoppin'. I picked up the tab for lunch, and then Walt, Dean, and I retired to the bar where we could do some more catchin' up. After five or six drinks, Walt mentioned that he'd seen old Shorty Daniels down at Pat's Club earlier that day, so we set out in search of Shorty.

Half a dozen stops and several drinks later, Elaine found us. She didn't seem too interested in the fact that we hadn't found Shorty yet. She had quite a few things to say to Walt and almost as many to say to me. None of 'em were very complimentary, though. She brought up things that'd happened years ago, things I'd all but forgotten. Elaine hadn't. She was sure bristled up and on the peck when she drug poor old Walt out to their pickup. And that damn Dean, he just stood there with that silly grin on his face the whole time she was a-carryin' on.

I's sorry that the boy had to see what a grown man sometimes has to put up with once he decides to get hitched and is pullin' in a double harness. I's even sorrier that he had to hear the things that Elaine said to me. She took some minor little incidents that happened years ago and blew 'em all out of proportion.

Sure, it's true that I'd talked Walt into goin' into town with me once or twice when he shoulda gone home. And maybe he had gotten fired that last time 'cause we didn't get back to the ranch for a week or so. But hell, I never tried to get him to marry that little gal down at Sue's. That'd been his own idea. And he was the one drivin' when we wrecked their pickup on the way back from Battle Mountain. I sure couldn't see how Elaine could blame me for all that.

When we stepped outside, it was still fairly early, but it was already dark. I hadn't told Dean that I'd left most of my money back at Lonney's and I'd spent the last of it to buy a round or two of drinks. I knew Dean had most of his paycheck. Rather than tell him what I'd done right then, I suggested we call the Wilcoxes and go get a place to sleep.

We drove down to the Nevada Hotel, got a room, and used the pay phone in the hall. I told Mr. Wilcox that if the job was open, we'd be there in two days. He said that'd be fine and gave me directions. Then we went up and turned in.

The next mornin' Dean and I were both up early. I figured I was gonna have to tell him sooner or later what I'd done with my wages, so while Dean was gettin' dressed, I gave him the news. He was sittin' on the edge of the bed, pullin' his boots on, when I told him I's broke.

He just sat there for a minute or two; then he started to laugh.

I asked him what was so damn funny. I knew the kid had kind of a strange sense of humor, but it was then that I found out just how warped his mind was.

He said he thought I had most of my pay left, so he'd given Lonney's mom all of his except for ten dollars. He'd spent a good part of that last night. Now we were both busted, the truck was about outta gas, and we still owed the hotel for our room. I didn't think it was all that funny.

We'd taken most of our things outta the back of the truck the night before and had 'em in the room with us, so we started rummagin' through our gear to see what we could find to sell. About the only real extra tack that either of us had, 'sides some wore-out ropes and ol' saddle blankets, were the silver bit and spurs that I'd bought in Fallon. I sure hated the idea of gettin' rid of those spurs. They were about the only pretty thing I'd bought for myself in a lot of years. Dean said he thought we could get enough for the bridle to get us to Oregon. We sneaked out through the lobby and went out to see if we could find a gas station that would take the horse jewelry in on trade.

We wandered around town, stoppin' at every gas station we come to. Almost all of 'em would take the bridle on trade for one tankful, but none of 'em would give us any extra money.

Around nine, the pawnshop opened, and we went in. The guy behind the counter was a kinda snakey-lookin' little dude with a skinny black mustache and sunglasses. I've always been suspicious of people who wear sunglasses inside a buildin'. I figure they don't want you to know what they're lookin' at, or they don't want you to know they can't look you in the eye.

I knew the whole setup—silver bit, rawhide reins, headstall, and silver conchos—was worth easily $250. If I could have found the right person, I think I might even have been able to get $300. The price would be twice that today. The little man offered to loan us $50 for the outfit or buy it outright for $75.

Dean and I talked it over. Neither of us was sure how much it was gonna cost to get us up to the Wilcox place, so we decided to take the $75.

We went back, paid our bill at the hotel, and filled the truck with gas. We decided not to eat any breakfast and that we'd buy our other food outta grocery stores till we saw how far our money was gonna get us. Then we pulled out of town and got back on 95, headed north again.

Soon Dean and I were goin' past the turnoff to Paradise

Valley, and a thousand memories came rushin' back into my mind. It was right over the hill from here where I'd met Rose Mindeola. God, but she was a pretty girl. A little chunky, like a lot of Basco gals, but still prettier than a filly colt on a spring mornin'. She had long brown hair and big brown eyes that always seemed to sparkle and dance. From time to time, I still catch myself wonderin' whatever become of her. It was to Rosie that I come closest to gettin' married.

Right after World War II, there were thousands of mustangs on the ranges from the Black Rock over to Battle Mountain. The two Archuletta brothers, Albert and Pete, hired me to help 'em gather some. We were doin' it the old way, with saddle horses and pole traps.

When their two cousins Santiago and Jose Mindeola got discharged from the army, there was an old-style Basco family homecomin', and everyone in the area was invited.

Two things happened at that get-together. First off, the five of us formed a partnership and a small company to gather horses. The second was I met the Mindeola boys' sister, Rose.

We pooled our money and bought a little Piper Cub airplane and a stock truck. Jose had learned to fly in the army, and we figured with that plane we could really run hell out of the wild horses.

No one had used a plane to chase horses in that area, and they were easy to handle with it. Jose's brother, Santie, would fly along with him, and if any old breakback mare made a run for it, Santie'd dust her hide with a load of bird shot from his twelve-gauge.

A lot of other people were gatherin' horses about that

time, but we were the only ones with a plane, and we were sure cleanin' up the area. With the two Mindeolas in the air and me and the two Archulettas horseback on the ground, we were able to catch and ship almost 500 head every twenty or thirty days. Even at three cents a pound, we were averaging over $1,200 a month. It wasn't long 'fore we had the plane and truck paid for, free and clear, and were puttin' better than $200 a month in each of our bank accounts. That was a hell of a chunk of money back then when a top cowboy was makin' less than a hundred.

While all of this was goin' on, I'd got to takin' Rosie out every time I got a chance. She was teachin' school over north of Leonard Creek, and we didn't see each other all that often. When we did get together, though, we had a lot of fun, and I got to thinkin' of her as my girl.

One afternoon, we were on a picnic with her brothers and their wives when Rosie says, "Tap, you ought to start thinking about settling down. You're making good money now, but the horses aren't going to last forever. You ought to find yourself a little place and think about putting down roots and raising a family."

Well, I read all sorts of things into that little statement, and my old heart was a-beatin' like a bass drum. I figured she was tellin' me what she'd kinda like to do, and if she was a-wantin' to settle down with me and raise a litter of crumb snatchers, that sure suited me just fine.

A couple weeks later, I heard about a little three-hundred-head outfit up on Willow Creek that could be bought for $30,000, so I went up and took a look at it. The house wasn't much, but it could be fixed up without a lot of work. I'd have to do some hayin' in the summer to get all the cattle through the winter, but the meadows were in pretty fair shape, and it had good water rights. I offered the owner $25,000 for the place if he'd throw in the machinery and the work teams. He grabbed it so fast that I think I coulda given him considerably less. I paid him all the money I had in the bank as a down and agreed to let him stay on the place till fall. He was to keep that year's calf crop and gather the cattle for me.

I never said anything to anyone about what I'd done. I just kept sendin' the owner all the money I was makin' off the horses, with the idea that come fall, I'd surprise Rosie by takin' her out to see the place and askin' her to marry me at the same time.

It wasn't long after that when we got word that there were lots of horses down east of Tonopah. A couple of the ranchers there would not only let us keep what we caught, but would furnish the fuel for the plane and trucks, along with our groceries, if we'd come down and gather 'em.

We loaded up camp and moved. We ran horses way into October without a break. I have no idea how many we shipped out of that desert country, but we had to buy another truck and hire two drivers to haul all of 'em. When the boys decided to go home and visit their families, I went along with 'em. I figured it would be a good time to go out and count my cows and pop the question to Rose.

While we were at Santie's house, the first night back, his wife told him that Rose had gotten engaged to some feller that worked for the Forest Service and was fixin' to get married on Thanksgiving. Everyone joked and kidded with me about bein' too slow. I smiled and laughed right along with 'em, but when they loaded up to go back to Tonopah, I let 'em leave without me. That was the winter I drifted over to Elko and worked for the Spanish Ranch.

Dean and I made it clear to Baker, Oregon, 'fore I had to sell my silver spurs for more gas money and to get a flat tire fixed. I sure hated to get rid of those old things, but there wasn't much else we could do.

The feller at the fillin' station where we sold the spurs had given us a fair enough price for 'em. In fact, we even had enough left over to buy a decent meal, with a few dollars extra to travel on.

We spent the first part of that night sleepin' in the back of the truck out on the edge of town. About midnight, though, it started to rain, so we crawled in the cab and spent the rest of it tryin' to sleep sittin' up. I woke the next mornin' with a stiff neck and a back that felt like I'd been run over by a tank. From the way that Dean walked when he crawled outta the cab, I don't think he felt any better.

The rest of the trip up to the Imnaha country went by without any excitement. We stopped once and gassed up in La Grande. At a campground near Wallowa Lake, we washed and changed clothes.

We pulled up to the gate that led down to the Wilcoxes' Imnaha Land and Cattle Company sometime in the early afternoon. We were out of the sagebrush country now and not far enough north or high enough in elevation to be in the heavy timber, although there were some fairly large patches of trees.

When Mr. Wilcox had said that the area was rough, he sure wasn't kiddin'. The only places I'd ever seen that came close to it were the Bruneau River Canyon in Nevada and the area around Riggins, Idaho. Almost all of this land was steep, but there were a few little spots that, if I used my imagination, I could call rollin' hills. One thing about it, though, it had some of the finest grass I'd ever laid eyes on.

The windin' dirt road that led to the Wilcox headquarters was narrow. In several places, the sides of the canyon closed in so close, I think I could have reached out the window and touched 'em. The few cows I saw were in good shape and also of good quality, mostly blacks and black ballies. The fences were all up and in good repair, too.

The headquarters for the outfit sat at a wide spot where two steep little canyons came together. It consisted of an older, two-story house and a smaller new one, a metal shop, a single wide trailer that was used for a bunkhouse, and a log barn with a good set of pole corrals. All of this was crammed into an area smaller than ten acres, 'cause that's all the flat ground there was.

A little creek ran down past the back of the older house, and big cottonwood trees grew wherever they could take root. Both of the houses were painted up real nice and the yards were well kept, too. The machinery was all lined up out back of the shop. The seats on the tractors and haying equipment had been covered to protect 'em from the sun and rain. All in all, it made you feel like you were on a well-run outfit that made all of its income from the cattle it raised and not from some outside source, like a lot of places are doing today.

When we pulled into the driveway between the two houses, a younger woman came outta the smaller place, and a pack of black-and-white dogs appeared from every direction. The lady was slender and wore a long dress that came almost to her ankles. She wore her brown hair tied back in a bun. She asked if we were the two new men from Nevada, and when we told her that we were, she had us take our gear over to the trailer. She said the rest of the family was down at the lower place, weanin' some calves. It was hard to carry on much of a conversation with all the racket them pot-lickers were makin', but I did hear her say supper would probably be about seven and for us to go on over and rest up till then.

Dean asked if there was someplace where we could put our saddles. She pointed out a door at the end of the barn and said there was a tack room behind it. While we were unloadin' our gear, another half a dozen dogs came out from the back of the barn to take a leak on the tires of the truck and to sniff at our pants legs.

I'd just come out of the barn after takin' in the last load of our stuff when I looked up and saw the damnedest creature I ever laid eyes on. At first I wasn't sure just what it was, then I finally recognized it. Dean and I, neither one, had ever seen a baby buffalo before. It was about the size of a three-hundred-pound calf and uglier than sin. It came wanderin' over and rubbed up against Dean's leg. It was as gentle as a pet lamb.

After we got the truck unloaded, we started movin' into the trailer. Like everything else on the place, it wasn't fancy but it was neat and clean. There was no electricity, but it was rigged up with propane lights. It had runnin' water in the kitchen. The bathroom had been converted into a closet, but out back in the trees, where I couldn't see it, was an outhouse.

The beds looked inviting. I took the lady's advice and crashed on one of 'em.

It seemed like I'd no more than closed my eyes when the clangin' of a dinner bell woke me. Dean and I weren't sure just what we were supposed to do, so we wandered on over in the direction of the house where we'd met the lady. The buffalo came around the corner of the trailer and followed us.

We were standin' around out front when an older gentleman came out of the side door and motioned us over. He introduced himself to us as George Wilcox and invited us to come in and eat with his family. When we got inside, we found that the house was a lot bigger than it appeared from the front. In the dining room, three little kids and a younger man sat around a long wooden table. The man turned out to be the lady's husband. He was also George's son, Lonell. Sarah, the lady we'd first met, was in the kitchen finishin' up the last of the cookin'. This house, too, was lit by propane lights and a big, double-mantle Coleman lamp that hung over the table. The walls of the dining room were covered with photographs of ranch scenes and people who were friends and relatives.

From here on, I could take up a lot of time and tell about what all Dean and I did on a day-to-day basis for the next eight and a half months, but it wasn't all that exciting, so I'll just fill in the general details and a couple of the high points.

The Wilcox family turned out to be some of the finest people I ever met. Great-grandpa Jacob Wilcox and his brother George had come out to this part of the country as missionaries for some church based back East. That was sometime in the 1860s. They'd come out to work with the Indians.

When this religious outfit got word that Great-grandpa Jacob had fallen in love with one of his converts and married her, they cut off his funds and took away his preachin' license. His brother George was so upset over the church's attitude that he turned his collar around and quit, too.

The two brothers drifted to the Imnaha country and started a sheep outfit. From time to time, Jacob had some of his wife's red relatives work for him. This didn't make Jacob or George any too popular with their white neighbors.

When the Nez Perce Indian War started in the late 1870s, Jacob's brother-in-law was staying at his place. A group of local whites heard about it and decided to come over and string up the young buck. Jacob threw such a fit that one of his neighbors shot him, and the rest of the crowd went ahead and hung the brother-in-law.

Jacob's wife and their two kids, a little boy and girl, were hidin' in an ol' dugout back of the main set of buildin's. The mob didn't find them. When Jacob's brother George got back from tending camp and checkin' on their herders, he found all of the buildings burned and his brother dead. Later on, he married Jacob's wife and raised her two kids. He never had any children of his own.

The little girl grew up and married an Indian from up around Craigmont. The boy (I think they told me his name was Meshack or somethin' like that) stayed on the ranch, runnin' sheep with his Uncle George. While he was up visiting his sister on the reservation, he met a white schoolteacher, and a year or so later they were married. They named their only child, George, after his uncle.

This second George grew up and had a whole passel of kids, one of whom he named George. That third George was the old man who had greeted us. The second George is the one who built the big house we saw when we first pulled in. He's the one that switched from raisin' sheep to raisin' cattle.

Sometime in the early 1920s, there was an outbreak of influenza in this part of the country, and it wiped out the whole family except for young George. After his family all died, young George went to live with relatives up on the Nez Perce reservation, east of Lewiston. Because he's underage, the state or county leased out the ranch to neighbors.

George got to be quite a cowman and a hell of a horseman livin' there on the reservation, but he said he was never really accepted. When he was twenty-one, he went home and took over the ranch again. I guess he had one heck of a fight gettin' the place back from the neighbors that'd been leasin' it. They'd got to thinkin' of it as theirs, they'd had it for so long.

George ended up marryin' a daughter of one of these neighbors, which shoulda brought peace to the valley, but it didn't. His wife died a year later, givin' birth to Lonell. That started the feud all over again. Her folks blamed George for their daughter's death. That was thirty or forty years before we got there, and the families still had hard feelin's for each other.

I'm not sure just who helped George raise Lonell, 'cause he never got remarried. But Lonell did grow up and go off to college, where he married Sarah, the lady who had greeted us when we drove in.

The Wilcoxes only ran about 600 head of mother cows with another hundred or so head of replacement heifers. Their operatin' program was pretty much standard for that part of the country. They started calvin' the heifers in February, and the main cow herd started calvin' the latter part of March. They branded their calves in May and June, and then the cows ran in the higher country during the summer and were brought down nearer the house in September. It was also in September when they weaned the calves from the heifers. They weaned the main cow herd in October.

Somewhere along the line, one of the early family members had put in some irrigated pasture down in the bottoms of a couple of little valleys. They irrigated these fields with wheel-line sprinklers and cut them for hay. They used this hay to feed the calves after they'd been weaned and to feed the first calf heifers and older cows through the winter. The main herd was wintered out.

The third thing that made this operation so different was that the cattle spent six months of the year on the Oregon side of the Snake River. Come mid-October, the main herd was moved to the Idaho side of the Snake and wintered over there.

In the ol' days, they swam the cattle from one side to the other, but now the Wilcoxes had rigged up a barge that ferried the cattle across. This barge system was quite the deal. It consisted of two sets of corrals, one on each side of the river. These corrals were set up where the river was about 250 yards wide. They were laid out in two pens, a big one and a smaller one. A crowding alley led from the smaller pen down to the river's edge, where it opened at the place the barge was tied. The whole setup was made of stout logs, standing about six-and-a-half feet tall.

The cattle were herded into the corral, where they were cut into drafts of twenty head. The animals were driven down the alley to the barge and ferried from one side to the other. The barge itself was a large, flat-bottomed boat about twenty feet long and maybe fifteen feet wide.

There was an inch-and-a-half cable that ran across the river from one set of corrals to the other and was suspended above the water by two large, steel-framed, A-shaped structures. On the Oregon side was an old diesel engine that powered the pulley system, towing the barge back and forth.

The Forest Service or some other government agency wouldn't let the Wilcoxes leave the cable up across the river all year long, so when it wasn't in use, it was taken down and stored on a big roll. To rig it up, a nylon rope was tied to the loose end of the cable and this rope was towed across the river by motorboat. The rope was then used to pull the cable across.

Ferrying the cattle was a slow process, and it took us two-and-a-half days to get all 500 head from one side to the other, but it was still a lot safer than swimmin' the cattle across the Snake.

Dean and I were to spend the winter in a camp on the Idaho side. It consisted of a nice two-story log cabin, a log barn, a good set of pole horse corrals, and a sixty-acre roundup field. Down by the water, not far from where the shippin' corrals were set up, was a boat dock and a storage shed. Protein block was kept in the shed. Part of our job was to haul this block out to the cattle.

The land on both sides of the river was steep, but the Idaho side was the steepest. It was flat for about a quarter of a mile back from the river, then it started to climb pretty fast. The elevation at our camp was between 1,500 and 2,000 feet. It climbed to about 7 or 8,000 feet at the summit, but the cattle never got that high 'cause of the snow. This snow acted as a natural fence, keepin' the cattle on our side of the mountain. It rained a lot down in the canyon and snowed occasionally. Sometimes there were long periods of heavy fog.

The winter range was divided into four units, or fields. The cattle were kept in each unit for about six weeks and then moved to the next one. We started out usin' the fields farthest from our camp. That way, each time the cattle were moved, they got a little closer to the roundup meadow.

Drift fences ran from up in the higher country down to the river. In a lot of places, natural rock barriers acted even better than fences. Part of our job was to put up the fences and close the gates before the cattle were moved to that area. The fences in the lower country were usually in pretty good shape, but there was a lot of snow damage the farther up the hill we went.

Before Dean and I ever got moved to the Idaho camp, we spent a week or so helpin' gather the cattle off the fall range. When that was done, we brought 'em in and finished weanin' the calves.

Durin' the week or so we were waitin' for the cows to

quit bawlin', we ran 'em through the chute, where they were vaccinated for half a dozen diseases and preg tested by a vet. The old broken-mouth cows were sold, along with the ones the vet had called open.

It took us about three weeks to get all of this cow work done, along with gettin' our camp set up and some of the fences fixed over on the Idaho side.

CHAPTER *20*

After Dean and I'd been at the Wilcox head-quarters about a week, Lonell asked if I'd like to ride into town with him. He'd made arrangements to give the buffalo calf to a small private zoo south of Boise. They were supposed to meet him in La Grande and take the calf from there.

Durin' the drive into town, Lonell told me that the calf had been given to his kids by some of his Idaho relatives. They'd raised it on a bottle, but now it was gettin' too big to keep around as a pet, and he figured they'd best get rid of it while it was still small and cute.

We had the calf inside the stock racks on the back of Lonell's pickup when we met the people from the zoo out on the edge of town. They showed up in a car, pullin' a small trailer. They'd probably had the trailer made to haul sheep and goats around, 'cause the sides were only about three feet high. After we got the buffalo loaded, he stood a foot or so taller than the sides of the trailer.

By the time we finished movin' the little animal and

visitin', it was close to noon, so Lonell said he'd buy everyone a sandwich if we could find a place close by. The people from the zoo said they'd passed one of them convenience stores back up the road a ways.

When everyone got there, we all went inside and picked out some ready-made sandwiches and some soda pop. We were leanin' up against the pickup when one of the zoo men looked over at the trailer and let out a gasp. The buffalo was gone!

All of us threw our sandwiches in the front seat of the pickup and took off, runnin' up and down the street in different directions. We'd only been in the store about fifteen minutes; we didn't figure the little beast could get too far in that length of time, but no one we talked to had seen it.

We'd all gotten back together and were discussin' what to do next when we heard a whole army of police car sirens come blarin' down the street. Without sayin' a word, everyone jumped in the pickup, and we took off in the direction of the sirens.

When we stopped, there were three police cars pulled up in front of a small house on a quiet side street. Out front a man was tryin' to quiet a hysterical woman while a little boy of about five stood by. The police were checkin' their weapons and discussin' battle plans.

Lonell jumped outta the truck and ran up to the policemen. I didn't get there in time to hear what he said, but he and one of the officers started off in the direction of a side gate that led to the backyard. In a few minutes, Lonell came out of the yard, leadin' the little calf. The baby buffalo had a dress hung over its head, and its eyes were bugged halfway out of their sockets. I could tell he was almost as terrorized as the hysterical mother.

Lonell held the calf while the two zoo people took a truck back and picked up their car and trailer. While they were gone, the lady's husband told us the story of what'd happened.

It seems he and his wife had been in the kitchen, workin' on a plugged drain, while their little boy was out front, playin' in the yard. I guess the buffalo calf came wanderin' down the street and saw the little boy. He's about the same size as Lonell's kids, so the calf went over to visit. The kid took off screamin' into the house, yellin' that a monster was after him. Junior was so scared he forgot to shut the front door. The buffalo followed the little guy right on in.

When the father and mother came into the room to see what all the racket was about, they found the kid treed up on the couch, with the buffalo tryin' to lick his face. They didn't know the animal was a house pet and thought it was tryin' to hurt their little darlin'. The woman attacked first with her broom, and the father came in second with a baseball bat.

With the parents beatin' on him and screamin' like crazy people, the buffalo took off, tryin' to get away. I reckon from what they said, a bull in a china shop can't do near as much damage as a baby buffalo in a living room. What he didn't knock over and break, he crapped on. Lonell went in and looked, then came back and told me that the place was sure 'nough a wreck.

The zoo people arrived about then, and we loaded the terrified little creature back into their trailer. We were just about to pull out when the father came over and wanted

175

to know who was gonna pay for all of the damage.

Lonell looked over at the zoo men and said, "He became your animal when we loaded him into the trailer the first time. You answer the man." And with that he and I got in the pickup and took off.

It had been a long time since I laughed as much as I did that afternoon on the way back to the ranch.

Once the cattle were all across the river, the four of us—George, Lonell, Dean, and I—moved 'em north to the farthest unit. It took us two days to make the drive. It wasn't all that far. It was just slow goin' 'cause the country was so steep and the trail was only one cow wide in a lot of places. Those Wilcoxes had some hellacious good dogs, and if it hadn't been for them mutts, it might have taken us even longer.

After the cattle were all settled down, Dean and I set up our own routine. We got up every mornin' 'bout five. One of us would go down and grain the pack string and saddle horses, while the other one fixed breakfast. After we ate, we'd saddle up our ridin' horses and put the pack outfits on eight head of old, gentle, camp horses. We'd lead the pack string down to the storage shed near the river and load four protein blocks on each animal. These blocks weighed fifty pounds apiece, so we were haulin' out a little over three-quarters of a ton everyday.

We'd drag those poor ol' pack horses up and down the trail everyday, except for when we'd be changin' units or fixin' fence. Of course, there were times when the weather would shut us down for a day or so, too. The canyon was so deep and narrow where the camp sat that it was always dark when we left and dark when we got home. When the cattle were in the two farthest units, we never got back before nine at night. Later on, after the cattle were moved a little closer, we started gettin' in at a decent hour.

Ol' George'd come over at least once a week. He'd bring us our groceries and ride with us. He usually came over the night before so as to be there in the mornin' while we were saddlin' up. I don't know that George wanted to check on us and the cattle so much as he just liked to ride and look at the country. He knew every rock and tree on his range, and he truly loved the land.

He kept an old motorboat on the Oregon side of the river, and that was his transportation back and forth. One night it quit on him 'bout halfway across. He drifted downstream for fifteen miles in the dark 'fore he found a place where he could get out and call Lonell to come get him.

On the evenings when George would come, we'd stay up late, and he'd tell us stories about the history of this part of the river country. He'd also bring us newspapers, and he liked to discuss all of the political news that was in 'em.

Most nights, though, we'd just come in and fix supper. Then I'd read for an hour or so, and Dean would write letters. He was the writin'est cuss I ever saw. I think he wrote to everyone he ever met.

As I mentioned before, this was about the easiest, most unexciting winter I'd spent in a long time. The eight saddle horses were all gentle, and the eight head of pack animals were even gentler. The weather was fairly mild and pleasant, except for the fog.

Also, as I told you before, the Wilcoxes were some of the finest people that ever walked the face of the earth.

Almost every week when George would bring over our groceries and Dean's mail, there'd be a big batch of cookies or a pie or cake. There was always fresh bread, and the store-bought food was the same stuff they put on their own table.

At Christmas, Mrs. Wilcox sent over a huge basket of homemade candy and cookies. She also made each of us a new shirt, and Lonell gave us both a folding buck knife. Ol' George just stuck in two $50 bills with a note that said, "Thanks for doing such a good job."

In that same Christmas basket were my silver spurs that Dean and I'd sold in Baker. The Wilcoxes said they didn't know how they got there, and Dean denied askin' the Wilcoxes to buy 'em back for me. I'm a little too old to start believin' in Santie Claus again, so I'm pretty sure Dean put them folks up to it. In any case, I's sure glad to see them spurs again, and I got kind of a lump in my throat when I found 'em.

Dean took a week off at New Year's and drove into Boise. From there he took a plane down to Reno, where he met his dad and spent a few days with him. I guess they hadn't seen each other for quite a spell.

The only thing of any consequence that happened that winter took place sometime in February. It wasn't much, but it did kinda break up the routine and gave us somethin' different to talk about for a few days.

On this particular occasion, Dean spent the day fixin' fence up near the snow line in the third field, while I hauled out a load of protein block. When he got in that night, he told me that he'd met two Indians up there. He said they were both afoot and dressed in old-style clothes with lots of fur and skins. They had long hair worn in braids. He said they looked like something you woulda expected to see a hundred years ago, except for their guns. They both wore big .44 Magnum six-shooters and carried modern rifles with telescopic sights.

They spent the noon hour with Dean, talkin' about nothin' in particular. They swapped their homemade jerky to Dean for his Spam sandwiches. After lunch they drifted back into the snow country.

Later that week when George came over to ride with us, Dean told him about the visitors. It was hard to see the old man's features in the light of the kerosene lamp, but I saw him rub his chin and shake his head. Then he said, "No one I know's seen those two for some time now. Most folks figured they's dead."

Well, you can't make a statement like that without tellin' the rest of the story, so with a little coachin', Dean got old George to fill us in on the details.

It seems that when these two were just kids, they were always playin' like they were raised in the old days. They'd go out and live off the land, eatin' wild plants and animals. When they were in their teens, they got into some sorta scrape with a game warden over an elk they'd killed. No one knows what really happened, but the game warden ended up dead, and the two kids lit out for the backcountry. Over the years, they were reported bein' seen all the way from the Selway to the Seven Devils.

The shootin' had taken place several years ago, and the boys would now be grown men. Most people who even remembered the incident figured they were dead, 'cause it had been so long since there'd been any sightings. We never saw 'em again, but every now and then we'd see what looked like a moccasin track in the mud or snow.

A year or two ago, Lonell sent Dean a letter and a newspaper clippin'. I guess the two men had gone back to the reservation to visit relatives, and someone turned 'em in. In the ruckus that followed, one of the boys was killed, and the other hung himself in his jail cell.

When the first of March came, we helped string up the cable for the barge and began ferryin' the cattle back across the river, because the Wilcoxes wanted the cattle on the Oregon side 'fore they started to calve and 'fore the river got too high. Dean and I got in on the last part of calvin' the heifers and stuck around till the middle of April 'fore we decided to drift on.

We could tell that the Wilcoxes didn't really need us anymore. An outfit as small as that can't afford two full-time men. Dean and I talked it over, and one evenin' after supper, we told George and Lonell that come the end of the month, we'd be pullin' out. There were a lot of halfhearted attempts at askin' us to stay, but you could tell they's happy that they weren't the ones who had to let us go.

Come the night of April 29, Mrs. Wilcox had a special dinner for us. The next day she packed us a huge dinner basket to take along. George came out and gave us our checks. Even with all of the social security and taxes taken out, we each still got close to $2,000. Then he slipped us both another hundred-dollar bill. Lonell went into the house about this time and came back with two big boxes. In them were two brand new hats, just like the old beat-up ones that we were wearin'. Then the kids all came up and hugged us and began to cry.

As we were leavin', Lonell asked where we were headin'. Dean said we'd know that when we got there. Ol' George said, "Why don't you give the Lazy J a call? When I's in Baker last week, I heard they's lookin' for help down south."

With that Dean and I pulled out of the yard and headed for the blacktop.

CHAPTER 21

ean and I stopped at the little town of Joseph and bought a case of beer. It was the first alcohol that either of us had had to drink in seven months. By the time we'd driven the five or ten miles to Wallowa Lake, we were both pretty light-headed. Dean decided to pull off the road at the lake and wait till he sobered up 'fore drivin' any further.

We found an open campsite and parked. I laid down under a big tree with the rest of the case beside me. It was cool layin' in the shade. I'd doze off for a while, wake up, drink another beer, and sleep again.

Dean went down and jumped in the ice-cold lake. Then he came up and laid down, too. As soon as his pants were dry, he'd go down and jump in again. After about an hour of this, I was dead drunk and Dean was stone sober. I don't remember anything about the trip back to Baker City, not even gettin' in the truck. The next thing I do remember was wakin' up the followin' mornin' in the motel room.

We spent that day gettin' haircuts and buyin' all new clothes. I got four pair of Levi's, seven new shirts, and half a dozen sets of underwear and socks. I think Dean bought about the same number of the same things, only he bought a swimming suit, too. There was a covered pool at the motel, and he planned on usin' it.

In the afternoon, we found a little western store where I got a new saddle blanket, and Dean bought a slicker. While we were payin' our bill, we asked the owner about jobs in the area. He said that there were only a few outfits that ran cattle year-round. He thought the country was too high and got too much snow to be a good cow-calf location. The people who did run cows through the winter spent their summers irrigatin' and puttin' up hay and their winters feedin' it out. He suggested that we try some of the places that ran yearlings. He gave us a list of half a dozen but didn't seem to think we'd find the type of jobs that we were lookin' for.

For right now, though, we were in no big hurry to find anything. We bought a couple more cases of beer and a half a dozen sacks of ice. We took all of this home to our motel room, where we turned the bathtub into a giant cooler. I spent the next couple of days layin' in bed, watchin' ol' western movies on TV, sippin' my cold beer, and eatin' chips. In the evenin's, we'd go out and have a good meal at one of the restaurants. Then it was back home to the TV for me. I was havin' a great time catchin' up on all the ol' movies that I'd missed as a kid. I couldn't seem to get enough of Hoot Gibson, Tom Mix, William Hart, Tex Ritter, and the rest of 'em.

Dean spent his days layin' around the pool, soakin' up

the sun. At first he looked a little silly, 'cause his whole body was as white as a sheet except for his hands and his face. They were tanned dark brown. He looked like a ghost with gloves and a mask on. By and by, he struck up an acquaintance with the little gal who tended the desk at night. When she'd get off from work at two in the mornin', he'd take her out to eat. He usually wouldn't get back till sometime around eight.

We followed this pattern for a week or so until one mornin' when Dean came stompin' in and woke me. He said, "Let's get packed up and start lookin' for work. We've been layin' around here long enough."

From the sound of his voice, I could tell he'd had some sorta fallin' out with his lady friend. I could also tell from the sound of his voice that this wasn't the time to be askin' about it. While I's showerin' and shavin', Dean got on the phone and started makin' calls. He lined up a couple of people who wanted to talk with us. By the time I got outta the bathroom, he had the truck packed and was waitin'.

The very first place we stopped was the headquarters for the yearling operation of the Lazy J. That was the outfit George had told us about as we were leavin' the Imnaha.

Very few people in the cow business haven't heard of the Lazy J. They have a big feedlot down in California, a large cow-calf operation in southern Oregon, and several other ranches where they run yearlings through the spring and summer months.

Their headquarters was a few miles north of town, just off the main road. It was sure an impressive place, with all of the big irrigated meadows, manicured lawns, and freshly painted buildin's. It turned out this was just one of several ranches they owned or leased in this area.

We pulled up in front of a comfortable little buildin' that sat back in the shade of some big trees. It had a sign over the door tellin' everyone who could read that it was the office. We introduced ourselves to a young lady inside and told her why we were there. She picked up a microphone from her desk and talked into it. As soon as she was done, out came a bunch of squawkin' and poppin' noises, with a few other sounds that could kinda be mistaken for English. Then the lady turned to us and explained that the manager was someplace on the ranch in his pickup, and that he'd be back in a few minutes.

A half hour or so later, a pickup came to a stop out front, and a tall slender man in his early forties got out. He wore western slacks, shined boots, a short-sleeved shirt, sunglasses, and a western hat. When he came inside, the lady at the desk introduced us and told him why we were there.

He shook hands and pointed toward a side door without ever sayin' a word. Dean and I followed him into his office. The walls were plastered with maps, framed awards, degrees from different schools, and signed pictures of different rodeo stars. On a shelf in back of his desk was a big glass-covered case with twenty or thirty oval trophy buckles in it. Even though I couldn't read the inscriptions, I could tell they were for team ropin' and calf ropin' by the little gold figures on 'em. He was a perfect example of the modern-day cowman, the kinda person who causes changes and makes things happen within the industry. He was educated, confident, and a little arrogant. I didn't like him. He made me feel unimportant. He also represented change and progress. I's happy with the way things used to be.

He didn't waste any words with small talk or social chatter. He asked if that was our truck out front and our gear in the back. I knew then he's smart enough and had been around enough to size up a man by his tack. He could tell from our dirty bedroll tarps we weren't fresh from the city. The slick fork, high-cantle saddles told him we were probably from the northern part of Nevada or California or the southern part of Oregon or Idaho. Our long ropes and latigo-wrapped saddle horns meant we were most likely outside men, not arena ropers. The fact that the truck was clean and our saddles were well oiled may have told him we took pride in our work and were probably conscientious.

At this point, he looked us both in the eye for a second or two. Then he leaned back, locked his hands behind his head, and said, "Gentlemen, the Lazy J is a large, integrated, livestock operation. We have ranch holdings from California to the Canadian border. We have a feedlot in Fresno that fattens over a hundred thousand head of cattle every year. Most of these animals we either own outright or are partnered in a joint venture with other investors. We have our own slaughterhouse and are exploring the possibility of marketing the meat that we produce under our own trade name. We hire hundreds of people and offer not only top wages but an excellent fringe-benefit program for our permanent employees. For those people who work for us and then decide to leave for some reason, if they have given us fair notice of their intent to terminate and have performed adequately, their names are entered on a computerized list. They are then given preferential treatment and consideration should they decide to come back."

The fancy-dressed man stopped for a second, probably to get his wind. Before he got started this time, though, Dean leaned forward and said, "Save the B.S., mister. We came here lookin' for ridin' jobs. We aren't interested in any fringe benefits or retirement programs. All we want is a string of horses and some cattle to look after. If you need someone, say so; if not, let us know, and we won't take up anymore of your time."

I coughed and then swallowed. This was a side of the kid I'd never seen before. I figured that was the end of this interview and was gettin' ready to get up and leave when the tall man unfolded his arms and turned to the computer that sat on the side of his desk. He typed in some letters and numbers. A list appeared on the screen. He scanned it and said, "At eight o'clock this morning we needed one pen rider in Fresno and two buckaroos at the southern Oregon ranch. We can also use three tractor operators, a mill man, and two killing-floor employees. Are you interested in any of these jobs?"

Dean said, "We'll take the two ridin' jobs on the southern outfit."

The manager picked up the phone and dialed a number. Then he laid it in a little holder that was wired to the computer. He typed in some more letters and then asked for our names and social security numbers. When we'd given 'em to him, he typed them into the computer too. With that, he hung up the phone and turned off the computer.

He told us we were hired and would be expected to be at work within forty-eight hours. If we didn't show up by

187

then, the jobs would be reopened. He also told us to keep the receipts for our gas and to turn them into the ranch office when we got there. We'd be reimbursed for our travelin' expenses at the time we received our first check.

With that, he got up, indicatin' that the interview was over. He never offered to shake hands or even say good-bye. He walked out of his room, leavin' us to follow. At the desk, he told the girl to give us a company employee's folder and map to the southern ranch. While we were waitin' for our map and folders, he got in his pickup and drove off.

When we were in our own truck, I asked Dean what in the hell was the matter with him.

He laughed and told me that he hated bein' talked down to. Then he fired up the little truck, and we were off again. He looked at the map that came with the employee's packet the secretary had given us and said we'd head on down to Ontario, cuttin' west towards Burns.

We stopped that afternoon and had lunch in Vale. After we finished eatin', we gassed up the truck, and I bought a case of beer. Dean wouldn't have any part of the drinkin' now. He's like that. He'd party with you for just so long, and then he was through for a couple of months. That suited me just fine.

We drove along, followin' the Malhuer River over to Juntura, where we stopped to use the restroom, and I bought another case. By now it was startin' to get on toward evenin', and I was pretty well on my way to gettin' real soused. Dean went into a little diner and bought himself somethin' to eat. I stayed in the truck and drank my supper.

I think I either fell asleep or passed out, 'cause the next

thing I knew, it was just startin' to crack dawn. I squirmed around on the pickup seat and started to sit up. The movement sent my head to throbbin' and my stomach spinnin'. In an instant, I knew I's gonna be sick. I only hoped I'd be able to get the door open 'fore I puked. I was hangin' on the side of the truck, heavin' my guts out, when Dean crawled out the other side and walked over to where I was gaggin' and moanin'.

He looked at me, grinnin' that big silly grin of his, and said, "You look like hell. What'd you do, pee your pants or spill your beer?"

I looked down at the big wet spot in the front of my pants and shook my head. That started the world to spinnin' again, and I started gaggin' and retchin' all over again. Nothin' was comin' out but the noise.

Dean crawled over the tailgate into the back of the truck and started diggin' out some clean clothes for me. He mumbled somethin' about the pleasures of social drinkin'.

I couldn't make out what he said, but I let it pass 'cause I figured it was just another one of his smart remarks.

By and by, my stomach began to settle down, and I was able to let go of the side of the truck. I straightend up and looked around. I saw we were back in the high-desert, sagebrush country again. The land was fairly flat with a big string of mountains way off to the east. There wasn't a tree in sight. The truck was parked off to the side of a dirt road that was fenced on both sides. About fifty yards ahead was one of those big archway gates with a sign hangin' from the crosspiece. From where we were, I couldn't read what it said.

Dean handed me my clean clothes and said, "Hop in.

We passed a stock water pond back aways. We'll go there and you can clean up a bit."

We had to drive past the gate to find a place wide enough to turn the truck around. As we did, I looked up and read the sign. As soon as I did, my stomach started to churn all over again. This time I wasn't sure if it was from the booze or from what the sign read. In big white letters it said, "FLYING D RANCH." Under that, in smaller letters, it read, "Lazy J Cattle Company."

Everyone I knew had heard of the Flyin' D. It was as well known as the ol' Miller and Lux outfit. Only I didn't know it was part of the Lazy J corporation. The last I'd heard, it was supposed to be owned by some insurance company. I looked over at Dean and asked, "Haven't you ever heard of the Flyin' D before?"

Dean shook his head.

I told him that for as long as I could remember, the Flyin' D had had a reputation for havin' the rankest horses in the country. When I's a kid, it was said that if you could ride an average string of Flyin' D horses, you could ride rough string for any other outfit around.

The last thing I'd heard about the ranch was that they had some crazy bastard by the name of Red somethin' or other for a cow boss. The story was that he'd come there as a kid from a reform school up in Portland. The school had paroled him to the ranch on the condition that if he made good, he wouldn't have to spend his time behind bars.

This Red was such a rotten little creep, the cowboys had tried to kill him every way they could, short of shootin' or stabbin'. They cut him a string of horses that got him bucked off four and five times a day. They put him in the crowdin' alley afoot to sort cattle and then tried to drive the whole herd over the top of him. In the summer, they made him night herd the cavvy and then wrestle calves all day. One time they sent him out with a pickup load of salt to take to the farthest camp, only they didn't tell him the gas gauge didn't work. He had to walk thirty or forty miles back in the summer sun. At different times they put sand in his bed, salt in his coffee, and Ex-Lax in his food. One winter they put him in a camp with a man they knew was nuts. Rumor had it this crazy feller had even killed a man or two.

But Red had sand, and he stuck. In a year or two, he became the rough-string rider, and a few years after that, he was made buckaroo boss. Now he was the man pullin' the strings and makin' everyone else dance. It was said that at twenty-five, he was a top hand with either a horse or a rope and really knew how to handle cattle. But, it was also said that he was big, tough, and mean.

I told Dean all of this while I was washin' up in the warm, muddy water of the stock pond. After I crawled out and got my clean clothes on, I began to feel a little more human. After tellin' him all these war stories, I was hopin' Dean would decide that maybe we should look someplace else for a summer job. But he'd made up his mind about goin' out with the wagon of a big outfit, and he wasn't gonna let a few wild tales get in his path. In a way, I think he was lookin' at this job as sort of a test. He wanted to see just how well he measured up to a crew of real wild, wooly, bronc-stompin' buckaroos. In his mind there was the question, "Am I good enough to make it on one of these big outfits or not?" I'd felt that way once, but that had been a lotta years ago.

When I was done washin' and gettin' dressed, we built a sagebrush fire on the bank of the pond and heated up some water. Then we both shaved. When he was done, Dean ate the last of a bag of cookies he'd bought someplace the night before. I couldn't even stand to watch him put one in his mouth, let alone eat one of the damn things myself. I judged it to be close to seven when we got back in the truck and headed down the road that led to the headquarters of the Flyin' D.

When we took off, I could tell Dean was pretty buzzed up. He was startin' to talk more and ask a lot of questions. He did that when he got nervous. In most cases, I'd had too many years and too many places behind me to start gettin' excited over the prospects of a new job. But, I had a feelin' this time that this one was gonna be somethin' to remember—if I lived through it.

CHAPTER *22*

From the road I couldn't see the long winding meadow that made up the main part of the deeded ground belonging to the Flying D Ranch. It sat down in a valley where several small creeks come together at the head of a canyon, makin' one larger one. Through the years it was this larger stream that had cut and widened the valley.

In the early rush to settle California and Oregon, no one paid much attention to the willow-choked canyon. It was a good place to camp and rest the stock for a few days, but the idea of settlin' there never entered anyone's mind. There was so much good open ground farther north and west that tryin' to carve a homestead in the dry open country just didn't seem worth it. By the late 1800s and early 1900s, though, most of the better ground in the West had been taken up. People were now willin' to work a little harder to get a place of their own. That was when the settlers started movin' into this area.

Over the years, five families settled along the creek. They cleared the willows from the bottoms, irrigated the new ground with water from the stream, and ran their cattle up on the desert durin' the early spring and into the summer. While the cattle were off the meadows, they irrigated and cut hay in the canyon. The only fences in the country then were around these meadows.

When what little natural water there was on the desert dried up, the early settlers brought the cattle down to the meadows. They pastured the stubble until it was gone. Then they started feedin' the hay they'd put up durin' the summer.

In those days, it didn't take as much to keep a person happy, and none of these early ranches ran more than a hundred and fifty head. They lived in small houses made of native rock and built their corrals outta willows.

As the years passed, more and more water was developed up on the desert flats. Dirt storage tanks and reservoirs were dug, and dams were built across the little washes. Durin' the Depression of the thirties, President Roosevelt had the CCC boys put in windmills.

The five separate ranches were bought and sold back and forth by the different neighbors. Sometime in the mid-thirties, they all came under the ownership of one family named DeWitt. In the early sixties, the Dewitts sold to a big California corporation. This corporation drilled some deep wells and put in several circular-pivot, irrigation systems at the south end of the canyon. They also started cross-fencin' the big desert allotments.

In the end, the Californians went broke and lost the ranch to an insurance company that ran it for a few years. The insurance people sold it to the Lazy J outfit. There was now enough water on the desert to summer

6,000 head of mother cows. In the fall they were brought in and pastured on the irrigated fields at the south end of the valley. The calves were weaned and shipped while the cattle were down there. As winter came on, the cattle were moved farther north into the deeper more protected part of the canyon, where they were fed after the fields were pastured off.

These were the facts that Dean and I learned over the next four months while working at the Flying D. But when we first drove under the big arch gate, we knew nothin' of the history and had no idea where the road we were on was goin'. That's why it was such a shock to us when we suddenly came to a spot where the road seemed to end. What it actually did was run up to the rim and then drop over the edge in a series of switchbacks to the valley floor.

When we stopped there, we saw a beautiful green valley stretched out below us. It was probably a quarter to half a mile wide. We could see a large reservoir at the head of the valley and another about halfway down. The water from the wheel-line sprinklers that were irrigatin' the meadow looked like silver ribbons in the mornin' sun.

At the foot of the rim, sittin' in a grove of large poplar trees, was the headquarters. Lookin' south a couple of miles, I could see two more stands of big poplar trees. The road leadin' down was fairly steep but not all that bad. At the two places where it switched back, it had been widened. Still, it woulda been hard to run big cattle trucks up and down right here. The road they used was farther to the south, where the valley wasn't as deep and not as steep.

Within an hour after we'd arrived at the headquarters, we'd each been issued a tepee and shown where to store our extra gear and Dean's truck. We had loaded our bedrolls and tack into a company pickup and were ready to be hauled out to the buckaroo camp.

While we were switchin' our stuff from one truck to another, Dean told me that you could tell this was "a well-organized, fast-movin', smooth-runnin' operation, geared for maximum production. People here were just another type of machinery necessary for the operation of the business." This was a big change from the Williams' place where we felt like part of the family.

Our driver was one of the hay hands. They called 'em "rawzin jaws" in that part of the country. This guy was kind of a talkative cuss and was willin' to tell us everything he knew about the company, the people who worked on the ranch, the economy of the nation, and the social problems of the world. I thought his views on the ranch were kinda interestin', considerin' the fact that he said he'd only been there for three months.

We drove south down the valley, passin' acre after acre of irrigated pastures. I've no idea how many wheel-line sprinklers we went by, but it musta numbered in the hundreds.

A few miles down the valley, we came to a side canyon and turned. A road led up to the rim, and we climbed out of the valley on it. We drove for another forty miles in a southwesterly direction. At first, the country was fairly flat, but gradually it began to change and became more rollin', with large outcroppings of lava here and there.

We drove for better than two hours. Durin' that time

we never passed another vehicle, buildin', or man, not even a cow. We only crossed two fence lines. We did go by quite a few dirt water tanks, and I saw several windmills.

Sometime around noon, we pulled up on a little ridge. The feller doin' the drivin' stopped and used the radio in the pickup to call headquarters to tell 'em that he'd made it that far okay. Down below us at the foot of one of the lava buttes lay the camp. I could tell there was a natural spring there by the small stockade corral built around a water trough. Over closer to the foot of the butte sat the camp itself.

There was a military, four-wheel-drive truck with a twenty-foot box on the back. This rig turned out to be the cook wagon, and the box was the kitchen. Parked next to it was another army surplus truck with a two-thousand-gallon water tank on the back. And next to these two rigs were two of those twelve-foot, canvas-covered, army trailers. All the vehicles were painted white.

Surroundin' this layout and scattered through the brush were half a dozen tepees. Out about a hundred yards and settin' off by itself was a small, sixteen-foot camp trailer. To the south a mile or so, I could make out the cavvy, grazin' 'tween two little hills. Looked like there was probably sixty or seventy head of horses in it.

When the driver was done with his radio call, we drove on down to the camp. The cook came outta the kitchen on the back of the army truck. He was a short little guy of about fifty. He spoke with some sort of an accent and introduced himself as Frenchy DuBeau. He invited the three of us in and poured everyone a cup of coffee.

We were told the crew would be back in a couple of

hours and for us to set our tents up anyplace we wanted. He said he usually served supper around five, but that depended on when the boys got in.

After a quick sandwich, the driver took off for the ranch, and Dean and I set about findin' a place for our tents. While I was gettin' my gear moved into mine, the cook came over and struck up a conversation. He was a likable little feller, not grumpy and sullen like a lot of those grub slingers. Over the years, I've found that most cooks are about half crazy. Old Mike Christensen once told me that standin' over a hot stove and smellin' all that burned grease affected their brains. In any case, Frenchy wasn't like that; leastways, not until Dean got him riled and he quit. That was a couple months later though.

Frenchy told me the cow boss's name was Red McKlosky, and the rest of the crew except for the horse wrangler were all nothin' but a bunch of snot-nosed kids. He said Red was a quiet sort except when he got stirred up, and then he was a tiger. Frenchy said it took someone like Red with his temper to keep this pack of juvenile delinquents in line.

He went on to say that one of these kids, a boy named Donnie, was probably nuts. He figured that, at best, this Donnie was at least a homicidal maniac. Another kid from California named Roy spent most of his time hidin' out in the brush, readin' his Bible. Frenchy figured Roy did that 'cause he believed Donnie was gonna kill him.

The cook called big Dan Walgamont "The Bear", 'cause he was covered with fur from foretop to fetlocks. About the only place he didn't have any hair was the soles of his feet and the palms of his hands. Dan wasn't quite as crazy as Donnie, but he ran a close second.

Everyone kept an eye on him 'cause he carried a big pistol on his left hip and spent most of his spare time shootin' at anything that moved. If he couldn't find any rabbits or other varmints to kill, he shot at anthills, sagebrush, rocks, and cans.

The twins, Tim and Tom, from over in Jordan Valley, probably came the closest to being normal. The only problem Frenchy saw with them was they'd been raised out in the brush and had never been away from home till that summer. When they weren't workin', they stuck closer together than two breedin' dogs. Frenchy believed the twins were scared to death of Don and Bear, and thought Roy was some sort of religious fanatic.

Ol' Pat, the horse wrangler, was a little guy about my age. Even though he was part of the crew, he never mixed with the younger men. He spent most of his time with the horses and always tried to time it so he wouldn't have to eat with the others. In fact, right then while we were talkin', he was over by the cook wagon, eatin' his supper. That way, he could take off when the boys came in. He was an honest-to-God loner. No one knew anything about him except he's from Arizona and he'd come up every summer for the past five years to wrangle horses for Red. When the wagon pulled into headquarters, he left and no one saw him again till the next spring.

Frenchy was just gettin' ready to start tellin' me about himself when another one of those big army surplus trucks came bouncin' in. This one had an eighteen-foot stock rack on the back. Up front, attached to the stock rack and hangin' out over the cab, was an extra seat.

Three men sat in the cab and two men rode on top. In the back were six head of horses.

While the stock truck was backin' into a wash so they could unload the horses, a pickup came in. There was only one man in this truck. As soon as he stepped out, I knew I was lookin' at Big Red McKlosky. My God, I thought, he's a damn giant! He stood six-foot-six and weighed around 250 pounds. He had flamin' red hair with a light complexion and freckles. His nose had been broken and never set straight. One of his front teeth was busted, and one ear had the top of it missin'. He walked with a slight limp.

The men led their horses down by the pen that surrounded the water trough. After they'd unsaddled, they led the horses into the corral and turned 'em loose to drink. Each of them was dressed differently and yet alike. By that I mean they all had on the same type of clothes, even if they showed different amounts of wear and were different styles. They all had on western hats, some with stampede strings and some without. The hats were all different colors and shapes, yet they all had about the same size crowns and brims. Each man wore a silk scarf around his neck; a few were rolled and tied tight while others flapped in the breeze. Each wore chinks for chaps. Some of 'em were fancy and some plain; some were just about worn out, and others looked new. All of 'em wore western boots that were so scuffed and dirty, they really did look alike. A couple of the boys had on spurs with wide bands, and others wore narrow ones. Some had big rowels and others small, but all of 'em were the ol' California vaquero-style, silver inlayed with long drop shanks.

The one thing that sticks out most in my mind about

those kids was the amount of horse jewelry they were packin'. There was more silver in that camp than the United States mint had in its vault. They had silver conchos at the corners of their headstalls and on their chaps. Their saddles had silver horn caps and cantle plates. They all had big hair tassels hangin' from their cinches, and a couple had little silver bells on 'em, too. Only one man had a nylon rope on his saddle; that was Roy, the kid, from California. All the rest had rawhide riatas. The twins and Red had big, long taps on their stirrups like Dean wore.

The whole bunch may have been a little crazy like ol' Frenchy said, but they damn sure looked like what buckaroos were supposed to look like.

From the description that the cook had given me, it was easy to tell just who each one was. The first to get his horse unsaddled was a big, stout kid. As soon as he's done and his horse was turned loose, he went bouncin' around the others, actin' like he was boxin'. He took a couple of quick fake jabs at one of the twins, then ducked and bobbed a bit 'fore shootin' out a quick left jab that knocked the youngster's hat off. Before the little guy could bend over to pick it up, the big feller reached down and snatched the hat from the ground. He placed it back on the smaller boy's head, sideways; then he bounced and weaved his way over to another kid who had his back to him. He made a few quick feints like he was throwin' punches at this guy's back, and then he reached over and pinched the boy on the butt. With that, he bounced and danced off in the direction of one of the tents. I figured that the dancer had to be the one that Frenchy called Donnie.

It was easy to tell the twins, not only 'cause they looked alike but 'cause they stayed off by themselves mosta the time. They were younger and smaller than the others. I never did get to where I could tell which one I was talkin' with.

The second man to get unsaddled had to be Dan Walgamont, the one the cook called The Bear. He stood close to six foot tall and was built like a brick. His shoulders and hips were about the same width. He had no stomach and no butt, and looked like a block with a furry ball on top. He had long, reddish brown hair, which needed cuttin', and a full beard. The backs of his hands had hair on 'em the same color as his head. This hair was about an inch and a half long. Later, when they were all down by the trough washin' up, I noticed that Dan's chest and back were just as furry as his hands and face. He really did look like a red bear or a rusty-colored gorilla. He never took off the big six-gun he wore except when he slept. Even then, it was said that he slept with it in his hand.

Through the simple process of elimination, I figured that the slender kid who had his butt pinched had to be the boy from California. He was about five-foot-eight and very slight built. He was shy and always acted like he was about half afraid of his horses and the other men in the crew. Why he stayed out there with all of the teasin' he got is beyond me. He musta had a lotta heart, 'cause a weaker man woulda pulled out long before the wagon came in.

Dean and I started over to introduce ourselves to Red McKlosky. We got there right after he'd turned his horse loose. When we shook hands, I couldn't help but notice that his hand wrapped completely around mine, with his thumb touching his middle finger. The man was huge. He just glanced at Dean, but he kept starin' at me. Finally he said, "Friend of mine once told me that Ross Dollarhide said there's a feller used to ride rough string for the ZX named Tap McCoy. Said this McCoy was about the best hand he ever seen with a cranky horse. That wouldn't be you, would it?"

I admitted I use to work for the ZX and that I'd rode their rough string one summer, but I didn't think I could be the one Dollarhide was talkin' about. Hell, that'd been thirty or forty years ago.

Then Red said, "I's over to Elko once, and the men got to talkin' about good riders. One feller said that Small Boy Fairchild told him a few years back he had a blue roan stud that dumped every man who ever climbed on 'im. Dumped 'em all but one. Said this feller rode the horse to a standstill. When he climbed off, this guy had blood runnin' outta his nose and both ears. Said this man went by the name of Tap McCoy."

I admitted that the story was kinda true, but you had to know Small Boy. If you did, the tale wouldn't mean so much. When I said that, Red gave me a look that scared the hell out of me. It was one of those sideways glances, where the feller nods his head and smiles at you, like the two of ya have some sorta mutual secret.

The reason that look scared me was that I knew this outfit had a reputation for havin' some tough horses, and I didn't want any part of 'em. If I'd ever been a rough-stock rider, it'd been a long time ago. Now, all I wanted to ride was good gentle horses that would stand next to a rock for me to get on and that never expended any more energy than it took to jump a ditch. I kept tryin' to explain that all of those things had happened long before McKlosky was ever born. But, Red just kept a-smilin' and noddin' at me.

I didn't eat a lotta supper that night and I didn't get a lotta sleep either. I almost made myself sick just imagining what was gonna take place the next mornin'. All night long I kept tryin' to think of some way I could get outta there.

I was awake long 'fore I heard Frenchy crawl out of his tent and start rustlin' around in the cook wagon. The mornin' air was cold, so after I slipped on my Levi jumper, I went over and got a cup of coffee from him. He's mixin' hotcake batter and fryin' eggs. The little cook wagon with its propane lights seemed warm and friendly, and I got to wonderin' if maybe Frenchy didn't need a helper. I'd never thought much about changin' occupations before, but I's sure thinkin' about it then.

By and by, I sorta bent the conversation around to the horses and the tales I'd heard. Frenchy didn't make me feel no better when he told me that almost every mornin' the crew rode from camp, he got to see someone go for a bronc ride.

When it was time to eat, Frenchy rang the bell, and the crew lined up single file at the backdoor of the cook wagon. Then the men filed into the kitchen where they picked up a plate and filled it with the food that was laid out on the counter. As soon as they'd filled their plates, they went out a side door and found a place somewhere around the wagon to sit. In bad weather, we'd set up a big tent next to the cook wagon to eat in. That first mornin', I was glad the cook wagon was too small for the crew to eat indoors. It was still dark outside where we had to sit. No one could see my cup shake or notice my plate was almost empty.

We'd barely finished eatin' when I heard the sound of the horses comin' in. Funny, I use to love the noise of horses bein' wrangled in the cool, dark mornin' air. That mornin' though, I hated it.

The twins and Bear grabbed the ropes off their saddles, and we formed a circle. Pat drove the horses into the middle, and we pulled the ropes up tight, making a single-strand rope corral. Each man called out the name of the horse he was gonna ride that day. Then Red would rope one and lead it over to Pat, who would put a halter around its neck and lead it outta the corral. He'd either give the horse to the man who had called for it or tie it to some sagebrush or one of the trucks.

That first day, Red roped a little bay for Dean and told him that the horse's name was Peaches. He snagged a shaggy little black with big furry fetlocks for me, smiled that sly grin again, and said, "I call this little feller Teddy Bear."

Each man led his horse over to his saddle. Then he hobbled the animal and saddled up. There was lotsa snortin' and whistlin'. I even saw the outline of one horse as he tipped over, but in the dark I couldn't tell who it belonged to.

I watched Dean ease his rig into place and let it set for a minute before he made a loop with his latigo to snag the cinch on the off side. He pulled the cinch under the horse's belly and took a couple of loose wraps 'fore easin' it up tight. The little bay humped up but never did much after that. Dean bent down, unhobbled him, and led the horse around in a circle. The bay walked like he's on eggshells, but he never did anymore than that.

Teddy Bear stood there as quiet as a kitten. I led him around, expectin' him to do somethin', but he never made a bobble.

When everyone was saddled, we led our horses over to the stock truck and loaded 'em. Donnie climbed into the driver's seat, and Dean and the twins climbed up on top. Bear and Roy jumped inside. I was lookin' around tryin' to figure out where to ride when Red motioned for me to get in the pickup with him.

We drove for better than half an hour, and by the time we stopped, it was daylight. Red never said much as we were travelin'. He didn't act sullen or anything; he just didn't have much to say. When we stopped, he had Dean, Roy, and me unload our horses. He sketched a crude map in the dust, showin' us where we'd rodear the cattle that day. Then he and the rest of the crew loaded up and drove off.

I led Teddy Bear in a circle to loosen him up, but he acted as though he was still asleep. I checked my cinch, hooked my elbow over my Mecáte, and pulled Teddy Bear's head around as I pushed my left knee into his shoulder and eased myself into the saddle. I was ready for the wreck, but nothin' happened. Dean's horse was the same; Peaches walked along for forty or fifty feet all humped up, but then he settled down and lined out too. Even as scared as I was, I still almost felt disappointed.

We scattered out and started pushin' the cattle we found in the direction of the rodear ground. Off in the distance I could see dust, and I knew it was one of the other riders headin' in the same direction.

The rodear ground for this particular day was a flat next to a dirt water hole. By the time all of us got there with our mornin's gather, we had somewhere around a hundred and twenty-five head. Two men held the herd while the rest of us went to bringin' in sagebrush for the brandin' fire. In twenty minutes, we had a pile six or seven feet high and about the same distance across.

Red parked the pickup near the fire and used the tailgate as a table to hold the syringes, vaccine, and dehorners. He drove a peg with a ring on the top of it into the ground. There was a rope tied to the ring, and the rope had a loop in the end of it. He let the fire burn for ten or fifteen minutes while the irons heated up. Then Red told the twins to start headin'. He had Bear do the heelin'. Roy and Donnie were holdin' the cattle. That left me, Red, and Dean to work the ground.

One of the twins would rope a calf by the neck and drag it outta the herd. When it got near the fire, Bear would rope it by the hind feet and drag it up to the peg, where Dean would put its front feet in the loop that was tied to the peg. Bear would back his horse and stretch out the calf. Dean would then sit down behind the calf, pull Bear's rope from the hind feet at the same time that he pushed the calf's bottom leg forward with his right foot, and pull the calf's top leg back.

They call this "flat assin' a calf." I guess they call it that 'cause you sit on your butt while you're holdin' the calf. Red and I did all the brandin', earmarkin', dehornin', vaccinatin', and casteratin'. We'd do about twenty head, then Red would call for us to change off. That way, everyone got to rope and no one got overworked on the ground.

Ropin' out of a loose rodear is a lot harder than draggin' calves in a corral or a brandin' trap. In a brandin' trap, I knew they couldn't get away, and most of the time, I's right next to one 'fore I made a shot.

In a rodear, I usually had to throw from a longer distance. If I went to swingin' my rope round and round my head, I'd never get a shot. Those kids were all good ropers, but Dean didn't have to take a backseat to none of 'em.

Toward the middle of the day we got down to the last little bunch, and Red called for me to heel while Donnie and him went in to head. By now the calves were restless. They'd been roped at all mornin' long, and they'd go scootin' through the bunch as soon as they saw a man on horseback. That was when I got to see a real roper at work.

Up to this point, all of the calves had been roped by the neck and dragged out. With his rawhide riata, Red could throw farther than any man I ever saw. Usually he'd heel 'em from the same distance that the rest of us had been headin' from. I'd seen it done before, but there was no gettin' around it: Red was sure damned good.

When the last calf was done, Red counted the pieces of the ears that he'd cut off and saved from each animal. Then he counted the bags from the steers. By subtracting the bag count from the ear count, he knew how many steers and how many heifers we did that day. He wrote the number down in his tally book, and we started packin' up the truck, gettin' ready to head back to camp.

That's pretty much the way we did it everyday we trucked from camp. When we changed campsites, though, which we did every week to ten days, we'd ride from camp for the first four or five mornings. On those days we'd drag a pack horse with us and take turns leadin' it. The pack horse carried the branding and dehorning irons on one side along with the peg and a sledge hammer. On the other side, he carried a cooler box with the vaccine and syringes in it. It was those days the rodeos usually took place.

For some reason, truckin' a horse thirty or forty minutes takes a lotta the edge off him. On the mornin's we rode from camp, there was no way to avoid a fight. If a horse wanted to buck, about all a person could do was take a deep seat and hang on. The rider might turn him around in a circle a time or two or try and get ready 'fore Red took off at a trot, but that was about it. It was just like Frenchy said, 'bout every mornin' we rode from camp we could expect a show of some kind.

After a week or so, I'd pretty well figured out that Red hadn't cut me any outlaws. In fact, I had the gentlest string there, next to the ones Pat used to wrangle on. A couple of mine would hump up, and I'm sure if I busted 'em out on a cold mornin', I coulda got a few jumps out of 'em. But, by hidin' behind the saddle horn and stealin' a ride for a few minutes, I's usually able to get outta camp without much of a battle.

With the kids it was a different story. First off, their horses were greener and crankier than mine. And secondly, if one of 'em had tried to cheat a horse the way I's doin', the others made so much fun of him that it was easier to get bucked off than to have to put up with the ribbin'. That summer I saw everyone of them boys go for several bronc rides, and I saw everyone of 'em get bucked off a couple of times too. That included Dean.

Red's horses were no better than the ones the boys were ridin'. If anything, he had several that were worse. But I never saw him get dumped. He wasn't a showy rider like a lotta fellers I've been around. He couldn't spur one from the shoulder to the cantle or do any of that other fancy stuff, but he was sure hard to unseat out in the brush. If I was ever any good when I was younger, then Red was better.

When we got in that afternoon, we pulled our saddles and turned the horses in on water. After they were done drinkin', Pat trailed these horses out to where the cavvy was grazin'. He'd spend the night out there, herdin' 'em till early the next mornin'. About three, he'd unhobble the ten or fifteen that he didn't trust and trail the whole bunch back into camp.

The next day, it was the same thing all over again. By the time we were done with our breakfast and ready to catch our morning mounts, Pat come trailin' the cavvy in. When all the men had a horse to ride, Pat would take the extras down and water 'em. Then he'd take 'em back out to graze. He kept a bundle of rope hobbles in a gunny sack on the back of his horse, along with a little sack of grain. He used the grain to catch the horses he wanted to hobble. After he's done with that chore, he'd trot on back to camp where he'd eat breakfast and go to bed. He'd sleep the better part of the day. This system was a little different than most of the other outfits that I'd seen, but it worked.

On the first of July, I got kicked pretty good shoein' one of my horses, so I didn't get to take the fourth off with the rest of the crew. I laid around camp for the next four days, feelin' sorry for myself and tryin' to heal up so I could get back to work when everyone got in on the sixth.

Red hauled all of the crew but me and Pat into head-quarters the night of the second. The twins took off for their home in Jordan Valley; Roy's family drove as far north as Alturas, where he met 'em; Dan left for a gun and sporting equipment show up north someplace; Frenchy went to the Basque Festival in Elko; Red never told anyone where he went or what he did; and Dean and Donnie went over to Owyhee where they were entered in the horse ropin'.

I kinda figured ol' Pat might loosen up and do a little talkin' now that there wasn't anyone around camp but me and him. He never changed his routine a bit though. He'd bring the cavvy in and water 'em. Then he'd take 'em out to graze for the day. In the evenin', he'd get up and fix himself some supper and a snack to munch on durin' the night, and off he'd go. He never offered to fix anything for me to eat, and he never stuck around to do any visitin'. Like I said before, he was an honest-to-God loner.

Red brought everyone back to camp the night of the sixth. Frenchy was about half lit and full of stories about the friends he'd seen in Elko. Dan had a new pistol and somethin' called a speed loader that made it possible for him to reload his new gun in half the time. The twins were all smiles and acted like they had a big secret. Roy said his family was fine, and they'd had a good time goin' on picnics and watchin' the fireworks display.

Dean and Donnie were both laughin' and jokin', but they looked like hell. They had bruises on their faces and were stiff and sore. Dean told me that they'd borrowed a couple of horses to rope off of and had placed third the first day but hadn't done any good after that. Later, they met Hooper John in one of the bars in Mountain City. Dean said Hooper was a lot friendlier this time than he was when we'd worked with him at Ben Bird's place.

Dean said Hooper was pretty wrapped up in a new activity called AIM, the American Indian Movement. Hooper was waitin' for some feller named Trudell to introduce him to Russell Means and Dennis Banks. Then they were all headed for South Dakota again to help the "traditionals" get a fair shake in the upcoming tribal election.

While they were sittin' at a table in the corner listenin' to Hooper tell 'em about the new organization, a couple of drunk miners come over and started givin' Hooper a bad time. Hooper took it a lot longer than Dean figured he would 'fore he popped the biggest and loudest one in the mouth. A couple more dirt diggers decided to jump in when they saw their friend was gettin' the worst of it. So Dean and Donnie helped Hooper clean out the bar. Then the three of 'em went across the street to another bar, where a bunch of drunk Indians started in on Dean and Donnie. Hooper helped them whip everyone in that place, too.

I reckon that goes to show that no race has a corner on bein' prejudiced.

CHAPTER 23

After we'd been there on the Flying D for five days, I'd remembered every reason that I use to love to go out on the wagon each spring. But, before two days were up, I could tell you all of the reasons I'd quit doin' it.

On the positive side, there's somethin' about wakin' up every morning before daylight and watchin' the sun come up over the horizon that makes a man feel alive and close to God; the sound and the outline of the cavvy, comin' in against the first light of a mornin' sky; the smell of sage and the chill in the mornin' air; the sight of six or seven dust trails, all headed for a central gatherin' point; the sound of a hundred head of cows and calves bawlin'; the smell of burnt hair and the taste of calf oysters, cooked in the ashes of a brandin' fire; and when I turn in at night, tired from spendin' the day ridin' and wrestlin' calves, I have a good feelin' about myself.

There's something else, and it's harder to explain. There's almost no law on a wagon. I can do just about anything I think I'm tough enough to get away with. This gives me a certain feelin' of freedom that most people never get to know. And finally, there's the companionship.

The top of the negative side has to be the dirt. I sleep on the ground, I work in the dust, and I eat outside. The dirt is everywhere—in my bed, on my clothes, and in my food. I spend weeks on end without ever gettin' clean. I think I'm gettin' a tan till I get too near a water trough. At my age, I find that a few nights of sleepin' on the ground goes a long way. I wake up so stiff, I doubt I'll be able to get on my horse. The cold night air makes all of my joints ache, and my nose feels like it's plugged for an hour after I get up. And again, there's the companionship thing.

With that in mind, let me tell a couple of stories about some of my companions on this little adventure.

This Donnie, who Frenchy thought was nuts, really did have somethin' the matter with him, but I kinda doubt he was really crazy. Dean told me once he thought Donnie was hyperactive. He couldn't sit still for two minutes. He was always movin' or singin' or talkin'. He played tricks and jokes on everyone, but poor Roy was his favorite target. One time he rode up alongside Roy while we were trottin' home. Without warnin', Donnie reached over and flipped the headstall that held the hackamore on Roy's horse's head. The bosal fell from the horse's nose.

Roy was left holdin' a set of reins that wasn't connected to the horse's head anymore. Then Donnie says, "Wanna race!?" and with that he whacked Roy's ol' pony across the rump with his quirt. The horse shot off across the desert at a dead run with Roy pullin' back with both hands, tryin' to stop him. Roy made it back to camp a good hour ahead of the rest of us.

Another time, Roy was ridin' a real flighty little horse called Brown Jug. We were movin' single file through some rimrock when I saw Donnie take down his rope and build a loop. Roy was in front of him and never had any idea what was goin' on. When they came to a place wide enough for him to get a shot, Donnie threw a heel trap around the hind feet of Roy's horse.

As soon as the loop went tight, Brown Jug was airborne. He shot straight out from the ledge and landed buckin' down through the rocks and boulders. I've got no idea how the kid ever managed to stay on, but when the colt finally stopped, Roy was still in the saddle. He was ghost white and shakin' like an aspen leaf, but he was right side up, with a leg on each side. Dean said he thought Roy was really bucked off on the first jump, he just happened to keep landin' where the horse was.

Donnie wasn't like a lot of bullies, though. He could take it as well as dish it out. One mornin' when he was ridin' his crankiest horse, the twins sneaked out and turned his saddle around.

Donnie came back from the cookwagon and saw the ol' pony standin' there with the saddle on backwards. He made out like he never even noticed. He stepped aboard, grabbed a handful of tail hair like it was his bridle reins, and said, "Let's get movin'." With that he threw both feet up in the horse's flank and hooked him. The horse blew up and fell apart. In three jumps, Donnie was lyin' on the ground, laughin' just as hard as the rest of us.

Donnie musta known a hundred dumb, little, one-line jokes, and he'd come out every mornin' and greet the first person he saw with one of 'em. Then he'd call that person by the name in the joke for the rest of the day. For instance, I 'member one mornin' he came up to me and said, "And how much would you like to donate to the Indian Relief Fund, Mrs. Custer?" For the rest of that day, everytime he had anything to say to me, he called me Mrs. Custer.

A few days later, he saw Dean first, and his greetin' to him was, "Other than that, how did you enjoy the play, Mrs. Lincoln?" For the rest of that day, Dean was Mrs. Lincoln.

Donnie thought of himself as quite a boxer and figured he's about half tough. Dean slowed down his shadow-boxin' with him about ten days after we got there. One afternoon right after supper, he come up to Dean, bobbin' and weavin' like he wanted to do some slap fightin'.

Dean answered by takin' up a boxin' stance, too. In no time flat, Dean blocked Donnie's left jab with his own left and slapped Donnie up alongside the head about three times on each side. Then Dean jumped in the air, spun around, and kicked the hat off Donnie's head. This all happened so fast that poor ol' Donnie wasn't sure just what'd taken place. But, he was damn sure he didn't want to shadowbox with Dean anymore.

From then on, he kept pesterin' Dean to teach him how to do that karate stuff. To everyone else's relief, Dean agreed, and every night after supper the two of 'em would go off by themselves and practice.

This gave the rest of us some relief from Donnie's constant talkin' and harassment. Whenever the two of 'em got together while we were ridin', they talked about "Katas" and "eons" one, two, and three and a bunch of other Japanese words that I can't remember.

Everybody there had a run-in with Donnie; mine was

over a snake. The wagon was camped near a place named Tendall Points, and a lot of rattlers were around. One evenin' just 'fore supper, Donnie killed an especially big one; musta been a little over three feet. He dragged the damn thing back to camp with him.

At supper that night he was showin' it off by tossin' it at the younger men. Pretty soon he says, "Ya' know, Tap, I think I'll sneak over and stick this thing in your bed. I'll tie a string around it, and about the time you're fallin' asleep, I'll start pullin it out. I'll bet that ol' tepee of yours'll take off and look like one of those rocket ships goin' up."

Well, he's sure right about that. I'll bet I woulda gone straight out of sight. He kept goin' on and on about stickin' that snake in my bed till I'd had enough. Finally, I walked over to my tent and got my ol' hog-leg pistol; then I came back. I took the shells out of it and asked him to count 'em. When he was done, I put 'em back in the pistol and shoved it under his nose, with the hammer back on full cock.

"Now you crazy son of a bitch," I said, "if that snake turns up anywhere near my tent, I'm gonna blow your ass all over this flat. I don't care if you put it there or if one of these other deliquent bastards does it, you're still a dead man. Do I make myself clear!?"

That was one time when Donnie did stand still; leastwise, he stood still till I headed back for my tent. Then he took off at a dead run for Red's trailer. I heard him yellin' at Red, tellin' him how I'd pulled a gun.

When Red asked why, and Donnie told him, I heard Red say, "I don't blame the old man a bit. If you ever put a snake around my place, I'll shoot you, too!" Then he went back inside and slammed his door.

Probably a lot crazier than Donnie was Dan Walgamont, the one Frenchy called The Bear. He always carried that big .44 Magnum pistol on his hip. He'd tell me about what he was gonna do if he ever came up on any rustlers. He told the twins he carried it 'cause he figured that someday a bunch of motorcycle bandits or Hell's Angels might show up. And he told Dean he wore it 'cause he wanted to be ready for the time when the people in the cities revolted against the government.

He cleaned it almost every night and practiced with it all the time. He was a crack shot and had books on the fast draw and combat shootin'. Sometimes he'd set up a few cans and then back off a couple hundred yards. All of a sudden, he'd take off runnin' at the cans, duckin' and divin' behind sagebrush. He'd jump up runnin' and screamin'. When he was about sixty or seventy yards out, he'd start shootin'. If he ran outta shells, he'd reload while rollin' around from one piece of cover to another. The game ended when all the cans were dead. I kept my distance from Dan.

Dean had a couple of funny little things happen to him while we were camped out there that summer, too. The first one took place not too long after we first got there. Dean was ridin' a little stockin'-legged, bald-faced horse called Headlight. It was Dean's turn to heel, and when he dragged the second calf up to the fire, Headlight got ticked off about somethin' and blew up. He went hoggin' it around the rodear ground. The little horse was only doin' a half-assed job of buckin', and pretty quick he was wantin' to quit.

The only problem was that on his last jump, he'd landed

in the brandin' fire. The horse was so mad, he didn't notice where he was for a few seconds. Dean tried to ride him out of the fire, but he was sulkin' now and had made up his mind he wasn't gonna do anything that a human wanted him to do. He musta stood there for a full thirty seconds 'fore he felt the heat.

When he came outta there the second time, he was damn sure turnin' the crank and tearin' up the country. Dean got him covered, but it was about all he could do to get it done. Everyone agreed that ride was the best buckin'-horse ride of the summer.

The other little incident took place the last week of July. All eight of us were trottin' back to camp when we crossed a little wash. When the first rider rode down into it, a big ol' bobcat come scootin' up the other side. In two jumps, the whole crew had their ropes down and were in hot pursuit.

Dean made a long shot that snagged Mr. Cat around the neck and one front leg. With the cat in tow, we struck out for camp again. The animal would bounce along in back for awhile, and then he'd run out along the side. By the time we got to camp, he was wide-eyed scared and sure 'nough mad.

No one had any idea just what we were gonna do with the damn thing now that we had it caught, but we figured Pat and Frenchy oughta see it. This time we were camped at a place called Dry Lake. There wasn't a thing growin' there taller than a blade of grass.

For no reason in particular, all of our tents were pitched a lot closer than normal, and we rode right into the middle of 'em. The flaps on all of 'em were tied closed, except for the one Frenchy the cook slept in.

Frenchy was lyin' on his bed readin' an ol' newspaper when we came draggin' the frightened bobcat into camp on the end of Dean's rope.

The cook's tent musta looked like a good place to hide, 'cause as soon as the ol' tom saw it, he dove for the door.

Dean saw what was happenin' and stacked on his dallies at the same time the cook heard us and laid down his paper. The cat hit the end of the rope in full stride, but the rope stopped him in midair. The sight that met Frenchy's' eyes as he put down the newspaper was a terrified bobcat with every hair on its body fuzzed out and its claws extended. The impact of hittin' the end of the rope at a full run and in midair caused the wildcat to scream like a banshee.

The sight of the frizzed-out cat silhouetted spread-eagle in his tent doorway, combined with the unearthly scream, scared the cook so bad, he actually tore the back out of the tent tryin' to get away. All of us were laughin' so hard that a couple of the boys fell off their horses. But, Frenchy wasn't laughin'. He was so mad that he quit right there on the spot. No amount of apologizin' on our parts made any difference. He was done.

CHAPTER 24

Red took Frenchy into headquarters the next mornin'. When he got back in the afternoon, he called us all together and told us he had bad news. Red said the hay hands had all gotten drunk, and a bunch of 'em had quit. The superintendent wanted him to bring in the buckaroo crew. They planned on all of us, except the horse wrangler and Red, to start puttin' up hay. For doin' this, the company would give each of us a $50 bonus at the end of hay season, and we'd all be back ridin' by the middle of September.

No one said anything for a few minutes. I guess we were all rollin' the idea around in our minds. The twins were the first to speak up. They said if they had to put up hay, they'd just as soon be doin' it at home for their dad, so they reckoned they'd be pullin' out.

Then Roy cleared his throat and said he had hay fever and asthma too bad to be workin' in the fields, so he didn't think he'd take 'em up on the offer either. Donnie pretty well sized up the way Dean felt when he told Red he didn't care if there was a fifty-dollar-a-*day* bonus; he wasn't out here for the money. He said he liked to rope, and he liked to ride. If he couldn't do it there, he'd go someplace else where he could.

Dan said he'd stay out in camp for nothin' till the ridin' started again. He'd even pay the ranch for his grub if he had to, but he wasn't goin' in and be no rawzin jaw.

Then Dean told Red that over the Fourth of July he'd heard there was an outfit east of Lake View called the Turkey Track, and they was needin' some help on their brandin' crew. He figured he'd give 'em a call.

Red looked over at me and said, "Well, old man, what're your plans?"

I told him that Dean was kind of a leppie bastard who needed someone to bottle-feed him, so I reckoned I'd see if this Turkey Track could use an old reprobate like me, too.

With that settled, all of us but Dan the Bear, old Pat the horse wrangler, and Red, left to roll our beds and take down our tents. An hour or so later we loaded all of our tack and beds in the back of Red's pickup and headed for the main ranch.

Red had called ahead on the pickup radio and told 'em to have our checks ready. When we pulled up in front of the office, there was quite a little reception committee to meet us. It just so happened that one of the big bosses was up from California to check and see how things were goin'. He was kinda upset to find half the hay crew had quit right in the middle of the season. He was even more disturbed to hear the whole buckaroo crew would quit rather than help out the company when they were in a jackpot.

Next to this California boss stood a short, squatty guy I

bet could sure be mean and tough. On the far end was a gunsal-lookin' feller who resembled a younger, less-experienced version of the man who ran the steer operation in Baker City. These two men turned out to be the ranch superintendent and his assistant.

The reception speech started with the man from California givin' us a pep talk on company loyalty. It ended with the young feller threatenin' not to put our names on the preferred employees list. He said somethin' to the effect that although we'd performed adequately, we had not given sufficient notice of our intent to terminate. Therefore, our names could not be included on the list of persons who were to receive preferential consideration should they decide to be reemployed with the Lazy J.

When they were done, Roy apologized for leavin' but said he had asthma, and workin' in the hay fields would aggravate his condition. The twins said they were gonna have to leave to go home soon anyway, as their folks needed 'em to help with their own hayin'.

Donnie rocked up and down on the balls of his feet the whole time that everyone was talkin'. When the twins were through, he reached up, took off his hat, and looked at the three bosses kinda humble-like. Then he added his little bit. "Since I started here, I been workin' fourteen hours a day and sleepin' on the ground. The only shelter I've had over my head when it stormed was a leaky, old, canvas tepee tent that you charge me ten dollars a month rent for. I been ridin' cranky horses most outfits woulda chicken fed. I haven't had but four days off in the past four months. And now, now you tell me 'cause I wanta keep on livin' and workin' like this that you won't put my name on your preferred employee list. Well, friend, as far as I'm concerned, you can take your list and use it to wipe your rosy red ass!" With that he flipped his hat some way so it seemed to roll up his arm and landed on his head at a cocky angle. Then he stuck out his hand and said, "Check, please."

I guess I don't need to tell you that ended our little pep rally. The two older dogs stormed back into the office, leavin' the duded-up pup to hand out the checks.

I looked over at Red about this time, and he was smilin' like the cat that just ate the canary. We all shook hands with him, and he wished us good luck 'fore he went into the office, too.

After we'd loaded our gear in Dean's pickup, we headed for Burns. This was the exact opposite direction from where we wanted to go, but it happened to be the closest place where there was a phone. We got in there just before dark. Before I could even buy one drink, Dean was on the phone and had gotten us jobs down south on the Turkey Track. Donnie wasn't five minutes behind us, and he got a job on his first call, too, only his was up north on the Grind Stone.

We ate, gassed up the truck, and headed south. Dean drove most of the night, and when the sun came up, we were sittin' in front of the cookhouse of the Turkey Track. This outfit wasn't anywhere near as big as the Flyin D, but it still ran close to two thousand head of mother cows. It was owned by a group of investors who were out to prove cattle and wildlife could both be run on the same range without interferin' with one another.

Besides the ranch crew, there was a whole city of biologists, zoologists, bugologists, and other college types runnin' all over the place, countin' everythin' from blades of grass to rabbit pellets. Luckily, these people all ate with the farm crew in the main cookhouse.

Dean and I got there in time to have breakfast with the buckaroo crew in the smaller cowboy cookshack.

It turned out that 'cause the ranch was managed by an advisory committee made up of college professors, tree huggers, and bunny breeders, it was hard for the Turkey Track to hire decent help. They'd had to take to hirin' a lot of kids from the city, who wanted to be buckaroos. They were all good boys, don't get me wrong, but not one of 'em woulda made a pimple on a decent cowboy's ass, and that included their buckaroo boss.

The head cow chaser was a college kid, too. He's only about twenty-two or three. His crew was made up of five kids, with the oldest one bein' no more than eighteen, and an older man of about forty who did the cookin'.

I can't 'member any of these people's names except for the cook. This guy was a loud, heavy-set feller. His name was Bill Anderson, but he told us we could just call him Wild Bill 'cause that was the name he went by when he was boxin'. In the time it took us to eat breakfast, I could tell it was this Wild Bill who ran the crew. Most of the mealtime chatter was dominated by him. He was the center of attention, and I could tell that he enjoyed it that way. The college-boy cow boss had to ask him when he would like to have everyone in for supper. Some of the younger men even called him "Mr." Anderson.

This crew didn't work out of any camps. They lived in a permanent bunkhouse and rode or trucked from there everyday. In a way, it was kinda nice, but the cook wouldn't fix breakfast before six, and he wanted the men back by six that evenin' for supper. That meant they didn't get out to where the cattle were till late in the mornin', and they had to head in pretty early, too. This made for an awfully short workday.

The government employee-type of work schedule, along with their being shorthanded and usin' a green crew, caused the ranch to be so far behind with its summer brandin'.

At first, this Anderson didn't seem all that bad. He came down to the barn while Dean and I were shoein' up our horses and brought us some iced tea to drink. He spent a couple of hours there with us. During that time, he told us a little about the ranch, but mostly he talked about his boxin' days and his love life.

Later in the afternoon, he brought some sandwiches. In return, we had to listen to more of his stories of conquests in the ring and the bedroom. It struck me and Dean kinda funny the way Bill nursemaided over the boys and ordered the college-kid boss around. For instance, that evenin' at supper Wild Bill sent one kid back to his room to take off his spurs and sent another out to rewash his hands.

The next day after breakfast, we trucked out and made a circle, gatherin' to a brandin' trap set in a fence corner. When we got there with the day's gather, there were about a hundred and twenty-five pairs in the little pen. The boss sent me and one of them kids in to rope first.

That boy couldn't rope for sour owl crap, and I ended up draggin' most of the first twenty or so calves. Then the boss had the young feller change off with Dean but left me in to keep on ropin'.

Well, the longer I roped, the hotter my luck got. I was makin' shots I hadn't been able to get away with in my whole life. I'd started out just throwin' plain heel traps, pickin' up two feet and goin' to the fire. As the day wore on, though, I got to tryin' all sorts of fancy throws and some of 'em from a good long distance, too. I threw backhand shots, underhand shots, rollovers, culos, and every other throw that I'd ever seen made. Almost everyone took. I swear, I coulda thrown my rope straight up in the air, and a calf woulda flipped over on his back so it got him by the hind feet.

I roped all day 'cept for a couple of hours' break in the middle of the afternoon when my horse needed a rest. My grand finale came that afternoon on the very last calf. I was sittin' on my horse out by the brandin' fire, coilin' up my rope, thinkin' we were done. The kid who was ropin' with me spotted another one we hadn't seen and started followin' it around, tryin' to get in position for a shot. Before he got set up, I'd built a new loop and was gettin' ready to ride in if the boy missed. Suddenly, the calf popped out on the outside edge of the bunch. Without untrackin' my horse from where I'd just turned the last calf loose, I made a forty-foot, underhanded throw, hopin' that if I's lucky, I'd snag this one around the neck. My loop was too big, though, and the calf jumped through it. I jerked my slack anyway, and I'll be damned if I didn't end up with the two hind feet again.

It was then I knew the true meanin' of the old sayin', I'd rather have luck than skill anyday. I couldn't believe some of the shots I made that day, but neither could those kids. The way they were carryin' on was almost embarrassin'. I never let on that I'd never had a day like that in my life. I just made out like that was the way it was supposed to be done.

Well, at supper that night the boys were still a-goin' on about my ropin', askin' me to teach 'em how to throw different shots and wantin' to know where I'd learned 'em. But Wild Bill didn't have a hell of a lot to say. In fact, he was right down sullen.

Right then I didn't care about Bill's feelings. I was enjoyin' bein' a celebrity and the center of attention. After I put my dishes in the sink and was headin' out the door, the college-boy, buckaroo boss come up to me and said, "Tap, I was kinda worried about you at first. You know, you being so old and all, but you're all right. I'm glad you're here. Now, maybe we'll get done with this brandin' before the snow flies."

Then Dean came up and says, "Ain't no gettin' around it, Pard, that had to be some of the fanciest ropin' I ever saw anyone do."

I tried to act all humble, like it was just an average day for me, but I felt about ten feet tall, and I know my hat size was a good two inches too small for my head. I had no idea what I's gonna do the next day when my luck was back to normal. For that night though, I was just enjoyin' the feelin' of being someone special for once.

The next mornin' those boys were still a-carryin' on at breakfast. As we were fixin' to leave, one of 'em asked me to teach him to make some fancy shot, but 'fore I could answer, Wild Bill interrupted.

"Tap will have to teach you that some other time, Son. Today he's gonna be my swamper. He forgot his cup last night, and you boys know the rules. If you leave any of your eatin' gear on the table, you got to help the cook the next day. Tap, here, ain't no exception. After he gets through moppin' the floor and cleanin' out the garbage cans, maybe I'll be able to get him to teach me some of those fancy rope tricks too. Right, Old Man?" And with that, he gave me a mean sneer of a smile.

I knew damn well I never left no cup on that table; I knew even better that I wasn't gonna be no cook's flunky, and I told him so. I told him in just about those same words, too. I ended by sayin' that I'd roll my bed 'fore I washed a single spoon for him.

He said somethin' to the effect that I might quit, but I wasn't leavin' the ranch till I spent the day washin' dishes and cleanin' the kitchen for him. The room was dead silent, and the kids was all starin' bug-eyed at the two of us.

At that point, I told him he could take his kitchen, his boxin' career, and his love life and stick 'em all where the sun don't shine. Then I turned my back on him and started for the door. I never saw the punch that caught me on the back of the head and knocked me across the room. But, I did see the foot that kicked me square in the ribs as I was layin' there on the floor. It knocked all the wind outta me and left me gaspin' for air.

Bill was fixin' to kick me again when Dean came sailin' through the air and smacked him square in the back with one of his flyin' jump kicks. It sent Anderson sprawlin' over the top of me, but other than knockin' him off balance and surprisin' him, it didn't do any real damage.

For a big man, Bill got to his feet amazingly fast and turned to face Dean. He was takin' up a boxin' stance when Dean came in, faked a punch at his face, and took Wild Bill to the floor with a sweep to the older man's left leg. As fast as Bill was, Dean was still quicker. The boy was on his feet first, and as Anderson was comin' up, Dean was comin' down—he's comin' down with one of the wooden chairs from next to the table. The chair caught the big man on top of the head and busted into a dozen pieces.

Bill went to his knees from that one, but was startin' to regain his feet when Dean picked up one of the chair legs and hit him a solid blow square in the face. That put the ex-boxer down on the canvas but still not for the count. Once more he was startin' to stagger up when Dean kicked him in the ribs so hard that you could hear a couple of 'em crack, clear outside.

I struggled to my feet and was crossin' the room when Dean picked up the chair leg again and hit Anderson across the back of the shoulders. That blow laid the big man out face first on the floor. I caught the kid by the arm just as he was gonna bring the leg down on the man's head. "That's enough, boy. Let it be."

Dean hesitated for a minute, and then threw the piece of wood across the room. He put his arm on my shoulder and asked if I's okay.

I said, "Sure," and we started for the door.

But then, Dean stopped and walked back and looked down at Wild Bill. He reached down and rolled the big man over so that Bill was layin' face up. Suddenly, 'fore I could stop him, Dean straightened and kicked the boxer two more times in the ribs and once more in the face. The kick to the face splattered blood all over the floor and sent several teeth flyin' across the room.

The older man's body jerked and convulsed once or twice 'fore relaxin' and goin' limp. His jaw hung at a funny angle, and only the whites of his eyes were showin'. I was fairly sure Dean had just killed Wild Bill Anderson. I'd seen a couple of other men die, and that was the way they acted just 'fore they checked out.

Everyone in the room was standin' there starin' like they were in some sorta trance, so I said loud enough for any of 'em that was listenin' to hear, "Come on, let's get our stuff loaded. I know a place where we can stay over in Wyoming." I had no intention of headin' in that direction, but I figured when those kids told the sheriff what they'd heard, it might buy us a little time.

We never rolled our beds or nothin'. We just heaped everything we owned in the back of Dean's truck and headed south for California.

CHAPTER 25

e shot outta there doin' ninety and headin' south. Dean was fightin' hard to hold the little pickup on the dirt road as we roared away with the dust a-boilin' and the gravel flyin'. We drove all day and most of the night, stickin' to the back roads as much as we could. Our plan was to head south. I had a friend livin' out in the desert east of San Diego. We weren't sure just what we'd do after we got there, but this guy's place was close to the Mexican border.

While we were rollin' down the road, I asked Dean what had ever caused him to work poor ol' Anderson over like that after he'd already whipped him.

He shook his head and said, "Hell, I don't know. I went over to see if he's all right, and when I rolled him over, I remembered him kickin' you while you were down. The next thing I knew, somethin' kinda snapped, and all I wanted to do was kill the fat bastard."

Travelin' on those secondary roads took up a lotta time, and come midnight, we were still just a few miles north of

Sacramento, up in the foothills. We pulled off the road at a little public campsite and got a few hours rest.

We got up 'fore the sun the next mornin', changed our clothes, shaved, rolled our beds, and straightened up the gear in the back of the truck. Then we drove on into Placerville, where we gassed up again and ate some breakfast. While we were eatin' we dug out our billfolds and took stock of our finances. Between the two of us, we had a little over $1,800, with most of it bein' mine for once.

We kept on followin' Highway 49 as it wound its way through the foothills of the old gold-minin' districts. The weather was hot, and the country was already dried out with the wild oats, now a bright yellow. Around ten in the mornin', we turned out of the foothills and took another side road that headed west to the main highway. We knew from our map that we were now a few miles northeast of Fresno.

As we came outta the rollin' country and were just gettin' into the valley, we smelled the unmistakable odor of a feedlot. A few miles farther, we topped a rise, and then we saw it. There spread out before us was one of the largest feedlots I'd ever seen. There musta been well over 600 acres of pens alone, not countin' the farm ground around it.

The road we were on went past the feedlot, and as we were goin' by, I saw a big sign that read "ALAMO CATTLE FEEDERS" and in smaller letters, "Lazy J Cattle Company." Dean hit the brakes and backed up to make sure he'd read the sign right. Then he looked at me and said, "Oh, what the hell."

I didn't have any idea what he meant by that, and I had

no idea at all what he had in mind when he pulled off the highway and drove down the road that led into the lot. He stopped in front of the main office and said, "Let's see if they really do have a preferred employees list."

He got outta the pickup, and I trailed after Dean into the air-conditioned main office. I followed him up to the desk where he told a pretty young girl receptionist that we'd like to know who to talk to about jobs as pen riders.

She smiled at him in a way that was a lot friendlier than the job required and indicated an office down the hall, asking us to wait one minute. She pushed a little buzzer and talked into an intercom system for a few seconds, all the while smiling at Dean.

In a minute an older gentleman in faded jeans and a white shirt came outta the office that the receptionist had pointed at. He introduced himself as Gene Turner and said he's the yard foreman. Then he asked if he could help us.

Dean told him we were interested in jobs as pen riders and asked if they had any openings.

Mr. Turner said that, as a matter a fact, two men had just quit the day before. Then he asked if either of us had any feedlot experience. I told him I'd worked for Clatterbuck in Colorado some years back, and Dean said he'd worked for McElhaney's down in Arizona. I was tellin' the truth, but I think Dean was lyin'.

After that, Mr. Turner invited us into his office. I was sure we were gonna get the routine, Lazy J introductive spiel about it being a large integrated cattle operation. Instead, he showed us a big map of the feedlot, then pointed out where we were to work and gave us the names of our bosses. It turned out that the feedlot was so large, it had four separate cowboy crews, and Dean and I were each on a different one.

Then Mr. Turner explained that this feedlot still paid by the month rather than by the hour, like most of the others were startin' to do now. He said we would start at $650 a month and would receive an automatic $50 a month raise at the end of six months. After that, all raises would be based on performance. I almost choked when he told us our starting salary. I'd never made over $400 a month in my life.

He asked if we had a place to stay yet, and we told him no. He said the company did have some apartments for single men, but he didn't think we'd like 'em. The company deducted $75 a month from employee's wages for the use of these places. Dean and I talked it over; then without even seein' 'em, we told Mr. Turner we'd take one till we could find another place.

He took us down the hall after that and introduced us to another lady who gave us one of those employee's folders with our job description sheet and some little pamphlets that told all about the company and the many benefits it offered. She also gave us a key to one of the apartments and directions on how to get there.

Mr. Turner told us to use the rest of the day to get moved in and to take a look around the feedyard. He said he would tell our bosses we'd be startin' work the followin' mornin'.

We drove over to the company's housing unit for the single men and found our apartment. It wasn't much, but Dean and I'd both lived in a lot worse. It was just a simple room with two double beds in it. There was a stove, refrigerator, and sink along the back wall, and a table in the middle. It was clean but hotter than the hubs of hell inside. There was only one window and no air conditionin', not even a fan.

After movin' our gear inside and drivin' around the lot, we went to look at the countryside. There was a little town about three miles away, made up mostly of Mexican families who worked at the feedlot and the surrounding farms. There were a couple of small grocery stores, a filling station, and three bars in the town.

We checked around and found that the man who owned one of the fillin' stations also owned an old motel. He'd converted it into apartments that rented by the month. They came with air conditioning and televisions, so Dean and I put our names on the waitin' list. Only a couple of people were ahead of us.

We bought some groceries at one of the stores and went back to our room. After we'd cooked our supper, it was so hot in the room it was darn near impossible to sleep inside.

Later in the evenin' as the men got off work, we found that almost all of the other people who lived in the single-men's complex were Mexicans. They worked at the feed-mill or on the farm. We were the only two cowboys and the only two gringos.

Our neighbors stayed up half the night, sittin' outside, talkin' and playin' their guitars. It was too hot for them to sleep inside as well, and many of 'em simply laid down where they'd been visitin' and slept right there.

The next mornin', we were up at five and down at the lot by five-thirty. Dean dropped me off at the barn, where I's to meet my boss, and he took off for where he was to start.

Seven men, countin' the cow boss, were on each cowboy crew. Every crew had about 25,000 head of cattle they were responsible for. Every man was responsible for the cattle in an assigned set of pens. If he found any sick ones, he'd cut 'em into the alley and later took 'em up to the hospital where a company vet and his crew doctored 'em.

Each man had three horses to ride. The company kept 'em shod for him. If he wanted to shoe 'em himself, the company would pay him $8 extra for each horse.

Every day, we started work at six. We'd saddle our horses and then go over to the cowboy shack where we'd get a cup of coffee and find out what pens of fat cattle were to be sorted that mornin' and how many truckloads were goin' out. Then we went down and brought those pens of cattle up to the sortin' alley near the scale. There the buckaroo boss or Mr. Turner sorted off the cattle we were to weigh and ship that day. When that was done, we usually had another cup of coffee and started ridin' our pens.

At ten-thirty, we had another fifteen-minute coffee break and then returned to ridin' pens. We got an hour off for lunch. In the afternoon we checked pens till we were done. Then we went up to the hospital where we sorted and returned the cattle that were considered well enough to go back to their various pens. We were usually done by six in the evenin' but were expected to stay longer if necessary. The only time this routine varied was when we were receivin' new cattle that sometimes came in at night or when we were processin' 'em. Then the days could get a lot longer.

Two months after we were there, three things happened. The first one was we got a card sayin' a room opened at the little motel downtown. We grabbed it in a minute and were moved in by nightfall. The second thing was that Dean got word that Bill Anderson had lived through his beatin' and there was no warrants out for our arrest. The third was that Dean got transferred to the veterinary crew and was made an assistant to the company vet. He liked that a lot better than ridin' pens.

After our move to town, our whole lifestyle changed. We still kept the same hours, but now we got to watch TV at night, and we ate out a lot more. We were livin' like regular townspeople with normal jobs. We got up at a decent hour, went to work at the same time, and usually got home at about the same time. I was makin' more money than I'd ever made in my life.

By the time the first year was up, Dean had taken me down and gotten me signed up for social security. That gave me even more money. I had so much to spend, I didn't really know what to do with it all. For the first time since I'd worked as a mustanger, I opened a bank account and started savin' a little nest egg. I had nice clothes to wear, and I took 'em to a cleaners rather than wash 'em myself. We always had cold beer in the refrigerator, but I found that I didn't drink as much of it as I thought I would if I had it around all the time. I usually ate at least one meal a day in one of the restaurants, and I liked that a lot better than my own cookin'. People around town had gotten to know us, and most everyone spoke to me and was friendly. The men on the feedlot crew were all a lot younger than me, but that was nothin' new. I did my share of the work, and we all got along fine.

The weather took a little gettin' used to 'cause it was

awfully hot in the summer, and the dampness made my old joints ache in the winter. Still, it beat the hell outta those forty-below mornin's. All in all, life seemed pretty good.

Dean was happier workin' on the vet crew than he was ridin' pens. When he was a pen rider, he used to kid with me and say that he could always tell what time it was by the pen he was in, 'cause you were always in the same pen at the same time everyday.

By the end of the first year, I could tell Dean was startin' to get restless. I think the only thing that kept him around for as long as he stayed was that he had got to datin' that pretty little gal at the front desk in the main office. I don't think either of 'em ever got too serious, but they seemed to enjoy bein' together. I could read the signs though, and even she wasn't gonna hold him there too much longer. Bein' confined to the same place and doin' the same thing everyday was gettin' to be a lot like bein' in jail for him. He missed the wide-open spaces and the smell of sage. Most of all, he missed the excitement.

To break up the routine during the two Christmases we spent there, Dean took time off and went to visit his dad. I still wasn't sure just where he lived or what he did. Dean was real closemouthed about his family life. I figured there'd probably been some problems sometime back. They musta started gettin' along a lot better, 'cause Dean would mention talkin' to his dad on the phone every now and then.

One year when he came back from a Christmas visit, he brought me the prettiest pair of beaded Shoshone moccasins I ever saw. They were made of home-tanned buckskin and still smelled of sage smoke. The beadwork on the top covered the whole foot from the toe to the ankle. They were one of the best-made pairs I'd ever seen. I used 'em for house slippers. The big, round, metal container I gave Dean to keep his ropes in seemed cheap by comparison.

After that second Christmas visit back home, I knew the time was comin' when Dean was gonna want to move on, and I'd made up my mind I wasn't goin'. Wanderin' around the country is fine when you're young, but when you get to be as old as me, it's kinda nice to know where you're gonna be sleepin' that night. New country, strange horses, and different people to work with didn't hold the call to me it had when I was young.

Dean was still writin' letters to everyone he'd ever met, and every now and then, one of 'em would stop by for a visit. One afternoon Dean come home to find a letter from ol' dumb Donnie. He's over on some outfit north of Austin, Nevada. In the letter Donnie said he was the cow boss on the place where he was workin', and he had a job there for the two of us. Later in the letter he said the neighborin' outfit was lookin' for a couple of men to start a string of colts. He said the job he had would pay us $300 a month, and the one on the other place paid $500 apiece.

When Dean told me about the letter, I didn't even let him finish 'fore I said there was no way in hell I'd ever consider workin' for that dim-witted bastard. And no man in his right mind would consider hirin' a feller that was over sixty-five years old to start a string of broncs, so that place was out, too.

Dean acted like the thought had never crossed his mind, but every now and then he'd drop some little hint about how he really felt. One evenin' while we were sittin' there watchin' television, he got to talkin' about the ol' times at the pack station and our first camp job together at Ben Bird's place. When he was done, I told him that those were sure 'nough good times, but they were over for me. I told him I's old now, and the idea of ridin' cranky horses and sleepin' on the ground made for good memories, but it damn sure wasn't anything I wanted to do again.

Tryin' to tell a young person what it's like to be old is a lot like a starvin' man tryin' to tell someone who has just eaten a big dinner what it's like to be hungry. He can kinda get the idea, but he just don't get the real feelin' of what you're sayin'.

Finally, one evenin' in late January, a little over two years after we first started at the feedlot, Dean says, "Tap, I'm headin' back for Nevada, and I want you to come along with me. I plan on givin' my notice tomorrow. I'll stick around a week or so after that, but then I'm headin' out."

I told him I sure understood how he felt, and if I's a few years younger, I'd be sittin' right beside him 'cause I missed the mountains and the big sage flats, too. But a man's got to face up to the facts of life, and one of 'em is we all got to get old someday, if we live long enough.

That night as I laid in my bed, I got to thinkin' over what it was gonna be like livin' without the kid. We'd been together goin' on five years by then. What was it gonna be like livin' the rest of my life out alone? That boy was about as close to family as I'd had in a lot of years. And, I was tellin' him the truth when I said I missed the high-desert country.

God Almighty, how I did miss it! Hardly a day went by that I didn't think about the sights, sounds, and colors that had made up my life for so many years. I could close my eyes and see the shadows of the other riders saddlin' up through the purple haze just before first light. I could smell the fragrance of wet sage after a sudden summer shower. And I could hear the sound of a thousand head of cattle, bawlin' for their calves at weanin' time. The idea of never bein' able to experience these feelin's again made me wish I was dead already. But I wasn't, and I had to make the best of it till my time did run out.

The next two weeks were some pretty sad times for me and Dean. We talked a lot about all the good times and rehashed a lot of ol' memories. We promised each other how we was gonna write and come out and visit and all the other things ol' friends do when they're fixin' to say good-bye.

When that final mornin' came that Dean was to leave, I was feelin' like I was goin' to the funeral of my best friend. Dean had packed his truck the night before, so about all he had to put in it was his bedroll and saddle.

I helped him carry these last few things out, and we shook hands. Neither of us said a word. I didn't 'cause I had a big lump in my throat, and I didn't think I could get any words to come out around it. I reckon Dean musta felt the same way. I just stood there starin' down the road for ten or fifteen minutes after he left. Then I sat down on the front step and started to cry.

Yes sir, I said I cried. I hadn't done that since my grandfather had died, and that had been over fifty years ago. I cried 'cause I missed the boy, I cried 'cause I was alone, I cried 'cause I missed a way of life that I couldn't have any more, and I cried 'cause I was old.

By and by, I kinda got myself under control, and I went

into the house. I'd just finished shavin' and was gettin' myself ready for work when I heard a truck pull up outside. I was expectin' one of the other men I was workin' with 'cause I'd made arrangements to share the gas bill with him for a ride.

I stepped out the door, and there sat Dean's pickup. I figured he musta forgotten somethin'. He motioned for me to come over and get in. When I sat down, I saw that his eyes were red and his cheeks were all puffy. He said, "I can't do it. If you won't come with me, I'll just have to stay. You reckon I can get my old job back?"

I said, "Do you really want to go, boy?"

He just nodded his head, then he said, "Want to go bad, but I don't want to go bad enough to leave you back here, so I reckon I'll have to stay too."

I got choked up all over again, and finally I said, "The hell with it! Come on in and help me get my stuff packed. If we stay around here, you'll just sulk and pout, and no one'll be able to stand you. I might as well do what you want 'cause you won't be fit company if I don't."

Then we both started to laugh.

CHAPTER 26

Well, Dean and I didn't go to Nevada, not at first anyway.

While I was packin', we talked it over and decided that 'cause it was only the first of February, it might be a little rough to get a decent job there. Mosta the good ones would already be taken, and none of the big ranches would be turnin' out for a couple of months. In that part of the world we figured about the only jobs we'd be able to land would be calvin' heifers or forkin' hay to hungry cows, so we headed south.

In a way, it felt good to be on the drift again, but for the first time in my life, I's afraid of what it might mean. I'd gotten used to the security of a steady job and sleepin' in the same bed every night. I also realized I was gettin' old. That meant a lot of people wouldn't hire me. Others would give me a chance but would be watchin' me just like you do a green kid to see if he can handle the work. Thinkin' about these things made me lean back and take stock of our situation.

I was goin' on sixty-seven years old. My health was good, but I could tell I was slowin' down. On cold mornin's or when it was damp, every bone I'd ever broke told me where it was located. Financially, I was in better shape than I'd ever been in my life. I had over $800 in my pocket and a little over $4,000 in the bank. I had a footlocker full of clothes, all fairly new and and fresh out of the laundry. I had a good work hat and a new dress hat. I had two pair of new custom-made boots, one built by Blucher and the other by Paul Bond. I had traded in my ol' wore-out saddle on a good, custom-made Capriola rig with a three-and-a-half-inch post horn and a five-inch cantle.

Dean had turned twenty-six in December. He stood six-foot-one and weighed 165 pounds. As the old-timers used to say, "He was in his natural prime." For the past year and a half, he'd been workin' out three nights a week at a gym on the outskirts of Fresno. At first, he'd gone down to get some exercise and brush up on his karate. Lately, he'd gotten into kick boxin' and this bodybuildin' stuff. He looked skinny till he took off his shirt. Then he'd scare you. His forearms were the size of my thighs, and the horizontal muscles in his stomach and back stood out like old scars.

I don't know how much money he had on him, but I'd guess that it was close to a thousand dollars cash. Durin' the time we'd been at the feedlot, I'd saved a good part of my wages, but he'd spent a lot of his. Yet, I'd still bet he had another thousand in the bank. Like me, he had a footlocker full of good clothes and a couple pair of new boots.

He had his ol' flower-stamped, center-fire saddle, but he also had a good, low-cantle, ropin' saddle with a nice, three-inch, rubber-wrapped dally horn. He'd bought it right after we started at the feedlot to keep his old one out of the mud and manure.

After we were there for a month or so, he got to goin' to a few of the practice team ropin's they held around the area. Pretty quick, he's ropin' two and three nights a week. He'd been doin' that for two years now and was gettin' to be some pretty tough competition at the little jackpots they held. If he was ridin' a decent horse and had a good heeler behind him, he could stretch 'em out pretty regular in the eight-second range. In that part of the country, some of the best arena ropers in the world compete. Dean wasn't one of 'em. Still, he could hold his own with most of the backyard and weekend cowboys.

He'd gotten to drinkin' a lot more than he used to, and I was drinkin' a lot less. When he drank, it didn't take much to tap him off, and he'd go to fightin' at the drop of a hat. It got to where I didn't even like goin' out with him. After we left the feedlot though, he cut way down. Within two years, he'd quit completely. Now he won't touch a drop.

We landed our first Arizona job down at Oracle Junction, just north of Tucson. We stayed two weeks and pulled out. The weather was hot and the country was some of the roughest I ever saw. The whole area was covered with cat's claw, cholla, and a dozen other kinds of stickery plants. The feller that hired us told Dean that everything on the ranch had horns, teeth, or stickers. He wasn't kiddin'.

We headed back north to Flagstaff. When we left Oracle, it was close to eighty-five degrees, but when we got to Flagstaff it was snowin'. We spent about a week chasin' job leads, mostly on ranches off the mountain and over to the east. It seemed we were always just a day or so too late.

Then one afternoon we heard about a lumberman by the name of Wilson who lived there in Flagstaff. He was supposed to have a good-sized place down south, just west of the big Apache reservation.

We finally tracked him down at his office. He told us that he did own the ranch, but he left the complete runnin' of it to his foreman, an Indian by the name of Sam Winzlo. He told us this Winzlo had been on the ranch through four different owners. One had tried to run it for awhile without him, but in the end had hired Winzlo back.

Mr. Wilson liked talkin' about his ranch, and we spent a couple hours with him. Durin' that time, he told us he'd bought the ranch as an investment, and as long as it made a small profit or just broke even, he was happy. He'd been pumpin' a lot of money into the place, fixin' it up 'cause he planned to retire out there in a few years. His arrangement with his Indian manager was simple enough. Winzlo ran the ranch, and Wilson paid the bills. As long as it broke even, Sam Winzlo had a job. If the place lost money, Wilson would put it on the market. So far, this Winzlo had been able to make the place pay, and Wilcox was happy.

The lumberman told us that the place carried about 1,400 head of mother cows. The cattle ran down in the valley durin' the winter and summered up in the mountains in the Tonto National Forest. They didn't put up a lick of hay on the ranch and never fed any supplement. It took six men to brand the calves in the spring and move the cattle to the summer range. During the summer, it only took three men to shuffle the cattle from one allotment to another and keep the springs and fences up. In the fall, they went back to a six-man crew again to gather and work the cows. He never said how many men it took to run the place in the winter.

The crew operated out of three camps. The summer camp was up in the mountains and had been a dude ranch at one time. It was all fixed up with nice log buildings, barns, and corrals. It even had its own rodeo arena, with a ropin' box and buckin' chutes.

Mr. Wilson gave us a map and directions on how to get to the ranch but said he didn't know if his foreman needed any help or not. There was no phone at any of the camps, so the only way we could find out was to drive out there. Then he mentioned that Sam usually hired local Indians from the San Carlos and Fort Apache reservations. When he hired other people, they didn't seem to stay very long. There shoulda been a message in that little statement, but he said it so casually that it never sank in.

It was about a three- or four-hour drive southeast to the ranch, but we decided to take a run down there anyway. We left early the next mornin'. About ten-thirty or eleven we pulled up to a little general store and restaurant at a place called Grassey Springs Station. Mr. Wilson's map showed it as bein' about ten miles from the ranch's main camp down in the valley. It was only a few more miles to the reservation line.

Grassey Springs made most of its money sellin' groceries, gas, and beer, but they also had a little restaurant. Their main customers were the tourists and local Indians. The place rented out half a dozen cabins to people who wanted to fish, hunt, and camp in the area but didn't like to sleep on the ground.

We decided to get a bite to eat before headin' out to the ranch. While we were waitin' for our food, Dean asked the little man behind the counter how far it was to the Three Dot. That's what Mr. Wilson called his place.

The man nodded in the direction of the ranch and said, "Maybe eight or ten miles. You ain't fixin' to go out there to work, are ya?"

Dean told him that we were gonna go see if they needed any help. Then Dean asked why the man sounded so surprised that we'd be goin' there to look for a job.

The feller just sorta shrugged his shoulders and said, "Oh, I don't know. It's just that most white folks don't seem to stick around the Three Dot very long." Then he leaned over the counter and whispered so as no one else could hear, even though we were the only ones in the place, "Been some stop in here on their way to the ranch that I ain't never seen again." Then he straightened up, looked around to make sure no one had heard him, and went back to check on our hamburgers.

When he came back, Dean asked if he knew this Sam Winzlo that ran the place. The feller said everyone in these parts knew Sam Winzlo. He'd been a top saddle bronc rider back in the late forties and early fifties. He'd been runnin' the Three Dot for over twenty years now. He went on to say Sam was a big, black, sullen bastard who never talked to no one. Injuns and whites alike were scared of him. The skinny little guy said Winzlo came in here every Friday afternoon on his way to pick up supplies and the ranch's mail. "Always buys the same thing—a package of salted peanuts and a Coke. Dumps them nuts into his drink and walks out without sayin' a word to no one." The way this little guy talked made it sound like buyin' nuts and a soda pop was a very suspicious thing to do.

When we got out to the truck and were fixin' to leave, Dean looked over at me and said, "That feller's kind of a weird little duck, ain't he?"

I nodded in agreement but I was thinkin' more about the things the man had said and hinted at. I'd only worked around one or two Apaches, and they were sure a different breed of cat from the Shoshone and Bannocks I'd been raised around up north. I thought about these things all the way into Mr. Wilson's winter camp.

I've always thought of a cow camp as kind of a primitive place with real limited livin' facilities. This place of Wilson's was anything but that. There were only three buildings: a barn, bunkhouse, and main house. All of these buildings were built long and low and made of cinder blocks. They were all painted white and had red roofs. The corrals in back of the barn were made of steel pipe. There was a white board fence that ran from the gravel road into the yard. Hundreds of poplar trees lined both sides of the road. The trees were only fifteen or twenty feet tall, so I knew they hadn't been there too long.

As soon as we stepped outta the pickup in front of the bunkhouse, I heard the ol' familiar poppin' noise of a Woody generator. The cookhouse faced east, with the front door set in the middle of its east wall. There was a kitchen and dinin' area at the north end and a kind of rec room at the south end. In the middle were eight rooms, four on each side of a big bathroom and shower. The walls in the bathroom and kitchen were made of stainless steel so they could be hosed down and wiped off. Each of the bedrooms had a window that faced the mountains to the west. They were furnished with a twin bed, a closet, and a dresser.

When we stepped into the building, Dean and I could hear someone in the kitchen, so we headed down the hall in that direction. We found a fat, Mexican-lookin' cook, fixin' supper. Dean asked if he knew where we could find Sam Winzlo. The Mexican looked at us suspiciously and said the cowboys would be back in an hour or so.

Dean looked around the kitchen and dinin' area and then asked the cook if he knew if Sam needed any more riders. The man almost dropped the pan he was holdin' when Dean asked that. "You want a job here?" he asked like he couldn't believe what he'd just heard.

Before Dean could answer, the Mexican went on to say, "Do you know where you are? This is the Three Dot. Sam Winzlo is boss. What's the matter with you?" Then he walked into the kitchen, shakin' his head.

Dean and I walked back to the rec room and sat down. Each of us picked up a magazine and started thumbin' through it. I wasn't payin' much attention to mine. I was thinkin' that there was somethin' awfully strange about the way people acted toward this place.

An hour or so later we heard a pickup pull into the yard, so we got up and headed for the door. As we stepped outside we saw the truck stop down by the barn. It was pullin' a big, twenty-foot, goosenecked, stock trailer with four horses in the back. Three men got outta the front of the truck, and one climbed outta the back. Two men had on batwing chaps and the other two had on shotgun leggin's.

As we walked up, I saw that all four men were Indians. They looked to run in age from about thirty-five to fifty.

251

Each was over six feet tall, and none of 'em weighed less than two hundred and twenty-five pounds. They were all dark, but one was the blackest Indian I'd ever seen.

By the time we reached the truck, they had their horses out, and I got a chance to get a good look at their outfits. The saddles were sure a big switch from the fancy buckaroo rigs that the men up on the Flyin' D rode. These saddles were all swell-forked, double-rig outfits with small horns and low cantles. None of 'em had any stampin' or carvin'. There wasn't a speck of silver or horse jewelry in the bunch. The catch ropes tied or buckled to the forks were all short, heavy nylon. The longest couldn't have been over thirty-five feet, and each had a horn knot tied in the end. They all rode grazer bits. Two of the men were even ridin' with their halters under their bridles.

Dean and I walked up, and I asked if one of them could tell me where I could find Sam Winzlo. Three of 'em acted like they never heard me. The fourth one, the darkest of the bunch, said he was Sam.

Dean stuck out his hand and introduced himself and me. For a second or two I didn't think Winzlo was even gonna shake with him. While Dean was doin' all the talkin', I started sizin' up this Sam Winzlo. He was a fairly big man but not as large as one or two of the others that had taken their horses into the barn. I'd say he's only about six feet tall, same as me, but I'll bet he outweighed me by sixty or seventy pounds. His shoulders were a good ten inches wider across than mine, and that made him look like he was almost as wide as he was tall. His head was huge, and he didn't seem to have any neck at all. His hair needed cuttin' but wasn't any longer than a lot of white people I've worked with. It was startin' to turn gray in front of his ears and along the back of his neck. I found out later that he was in his late fifties.

The most strikin' thing about Sam was his color. Like I said before, he was the darkest of the four cowboys, but that's kind of an understatement. I think Sam Winzlo musta been the darkest man I ever met who wasn't black. People are always kiddin' me about how black I am because of my Bannock Indian blood on my father's side, but next to him I looked like a glass of milk.

Dean was still rattlin' away when Sam cut him off. He said, "You want job, I give you a try." Then he turned and walked into the barn.

Dean and I went over and started movin' our saddles into the barn and our bed and clothes into the bunkhouse. When we were done, it was still a half hour or so before supper, so I slipped on the beaded moccasins that Dean had given me and went into the rec room to find somethin' to read. Dean went in to take a shower.

While I was sittin' there lookin' at the pictures in an old *National Geographic,* one of the other Indians came in, picked up a book, and sat down beside me. Pretty soon he said, "What kind Injun make them shoes?" I never even looked up. I just said, "Shoshone." That seemed to satisfy him, and he sat back and went to lookin' at his book.

Pretty soon one of the others came in and jabbered somethin' to him in Apache, and they both went down the hall to the bathroom. Then I saw another and another and another, all makin' a trip into the bathroom. A few minutes later, Dean came prancin' out with a towel wrapped around him, and he went into his bedroom.

Then I figured out what was goin on. They were takin' turns goin' in to look at the kid. I'm not sure if it was 'cause of his color or 'cause of his build. Either way, I thought it was kinda funny.

No one spoke another word to either of us till the next mornin'. We were all standin' around the barn, waitin' for one of the men to get in with the cavvy, when the one they called Charley Brown come up to Dean. I'm not sure if that was his real name or just a nickname, but that's what he went by. He looked Dean in the eye and said, "You have pretty big muscles. Maybe you pretty strong. But what you do someday when you meet bad Injun with big knife?"

It was then that I noticed he was holdin' a big, foldin' buck knife in his right hand and was testin' the edge of it with the thumb of his left hand.

Dean was standin' kinda sideways to the other man when he smiled that silly grin of his and said, "I'd kick his damn head off," and with that he shot out a wicked side kick that landed against the barn wall, just to the left of the startled Indian's head. The dust on his boot left a perfect print on the wall. It happened so fast that I don't think Charley Brown really realized what'd taken place for a full second or two, but it was enough to surprise him, and he cut his thumb on his own knife.

The horses Winzlo cut me and Dean to ride that day had to be some of the sorriest animals I ever strapped my saddle on. Mine was a big paint horse that musta weighed 1,400 pounds and was almost as old as me. He had a rein on him like a green-broke mule and was so damn lazy and slow, I could hardly get him out of a fast walk. Sam called the horse War Paint.

Dean's was a big bay about the same age and temperment. When the boy got tired of kickin' the horse, he used a green switch to swat him down the hind leg; then the bay would come to a complete stop, jump, and kick backwards.

We were gatherin' the lower country and movin' the cattle up toward the spring range. A few of the cows had small calves followin' 'em, and we had to go pretty slow. For that reason alone, I's able to keep up with the others, even at War Paint's slow pace.

By the time we got in that evenin', I's probably just about as tired as I'd have been if I'd walked the same distance. I'd been kickin' and poundin' on that poor ol' wore-out pony till my legs were shot.

After the incident with Charlie Brown in the mornin', the rest of the crew had decided to Injun up on me and Dean, and no one spoke a word or even looked at us. That was their way of sayin' we weren't important or didn't exist.

That night after supper, Sam left with the pickup and trailer. I don't know were he went or when he got back, but the next mornin' there were three new horses standin' in the corral. When we went down to catch our mounts for the day, he pointed at the three strange animals and told Dean they were his new string.

Sam told me I could put the bay horse that Dean had ridden the day before in my string. Then he pointed out a little mustang-lookin' outfit that didn't weigh over 800 pounds and probably only stood about twelve or thirteen hands. The horse had a head as long as a pick handle and a Roman nose. In his pidgin English, Sam said, "That be your third horse. Call him Speedy Gonzalas."

None of the three new horses were very big, maybe only fourteen hands and weighin' around a thousand pounds. Two were brown and one was a palomino. As soon as we stepped up to the fence, they backed away and started movin' around kinda nervous-like. They all had old, white, saddle marks on their backs, so I figured they'd been ridden a few times at some point in their lives. The palomino musta had fifteen brands.

I caught Speedy and got my saddle on him. Then I went out to help Dean get ready. He was havin' a hell of a time gettin' one of the brown horses cornered up and caught. We'd back him against the fence, but as soon as Dean would step up to put his lead rope around the horse's neck, the knothead would dive straight ahead and run over anything that got in his way.

After about three episodes of this crap, I was gettin' fed up. I could tell what Sam was tryin' to do, and it really ticked me off. He and his little band of friends figured if they made it uncomfortable enough for us, we'd pull out, and they could have a few laughs at our expense in the process.

I walked into the barn and got the rope off my saddle. As I walked back into the pen with Dean, I shook out a good-sized loop. I waited for Dean to back the brown into the corner again. This time when the kid stepped up to the horse and he bolted, I rolled out a front foot trap. As soon as I saw I had both feet in the loop, I sat back on the rope and tipped the dirty little brown bastard over on his nose. Before he quit slidin', Dean was on his neck and had his nose halfway into the halter.

Dean was gonna start saddlin' the horse, but I told

him to turn it loose again. We dumped that little spoiled nag four more times. I was gettin' ready for a fifth one, but this time he wouldn't move when Dean started for him. That's not the way the professionals say you're supposed to get a horse to stand for you, but it works when you're in a hurry and don't care much about what happens to the horse.

I know how to break one to stop and stand by chasin' him in a circle in a round corral. If I take the pressure off of him when he wants to stop, pretty quick the average horse figures out that it's easier to stand still than it is to run, but that takes time. This way gets their attention a lot quicker.

Dean got his saddle on without much trouble, but the horse was all humped up like he was pretendin' to be a camel. Dean tried to loosen the animal up by leadin' him around in circles, but the pony wouldn't let down. Dean turned him loose and chased him around the corral. The horse bucked and squealed but still stayed tight.

Finally, Dean said, "The hell with it," took aholt of the lead rope, and stepped on. Before the little horse even realized Dean was on his back, the kid drove his spurs into the brown's belly, clear up to the chap guard. The horse let out a fart and jumped straight ahead. He hit the ground with his head between his legs and went tearin' around the corral. The little horse was squealin' and squallin' but was doin' an awfully poor job of bein' a buckin' horse. He was doin' a lot of stiff-legged crow hoppin' but wasn't gettin' more than a foot or so off the ground.

After a couple of minutes of Dean stickin' holes in his belly, the horse was ready to quit for awhile. Dean stepped off and went to lead him outta the pen, but the damn thing had sulled up and wouldn't take a step. I took the tail end of my rope and proceded to warm his hocks with it. By and by, the horse figured it was better to try and move out than to stand there and get his legs whipped raw.

As we were loadin' the six horses in the gooseneck trailer, Sam walked up and said to Dean, "His name Bed Bug."

Me and Dean and one of the "big three," that's what Dean and I'd taken to callin' 'em, rode in the back of the pickup, while Sam and the two others rode in front.

When we unloaded and went to start the mornin's gather, it was the same show all over again with Dean and Bed Bug. This time, though, the horse wouldn't move after Dean got on. He clucked, spurred, and jerked, but the horse stood there like his legs was stuck in cement. Finally, the kid jerked down his hobbles from the keeper on the left side of his saddle. He took aholt of the buckle with his right hand and went to over-and-underin' that Alpo reject.

It musta taken ten or twelve good swats 'fore Bed Bug untracked and started crow hoppin' out through the brush. Dean never let up till the horse's head came up and he went to stampedin'. The boy bent him in a wide circle back to where we were waitin'.

Sam gave us directions in English on where he wanted us to go and gave the other three their directions in Apache. When we went to take off, Dean had to go through the same program all over again with Bed Bug to get him away from the other horses.

Speedy Gonzalas, the horse I's ridin', was like bein' on one of those fancy parade horses. He danced and pranced and jigged sideways, fightin' and chewin' at the bit the whole time. In just fifty feet, he was covered with sweat. The one thought that consoled me about him was that he was small enough so that he'd have to get tired and slow down 'fore the day was over. I was wrong. That night when we got in, I was just as wore-out as I'd been the day before when I climbed off poor old War Paint. Dean thought the whole thing was kinda funny and said if it never got no worse than this, we'd make out okay.

On this outfit each man only had three horses in his string, so the next day it was my turn to ride the bay that Dean had ridden the first day. Sam called him Alamo. I had tried to come up with some trick or gimmick to use to make poor old Alamo walk out and at least try to keep up with the other horses, but I couldn't make any of my ideas work.

Dean caught the second brown without near as much trouble as he'd had with Bed Bug. Sam called this one Prescot. He saddled him in the corral, and as soon as his cinch went tight, ol' Prescot went up in the air and over on his back.

"Kinda cinchy, ain't he?" was all that Dean had to say. When the horse was back on his feet, Dean led him out to the middle of the parking area and stepped on. Prescot went runnin' backwards for about thirty feet and tipped over again. If Dean hadn't been as quick as he was, the horse woulda landed on top of him. As it was, the boy was fast enough that he stepped to the side, and the horse missed him.

The next time Dean went to get on, he turned the horse so the animal was about ten feet from the side of the trailer. This time the pony went sailin' backwards and hit the gooseneck. It startled him so badly that he jumped ahead,

259

and Dean drove the steel to him at the same time. Prescot was fine after that when Dean rode him around the yard.

That evenin' when we got in, the kid could get on Prescot any place without a fight. When we were alone, I asked him how he'd done it. Dean said that everytime he came to a ditch or washout that was over six feet deep, he'd get off, reset his saddle, and face Prescot away from the cut. Then he'd step on. The stupid horse would go flyin' backwards or flip over, just as Dean jumped off, lettin' the dummy land upside down in the bottom.

Dean said he wasn't sure a couple of times if the horse hadn't broke his neck. At one point the kid had lost his temper. When he found a washout that was ten feet straight down, he pulled his little trick on Prescot there, too. Dean said he got control of himself and realized that if he kept that up in those deep places, he's gonna wreck his saddle.

The boy told me that what he thought really did the trick on ol' Prescot was letting the horse flip over into one of the stock-water ponds. While the horse was down, Dean had waded out, jumped on the horse's head, and held him under till Prescot fought so hard that Dean couldn't hold him down anymore. After that, the brown horse had been pretty good.

This was also the day the big three decided to put the "evil eye" on us. They must have gotten together and planned out their strategy the night before, 'cause startin' at breakfast, everytime we looked up, one or all of 'em would be starin' at us. No smiles, no words, just cold, hard, mean-lookin' stares. They kept this up all day whenever we were around.

The next mornin' it was the yeller horse's turn for

Dean, and old War Paint again for me. The palomino was called Road Map. I guess he's called that 'cause of all the brands on him. He was easy to catch and saddle, but I knew he had a hole in him someplace 'cause of all of those brands—not that many people woulda traded him off if he'd been worth a damn.

Dean chased him around the corral without the horse even humpin' up. He climbed on and rode him around in there, too, with no trouble. After he figured the horse was warmed up, he had me open the gate to let both of 'em outside.

The boy was trottin' the yeller horse around the parkin' area when it happened. For no reason at all, that palomino grabbed himself and fired. He went up in a long straight leap and hit the ground hard. Each jump after that seemed to be gettin' higher. Dean had a Mecáte rein in each hand and was doin' all he could to get the horse's head up, but he wasn't havin' much luck. When the little horse sucked her back to the left in a perfect one-eighty without breakin' stride, Dean went sailin' straight ahead and landed in a heap.

Dean got up and brushed himself off while he watched the horse buck around the parkin' area for another minute or two. When he stopped buckin', he let one of the Indians walk up and catch him. Dean walked over and climbed on again, but Rode Map was done, and he'd do anything that Dean asked of him.

There ain't much use in goin' into all the wrecks that took place the rest of that day. Just let me say that Dean got dusted nine more times 'fore we got in that afternoon. The rest of us spent most of our time catchin' the yeller horse. There were a couple of times when it actually looked like the boy was gonna get the horse covered, but the truth is, he never made it. Not once. If Road Map bucked, Dean got dumped.

Two more things happened that day that are worth tellin'. One took place in the afternoon and the other in the evenin' at the supper table.

About noon, we were all sittin' around restin'. Dean had already been bucked off six times. He was sore, and the rest of us were tired from havin' to run his horse down. Sam was off to one side by himself, and the big three were grouped together. One of 'em was sharpenin' a big sheath knife on his boot top. All of 'em were starin' at us. Dean and I were sittin' far enough away that they couldn't hear us talkin'. Dean said, "Which of them three you reckon is the ringleader?"

"I don't know, but I'd guess it's that one over there on the left. The one I think they call George," I said.

Then Dean said, "I bet you're right. Let's have a little fun of our own. I'll draw a circle on the ground. When I do, I want you to put four piles of sticks in it. Each pile is to have four sticks. I want one pile placed at each point of the compass. You know, like north, south, east, and west. When that's done, I want you to make sure he's lookin' at us, and then you point at him while I make a cross on the left side of this circle."

I asked Dean what the hell all of that was supposed to mean. He told me he didn't know, but then neither did George. When we were done with this hocus-pocus ceremony, Dean looked over at the Indian on the left and, without takin' his eyes off of him, he picked up the pile of four sticks that was on the left-hand side of the circle. Without sayin' a word, Dean crossed the distance from us to them.

He held up the four sticks in front of him. Then slowly and deliberately, he took out one stick, put the other three in his pocket, and with a vicious snap, broke the remaining stick, throwing it at the ringleader's feet. The boy turned and marched back to where I was sittin' and sat down beside me. The three of them went into a huddle and when they looked up, Dean was matchin' 'em, stare for stare.

Later that day between buck-offs, Dean rode up alongside this chief instigator, stared at him while he took another stick from his pocket, and broke it like he had the first one, throwin' it at the feet of the other man's horse. That evenin' as we were loadin' the horses into the trailer before startin' back, Dean did it again. He took out the fourth and final stick after we'd gotten home and put the horses away for the evenin'. The other man was the last one to come outta the barn, and Dean was waitin' for him.

Givin' the big man the same evil stare he'd been doin' all day, Dean broke the final stick and threw it at his feet. Then Dean faced east to where the sun comes up, made the sign of the cross, kinda like the pope blessin' a crowd, then he turned back toward the Indian. With a kind of low growl he drew his right hand from left to right in a horizontal motion, turned, and walked away.

The Indian took off at a dead run to catch up with his friends. Just as he got there, he tripped and fell. They went into another huddle. When they came out of that powwow, the evil-eye contest was over.

As stupid as it's gonna sound, the thing that happened next at the supper table that night probably had more to do with changin' our lives than anything up to that point.

When we sat down to eat, no one was starin' at us anymore, but no one was talkin' to us either. About halfway through the meal, Dean says loud enough for everyone to hear, "Hey, Sam, you ever hear the story about the two trappers that scalped the Indians back in the old days?"

I'd heard the joke, and I couldn't believe I was 'bout to hear it again; leastways, not there.

Sam looked up slowly from his plate and over toward Dean. "No, never hear no story like that," he said in his high-pitched Apache accent.

I looked up toward the ceiling and prayed as loud as I could without openin' my mouth, "Please, God, please close his ears so he don't hear it now, or else seal this dumb kid's mouth." Dean started in with his story, and I started easin' my chair back from the table; I wanted to be ready to run.

"Seems there was these two trappers named Pete and Charley. They'd trapped all winter long, but when they took their pelts into the tradin' post, they found prices had slipped, and they were only able to get forty-five dollars for the whole pile.

"They bought a jug of whiskey with part of their money and started out the door. As they's leavin', they seen this sign in the window that said, 'Fifteen Dollars CASH for Apache Scalps.'

"They took their bottle and sat on the porch, sippin' at it, cussin' their luck and everyone who had anything to do with prices bein' down. When they's done, they headed back for their camp down in the meadow. On their way, they came on an old Apache man. They snuck up behind him and knocked him in the head. Then they scalped him.

"A mile or so from their camp they came on a little girl and a woman pickin' berries. The trappers snuck up and killed both of them, too. That night they decided this scalpin' Injuns was better than trappin', so they figured they'd stick around the area and see if they could find some more Apaches. After all, they'd already made as much in one afternoon as they'd made all winter.

"Next mornin' Charley woke up early 'cause he heard a noise outside their tent. He rolled up the side a little and peeked out. There, surroundin' the meadow, was five hundred Apache warriors, all painted for war and lookin' mad.

"Charley let the side of the tent down real easy and rolled over and shook Pete as gently as he could. When Pete turned over, Charley whispered, 'Wake up, Pete.'

"Pete whispered back, 'What is it, Charley?'

"Charley looked out again at the five hundred warriors and said, 'Pete, I think we're 'bout to become millionaires!' "

By the time Dean was done, I had my chair completely away from the table and was ready to break for the door. There was dead silence in the room. Slowly a corner of Sam's mouth started to twitch; then it turned up, and he started to laugh. "Charley pretty dumb white guy!"

Then he started in jabberin' in Apache, tellin' the other three what he thought of the story. In a minute or two they were all laughin'. Before they'd quit, Dean said, "You ever hear about the football game 'tween the Hopis and Navajos?"

When they shook their heads no, Dean began, "Seems the people who worked for the Bureau of Indian Affairs thought that if they could get the Hopis and Navajos involved in sports against each other, maybe they'd quit their squabblin' and feudin', so they arranged for 'em to have a football game.

"The day of the big game, the Navajos from all over the reservation came—some from Utah, some from New Mexico, some from Arizona, some from Colorado—from everywhere they came. The Hopis came down from up on the Mesas. The Navajos lined up on one side of the field and the Hopis on the other.

"To start the game, the referee blew a whistle and fired a pistol in the air. When they heard the shot, the Hopis thought the Navajos were startin' a war, and they all ran away. Two hours after the last Hopi'd left, the Navajos scored their first touchdown."

Sam really liked that one.

"Weak-hearted Hopis all go home! Ha, Ha. Dumb Navajos can't win when play against nobody! Ha, Ha. You know more Injun stories?"

Dean said "Sure, did you ever hear about the man from San Carlos who took the white men huntin' at Willow Mountain?

"There once was an Apache from San Carlos City that made a deal with two white men to take 'em deer huntin' on Willow Mountain.

"He hadn't been there for a couple of years, and when he got to the canyon where he wanted to take the hunters, there was a new fence with a locked gate. They drove back down the canyon till they came to the house of an old man. The Apache from San Carlos left the two white men in the pickup and went to ask if he could get a key. The old man told him he'd give him a key if he'd do a favor for his family.

"The old one said he had four horses up in the canyon. Three were very good, but the black one was old and blind. The old man said that all of his children had learned to ride on the black horse, and it was like a member of his family. He did not like to see the animal gettin' skinny and sufferin', but he had too much feeling for the horse to shoot it himself. He asked the man from San Carlos if he could put the old black horse to sleep for him. The old man went on to say that you could tell the horse from a distance 'cause he always stayed with a gray, a brown, and a sorrel.

"The Apache said he would do it, but on the way back to the truck, he decided to play a trick on the white men. When he got in the pickup, he told 'em the old man had given him a key, but he had to beg to get it. All the way to the canyon he talked about how he was gonna get even with the people that lived out in the country. About halfway up the canyon, they came on the four horses eatin' in a meadow.

"The Apache told the two whites that this was his chance to get even. They looked at him in surprise when he took his rifle out of its case. Slowly he took aim on the old, blind, black horse. Boom! went his rifle, and the black dropped in its tracks.

"Then he heard boom, boom, boom, and one of the white men shouted, 'Quick, we got the gray and the brown, but the sorrel got away!'"

Well, that's the way it went for the rest of the evenin'. Dean told every ethnic and racial joke I ever heard, only he twisted 'em around so they were about Indians, and Sam loved it.

CHAPTER 27

Later, after supper, I went over to Dean's room. I found him lyin' on his bed, readin' a six-month-old issue of *Western Horseman*. We joked and kidded for a few minutes 'bout his stories, and then I got to the point. I told him I thought we better start thinkin' about pullin' out in the next day or so.

Dean looked at me like he couldn't believe his ears. When I was done, he asked, "Why?"

Then it was my turn to look at him like I couldn't believe my ears.

"Why? What do you mean, why?" I asked. "Son, it's as obvious as sin on Sunday. These four people don't like us. One of 'em is doin' everythin' he can to get you hurt. The only reason we got hired in the first place was so they could get a few laughs at our expense. This is a big game with 'em."

Dean was sittin' up now. I could tell that the things I said had made him feel bad. He was sittin' there with his head down, starin' at the floor. He had about the same look on his face he'd had five years earlier when Lonney had told him that he was gonna have to let him go if he couldn't handle the horses at the pack station.

I don't think Dean could believe there were people who could dislike him for no reason. Usin' that kinda logic meant he'd done somethin' wrong and he didn't know what it was. Finally he said, "We quit that feedlot job 'cause we were bored. Now, you gotta admit that life here has been anything but borin'. I've had more fun in the last few days here than I have since we left the 'D' up in Oregon.

"I don't think these guys actually hate us. It's just that we represent somethin' different. We show up here with our slick fork saddles, long ropes, and chinks, and they take it as a challenge to prove their ways are better than ours. Hell, if some feller had landed there at Ben Bird's place with a double-rig saddle, tied hard and fast, and wearin' batwing chaps, old Ben woulda done the same thing this Sam Winzlo is doin'. He woulda cut him a string of horses that woulda made Casey Tibbs hunt a hole. And we would have all sat around and laughed at the stranger's misfortune.

"I like this Tonto Basin area. It's some of the best cow country I've ever seen. I'd kinda like stickin' around for awhile longer, but if you want to quit, we'll roll 'er up in the mornin'."

I thought it over for a few minutes and then I told him, "Maybe you're right. Let's give 'er a try for another ten or eleven days. That'll give us two weeks here. If things aren't any better by then, we'll pull out, okay?"

We didn't have to wait ten days for the changes to start.

Granted, they weren't big ones, but they were for the better at least. The first one took place just 'fore breakfast. Dean was headed for the bathroom, staggerin' along with his head down about half asleep. Just as he went to open the door, George stepped out. It kinda startled Dean, and he jumped back.

"Ha, Ha. You look like Charlie in your story when he looked out his tent and seen all them Injuns," George said as he went laughin' down the hall and back to his room.

At breakfast they passed the food to us without our havin' to ask for it. And even if we couldn't understand 'em, they joked and kidded among themselves a lot more openly than they had before. I know that ain't much, but it was the first thing any of 'em had said or done that was close to bein' civil.

Down at the corral when we went to catch our horses, even the animals acted better. We cornered Dean's little brown horse, Bed Bug, the one that was so hard to catch. When Dean headed for him, the horse crouched like he was fixin' to make a break for it; but as soon as he saw me roll my rope back and get ready to throw, he froze and let Dean walk up and tie the lead rope around his neck.

War Paint was the same ol' deadhead he'd been the first time I rode him. I guess a man shouldn't complain though. Gentle is a pretty good color on any horse when you're my age.

While we were loadin' the horses in the trailer that mornin', Sam looked over at Dean's outfit like he was seein' it for the first time. He looked at the old slick fork saddle with its silver conchos at the base of the saddle strings, the silver horn cap, and the little silver bell on the cinch. Then Sam looked at Dean's snaffle bit. This bridle setup had two big silver conchos at the corner of the headstall where the brow band fastens to the cheek piece. A hair tassle hung from the throat latch, and basket-stamped slobber straps held the hair Mecáte to the bit. The boy's old-style California spurs were inlaid with silver and had big silver conchos on the outside of the straps. Dean's short buckaroo-style chink chaps had three silver conchos down each leg.

When he was through givin' Dean the once over, Sam said, "You friend have more silver on him than a Navajo pawnshop." Then I think he repeated it in Apache to the others, just in case they'd missed what he said. Everyone chuckled.

When we unloaded and got ready to start makin' our circle, Bed Bug sulled up for a minute, but after Dean drove the steel to him for the fifth time, he made a couple of little hops and was all set to go to work.

The next mornin' when we got ready to take off, Dean backed Prescot, the brown that had tipped over so many times with him, against the trailer. Then he stepped halfway up so he was standin' with all of his weight in the left stirrup. Prescot took a couple of quick steps backwards, bumped into the trailer, and froze.

When the boy saw the horse wasn't gonna flip over, he brought his right leg over and eased into the saddle. I guess ol' Prescot had remembered the wreck at the pond where Dean had tried to drown him three days before, 'cause he never pulled any of that crap again.

That wasn't the case with the yeller horse, Road Map, though. He still bucked Dean off five times on that second ride. I'm not sure if Dean was gettin' better or if Road Map got to where he wasn't tryin' so hard, but Dean did manage to get him rode through one or two other storms that day. The reason the horse was so hard for the kid to ride was that he never blew up when you were expectin' it. He might go an hour or so 'fore he'd grab himself. When he did decide to break in two, there was no warnin'. He didn't tense up or even hump up. He'd just be walkin' or trottin' along and all of a sudden his head would disappear 'tween his front legs.

His style looked like it would be pretty hard to handle, too. He'd make two or three hard, stiff-legged, back-jarrin' hops, and then he'd start gettin' airborne. He'd get to goin' higher and higher each jump. Then right in the middle of about the fourth or fifth of these, he'd do a 180 and suck her back, usually to the right but not always. It was on these turns that he'd lose Dean.

That evenin' when we got in, the kid caught old Sam off to one side by himself and said, "Everyone tells me you were one of the best saddle bronc riders to ever come out of this country. Could you have ridden that yeller horse when you were younger?"

Like most of Sam's answers, this one was short. "Yes." Then he started to walk off.

Dean wasn't ready to let it end there, though. "Can you teach me to ride him?"

Sam stopped in his tracks and turned around to face the boy. "You want to learn to ride saddle broncs? You want me to teach you?"

Dean just nodded.

Sam looked him up and down and, 'fore walkin' away, said, "Okay."

That night Sam took off again after supper with his pickup and trailer. The next mornin' there were four new horses in the corral. After breakfast, Sam tossed an old canvas bag to Dean along with a can of saddle soap and a jug of olive oil. He told Dean to clean and oil everything that was inside.

When Dean dumped out the bag that evening, he found an association bronc saddle, a pair of short-shank spurs, a leather halter with a braided bronc rein, a pair of green chaps with white fringe, and a pair of boots. Sometime in the past, Sam had taken the boots in and had the arches removed. Now the soles were more like a pair of house slippers or moccasins. Later, Sam told Dean that the soft soles made it easier to hold a stirrup. All of the gear was dry and cracked. Some of it was covered with white mildew. It took Dean all evenin' to clean everything. He got up the next mornin' at three and oiled all of it.

That afternoon when we got in from work, Dean took the bag of gear over to Sam's room for his inspection. They had to replace the latigo and the little straps that hold the fenders forward on the saddle, but the rest passed Sam's inspecton. He and Dean went down to the corral where they rigged up one of the gates that swung all the way around to use as a bronc chute.

They ran in Alamo, the old bay horse that Dean had ridden that first day and was now in my string. On this old gentle horse, Sam taught Dean how to set his rigging, how to measure his bronc rein and mark it with a piece of mane hair, and how to get down on his horse when they were in the chute. When Dean had these fundamentals pretty well figured out, Sam had him practice startin' his horse out of the chute, with his spurs hooked in the point of the horse's shoulders.

Sam explained to the kid that it didn't matter how good a ride he made, if he missed his horse comin' out and didn't have his spurs up past the point of the shoulders, it was an automatic zero for a score.

For the rest of the evenin' till it was too dark to see, Sam had Dean ridin' around the arena with his right arm out in front of him, holdin' the bronc rein while he practiced spurrin' the horse from the shoulders to the cantleboard of his saddle.

They did this for two more evenin's 'fore Sam decided Dean was far enough along to try a ride on a real buckin' horse. Those first few rides were sure somethin' to watch. I can remember one where Dean went the whole ride with his spurs up in the horse's shoulders. Another time, he went to jump off and misjudged his distance. He landed in front of Sam, who was on the pickup horse. The horse tripped over the boy, and all three of 'em ended up in a big pile with Dean on the bottom.

Two things were obvious from the very start. Dean was hard to buck off, but he had a hard time spurrin' his horses. He rode too tight and never loosened up. I've seen people who could take a common dink and make him look like he's National Finals Champion. They did it by sittin' loose and lettin' the horse jerk and pop 'em around.

Dean wasn't one of these. He just never seemed to get the knack for showin' his horses. He could start 'em fine, but he seldom ever spurred much farther back than his cinch, and he was always tense. Still, he seemed to really get a big kick out of ridin' buckin' horses. It was almost like he got some sort of a buzz out of the excitement that went with it. I've heard people refer to this as an "adrenaline high." Whatever it was, it seemed to fill a hole in the kid's life, and he was as happy as a preacher at Easter.

It turned out that the four extra horses Sam had brought were practice horses for Dean to ride. They were pretty common as far as buckin' horses go. They jumped and kicked and went straight away but didn't buck too hard. None of 'em fought much in our makeshift bucking chute, and all were easy to get down on. They were just right for someone to learn on.

Every evenin' after work, the whole crew would go down to the corral to watch Dean and give him advice. He rode each horse one time every night for a week and a half. That's over forty head of practice stock, not countin' the workout Road Map was still givin' him every third day. The boy was sore and black and blue, but he seemed to be lovin' every minute of it.

This interest in buckin' horses really built a strong bond 'tween Dean and Sam. Even later when it was obvious that Dean would never be the bronc rider that Sam had been, they stayed close.

At first, Sam gave the crew three days off at the end of every second week. Later, after the brandin' was done and the crew was cut down, we got every Saturday and Sunday off. I'd never worked on on outfit that gave the cowboys so much time off; but the men knew the country, and Sam was so well organized that eveything went like clockwork. Except for havin' to catch Dean's yeller horse half a dozen times every third day, there were very few wrecks or mistakes made by the Three Dot crew.

The afternoon 'fore the first weekend that Dean and I got off, Sam asked Dean if he'd like to try his luck at a little rodeo up near Holbrook. Sam went on to say it was only a couple of hours drive, and we could stay at his place that night. We'd drive up the followin' day and camp there overnight. He said he was goin' anyway cause' he was entered in the team ropin' with one of his brother's little girls. She was also a barrel racer. It turned out later that this niece was one of the top-ten barrel racers in the whole Southwest.

Every weekend he got off, Sam and his wife would pack their campin' outfit in his old car, hook on his four-horse trailer, and haul this girl to a rodeo someplace in Arizona, New Mexico, or Southern California. Sometimes, Sam would take his rope horse along and team rope with her.

Sam tried to tell us he did this for the little girl. He said it gave her a chance to see some country 'sides the reservation. The truth is, Sam did it for his own self. He loved rodeos. He liked to visit with people he used to know when he was a contestant, and he liked bein' remembered. When he was on the road, he was totally different than he was at the ranch. He talked and joked and seemed to be completely relaxed.

On this particular Friday, we got in early. Everyone but Salvadore the cook got cleaned up and headed for the reservation. Dean and I rode in the pickup with Sam.

On the way in, Sam told us he wanted to stop by his brother's house and check on some horses he kept there. He warned us ahead of time that his brother's family was not gonna be very friendly toward us. He said his brother lived near his wife's folks, and the whole clan was pretty old-fashioned and followed a lot of the old ways. None of 'em liked whites.

As we were goin' by Grassey Springs Station, Dean asked Sam to stop for a minute while he ran in and bought somethin' for us to snack on. When Dean came out, he had a soda pop and candy bar for me and him, but he handed Sam a Coke with a small bag of salted peanuts dumped in it.

That ol' man looked at the drink for a long time. Then he looked at Dean. "How you know to buy this for me?" he asked.

Dean looked at him and smiled. "I don't know. You just look like the kinda person who would drink Coke with salted peanuts." Then he glanced at me and winked.

CHAPTER *28*

Sam's brother lived a little way outside the reservation town of Whiteriver. The drive from the ranch to his place took us about two hours and was through some of the prettiest country I'd ever been in.

About three, we pulled up in the front yard of a neat little house that looked just like half a dozen others that were built in the same area. Sam told us that all the people who lived around there were related to his sister-in-law, mostly other sisters and their married children. The houses had been built within the last few years.

When Sam stopped the truck, the front door opened and a young woman of twenty or so stepped out. She was a little overweight and was every bit as dark as Winzlo. She and Sam talked for a few minutes to each other in Apache 'fore she pointed to the back of the house.

When Sam got in the truck, he told us the girl was his oldest niece, Lydia. She was married to a boy named David Bentiece. They lived in her parents' old house down the road a-ways. David worked construction off the reservation and only came home on weekends. Since their baby had been born, Lydia spent a lotta time at her folks' new place. The old house didn't have indoor plumbing or electricity.

Sam said Lydia had told him that everyone was down at the corral, watchin' her younger sisters practice their barrel racin'. She also told him that they had his horse all saddled and were expectin' him to do a little practice ropin' with one of the girls.

We drove around back, past an ol' rickety barn and some half-fallin'-down pole corrals; then we came to a stop beside a nice new ropin' arena. Standin' next to the fence was a man who looked so much like Sam, I knew he had to be a brother. They both had the same heavy and powerful build, large head, and dark complexion. Beside this man stood a woman I wasn't even sure was Indian. She was kinda chunky but built small for an Apache. The color of her skin was way lighter than mine.

A girl in her teens on a coal black, thoroughbred-lookin' horse stood near the gate that opened into the arena. She was small like the woman but was a little darker. She had on a pair of blue jeans and a white shirt. From under a black hat, two long dark braids hung down her back and almost to her waist. I'd have to say that she was good-lookin', but the expression on her face was so serious, I didn't notice how pretty she was at first.

Comin' around the last barrel and headin' for the gate at a dead run came another little girl on a long-legged buckskin. She shot through the gate and started pullin' the horse to a dancin' stop. When she rode back to where everyone was standin', I saw she was younger than the girl on the black horse. She was just as light-skinned as the older woman and wore the same combination of clothes as the other girl. Her hair was short and she wore a baseball cap over it. I woulda guessed her to have been someplace around thirteen or fourteen. She was a little heavier than the girl on the black horse but was far from bein' anything close to what you'd call fat. She was pretty enough to be a model or a teenage movie star.

The three of us got outta the pickup and walked over to the little group who was lookin' at a piece of paper with numbers that the older woman had written. She checked her stopwatch again and added another figure to the list.

Sam and the three of 'em talked to each other in their own language for a minute of two; then Sam introduced us to his brother John, sister-in-law Rita, and nieces TenaRay and Joliene. The older couple mumbled some sorta greetin' and nodded in our direction but none of 'em offered to shake hands. Only the youngest girl, Joliene, bothered to look at us. The other young woman, TenaRay, didn't even come over.

The four Indians talked back and forth; then TenaRay rode off to the barn on her black horse and came back a few minutes later, ridin' a big stout bay and leadin' an even larger, chunky-built brown. Both horses had on double-rig ropin' saddles with breast collars. The brown had a tie-down rigged up from a cable bosal on its nose to the front cinch.

Sam climbed on the big brown and rode to the center of the arena where he started lopin' the horse in circles to warm him up. While he's doin' that, the two girls rode over to a small field next to the barn and gathered up half a dozen ropin' steers and began herdin' 'em back toward the arena. When the girls had the steers in the pen in back of the chute, Sam came over and asked Dean if he'd go down to the catch pen at the other end of the arena and take the ropes off.

John went around to the left side of the chute and took aholt of the release lever. Rita took a position about halfway down the arena where she could record their time. Joliene tied her horse to the fence and went back to load the steers into the chute. Sam and TenaRay backed their horses into the box and got ready for the first steer.

When both ropers were ready, Sam nodded; John rattled the chute gate and then threw it open. The steer shot out and headed for the safety of the catch pen. Sam was right on top of him but never threw till he was over halfway down the arena. As soon as he made his catch, he jerked his slack and turned off. TenaRay came flyin' in and picked up two hocks. The ropes went tight and the riders spun their horses to face each other. Rita called, "Fourteen-two."

They ran all six steers, with their best time bein' twelve-five. Sam never missed a loop, but he was far from bein' as good a team roper as he'd been a saddle bronc rider. Like a lotta outside ropers, he had a tendency to chase his cattle too far, makin' sure of his shot. Also, he was used to ropin', tied hard and fast. Dallyin' was a foreign movement to him, and he had to look down at his horn each time 'fore he took his turns. All of this cost him time.

His niece TenaRay, on the other hand, was smooth and fast. She was always right there when Sam turned off. She never swung her rope more than three times 'fore poppin' her loop around the hind feet. She took her dallies quickly and effortlessly. Sometimes she only picked up one foot, but still, she was by far a much better roper than her uncle.

When they'd chased the last steer, they rode down to the catch pen to bring 'em back for a second run. While they were gettin' the animals outta the little pen, Sam looked over at Dean and said, "You ever do this stuff?"

Dean nodded his head up and down and said, "A few times."

As soon as Sam heard that, he stepped down from the big brown horse and handed Dean the reins. "Good! You go chase 'em for this girl. Let an old man rest." TenaRay jabbered somethin' to him that anyone could tell was a protest, but Sam just walked off.

Dean stepped up on the brown, then climbed down and adjusted the length of the stirrups. When he climbed back on, he shook out a loop with the short thirty-five-foot rope and began to swing it while he and TenaRay pushed the steers up to the other end of the arena.

After the ropin' stock was penned behind the chute again, Dean rode out to the center of the arena and loped the brown horse in a couple of big circles to get the feel of both the strange horse and different saddle. When he felt comfortable, he rode back to the roping box.

TenaRay rode her horse in while Dean backed his. When the horses were set, Dean reached up and pulled his hat down tight, folded the loop of his rope up, and tucked the loose end under his right armpit. Then he looked over at TenaRay. She nodded to him that she was ready, and Dean nodded to her father, who threw open the chute gate just as Joliene hit the steer in the rump with a hot shot.

The Corriente exploded from the head gate doin' ninety, but the big brown horse was hot on his heels. In three jumps, Dean was within throwin' distance. He took two swings to open his loop and threw. The rope went out flat and fast. It settled around the horns with the honda layin' on the steer's neck. Dean jerked his slack straight back and went to the saddle horn in the same motion.

Meanwhile, he'd started bendin' the big horse off to the left. Dean no more than felt the rope go tight on his hip when he looked back over his right shoulder and saw TenaRay pull her bay horse into position. She took one swing to open her loop, dipping it over her left shoulder with her right elbow pointing up. Then she threw. The rope flew down and around. When Dean felt the added jerk on his rope, he spun his horse around to the right and faced the steer. TenaRay's horse was braced off at the end of her rope that now held both of the steer's hind feet.

"Seven-five!" Rita hollered.

They ran the next five for an average time of eight-four, probably not good enough to win Chowchilla or Cheyenne but still respectable enough for a couple of kids out playin' games. By the time Sam had pulled the head rope off the last animal, the sun was startin' to set. Dean and the girls walked the hot horses around to cool 'em off while Sam and I fed the steers and looked at some registered mares and colts he was keepin' at his brother's place.

When the chores were all done, Sam, Dean, and I got in the front of the truck and the girls climbed in the back. We drove up to the house where the girls bailed out, laughin' and gigglin' and runnin' for the door. It was while they were on the porch with their mom and dad, talkin' with Sam, that I noticed how pretty TenaRay was. Up to that point, I'd only seen her on horseback. Standin' there on the porch, with her hands in her back pockets, lookin' up at her uncle, I got a good chance to see her.

She'd taken off the ol' hat and laid it someplace. The long black braids were hangin' down across the front of her shirt. In the evenin' light, her tanned cheeks looked as soft as velvet. Her face was oval shaped, and she had a high forehead. Her mouth was small and her lips were full. Now that she was around just her own family, the hard look in her eyes was gone and she seemed warm and friendly. She may not have been as cute as her younger sister, who had that wholesome, tomboy look, but she was still exotically beautiful. And Lord Almighty, for a young woman was she ever built. She had a figure that made even an old man like me look twice and cough to catch his breath. I looked over at Dean, thinkin' I'd catch him starin' at one of these beauties. I planned to tease him about it later.

Instead of starin' at the young women, he's lookin' off down the lane that led to the main road. Four yearlin' colts were rearin' and nippin' at each other in the field on the left side of the dirt road. He seemed to be way more interested in them than he was a couple of little high school girls.

Dean wasn't much for beatin' around the bush, and if somethin' interested or puzzled him, he'd usually just pop right out and ask about it. That's what he did as soon as Sam got back in the pickup. He just blurted out with, "Is your sister-in-law Indian?"

Sam looked at him for a second in the fadin' light, but 'fore he could answer, Dean went on, "Hell, she's whiter than I am."

I thought we'd gotten to be on pretty good terms with Sam, but still I figured that to be kind of a personal question. Especially considerin' most of these people seemed to act like they thought of whites as an inconvenience they had to put up with.

We were clear out to the blacktop road 'fore Sam answered him. He spoke carefully, weighing his words and struggling with his English. "The *Tinde,* what you call Apaches, were warrior and raider for hundred years. Men from Mexico to Kansas fear them. At first, their enemies other Indians; then Mexicans and whites.

"On raids, *Tinde* bring back food, horses, and clothes. Sometimes they bring back women and children. Many came to like their new life. All the children grew up knowing no other. They became *Tinde* in heart and spirit. They are *Tinde.*

"But, I tell you this; remember it well. Rita and her family are as much Apache as anyone living on this reservation. It would be a very bad thing to speak of these things." The expression in Sam's voice was enough to let Dean know that he'd best drop the subject right there.

Sam's house was about a thirty-minute drive from his brother's place. It set off by itself at the end of a little dirt road. The house was small and old. It had only three rooms, each one havin' been built at a different time and outta different materials. The front room was the original buildin', and it was made of logs chinked with cement.

The bedroom had been added onto the right side and was made from used railroad ties. The kitchen was built across the back and was made of sawed planks nailed to two-by-six studs. The little house sat in a grove of big cottonwood trees and looked like it belonged there. It was dark by then, and I could see the warm glow of a kerosene lamp shinin' in the window as we drove in.

We pulled up 'long the north side and went in through a back door that opened into the kitchen. In this room there was both a gas stove and a woodstove along with a gas refrigerator and a table. The house had been fixed up so that it had charm. It was paneled from one end to the other with tongue-and-groove knotty pine. There was no electricity and no indoor plumbin', but it was warm.

The livin' room had an ol' couch and two upholstered chairs. In the center of the room was an ancient wood-burnin' stove. The walls were covered with pictures of Sam durin' his rodeo days. There were dozens of 'em, mostly of him on different buckin' horses, along with several more showin' him receivin' different awards and shakin' hands with various celebrities from the past. In front of the couch stood a large, glass-topped coffee table. Under the glass was a shelf that held thirty or forty trophy buckles. The whole place was so clean, you could eat off the floor.

Sam's wife, Nina, was typical of the older women I've seen on the reservations. She was heavyset and had black hair that was startin' to turn gray. She wore a simple print dress that hung well below her knees. I'm not sure if Nina spoke English or not. I know I never heard her utter a word of it in all the time we were around her. In fact, not many of the people we were around ever spoke English unless they were talkin' directly to us.

That evenin' Nina fed us a big pot of stew 'fore we spread our blankets on their livin'-room floor. Sam teased Dean, askin' him how he liked puppy stew and told him if he was gonna keep hangin' around Injuns, he was gonna have to get use to eatin' dog. To this day I'm not sure how much of a joke this teasin' really was. I know that durin' the different times we stayed at Sam's house, Nina fixed us some very strange meals made of things I'd never tasted before. Most of it was good and none of it ever made us sick.

I's up 'fore sunrise the next mornin'. When I looked out the front window, I saw Sam standin' with his back to me, facin' east. Even from the back I could tell he's either talkin' or singin' to himself. When he's done, he unbuttoned his shirt and took out a little leather bag about the size of a silver dollar. It was hangin' from a string around his neck. He took a tiny pinch of some sorta floury-lookin' stuff and blew it to the four points of the compass.

Dean told me sometime later that the dust Sam blew was cattail pollen. Dean also told me that, in his own way, Sam Winzlo was one of the most religious people he'd ever met. It may have been true, I don't know. This was the only time I ever saw him do anything outta the ordinary. But then, Dean was around him a lot more than I was, so I guess he oughta know.

After breakfast, we loaded Sam's camp outfit in the back of his old sedan and hooked on his beat-up horse trailer. Then we drove over to John's place and picked up TenaRay, the two rope horses, and the black barrel-racin' horse.

During the drive north, TenaRay and Nina rode in the backseat and talked with each other, while Sam, Dean, and I sat in the front. TenaRay was her normal, friendly self. By that, I mean she wouldn't speak to either Dean or me, even when we tried to talk with her.

We got to the rodeo grounds about ten that mornin', and Sam drove around to the contestants' parkin' area in back of the chutes. There were already a lot of cars and trucks parked there, even though the first show wasn't till six that evenin'. This was one of the first rodeos of the season, and the ranch cowboys and wannabes with big hats were out in force.

We found a place to stay, clear to the back of the parking lot. There were several other camps already set up in the same area. While the three of us men took off to see about signin' Dean up and checkin' to see when TenaRay was to race, the two women started settin' up camp. That was one Apache custom that hadn't changed over the years.

When we got to the place they were usin' for a rodeo office, we found there were so many people signed up for the saddle bronc ridin' that Dean couldn't get in. Sam cornered the stock contractor who was puttin' on the show and by pullin' a few strings and bringin' up stories from the past, he got the man to agree to let Dean ride any turn-out horses they might have. These were horses that had already been drawn but their riders hadn't shown up.

There were also so many team ropers that they were goin' to have to rope almost all day before each show. Only eight teams would be ropin' durin' the actual rodeo, four each day.

The rough stock for this show had come off the Navajo

reservation up north. The bulls weren't too bad, but the horses were just a bunch of unbroken, untried range horses that had been run in. When they came outta the chutes, some of 'em didn't do anything but run. Others threw wild horse fits. Only one or two jumped and kicked straightaway so a man could make a decent ride.

Dean got to get down on two heads at this show. The first one came out and kicked over its head at the flank cinch so hard, it tipped over. In the process the horse hurt its back and hobbled out of the arena. The second one would run a little ways, squeal and kick at the flank cinch, and then run some more.

Sam and TenaRay never even came close in the team ropin', but Dean and she did win a couple of jackpots ropin' after the shows. TenaRay won the first go-round and placed third on the second day in the barrel racin'. That was good enough to put her in first place for the average. All in all, everyone had a good time and we went home in high spirits.

CHAPTER 29

The mornin' of our first day back at work, Sam told me that old War Paint needed a rest, and he gave me a new horse to take his place. He called this little guy Nantan. He turned out to be one of the finest horses I ever rode. He was quick as a cat and gentle as a kitten. He was a dream to rope from, and I never rode a better animal for sortin' cattle.

The second day, I got to retire Alamo and got a big bald-faced horse that was called Pale Face. He was nowheres near the horse that Nantan was, but he was such an improvement over Alamo that he seemed like a futurity champion.

Dean got to keep all of his original horses, but Sam did ask if he wanted to trade in Road Map. The boy told him that if it was okay, he'd like to keep the yeller horse. I think he wanted to use him as a yardstick to measure any improvement.

We kept movin' the cattle from the winter range to the spring range, but the work got slower and slower as more of the cows calved. By the time we got everythin' moved up, it was the middle of May, time to start markin' calves and movin' into the lower summer country.

We moved to Middle Camp and rode outta there while we were brandin'. This camp was a lot more like what I thought a cow camp oughta be. It was nothin' more than an ol' wood-plank bunkhouse and an even older cook-shack, where Sam and Salvador slept in the back. There was also a fenced pasture and a stockade corral for catch-ing horses. A brandin' trap stood at each of the six gates that opened onto the lower summer range. We'd gather the cattle into a different trap each day from the spring country, brand the calves, and turn 'em out on the sum-mer permit side. The thing that took the most time was sortin' off the pairs to be branded. We had to make sure they were straight 'fore goin' to the trap with 'em, or else we'd end up with a bunch of leppies to bottle-feed.

The men on this crew were all older than the kids up on the Flyin' D in Oregon, and there wasn't a lot of horse-play like there'd been up there. These men were all good ropers, but none of 'em threw any of the fancy shots that I saw thrown up north. These guys just rode in, heeled their calf, and rode out. Most of the time they never even bothered to turn their horse to face the animal while it was bein' worked.

Also, it didn't make any difference there if I caught one foot or two, I still came to the fire with whatever I had. Up north, no one woulda thought of draggin' in a calf by one hind leg. I guess it didn't matter though. The calves were small, and even if they were only caught by one foot, they were still easy to handle.

By the end of the first week in June, we were done with the brandin'. At supper that night, Sam told us he'd only be needin' two men to stay through the summer. These two men would help him move the cattle up to, and around on, the higher summer allotments. They would also have to go over the fences and repair the damage done by the snow and elk as well as clean out the springs and get the water in the troughs. They'd be bachin' for themselves as Salvador would be leavin' too. The place called Summer Camp had been used as a dude ranch at one time, and that was where they'd be stayin'.

None of the other three acted like they were much interested in fixin' fence and cookin' for themselves, so Dean says, "If no one else wants the job, Tap and me'll take 'er."

While all of this movin' and brandin' was goin' on, Dean had been goin' in with Sam every other weekend to a different rodeo. I went once in a while but not too often. I was tryin' hard to cut down on my drinkin', and I wanted to start savin' a little money. Both of these are hard things to do when you run with a rodeo crowd.

Dean'd managed to place in a couple of shows, but that was only 'cause everyone else had got bucked off. Anytime someone tells me he won a second with a score of fifty-five, I can pretty well bet the judges were just about ready to start payin' ground money.

The big change in his and TenaRay's rodeo program took place with the ropin'. It was obvious to everyone includin' Sam that Dean would never be a saddle bronc rider, so he'd gotten the kid to ropin' with TenaRay. Sam enjoyed the social life of the rodeo circuit, not the competition, so it was no big sacrifice on his part to let the boy take his place as TenaRay's partner.

TenaRay and the black horse she called Satan chalked up wins at almost every show they went to. If she coulda traveled and gone more, I'm pretty sure she coulda won the championship for the Southwest. But she's only makin' one rodeo every other week, while some of the girls were goin' to eight or nine in that same time.

Sometime after Dean had become Tena's regular partner, he came back from a weekend with her and her uncle and said to me, "You know, if either of them Winzlo gals was a little older, or if I's a little younger, I'd be tyin' ponies up out front of their ol' daddy's wickiup." It wasn't too long after he made that little statement that Dean talked me into goin' to a little rodeo down south with all of 'em.

I hadn't been out for several weeks, and the first thing I noticed was that Dean was startin' to drink again—not heavy like he had at the feedlot but more than he did when we first went with Sam.

The second thing was the difference in the way TenaRay acted. She still wasn't what you'd call overly friendly, but she would at least talk to both of us now.

Her little sister, Joliene, on the other hand, had turned into an out-and-out flirt. While Dean and TenaRay were practicing at her folks' place the night 'fore we were to leave, little Joliene did everything she could to make Dean notice her. Her sister's antics seemed to disgust TenaRay.

One Friday evenin' toward the end of June, after Sam had gotten back with the mail and groceries, Dean motioned me over to his bed. He dug a letter outta the stack he'd gotten and handed it to me. He said for me to read it and then tell him what I thought.

The envelope was extra large. Inside were three photographs. One was a big picture of a girls' basketball team. There were twelve or fourteen players in it. Above their heads was a banner that said, "HIGH SCHOOL GIRLS CHAMPION TEAM." One of the faces was circled and a line ran from the circle to a place at the edge where someone had printed "Me."

The second photograph was one of those little two-by-two high school pictures that the kids get every year. The girl in the picture had her hair brushed forward over the front of her shoulders. It reached down past her waist. Her small mouth was set, with no trace of a smile. I figured the photographer musta been white from the look that she was givin' the camera. Still, I couldn't help but see how pretty she was. Across the bottom of this picture was written, "TenaRay."

The third picture was a color eight-by-ten. It was of a young Indian girl seated and wearin' a buckskin dress. Her face had the same oval shape as TenaRay's, and the skin was the same light shade of brown as hers. But the eyes and mouth didn't look as determined. The expression was more of confusion or maybe even fear. The only two words I can think of that would describe the face in that picture are *soft* and *beautiful*. The ceremonial buckskin dress was a light yellow. It was beaded in several places and had a string of a hundred or more tiny silver bells hangin' from the fringe across the front and down one side. Her moccasins were unrolled and reached to her knees so that no part of her legs showed. The toes were turned up like all Apache footware. The dress, too, looked soft and beautiful. On the back of this picture Tena had written, "This was taken when I was fourteen at a special ceremony given for me. TenaRay Winzlo."

After I'd looked at this last picture for a long time, I put it down and picked up the letter that had come with it. It read:

TO DEAN McCUEN

For the past few weeks I have been thinking about you a lot and trying to straighten out the thoughts I have in my head.

There are many things about you I do not like.

I think you talk too much when you first meet people and are nervous. You do not have to tell everyone all that you know. You should learn not to show your emotions and be quiet more.

I do not like the fact that your life seems to have no purpose. You think only about having fun, with no thought for tomorrow. You should set some goals for yourself and walk in that direction.

I think you drink too much, and when you do, you fight and act stupid. It makes me ashamed to be with you. When you start to drink, ask yourself if you are drinking because you like the taste or if it is because you like the way it makes you feel. If it is because of the taste, try 7-Up or Coke. If it is because of the way it makes you feel, then you are weak and need the alcohol for a crutch to make you feel brave or smart. I would not like to be weak. I do not think you are.

And, I do not like the fact that you are white. That is not your fault, though, and I can see no way you can change it.

I have told you these things because I have other thoughts I do not understand. Lately when you are near me, my blood becomes warm like the summer sun, and my mind is at peace like the child that sleeps in the shade of a giant cottonwood tree.

When you are gone, my spirit becomes that of the big city in winter. Dark gray storm clouds roll across the sky and blanket the sun. The people walk the streets with their collars turned up against the cold and do not speak. So it is with me.

And when I think of your return, the blood flows through my veins like the forest stream as it bubbles and dances over the rocks and rushes toward the valley floor. My heart becomes one with the mountain meadow in spring, warmed by the sun and about to burst with the sight and smell of a hundred kinds of wildflowers.

I have thought long and hard about these things, and I tell them to you, Dean McCuen, because I think I am falling in love with you.

I have entered us in the team roping at the Fourth of July Rodeo. If your thoughts are not the same as mine, do not come to get me. It is better to end this now.

If you do not have a strong stomach, do not come to get me either. There will be many hard times ahead for us. I am only a seventeen-year-old high school girl and you are a grown man. I am an Apache and you are white. I know many people who will not see you as I do. I am sure you have friends that will see me only as a little, blanket-ass squaw, fun in bed but not the kind of girl you take home to your mother.

I will end this so you can think about the things I have written.

TenaRay Winzlo

After I'd finished readin', Dean asked me again what I thought about it.

I told him it appeared to me that the best he could

hope for if he went to see her again was a simple charge of statutory rape but that more than likely, he'd end up bein' shot by her father or scalped by some of her friends.

He laughed and said, "I'll bet you're sure right about that." Then he folded the letter and put it and the pictures in the footlocker at the end of his bed.

Dean never mentioned the letter or what his plans were, so I didn't figure he's too serious about either of the girls. Leastways, I hoped he had more sense than to get tangled up with 'em. I didn't care how cute they were, the fact was, they were still just a couple of little, high-school-aged girls. But, the way he didn't say nothin' had me sorta suspicious and wonderin'.

The evenin' of the second of July come, and Sam asked if I wanted to go to the big rodeo with him and Dean. They'd planned to leave the afternoon before and had told everyone we'd be down then, but we'd found a bunch of cows we'd missed when we changed allotments. We had to go back and get 'em while we still knew where they were. That made us a whole day late gettin' off.

I thought about Sam's invitation for a minute, then I said, "You bet. I wouldn't miss this for nothin'." I was wantin' to see what that kid was gonna do about Sam's two nieces. Sam'd told us they were fixin' to have some sorta special Apache celebration for Joliene durin' the Fourth of July vacation. He figured that's what I was talkin' about when I said I didn't want to miss this.

We were stayin' up at Summer Camp by then, and it took a lot longer to get to the reservation from there. By the time we got cleaned up, got some extra clothes packed, and drove down off the mountain, it was gettin' dark, even if the days were long.

We were just goin' past the turnoff to John Winzlo's place when Dean popped up and said, "Hey, it ain't all that late. Let's swing by your brother's place. I wanna find out if that brown horse is gonna be okay to rope off of tomorrow."

Sam looked over at him like he thought the kid was crazy and then said, "Hell, what's a matter you? That brown horse was okay last week. What makes you think he not okay now?"

Dean said, "Just a funny feelin' I have."

When the kid said that, Sam speeded up and shot off down the side road to John's. I guess he got to thinkin' about all that mumbo-jumbo crap that Dean had pulled on George and about how Dean had known he drank Coke with peanuts in it. In any event, we come screechin' to a halt in front of John's place a few minutes later.

The family inside musta heard the truck slidin' to a stop 'cause John, Joliene, and Rita all come out on the front porch. Sam started chatterin' away to 'em, and about halfway through it all, I heard him say Dean's name. When he did, TenaRay stepped into sight from back of the door. When she looked in the truck and saw Dean, she walked around everyone on the porch and stepped down in front. She was wearin' that blank expressionless look she used when she didn't want anyone to know what she's feelin'.

As soon as she stopped, Dean stepped outta the pickup on the passenger's side. He walked around the front of the truck and said to her, "Is the brown horse okay?"

Tena looked at him for a long moment, still with no sign of any kinda expression on her face. Then the slightest trace of a smile crossed her mouth, and she said, "He will have problems from time to time, but it will be okay now." Then she turned and walked back into the house.

When we were in the truck again and headed for the main road, Sam said, with kind of a suspicious sound in his voice, "My brother don't know nothin' about that horse bein' sick. How you know TenaRay think he don't feel good?"

Dean's answer was the same he'd given Sam before. "Just a funny feelin' I had."

I don't know what kind of an agreement Dean and TenaRay came to over that long weekend, but I couldn't help but notice the difference. I never did see 'em kiss and only caught 'em holdin' hands once. But when they thought no one was around, they talked openly and kidded and laughed together. I don't think I ever saw two people enjoy each other's company more.

After that weekend, Dean all but quit tryin' to ride saddle broncs, and he quit drinkin' completely. TenaRay tried to teach him some of the customs and the language of her people, but she ran into real problems there. White folks have a tendencey to believe everyone thinks, feels, and uses the same logic they do, but that's not the way the world works. Stories that make sense and are completely reasonable to an Indian are nothin' more than a bunch of unrelated ideas to a white man and vice versa.

As for the language—well, I don't think anyone who wasn't born and raised in an Apache home could ever learn it. An outsider might be able to say some words and get technical, learning how to put together a sentence properly, but there are sounds in that language English speakers don't even have letters or combinations of letters to make. On top of that, Apaches speak in a higher pitch than English speakers. But Tena kept tryin'. She was always pointin' at things and sayin' the Apache word for it, over and over, for Dean to repeat.

One evenin' Tena's father and mother brought her up to the mountain camp where we were stayin'. They wanted to check out the area and find where the chokecherries and pine nuts would be found in September and October. They dropped TenaRay off with us so Dean and she could get in some ropin' practice while they drove around the mountains on the back roads.

The kids used a couple of the ranch horses to chase eight or ten head of steers. Sam ran the head gate, and I took the ropes off at the catch pen. By the time they were done, it was coolin' off and the sun was startin' to set. Sam and I sat on the tailgate of his pickup and watched the two young people unsaddle their horses. They talked easily with each other now and joked and smiled a lot.

Sam and I sat there for quite a while, watchin' 'em without talkin'. Then without lookin' over at me he said, "What are you, old man?"

I thought about it for a long time, long enough I'd have made a white man nervous. Sam didn't seem to notice. Then I said, "I don't know." I's tellin' the truth cause I had no idea what he was talkin about. I didn't know if he meant was I a Democrat or a Republican or was I a cowboy or a buckaroo or a Christian or a Moslem. *I don't know* seemed like a good-enough answer to give him without havin' to ask what he's sayin'.

Sam nodded his head up and down and said, "I know what you mean." I's sure glad he did 'cause I had no idea what we were talkin' about. Then he said, "I have known others that have tried to walk both paths. Most of 'em never knew who they were either. You are too black and your face too coarse for a white man. Only the color of your eyes confuses me. I think you are just another red nigger like me. I like that. It makes it easier for us to be friends."

I knew then what he's gettin' at. "Does it make a difference?" I asked.

"It does to me," was his answer. "There may be a time when people look at the color of a man's heart and not at the color of his skin, but the time has not come yet. You and I are old. I do not think we will live to see it. I must live in a white man's world, but I do not have to like them." Sam stopped there and was quiet for a few minutes before he began again.

"It seems to me there are four kinds of white eyes. There are those that come and watch us dance at our powwows and then go home and never think of us again. There are those that feel guilty about the past and want to do something to make us forgive them. They usually tell you at some point that they are part Indian, too; Cherokee seems to be their favorite tribe. They say 'I am part Indian. My grandmother was a Cherokee.' The Cherokee must have had a lot of women. The third kind are the ones that want to help. They come to teach us how to farm or to teach us how to take care of our children. The ones that do it for a living go to work for the Bureau of Indian Affairs or the health services. Some are teachers that ask to come to the reservation. It makes them feel good to think they are taking care of us.

"The last kind are the ones that watch me walk by and then spit behind my back. They call us gut eaters, wagon burners, and war whoops. They hate us and want what little land we still have. They feel we are getting a free ride from the government. If I had to choose which one I had to live with, I would take the last one. I can understand him. The others puzzle me. I have never known an Apache who was sorry for what his grandparents did to the whites. I have never known an Apache who wanted to move to the city to help them. But I have known many who call the whites names and spit when they think of them.

"As I said before, I have to live in the white man's world. Much they have given us is good. I like having a warm roof over my head and a full belly. I like my pickup, and I like to watch television, but I do not like the white people."

After that speech, Sam was quiet for a long time. We sat there as the evenin' shadows closed in on us and watched Dean and Tena some more. They were through unsaddlin' their horses now and were teasin' each other with a garden hose that we used to water the ropin' steers. Tena had squirted Dean in the seat of his pants with it. Now he'd grabbed the hose and was tryin' to wrestle it away from her.

I broke the silence by asking Sam a question. "You say you and I won't live long enough to see the day when people won't look at the other one's color. What about those two?"

Sam smiled and gave a low quiet laugh. "They confuse me, too. I do not know if the skinny one is too dumb to know that we are different or if he is color-blind.

"The way TenaRay acts is even more strange to me. Of all

the families on the reservation, hers has the least use for the whites. Her grandfather is Jimmy Rich. He is a *di-yin,* what the white people call a medicine man. He is old now but still travels from one reservation to another, teaching the old songs and dances. He treats the people who believe in his medicine. He is in charge of many ceremonies. Jimmy has no use for the whites because they tell our people he can not make them well, and the churches say his gods are wrong. My brother lives near Jimmy's house. Jimmy has taught the grandchildren to feel as he does.

"Tena's father, my brother John, is on the tribal council. He has to deal with the soft-mouthed, empty-headed white administrators of the Bureau of Indian Affairs. They feel we cannot think for ourselves. He also has to deal with the white ranchers, hunters, and timber people. He has told me that almost all of them have tried to buy their ideas through the council. Sometimes it has worked and a few of our own people have sold out.

"John lives near town, and everyday he watches what drugs and alcohol have done to both our young and our old people. He blames this on the whites also. TenaRay has listened to these stories all her life. She has grown up with a bad taste in her mouth for the whites. She is the most prejudiced of all the members of my brother's family. She tries not to buy things from stores that do not hire Indians. She speaks English as little as possible. She practices many of the old customs and claims the Mountain Spirits watch over her because of this. Now she wrestles and plays with the skinny white guy like they have been raised together on the reservation. I do not understand."

Then Sam was quiet again, and we sat there in the early

evening darkness, listenin' to the two kids laugh and play. Life seemed good.

Things weren't always sugar and strawberries with them two, though. I 'member one afternoon at a rodeo down near Yuma. Nina was sittin' on a bale of hay, brushin' Tena's hair. Tena was sittin' on the ground in front of the big woman. Sam, Dean, and I were a few feet away, leanin' up against the horse trailer. Tena had won the barrel racin' and was gonna get a trophy buckle along with the winners of the other events later that afternoon.

Nina and Tena were gabbin' away to each other in Apache. The three of us men weren't talkin' about anything of much importance either when Dean looked over at Tena and said, "When you go out there this time, try smilin' for once."

Tena looked up and asked him what that was supposed to mean. Dean told her that everytime she won one of those buckles, she acted like she was doin' the judges a favor by acceptin' it. Now, I don't know if Tena was just havin' a bad day or if she was nervous and uptight, but the next thing I knew, she's on her feet and up in Dean's face.

When she started to talk, her voice had the sound of a snake hissin', and she seemed to spit out the words. I can't 'member what all she said, but she ended by tellin' Dean if he wanted to boss Indians around, he oughta get a job with the Bureau of Indian Affairs.

Dean stood there good-naturedly, listenin' to her carry on till she's done; then he reached down and picked up a bucket of water we had for the horses and dumped it over her head.

She shrieked like a bobcat caught in a trap and cussed him in both languages. At the same time, she bent down, grabbed a big rock, and threw it at Dean's head. He ducked, and the rock bounced off the side of the trailer. While he was gettin' outta the way, Tena picked up a piece of wood that was lyin' next to the campfire and came after him again. She took two or three roundhouse swipes that Dean ducked and dodged before grabbin' her by the wrist. Then he plopped down on the bale of hay that Nina had been sittin' on and jerked Tena into him and across his knee, where he proceeded to paddle her tail.

Dean got off three pretty good swats before Tena bit him in the leg and broke loose. She ran to the back of the trailer where her horse was tied, jerked the lead rope loose, jumped on the startled animal bareback, and raced off.

I looked over at Sam and I thought the old fool was gonna have a heart attack. Tears were streamin' down his face and he was rollin' around on the ground, laughin' so hard that he's about to be sick. Nina just stood there smilin' that quiet smile of hers and noddin' her head up and down.

Tena didn't come back till way after dark. Then she loaded her horse in the trailer and wouldn't speak to any of us all the way back to the reservation. I figured the big love affair was probably over; but sure enough, come the followin' Friday when Sam brought Dean his usual stack of mail, in it was a letter from Tena. Dean didn't offer to let me read it, but he said she never mentioned the fight and acted like it had never happened. He didn't press the issue, and everything went back to normal.

Another time, we were stayin' in a campground outside

of Kingman. It was the second afternoon of a three-day show. Dean had his borrowed bronc saddle sittin' on the ground and was practicin' his spurrin'. He sat in it, holdin' the fork where the horn used to be with his right hand. He'd roll the saddle to the left and shoot his right leg forward and then jerk it back to the cantle. He'd do this two or three times on one side and switch over and do it with his other leg.

Nina was cookin' some meat over an open fire, and Sam and I were standin' around talkin' with a couple of his Indian friends when Tena came stompin' back into camp. She'd gone over to one of the hot dog stands to get us somethin' to drink. She slammed the soda pop down on the fender of the horse trailer and jerked around to face Dean. "Your friends have dirty mouths!"

Dean stood up and said, "What brought that on?"

If any other girl had answered Dean's question with the same words as TenaRay's, it woulda sounded like she was poutin'; but comin' outta her mouth, they sounded more like a witch's curse. "It's that Tommy Tyree. He said if my pants were any tighter, I'd be on the outside looking in, instead of the inside looking out."

Like I said before, Tena mighta been young, but she had a figure that woulda made a blind monk look twice, and the skintight, red-satin bell-bottoms she was wearin' looked like they'd been painted on her.

Dean looked down first at the front and then at the back of the red pants. "Seems to me you ought to be happy about what he said. You keep tellin' me white people always lie. Now you find one that tells the truth, and you get mad."

Tena jerked back like she's gonna take a swing at him and then thought better of it. Slowly, that sly sarcastic smile she gets crept across her face and she looked over at Nina. She growled somethin' to the ol' woman in Injun, puttin' letters and sounds together the way only an Apache can, and they both started to snicker.

Sam was chucklin', too, so Dean asked him what Tena had said.

Sam said, "TenaRay say you should tell you filthy-mouth friend to look good next time he see her 'cause that is close as he ever going to get to seeing what's inside her pants."

Dean blushed, and all the Indians started to laugh.

CHAPTER 30

The month of August rolled into early September without much change in our schedule or routine. The weather was warm but there was a feel of early fall in the air. We'd already had a couple of light frosts, and the quakie trees had started to change color. A few had started to lose their leaves. It was a slow, peaceful time of year for us. The summer work was over and the fall work hadn't begun.

We had the cattle moved to the highest allotment on the ranch by then and were makin' plans to bring 'em in and ship the calves soon. The crew would be back in another week to help gather and move the cattle down off the forest.

There were still a few rodeos goin' on, but some weekends Dean would go down to the valley and help Sam or John around their own places. Each of 'em had seventy head of cattle, and each of their wives had seventy head that they ran in common with other tribal members. They both owned a lot of horses. This meant that there were always colts to halterbreak, corrals to repair, or fences to fix.

One evenin' right after Labor Day, Dean and I were both out in the bathhouse, gettin' ready to take a shower, when I found I's outta soap. I asked Dean if he had a bar I could borrow till one of us got to town. He said there's one in his footlocker and told me to go ahead and get it while he finished washin' up.

I went back to the bunkhouse and opened the big box. There pinned to the inside of the lid were two pictures of Tena; one was the picture of her in the buckskin dress and the other was of her receivin' a trophy buckle at some rodeo.

When I reached down to get the bar of soap, I noticed a stack of letters. The one on top was from her. I don't know what made me do it, but I picked up the envelope, pulled out the letter, and read it.

TO DEAN McCUEN

I went to bed early tonight, hoping that sleep would come quickly and take away the loneliness that I feel when you are not near me. But sleep does not come easily anymore.

Everything I look at seems to remind me of you. In the darkness I stare at the ceiling, and the shadows form an outline of your face. I look out the window at the stars and remember that they were the witnesses to our last good-bye. They saw you run your fingers through my hair and saw you cradle my face in your hands. They saw you brush your cheek against mine and saw the tears flow from my eyes as you drove into the darkness.

This thought is more than I can stand. I feel that the only way I can release the pain in my chest is to take a knife and slash across it, letting the hurt flow out with my blood.

I look toward the barn where you helped my father set the post for the new gate. The longer I stare at the spot, the more it seems that I can see the outline of your strong body as you stood there. Slowly, the picture becomes clearer. Now I can see the sweat running down the back of your neck and the muscles of your back ripple and shine in the sun as you drive the shovel into the ground. I like this thought. It gives me a warm feeling. The loneliness is not so strong now; it's been replaced by a strange feeling inside me.

Oops, there is my mother, hollering at me to turn out the light and go to bed. I wonder if she can tell my thoughts. They say some Apache women can do that. I do not think my mother is one of them. She would not like what she saw in my mind, though I think she probably felt many of the same things when she was young.

I will have to end this soon. Before I do, I would like to make a bet with you, Dean McCuen. You are always telling me I am only a child and call me a little girl. Well, I would like to bet you that when the time is right, you find that this child, this little girl, has the knowledge and imagination to come up with more than enough ideas to keep a skinny, old white man like you awake on many a cold, winter night.

With that thought for you to think about, I will close this letter.

Take care, My Man, and remember that I think of you often.

Yours forever,

TenaRay

When I finished the letter, I put it back where I'd found it. I felt myself blushing, havin' read such personal thoughts. I wanted to kick myself, ol' fool, for pryin' into the kid's business. I knew better.

The next day, Sam went into town. Before he left, he sent Dean and me out to go around the roundup field fence and make sure it was up. While we were doin' that, we saw that the spring box had silted in, and there was no water runnin' into the trough.

That afternoon we got some shovels and hip boots and went back. Dean and I were standin' up to our knees in the muck that surrounded the spring box when I told him that I'd read his letter the night before. Then I asked what his plans were.

He stopped diggin' and leaned on his shovel. "I don't know. Tena wants to finish high school this year and then go to college for a couple of years before we do anything. Hell, I don't wanna wait that long. Why, I'll be thirty-one before she graduates. I talked to my dad on the phone the last time I's in town and told him about her. He's pretty well-off, and he offered to back us in buyin' a small ranch if we can find one.

"The way I got it figured, with you and me doin' day work on the side and her takin' care of the place when we're both gone, we ought to be able to make it on a three-hundred-head outfit.

"I kinda thought maybe you and I could start lookin' around for somethin' up east of Flagstaff or the area just south of there. Even down around Roosevelt wouldn't be too bad. From what I've seen, that north Tonto and Mogollon country sure looked the best, though. Tena has pretty well made up her mind, she wants to stay somewhere close to her folks, and that area isn't all that far away. But, like I said, I'm not sure just what we're gonna do. I guess we'd best talk it over, though, and make some definite plans the next time I see her."

Dean and TenaRay never got a chance to have that talk. When we got in that night, Sam was back with the mail. In the stack for Dean was a letter from John and Rita Winzlo. Dean read the letter first and threw it down on my bed for me to read. I could tell he's mad when he stomped off and started gettin' cleaned up.

The letter said:

TO DEAN McCUEN

TenaRay has told us how she feels toward you. We do not like this. We think it is bad. We think you are sick in the head to think grown-up thoughts about a little girl. We are sending her away to another place to go to school.

Do not come to our house any more. Go find yourself a white woman your own age, and let our daughter grow up.

John and Rita Winzlo

A few minutes after I finished readin' the letter, Dean came back from the bathhouse. He's all cleaned up and dressed for town. He told me he's goin' to the reservation to try to get this mess straightened out. The way he roared off down the mountain in his pickup made me wonder if he'd make it there alive.

At supper that night, Sam told me he'd gotten a letter, too. His relatives blamed all of this on him for introducin' Dean to their daughter. Sam felt like it was his fault, too. He said he shoulda been able to see what was comin', but he thought the kids were just good friends. He went on to tell me that John had asked him not to help Dean find TenaRay. Sam said he liked Dean a lot, but he didn't like the idea of havin' any white man in the Winzlo clan no matter how he felt about him personally.

Dean didn't get back for two days. When he did show up, he looked like hell. I could tell he'd been sleepin' in his truck, and he didn't look like he'd had a whole lot to eat durin' the time he'd been gone. He only stopped in long enough to pick up his paycheck and his better clothes. He rolled his bed and packed up the rest of his stuff, leavin' it for me to watch.

While he was packin', he told me he'd been all over the San Carlos and Fort Apache reservations. The people he knew said they couldn't help him, and the ones he didn't know said they wouldn't help him.

He'd called his dad and told him what'd happened. His father said that the best thing Dean could do was to let it end now. But, his dad went on to say that if Dean really wanted to find the girl, he'd do all he could to help. To prove it, he was flyin' to Phoenix. Dean was to meet him there, and the two of 'em would check every reservation school in the whole Southwest if it was necessary. I knew Dean had been raised by an aunt back East, and he'd grown up in boarding schools. So, I'd just naturally figured his dad didn't have much time or use for the boy. I could tell now I was wrong.

I didn't see Dean again for over a month. By the time he got back, we'd finished gatherin' cattle off the forest and had shipped the calves. We'd moved the cows down to the lower country and were in the process of preg testin', mouthin', and vaccinatin' 'em.

313

Dean looked a lot better when he showed up this time. He had a fresh haircut and clean clothes. He even looked like he mighta gained a little weight. I could still tell he's hurtin' inside, but he was doin' a good job of coverin' it up now.

He told me he and his dad had found a place to leave the pickup truck in Phoenix, and they'd rented a car. They had traveled all over Arizona and New Mexico, even up into southern Utah. They checked every school that boarded children on every Apache and Navajo reservation in all three states. When that failed, they'd tried all of the private schools. Still, they had no luck.

Dean said his dad had foot the bill for the entire trip. When it became obvious they weren't gonna find her, the older man had suggested Dean go back to work. His dad said he knew a few people in Arizona, and he'd see what strings he could pull. If that didn't get any results, he said he'd hire a private investigator to look for the girl.

Now Dean was back and ready to pull out. He said he doubted Sam would let him stay, even if he wanted to. And right now, he didn't want to; he wanted to get as far as he could from this area and the memories that went with it.

I asked Dean where he planned on headin'. He told me he'd gotten us a job on a big outfit up in Elko County, Nevada. They were expectin' us in three weeks. That way I could give Sam fair notice I's leavin'.

There was only one problem with all of this. I didn't want to go. I'd wintered in Elko before, and I knew it could be a dirty, cold, snowbound, son of a gun. Besides, Sam and I'd done some deep talkin' while we were alone at Summer Camp, and he'd promised to keep me on all winter down in the valley with him. He said it got cold, but I knew it couldn't be as bad as northern Nevada.

There was one more reason I didn't want to head out with the boy. I'd been around him when he's unhappy there at the feedlot, and I didn't like it. It seemed all he wanted to do then was drink and fight. I figured this time he'd really be a tiger to be around. I was sure I didn't want any part of that again.

I felt stronger toward that kid than I did any person livin' on this Earth. I also felt we'd been together long enough that I owed it to him to be up-front and honest. So, I told him straight out just how I felt and what I's thinkin'. I told him I figured he'd be a miserable bastard to be around for the next few months. I went on and said I didn't like to be around him when he was drinkin', 'cause all he wanted to do was fight. The last thing I said was I damn sure didn't want to spend the winter in no snowbound cow camp up next to the Arctic Circle either. I don't know how I was expectin' him to take all this, but his reaction sure wasn't what I thought it'd be.

He started to laugh. Here I was gettin' all serious about him, and he was laughin'. When he stopped, he looked me in the eye and said, "Damn you, you old fart. You sure have a hard time figurin' things out. Don't you know you're more important to me than anything in this world. More than TenaRay, more than my dad, more than anyone?

"And as for my drinkin', well, if I wasn't countin' on gettin' that girl back, you might be right. But I do think I'll find her someday, and when I do, I don't wanna have to climb out of a bottle to hold her. Now, let's go tell Sam when we're leavin'. There's some other things I wanna tell that ol' man, too."

When he said that last part about wantin' to talk with Sam, his voice went cold, and a funny look came into his eyes for just a second. Then he slapped me on the shoulder and laughed again. "Come on! Let's get goin'. I wanna get outta here."

I wasn't lookin' forward to this meetin' at all. Both of these men were my friends, and I liked each of 'em but in different ways. I knew Sam felt like Dean had betrayed his friendship and trust. Also, John had made Sam feel guilty by tellin' him that this had all happened 'cause Sam hadn't kept an eye on TenaRay.

For Dean's part, he felt Sam had let him down by not stickin' up for him to Tena's folks and for not helpin' to find the girl. We went outside and found Sam down by the camp's generator. He was changin' the oil in the motor when we walked up. As soon as Sam saw Dean, he braced himself and bristled up like an ol' tomcat.

Dean had earned a reputation around the rodeo circut as quite a scrapper back 'fore he quit drinkin', and Sam had been there to see some of the fights. On the other hand, Sam had been known as a pretty rough character, too, in his younger days. Even now, people still talked about how tough he was. I knew, and I think Dean knew, that Sam Winzlo wasn't gonna back down or walk away from a fight, even if it was with a man half his age and twice as stout.

When we walked up, Dean looked him square in the eye and said, "Hello Sam."

Sam just glared back.

Then Dean opened the talks. "Tap and me'll be headin'

north in two weeks. If you want, I'll stay and give you a hand, finishin' up processin' these cows before we go. But, I want you to know somethin' before you say yes or no. You taught me a lot, and I owe you a great deal. But, I know that you know where TenaRay is. I also know you been holdin' the letters back from me that she's written since she left. I'm not gonna ask you to change your mind, and I'm not gonna ask you to help me. But I want you to know this: No matter how good of friends we were and no matter how much I owe you, I'll never forgive you for these things. Not now or ever.

"Now, do you want me to stay or do you want me to come back in two weeks and pick up Tap?"

Sam looked at him with a face that showed nothin' but total disgust. Then he spit at Dean's feet and said, "I don't need your help. I don't need no one's help to work these cows. If I have to, I do 'em all myself. You say you not gonna forgive me; well, I don't want you to forgive me. If I have to do it again, I do the same things.

"You say we were good friends; I thought so too, but all the time you pretending to be my friend, you sneakin' around with my niece. You make me look bad to my brother, who trusted the care of his daughter to me. When I think of you as a friend, my stomach is sick, and when I say your name, my mouth tastes bad. You can stay or you can go. You are not important enough for me to waste my time making thoughts about." With that he turned his back on us and went back to changin' the oil.

It'd be nice to say those two got to be friends again, but the truth is, they've never forgiven each other, even to this day. We went ahead and stayed there for two more weeks, but they never spoke directly to each other again. I guess that's not entirely true. One evenin' we were just finishin' up at the corrals when John and Rita pulled in.

Dean was on the other side of the squeeze chute where they couldn't see him when they drove up. Right when the three of 'em were in the middle of a deep conversation, the boy walked around the chute and over to their pickup. He walked up, put his arm on Sam's shoulder as friendly as can be, and said, "I'll put this vaccine in the icebox for tonight."

Then he looked at John and Rita and said, "Hi, folks. Say, why don't you come on over and visit with me and Sam tonight? We're gonna sit around and listen to Sam tell stories about the ol' days." Then he slapped Sam on the back and said, "See you at supper, Pard."

I have no idea how Sam talked his way outta that.

CHAPTER *31*

Durin' the next two weeks, Dean, Sam, and I finished gettin' the cattle preg tested, mouthed, and vaccinated. Everything went so smoothly, we were even able to get the culls shipped 'fore it was time to leave. I was the only one talkin' to Dean again, but he didn't seem to mind. He just did his work and kept his mouth shut.

The day we left, Sam gave me my check and told me if I ever needed a job or a place to stay, to come see him. He also gave Dean a check for the two weeks he'd helped. Dean tore his up and threw it at Sam's feet 'fore he walked off. I thought that was kinda stupid.

I'd made it clear to Dean from his first night back that I wasn't goin' to northern Nevada with him. If he wanted to leave, that was one thing; but I wasn't goin' to go up there and freeze my tail off for him or no one else. That was final. I wanted to stay in Arizona or Southern California while Dean was pushin' for the north country. We finally compromised and settled on southern Nevada.

We drove all over the lower part of the state, chasin'

down job leads without much luck. Sure, we picked up some day work here and there for people who needed a little help either gatherin' or fall brandin', but permanent winter jobs were scarce. It was no big deal, though. We both had plenty of money, and it was kinda nice just to be drivin' around, lookin' at the country.

We went to all the local points of interest and stopped to read every historical landmark sign we passed. If we weren't near a town when it got dark, we rolled out our beds and camped right there. If it was convenient, we stayed in a motel. Dean was back to his normal, happy, carefree self and was a real pleasure to be around.

We'd just finished helpin' a family over at Hiko with some brandin' when we heard about a man up on the Geyser Ranch north of Pioche. He's supposed to be needin' a couple of men for winter ridin' jobs. Dean gave the guy a call and made arrangements to meet him in town.

The town of Pioche had been a pretty lively place at one time, but now all of the mines were closed and the town was strugglin' to stay alive. It sat on the side of a hill overlookin' a big desert valley. The town was surrounded by abandoned mines and old mills.

We met the ranch manager just about noon, so all of us decided to go have lunch together. While we ate, we talked about the jobs he had and some of the places we'd worked. He told us a little about the ranch and the country, all the while tryin' to pick our brains to see if we were the kinda men he's lookin' for.

I could tell we weren't gettin' anywhere real fast with this guy, so when I's through eatin', I excused myself and went to the rest room. The booth we were eatin' in was right around the corner from the john. The cashier's desk was across from that. As I came outta the bathroom, I saw one of those bulletin boards where the local people post little announcements. It was around the corner from where we were sittin' and across from the cash register.

I stopped to take a look at it to see if anyone had listed any job. From where I's standin', I wasn't more than two feet from Dean and the man from the Geyser, but they couldn't see me. I was scannin' over the list of announcements when I heard the ranch manager say, "Look, Son, I can use you, but I'm not gonna put a man as old as your friend out in a camp fifty miles from headquarters. If you want the job, you got it, but your friend is out."

Then Dean said, "Well, I'm sorry to hear that. I'd like to give you a hand, but me and Tap been together too long to split up now." As I stood there, I got to thinkin' back to that first winter when I'd gotten us the job with Ben Bird up at Gerlach. I remembered how ol' Ben had said he could use me, but he didn't need no green kid. It didn't seem all that long ago, and yet here I was, hearin' another man say somethin' along the same lines to Dean about me. I kept hearin' the words, "I can use you, but your friend is too old," ringing over and over.

Finally, I walked around the corner and sat down. When I did, the man got up to leave. He thanked us for coming, looked over at Dean, and said, "If things change, give me a call." Then he left. I wondered what the kid was thinkin' about right then. I acted like I hadn't heard any of this, and asked Dean what the guy had meant by that last question.

The boy never lied, but he did kinda bend the truth a little. He told me the feller had said he could only use one of us right now. I started to tell him that I'd overheard their conversation but thought better of it.

We kept wanderin' around for another week or so, still not bein' able to find any permanent jobs. In my entire life I'd never been out of work for that long when I was really tryin' to find work. We were makin' a little here and there, but we were spendin' a lot more than what was comin' in. We were a long ways from goin' broke, but I didn't have to be an accountant to tell we couldn't keep up this kinda lifestyle forever.

Everytime we got turned down, I could hear that man from the Geyser say, "I can use you, but your friend is too old." Finally, I realized I was holdin' the kid back. I knew he could have landed a dozen jobs if it weren't for him packin' me around.

I made up my mind one evenin'. I was gonna have to make Dean get out on his own. I hoped maybe some other time down the road we could get back together for a visit or somethin'. I didn't like the idea, but I knew it was the best thing for him.

There was no doubt in my mind that I could talk Sam Winzlo into lettin' me have my old job back. Even if he wouldn't hire me, I knew he'd let me stay in one of the camps for the winter. With a place to stay, I could make it till spring on my social security check and the money I'd saved. There was always work then.

A day or so later we were over by Tonopah. We'd just been turned down for a job on the Pine Creek Ranch when I decided to make my move. We were sittin' in the parkin' lot of the Nez Pa Casino when I blew up and acted like I was mad at the kid. I told him I's tired of packin' him around, that if it weren't for him, I coulda had ten jobs by now, but no one wanted to hire me while I had a green kid followin' me around. I reminded him that he's the one that talked me into leavin' the feedlot to go bummin' around the country. And just recently he'd made me quit another good job. I ranted and raved and carried on like a crazy man, blamin' him for everything from contributin' to the national debt to the changes in the weather patterns.

The boy just sat there starin' at me. When I stopped to catch my breath, he said he needed to make a phone call, and that he'd be right back and we'd finish this talk then. When he returned from the pay phone, he looked at me with that little kid's face of his and said, "Look, Tap, I know you're just doin' this to get me out on my own, and you're probably right. Someday I'm gonna have to stand on my own two feet, but right now isn't a good time for me. I've just lost my girl, and I haven't got anyone else but you to talk to or to count on. I need you more now than I did when I didn't know which end of a horse the bridle went on.

"I just talked to that guy up in Elko, and he still has the job up there for us. Stick it out with me for this winter, and then we'll go our separate ways. Please? Just stay with me for the next few months. I really need a friend right now. I miss that girl bad, and if I lost you, too, I'm not sure I could handle it."

Well, I've always been a pushover for a sob story, and I knew he wasn't kiddin' about missin' TenaRay. Finally, I thought, What the hell. I guess I can survive a couple of months out in the cold if I have to. So I said, "Okay, one more winter and then it's over. Then I'm headin' south and I'm stayin' down there. Now that's final, I don't care how much you beg and plead." When he smiled at me this time, his whole face lit up, and it made me feel good inside.

We pulled outta Tonopah that afternoon and were in Elko a little after dark. We ate and got a room at the Commercial. The next morning we were up way 'fore daylight. We ate breakfast in the hotel coffee shop and were on the road headed north just as the eastern sky was turnin' pink. We drove for two hours 'fore we pulled up in front of the ranch office.

When we went inside and told the girl behind the desk who we were and what we were there for, she smiled and told us to wait just a minute. Then she walked over to a closed door, knocked on it, and went inside. A minute or two later she came out, still smiling, and said, "The owner will see the young man first." She motioned for Dean to follow her.

Bein' left out there like that really ticked me off. I felt like I's ridin' on the kid's coattail again, and I didn't like it.

After Dean was in there for a few minutes, I could hear the faint sound of laughter comin' from the room, and that made me mad, too. Don't ask me why; I guess I felt like I's bein' left out. The kid was in there for almost half an hour 'fore the intercom on the secretary's desk buzzed and a voice said, "Ask Mr. McCoy to come in, please." The girl motioned for me to follow her. She led me around the counter and down the hall to the room I'd seen Dean go into. When we stopped in front of the door, she paused and said, "The owner will see you now, Mr. McCoy," and with that, she opened the door.

When she did, I guess my mouth dropped open clear to my boot tops. There sittin' behind the desk with his feet propped up on top of it was the boy, Dean. He had a grin that was spread from ear to ear. Standin' next to him was an older man, not quite my age but still no spring colt. He had a smile almost as big as the kid's.

The older man motioned for me to come on in and then closed the door. I was still standin' there with my mouth hangin' open when the older man stuck out his hand and introduced himself. "Mr. McCoy, I'm Martin McCuen, Dean's father. I've heard a lot about you over the years."

We shook hands, but it was more out of instinct or habit on my part. My brain was runnin' ninety miles an hour, and nothin' was comin' up that made any sense.

Finally, Mr. McCuen offered me a chair and said, "I guess all of this is a little confusing to you, isn't it?"

I managed to close my mouth and nod as I sat down.

Dean had taken his feet from the top of the desk and gotten up so his father could sit there. Then the boy came over and sat down in a chair beside me.

Mr. McCuen said, "I guess you'd like an explanation about all of this wouldn't you?"

I nodded.

"You see, Mr. McCoy, I married a girl from a wealthy family back East. I met her while I was going to college back there. The West sounded romantic to her, but after we were married and moved out here, she hated everything about it.

"We were married for a year or so before Dean was born. Two years after that, his mother took sick. The doctors did all that they could, but she kept going downhill. On her deathbed, she made me promise that I would not let Dean grow up out here in this land that she hated.

"I disliked the idea but I kept my promise to her. When

Dean was five, I sent him back East to live with his mother's sister and her family. I went back to see him as often as I could, and he came out here once in a while but only for short visits. He went to a private boarding school. Shortly after he graduated, he got drafted.

"As soon as he was out of the army, he sent me a letter saying that he wanted to come home and help me run this ranch. I truly wanted the boy here with me, but I knew it would never work. I was afraid I would see nothing but his mistakes and never see the things that he did right. I would always think of him as the boy from back East who didn't know anything.

"My main fear was that, in the end, I would say and do things that would end up driving him away. I didn't want that. This place was homesteaded by his grandfather and added to by me. I want it to stay in our family for several more generations.

"I was sure that if he came here, knowing nothing about ranching, I would never notice the things that he learned and would always be afraid of turning any real responsibility over to him. In the end, I sent him his grandfather's old slick fork saddle and a letter telling him my feelings. I told him that when he felt that he was cowboy enough to ride that saddle, he was welcome to come home, but not until then.

"He has written me almost weekly since you and he met. He has told me about the places you've worked and of the things that you and others have taught him. When he and I were together a few months ago, looking for the little Indian girl, he said he thought he was able to ride that saddle well enough now, and he was ready for the two of you to come home. I believe he is right."

EPILOGUE

Well, that was seven years ago, and there've sure been a lot of changes in our lives since then. Dean's dad still runs the ranch, but Dean took over as the cow boss when ol' Willie Straton retired. He's been spendin' more and more time in the office lately, though. His dad wants him to start learnin' the books and business end of the ranch.

The boy has kept writin' to most of the people we met and worked with over the years, so we've been able to keep pretty good track of some of 'em.

Lonney Blain, the first manager of the Lost Lake Pack Station, moved to Wyoming and opened up a little saddle shop outside of Jackson Hole. Later, he married a real beauty with a bundle of money. She surprised him by buyin' a fancy-trained rope horse and a special-made saddle. Now even though he's still crippled, he goes around the country, ropin' and givin' lectures to physically impaired people about usin' horses as part of their therapy.

Slick's a vet with a practice down in Reno. He's bald, overweight, and takes medicine for his ulcers all the time.

Dave and Missy Robison, the couple who took over the running of the pack station after Lonney's wreck, eventually bought the outfit but lost it. The Forest Service put so many restrictions on how the place was operated that it became impossible to do everything they wanted and still make a livin'. They own a little feed store up in eastern Oregon now.

Ben Bird was killed in a car wreck. The newspaper clippin' we got said he was ninety-one and still runnin' his own place. Ben's sister in Susanville inherited the ranch. She hired Deak Iverstine to run it for her till she could get it sold. The new owners were from Texas, and they kept Deak on as manager.

Pete Courtley died of cirrhosis of the liver.

Hooper John was found dead on the road outside of a reservation back in South Dakota. One story we heard was that he'd been killed by a hit-and-run driver. Another said he'd been shot. In any event, it wasn't a very glamorous endin'. A hundred years ago, he woulda been considered a great warrior. Today, in the minds of many, he's just another trouble-makin' Indian.

Little Luther got off probation and moved back to the reservation, where he eventually got married and had a family of his own. He comes down every spring and helps with the brandin'.

Ol' George Williams, from up on the Imnaha, died of a heart attack. His son, Lonell, made the mistake of sellin' their deeded land on the Idaho side of the Snake River to some environmental group with the understandin' that he could keep on usin' it.

This group turned over the management of the land to the Forest Service. The first thing they did was cut the cow numbers and change the time of use. He finally got tired of fightin' with 'em and sold the whole place to some of his neighbors. He's drivin' a log truck over near Eugene now.

Big Red McKlosky is still runnin' cattle for the Flyin' D.

Donnie is workin' here for Dean. He got married and settled down a little. He's Dean's leadman. I imagine he'll take over as cow boss when Dean steps into his dad's job.

Dan, the kid who always packed the big pistol, got a job as a cop in a little town in western Idaho after he accidently stopped a fillin' station robbery.

No one ever heard of Roy after he left the Flyin' D.

The twins, Tim and Tom, are both married and runnin' their folk's place.

Dean never kept track of any of the people from the feedlot, so I can't tell you about any of them.

Sam Winzlo's wife, Nina, died of a heart attack, and Sam moved to the ranch to live permanently.

TenaRay's little sister, Joliene, is in college. She won all sorts of beauty contests after she left the reservation.

As for me—well, in the summer I go out on the wagon with the buckaroo crew. I've got a string of old pension horses that are damn near as old as I am. Me and them ol' ponies don't pull many big circles anymore; we just drag a few calves or help hold rodear.

Dean got me a neat little camp trailer to stay in, too. No more of them stinkin' tepee tents and sleepin' on the ground. In the wintertime, I mostly sit around the cook-shack and entertain the greasy hash slinger with stories about what it was like when the West was wild, and it took a real man to call himself a buckaroo.

Oh say, I almost forgot to tell you about Dean's family. We'd been at the ranch about two years when Dean and his dad went back East to visit Dean's aunt who had raised him. While they were there, his dad told Dean he'd heard about an Indian school down in Pennsylvania. He said they had kids there from all over the country. Mr. McCuen thought possibly there might be some children there from Arizona. If so, maybe they'd be able to give 'em a lead on TenaRay.

One afternoon, they took a little drive down to the school. They met the headman and told 'im they were looking for a girl from the Apache reservation in Arizona and asked if he had any kids in school from there. This boss teacher said that, as a matter a fact, they did have six or eight Apache kids enrolled; they ranged from little squirts clear up to college age. Dean's dad asked if they might speak to a couple of the older ones. This principal or whatever he was said sure 'nough.

He made arrangements for Dean and his dad to meet each one of 'em separately in his office. A half hour later, the first one to step through the door was TenaRay.

The truth was, Dean's old man had done like he said he would and had hired a private investigator. It had taken this guy two full years to track the girl to this school.

Dean and Tena's love life after that was still kind of a hassle. She wanted to finish her education, and Dean wasn't about to quit the ranch. They ended up spendin' a small fortune, flyin' back and forth to see each other on school breaks.

Ol' Martin McCuen thought TenaRay was the best thing that'd ever happened to his son, and he did every-thin' he could to keep the love affair goin', which included footin' the bill for most of the airplane tickets. After two years of college, Tena and Dean decided this long-range courtship was too expensive and too hard to keep up, so they went ahead and got married.

Actually, they got married twice: once down in Arizona

on the reservation by the girl's grandfather, and a day or so later in Elko by a justice of the peace. I went to both weddings and couldn't see a whole lotta difference in either ceremony. Neither of 'em made much sense.

Tena's folks tolerate Dean, but you'd sure have to use your imagination to say they like him. On the other hand, Dean's dad thinks the sun rises and sets in his pretty, black-haired daughter-in-law.

Dean and Tena have three kids. The youngest is a little boy about two months old. They call him John Martin after each of their fathers. The second is a little girl named Tena Joliene. The oldest is another little boy. He's damn near as black as old Sam Winzlo and ornerier than all hell. They call him Jimmy Tap after his Great-grampa Rich and me. Actually he's the cutest of the kids, but I don't tell that to everyone.

In the summer, when the wagon pulls out and Dean is gone most of the time, Tena takes the kids back to Arizona to stay with her folks. She's determined that those little crumb snatchers aren't gonna forget they're Indian.

Sometimes, while her folks are takin' care of the kids, TenaRay travels the country on a government grant. She lectures on "How to Maintain Your Cultural Heritage and Tribal Traditions While Living in a White Man's World."

Well, that's mine and Dean's story. Crazy how somethin' as simple as offerin' a stranger a ride can grow into a lifetime friendship. Somethin' for an ol' man to sit and ponder.

Kaan kwaisi kwaiyakka
(Shoshone)
The rat's tail came off

GLOSSARY

Ballies . . . Black or red cattle with white faces. Usually, but not always, an Angus/Hereford crossbreed.

Basco . . . A person of Basque ancestry.

Bosal . . . A noseband most often made of braided rawhide; however, some bosals are made of braided leather, rope, or horsehair. When held in place with a headstall and equipped with a Mecáte for reins, the complete outfit is called a hackamore.

Brow band . . . Part of a bridle headstall that goes across the horse's brow or forehead.

Cavvy (sometimes spelled cavie) . . . Short for the Spanish word *cavieta*. Because of the great amount of riding required to care for the cattle on the larger ranches, each rider has a couple of horses that he is responsible for and uses. This group of horses is called a string. A string can be as small as three animals or as large as ten. Five is the most common. All of the strings and the extra horses are kept in a herd. This herd is called a cavvy or remuda.

Chinks . . . A style of short chaps.

Corriente Steers . . . Corrienties are considered a breed by some people today. In truth, they are a cross of several breeds of cattle found in Mexico and come in a variety of shapes and sizes. They are popular with team ropers because they usually have large horns compared to the size of their bodies.

Culo . . . A style of throwing the rope so that it wraps around the rear of an animal and catches the hind feet from the back rather than from the side.

Dalleys . . . To take a wrap around the saddle horn with a rope.
 Some cowboys tie their ropes to the saddle horn while others "dalley," a word coming from a Spanish word that means to take a turn.

Deep Seat . . . The posture one assumes to get set to ride a bucking horse.

Drop-shank Spurs . . . Old California-style spurs named for the shank or piece that holds the rowel.

Forked Rider. . . A good rider. A hard person to buck off. To be referred to as a forked rider is a high compliment.

Gunsal . . . Another word for dude used in the Great Basin area. Some think it means hay hook in Basque. To be called a gunsal is not a compliment.

Gut Line . . . Slang for a rawhide rope or riata.

Gypo Trade . . . A trader who deals in junk cattle.

Headstall . . . The leather part of a bridle that holds the bit in the horse's mouth.

Honda . . . A lariat or catch rope that has an eye or loop in the end. This ring is called a honda. The free end of the rope passes through the eye, making the loop that is used to catch an animal. A simple honda is nothing more than a two- or three-inch eye tied in the end of the rope. More complex versions are made of rawhide and are fastened by backbraiding the rope around the honda. Metal rings can also be backbraided into the rope, making a nice, fast honda that will not pull down when an animal is caught.

Injun Sign . . . To bluff or scare an animal or a person.

Latigo . . . The leather strap that fastens to the cinch and holds the saddle on the horse.

Leppie Calves . . . Orphaned calves; also called bummers or dogies in some parts of the country.

Mecáte (McCartie is the anglicized version) . . . A Spanish word meaning hair rope, used for reins on a hackamore or a snaffle bit. Some Mecátes today are made of mohair or soft cotton rope.

Oreana Pairs . . . A cow with an unbranded calf. An oreana is any unbranded animal. In the Southwest an unbranded animal is called a maverick.

Over-and-under . . . To whip a horse first on one side, then on the other, while sitting on it.

Pack Outfit . . . An outfitter who either takes people on horseback camping trips or who provides them with the horses and equipment they need for such a trip. A pack outfit also refers to the equipment needed to make such a trip, as in, "He loaded his pack outfit on an extra horse and headed out."

Quirt . . . A braided, rawhide riding crop or short whip.

Rawzin jaw . . . A nonbuckaroo who works on a ranch, usually doing such jobs as irrigating, feeding cattle, and fixing fences.

Riata . . . From the Spanish *la riata,* a rope, usually sixty to eighty feet long, made of braided rawhide. It requires a great deal of work and skill to make a good riata. Like most handmade articles, quality varies from one to the next, but a well-made riata is the prize of any buckaroo.

Rodear . . . This word can be used as a noun or a verb. As a noun, it is a herd of cattle being held by a group of riders, as in, "We held the rodear while Jake sorted off the drys." As a verb, it means to hold a herd of cattle, as in, "We rodeared the cattle in a draw across from the dry lake."
The rodear is usually the larger herd from which the cut is made. When a certain class of animals is taken from the herd, they are placed in a smaller herd called a paratha.

For example, the oreana pairs are cut from the rodear and held in the paratha.

Rollover . . . A style of throwing a rope so that the rope actually turns over before catching the animal.

Round Ass . . . This term is the opposite of forked. A person with a round ass is easily thrown from a horse.

Sawbuck Saddle . . . A kind of pack saddle.

Shadow Rider . . . Almost all buckaroos take great pride in their riding equipment. Most of them have some silver on their bridles and saddles. Some riders carry this to extremes. These men are called shadow riders because they spend their time looking at their own shadows as they ride. The high point of their day comes if they pass a pickup window or a pond where they can see their reflections.

Suggans . . . Quilts or blankets.

Spade Bit . . . An old Spanish-style bit distinguished by its large, flat spoon-shaped mouthpiece.

Spur Rowel . . . The metal part of a spur is made up of three parts—the band that fits around the heel of the boot, the shank with its chap guard (the part that sticks out the center of the back band), and the rowel. The rowel is the round wheel that fits on the end of the shank. Rowels come in a variety of sizes and shapes.

Stampede Strings . . . A cord or string that fastens to a cowboy hat and runs down and under his chin. They are used to hold the hat on in heavy wind or while a cowboy is working. Most are made of soft braided leather, rawhide, or horsehair.

Sulled Up . . . A person or animal that is angry and refuses to work or move.

Tap Off or Top Off . . . To ride or break a horse.

Taps . . . Short for *tapaderos,* they are stirrup covers that were originally worn to protect the feet or boots of the rider. They come in a variety of shapes and lengths. In the Southwest, they are usually short and are called bull-dog or monkey-nosed taps. In the buckaroo area of the Great Basin where the brush isn't as heavy, they are longer; some are as long as thirty inches, but twenty-six inches is the most popular length. The most common Great Basin styles are the Eagle Bill and the Oregon or Lakeview patterns.

Trace Chain . . . A chain that is fastened to the end of the tugs on a harness, connecting the tugs to the single tree. Trace chains make it possible to adjust a harness to different-sized horses.

Tugs . . . The heavy leather straps on a harness that run the length of the horse and connect the harness to the single tree.